Secrets of the Jeweled Flask

Camille J. Severino

PathBinder Publishing LLC
COLUMBUS, INDIANA

Published by PathBinder Publishing LLC
P.O. Box 2611
Columbus, IN 47202
www.PathBinderPublishing.com

Copyright © 2025 by Camille J. Severino
All rights reserved

Edited by Doug Showalter
Covers designed by Kassondra Hattabaugh

First published in 2025
Manufactured in the United States

ISBN: 978-1-955088-93-0
Library of Congress Control Number: 2025904976

NO AI TRAINING ALLOWED

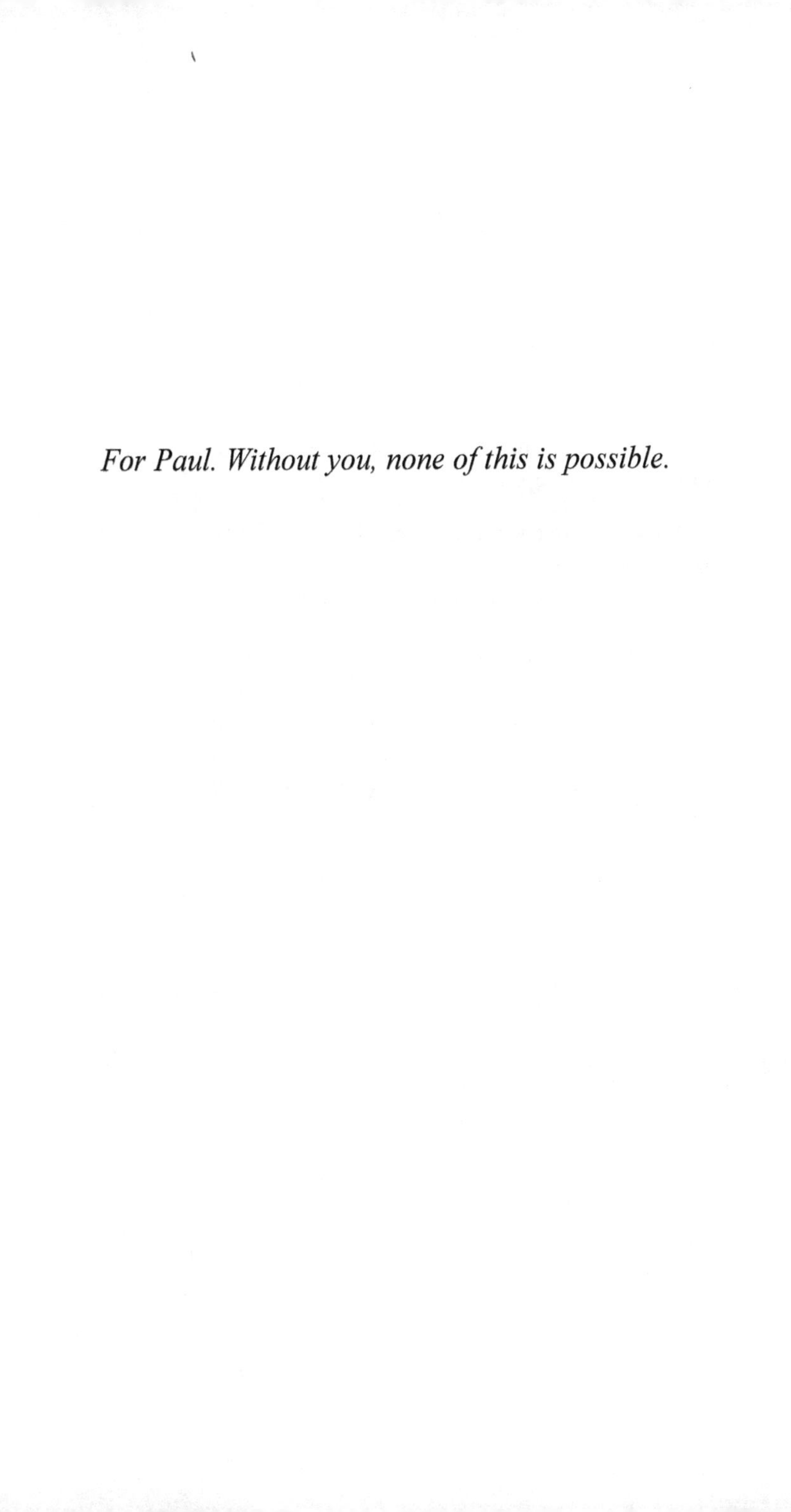

For Paul. Without you, none of this is possible.

Acknowledgements

First, I would like to thank my life partner, Paul Goeke, whose continual support of my creative endeavors was paramount to this first novel being published. I couldn't have asked for a better person to walk through time with. I want to thank my brother, John, and his children, Angelina and John. Your constant support and encouragement keep me moving forward.

I want to thank my publisher, Paul Hoffman, and his team of editors, cover designers, and formatting gurus for all your hard work and the care you took with my story.

I would like to thank Josie, Denise, and Elizabeth Ryan, who continually pushed me to finish this book. Additional thanks to Hillary Bullock Kane and Steve Mahoney for all the reading and feedback. I want to thank Teri Edwards for her amazing edits and beta reading and Teresa Crocco for her help with the Italian language.

I want to thank anyone out there who listened to me talk about this story, and the people who inspired the many characters depicted here.

— Camille J. Severino

"And if I ever lose my eyes
If my colors all run dry
Yes, if I ever lose my eyes
Weee eee ee ee eee
I won't have to cry no more."

— Yusuf "Cat" Stevens

La Porta[1]

The strange mist covered Vito like a shroud. Once again, he had no idea where or *who* he was. Every time he walked through the basement door, things were revealed that Vito didn't want to know. He assumed this time would be no different.

The smog clung tighter than any other time before this, which gave Vito the impression this latest adventure would reveal something unthinkable. He wanted to get it over with, so he waved his arms in front of his body in a vicious attempt to dissolve the cloud quickly. But it was no use. The powers that be wouldn't release him one second before they were ready.

Once Vito accepted this, the cloud began to thin and reveal his surroundings.

The haze lifted and Vito's eyes noticed the damp Chicago asphalt beneath his feet. He didn't have to guess where he was any longer. Vito knew. He didn't have to look down at his hands and body to know that this time he was a woman. He also knew exactly which woman he had become.

As if she could hear him inside her head, Vito felt his womanly legs begin to run. She was chasing a pair of red taillights pulling away from the curb. The unknown car sped off into the night air as Vito heard her voice emerge from the throat he now occupied. "GUS!"

The car didn't stop. Instead, the red taillights took a quick right and disappeared around a long row of bungalows.

Vito could hear a baby crying in the distance. The body he now occupied turned quickly and ran back to a house Vito had known his whole life. Once inside, he felt his arms reach out and pick up the wailing infant. Vito felt sobs pounding their chests. He felt her arms pull the baby tight to her bosom as they wept.

---

1   The door

Chapter One

March 16, 2007

Vito Glandell was an extraordinarily ordinary man. He knew mediocrity wasn't a good reason for embarrassment, but Vito despised his mundane existence all the same. When he was young, Vito tried to ignore his prison of nondescript days. But those days bled into weeks, into months, and into years, which, to Vito, resulted in a lifetime of nothing.

When he was young, Vito had dreams. While he waited out his youth, books and television took him to the places he could not go. But when eighteen came and went, every year that passed felt like a bullet picking off any chance he had of creating the life he wanted.

Now, nearing forty, Vito still lived in the home where he grew up having never left or experienced a life of his own. The more he turned the corner toward middle age, Vito sullenly accepted his fate.

One may wonder what makes a young man stay home and never leave his family. For Vito, it was a small seed planted into his young heart. A parasite he called "guilt." Over the years that pit of regret blossomed and now, Vito dwelt in a garden of fear. At thirty-seven, his fright was the size of an orchard and Vito was stuck.

"Vito!" his mother screamed from the kitchen. "You better hurry. You're going to be late for work!"

"Okay!" Vito hollered back. Conversations in their household didn't mean anything if the whole neighborhood could not hear them.

Vito got out of bed and found himself in the pink-tiled bathroom he shared with his grandmother and great-grandmother. Locking the bathroom door behind him, Vito opened the medicine cabinet. He looked at the nearly one-dozen yellow bottles with white child-proof caps inside. Each was prescribed to a different member of his household, but he knew most of them were there to induce sleep or reduce anxiety. If taken as prescribed, they could cure any mood.

"What if I took more than the recommended dose?" Vito wondered. "What if I took them all?"

Vito pulled a prescription bottle off the shelf. He wiped it down while inspecting the contents. Six pills. Was that enough to do it? He didn't know. While Vito struggled with depression, insecurity and crippling fear, suicidal ideation was new territory. He took another yellow bottle, recognized it as one of his own, and put it back. He'd been taking that crap since he was a preteen, and it did nothing. Vito reached for another as he considered how many pills he could pile up before dumping them into his mouth.

"Vito," he could hear his mother clenching her teeth outside the locked bathroom door. "We're making a special birthday breakfast for you. Get your ass moving."

Birthday. The word hit Vito's eardrums, and he hesitated. This annual reminder of his zestless life was the reason Vito was looking to put a stop to this mundane ride. Yet hearing the word birthday come out of his mother's mouth made him realize he had shitty timing.

"Okay," he called out. "I'll be right there."

Vito put all the pills back into the bottles from which they came, and back on the shelf, did what he needed to, and went up to his room to get ready for the day.

For the entirety of his life, Vito and his maternal mafia lived in a brick bungalow, a staple in the landscape of every Chicago neighborhood. Their notable traits are the solid structure and that they go long as opposed to wide. A Chicago-style bungalow has the ability to withstand a Peterbilt collision or a hail of bullets. They're typically a one-and-a-half-story home with a full basement. The half-story above served as Vito's bedroom.

While heading to his birthday breakfast, Vito looked at the yellow wall that connected the kitchen to the rest of the house. Some families put up pictures. Their household builds shrines. This hallway served as a makeshift memorial — lined with images of family and friends, many of whom were no longer among the living.

Every framed representation was held in place with more than nails. The love his mother, grandmother, and great-grandmother held for each soul on that wall suspended them as well. In Italian-American families, the dead are as important as the living, if not more so. They thrive in stories told and retold so many times, it is as if the dead person was sitting there, eating Nonna's pizza and drinking wine.

No matter what stylistic changes the hallway shrine had seen over the years, the wall remained yellow. While the color remained stagnant, the altar grew colossal.

"It's a color of sunshine bambino," Nonna Josie told him when he was six and had inquired why the wall was that color. "Yellow is the color of happiness. And da faces up there, they make a me happy."

If Vito had his way, the wall would be blue. He always found blue to be calming. Bright yellow made his nerves skyrocket. But, convincing Connie, his mother, to make the smallest changes to their home always proved to be difficult.

On his twentieth birthday, he asked her to take down a baby picture she had displayed on the wall. There he was, naked for everyone to see, lying on the proverbial white bearskin rug. When he brought it up, Connie put on her best pout, "Awwwww, but I love that picture."

"Can't you just put it somewhere people won't see it when they go to the bathroom?"

"What do you care what people think?" Connie asked, switching the subject to his insecurities.

"It's not that," Vito bit back.

"Yes, it is. Besides, you look sweet. Nonna and Bisnonna think so too." Vito's bisnonna, or great-grandmother, was Nicolette in Sicily, but she went by Nellie—the American name she had adopted after crossing the Atlantic. Her daughter, Vito's nonna, or grandmother, was Giuseppina until she reached the States. In America, her name became Josephine, and then Josie.

"You a momma is a right, Vito," Nonna Josie chimed in.

"But I'm an adult," he fought back.

"It stays up," Connie said, finalizing the discussion. "I had that picture taken the first Christmas after your father walked out. It's a reminder for us to thank God for giving me the strength to save us because we were left alone."

Once his father was brought into the conversation, Vito knew he had lost. Defeated, he walked out of the kitchen and never spoke of it again.

Seventeen years later, the nude memory of his father's abandonment was still there, right in the center of the yellow wall.

Vito had no memories of his father, not even his face. Gus left shortly after his son was born, and Vito had never seen a picture of him. Connie destroyed everything that reminded her of Gus in a sink fire soon after he left. All it took was some lighter fluid and matches for every image of Vito's father to be erased from their home. Whether it was her intention or not, this historical destruction ensured Vito wouldn't carry his father's face in his head. She even burned their wedding pictures. Not a single photo of Gus could be found in their house.

On one hand, this made Vito angry because he felt he should at least get to know his father's face. But Vito's procreator, Gus Glandell, decided one rainy night that being a father didn't suit him, so he walked out and never returned. To Vito, it could not be clearer. Gus did not give a shit about him and was never interested in being his dad. So why should Vito care what the man looked like?

But then Vito would look in the mirror and see differences from his other family members.

"Gus must've been tall," Vito would think as he towered over the other kids in his neighborhood. "He must've been lanky too." Vito could see some physical differences he had from his mother. While he and Connie shared the same color eyes and the general shape of their face, his mother, Nonna, and Nellie were short with curly hair. Connie's hair was jet black and his two grandmothers were gray now, but the wall shrine showed his grandmothers to both have pitch dark hair in their youth. Frank, Connie's brother, was also short with dark curly hair. Vito sprouted up when he was sixteen and his hair was lighter and straighter than anyone else in his family. He was thinner too.

Vito assumed these physical traits came from his father, even though he had nothing about Gus to recollect. He only had the memories his mother gave him. And none of those were ever any good. There wasn't a time in Vito's life when he didn't know the story of how his father walked out and his mother had been left alone to pick up the pieces, including him. Connie made sure Vito always knew the ultimate sacrifice she made by continuing on with her life after that tragic event.

As with any other neighborhood, word of Vito's father walking out on them made its way through the streets like fire. And, once Connie got a taste of the attention, she never missed a chance to share their luckless story.

She would tell parishioners after Sunday mass at St. Luke's about the difficulties of being a single mom. Connie would be the last person lingering at a parent-teacher conference because she let everyone there know how his father abandoned them. She even cried to strangers innocently squeezing Roma tomatoes at Naples Produce Market.

"Poor thing," young couples would whisper, throwing eye pity in her direction.

"The man should be hung," other mothers would say, shaking their heads and grasping the hands of their children.

"That's what she gets for not marrying an Italian boy," the neighborhood widows would say.

It was then that Vito realized they turned their noses down at him. Not only did they feel pity for them due to Gus walking out, but in grade school, Vito learned that the neighborhood considered him a half-breed. Half Italian, and half not-Italian.

When he was fourteen, Vito begged his mother to stop telling that story.

"But it's the truth," Connie defended herself, regarding the tale as part of her identity.

"It's embarrassing," he replied in one of his earliest attempts to get his way.

"Oh, Vito, you need to lighten up," Connie said, rolling her eyes. Then she pushed the shopping cart to the peppers section. Fourteen-year-old Vito followed obediently.

"Vito! You don't have all day," Connie called to her son, knocking him out of his head.

"Coming!" he yelled, pushing his memories back into the darkest box of his mind as he inched his way into the kitchen.

"BUON COMPLEANNO, VEEETO!"[2] Nonna Josie screeched as Vito walked through the kitchen door. She moved

---

2   "Happy Birthday, Vito!"

with the speed of light while wiping her hands on her pink floral apron. Once she was in front of her only grandchild, Nonna threw her arms around Vito's neck and pulled his face down to hers for a sprinkling of kisses. He didn't object, Vito never did. He knew the kisses meant more to her than they did to him, so Vito allowed his Nonna's spittle of adoration to cover his face.

"I have a sooprrrise for you," she said, releasing her love grasp and letting him stand up again.

Nonna Josie scurried over to the stove and pulled her favorite Corningware dishes from the oven. "I make flap a jacks, joost the way you like a them, with the little blueberries. We even gotta dat expenseeve maple soorup!"

"Real maple syrup? That's liquid gold!" Vito joked and kissed her cheek. "Grazie, Nonna."[3] He sat down in his usual seat next to his great-grandmother, Nellie.

"Veeto," he heard the nonagenarian say in a firm whisper.

"Si, Bisnonna?"[4] Vito replied.

Bisnonna Nellie's frail hands lifted a plate from her lap that had one lone Hostess cupcake with an unlit blue candle penetrating the plastic-like chocolate topping. She placed it on the table while Connie poured coffee and Nonna Josie began to serve the food.

Vito sat patiently as his great-grandmother pulled a book of matches from the pocket of her teal housecoat. She opened the book with hands drenched in wisdom and wrinkles. On the outside of the maroon cardboard, cream letters read *The Tap, Where Strangers Become Friends*.

The plates on the table grew in number as the scents of toasted Italian bread, scrambled eggs with zucchini and onion, fried potatoes, and pancakes moved from Vito's nostrils to his empty stomach.

All the while, Bisnonna Nellie attempted to strike a match with the speed of an ancient sloth. After a half dozen tries, she handed the matchbook to Vito.

He took it, struck a fire, lit the candle, and they all sang "Happy Birthday." All except the oldest of the group, who, at 98, could only clap her hands and smile along.

---

3   "Thank you, Grandma."
4   "Yes, great-grandmother?"

Somewhere between Vito blowing out the candle and the cupcake being split into four equal pieces; Bisnonna Nellie had bowed her head and closed her eyes. Her gentle snoring filled the room.

"You're getting close to forty," Connie said to her son while she drank her coffee and ate her toast.

"I don't want to talk about this, Ma," Vito replied, eagerly digging into his birthday breakfast.

"What do you mean?" Connie defended herself. "You're always so defensive. You have no idea what I was going to say."

"I don't?" Vito retorted. "So, you weren't going ask me about finding a wife?"

"Not at all," Connie huffed and took another drag of her cigarette. Then she turned her attention to her mother.

"Did you hear that the Abruzzo's cousin just moved to town?" Connie said and then paused for a few seconds. "She's from the old country. Palermo, I think."

"Ooh," Nona Josie responded with excitement like she always did when someone mentioned Italy, even though she hadn't been back since she was a girl.

Connie nodded at her mother. "I met her when I stopped by to say hi to Kathy the other day. Nice girl." Then Connie turned her attention to Vito, "Her name is Angelica."

"How a long is she in town?" Nonna Josie asked as she doused her plate with maple syrup.

"I'm not sure," Connie answered quickly and turned to her son once again. "But I told her you would call her. Maybe take her out to Leoni's for some ravioli. They make the best."

Vito didn't reply, knowing full well he wasn't going to call Angelica or take her to Leoni's for ravioli. He kept his eye on WGN's morning news show, playing on the kitchen television.

"Today, they are launching the latest in cellular phone technology," the anchorwomen informed. "Get ready to meet Apple's newest product, the iPhone."

"Well, I don't know how long you're going to make me wait around for grandchildren, Vito."

Instead of biting into his cupcake, Vito bit into her remark, "Seriously, Ma? It's my birthday. I don't want to talk about this."

"Okay, fine. I won't talk about it since it's your birthday."

Vito waited for the 'but' that he knew was coming.

"But I'm not getting any younger, you know? I'm coming up on sixty in a few years. Plus, you turned down Monsignor Benevento's offer to get you into the seminary."

"Just because I didn't want to be a priest doesn't mean I owe anyone grandchildren," Vito said between bites of food.

"You do owe me a couple of grandchildren for not becoming a priest," Connie retorted in a way that indicated he would never win that argument.

Vito said nothing and returned his attention to his plate.

"Maybe I'll get her to call you," Connie announced with the level of pride reserved for someone who'd solved homelessness.

"When Gina Tucci called me, you called her a slut and hung up on her. I didn't find out until I saw her in class the next day."

"That was when you were in high school. And I thought you were going to become a priest. It's 2007. All the girls are being aggressive now. Besides, I'm not getting any younger."

Nonna Josie frowned. "Girls who call boys are puttanas[5]."

Vito gulped his coffee and stood. "I'll be at the office late tonight, so don't make a huge dinner or wait up."

"But it's your birthday," Connie whined. "I'm your mother."

"I have some stuff to do," Vito said. "We can celebrate tomorrow."

He was lying. It was his birthday, and possibly his last night on Earth. Vito wanted to do something different. He wanted to have some fun. He wasn't sure what he'd enjoy, or where he would go, but he had eight hours to figure it out at the office.

Connie jumped out of her seat. "Wait! I made your lunch. Pepper and egg sandwich. It's Friday."

Vito hated pepper and egg sandwiches. They didn't reheat well in the microwave, and the bread always got soggy. "I don't have a taste for pepper and egg today, Ma."

"Then what are you going to eat, the food in the cafeteria?" Connie laughed as she grabbed the brown paper sack off the counter and handed it to her son. "Their cooking isn't as good as mine."

"Maybe I'll get a burger."

"WHAT?!" Vito's mother and grandmother shrieked in unison.

"It's Lent." Connie scolded. "And it's Friday."

---

5   Whores

"He's kidding." Nonna Josie took Vito's empty plate and put it in the sink. "Don't a hurt you mama's feelings like that," Nonna Josie said in her broken English.

In an unusual mood, Vito decided to stand his ground. "Maybe I like the food in the cafeteria. And they have vegetarian options."

"I spent all morning frying the peppers and then added the right amount of cheese," Connie's voice climbed to a decibel indicating her annoyance.

Vito sighed and took the greasy brown paper sack from his mother's hand.

"Have a happy birthday," Connie said, smiling victoriously before kissing Vito's cheek. Then she sat back at the kitchen table beside Nonna Josie, where they began flipping through the Chicago Tribune.

"Four hundred dollars for a phone?!" Connie exclaimed as Vito grabbed his briefcase from the hall chair.

"What is the i for?" Nonna asked. "I-a-phone? What's an i-a-phone?"

Vito let their voices fade as he closed the front door behind him.

***

Heading down the street toward the bus stop, Vito glanced around his neighborhood that sat on the western border of Chicago—or as he liked to call it, the Smelly Onion.

He once read that the city's name evolved from a Native American language. Miami-Illinois according to some. It's a derivative of the Algonquin tribe that had a habit of naming geographical locations after the growing vegetation. When this city had been nothing more than a lush forest, fragrant leeks grew along water lines. Thus, it was called *shikaakwa*, or stinky onion, by the local tribes, and that name eventually morphed into Chicago.

Vito always got a kick out of that story, though he wondered why he was thinking of it now. Perhaps it was just boredom, or maybe it was because shikaakwa was one of the ingredients in the odorous pepper and egg sandwich his mother had insisted he bring to work.

The moment Vito reached the corner, the Harlem Avenue bus pulled up. Picking up his pace, he got in line behind a woman in a janitorial uniform. The cold March air picked up and hit his neck. It reminded him there would be more cold commuter days ahead, at least until the end of April. Chicago weather is not for the sane. Typically for his birthday, the day was overcast and gloomy. A chill lived in the air that Midwesterners know as well as their mother's womb. Maybe even better.

A guy in a driver's uniform tripped and bumped Vito from behind. He looked back and saw seven people getting on board; he'd bet anything most of them worked at Chroma Paints, just like him.

As they boarded and put their coins into the slot, Vito recalled how well his interview had gone at age seventeen—the one that got him hired there twenty years ago. It was a part-time summer job sweeping up the factory. He'd seen a sign and taken a chance, knowing he was going to need money for college.

Vito plopped his thirty-seven-year-old butt into a window seat then turned his head away from the people getting on board. When the bus pulled away, Vito was happy to be alone. It wasn't long before they drove past the high school, which was the last place he remembered having hope.

In high school, Vito kept his nose in books and avoided other people. He found fiction to be less stressful and a great place to hide in plain sight. Book characters didn't make him feel weird, dorky, guilty or inferior. Mostly, people who lived in stories did not interfere with his life. He knew that one day, once he was out of high school, he would have to break his nose out of those pages and find a real friend. But in his teens all Vito could focus on was getting as far away from his mother as possible.

May 14, 1988

"I heard you were offered a job in sales?" Connie said the morning of his high school graduation.

"Who told you that?" Vito asked. He hadn't told anyone about his boss's offer.

Connie ignored her son's discomfort from her interference and began talking to her own mother.

"When his supervisor first told me, I was shocked. I mean, my son isn't exactly a social butterfly."

Connie laughed and looked back to Vito. "But your boss said you were the most likable kid he had ever hired. He thinks you'd excel in sales if you broke out of your shell a little bit."

"Why were you talking to my supervisor?" Vito asked, not wanting to let it go.

"I'm your mother, and I'll do what I want," Connie snapped back as she started clearing dishes from the table.

"I don't want that job," Vito said in defiance.

"Of course, you don't," Connie agreed. "You're going to be a priest."

"I'm not going over this again with you Ma," Vito argued.

"Why dohnna you wanna be a priest bambino," Nonna asked, excited at the thought.

"We've been going over this my entire life!" Vito began to shout.

"The Monsignor says that the priesthood is perfect for a boy like you. You were abandoned by your father and need guidance."

"Ma," Vito said exhausted. "Just because you work for the Monsignor and he's a close family friend doesn't mean I have to do what he says."

"But he's not saying it," Connie retorted. "I am. I'm your mother, Vito. And I made a lot of sacrifices to give you a good life."

Vito clammed up. He did not see the point of talking to someone who wasn't listening. Connie noticed she had pushed her son near the edge and decided to bring him back.

"We don't have to discuss it now. You can mull it over while you work on your theology degree at DePaul. There's plenty of time for you to be a priest."

"I'm not sure I want to go to DePaul," Vito said.

"I don't understand why you don't want to stay right here."

"Maybe I want a new experience," Vito replied. He hadn't told her that he'd applied to Tulane University and been accepted. Plus, he had already made up his mind; with the money he'd saved and what he had coming in grants, moving to New Orleans would not be difficult.

"But your boss said Chroma would be willing to work with your schedule when you start at DePaul next year."

"I never said I was going to DePaul," Vito repeated himself. Granted, he had never said he wasn't going to DePaul either. He was just waiting for the right time to tell them he was going to Tulane.

I know." Connie smiled and patted him on the head before continuing her housework. "You're going to make your big announcement tonight."

Nonna Josie helped clean up as Connie grabbed the pot from Mr. Coffee. Vito held up his cup for a refill.

"You've had two cups already," Connie said as she poured her fourth. "You're still growing."

"Does she still try and wipe your ass too?" Vito's Uncle Frank chimed in.

No one saw Connie's older brother come up from the basement, where he lived. Frank walked in the room as the scent of gin and cigarettes replaced the aroma of French toast, bacon, and biscuits "I'll take a cup of Joe, Connie," Frank said.

Connie frowned but grabbed a mug and poured him the rest of the pot.

Nonna Josie kissed Frank good morning. "Should I make more, Francesco?"

"Sure, Ma," he replied, taking a seat next to his nephew. "Now, what's this I hear about DePaul?"

"You already know, Frank," Connie said, lighting a cigarette. "The Monsignor pulled a lot of strings to get him into that school. It's one of the best in Chicago."

"True," Frank replied, "but maybe the kid wants something different. Maybe he wants some fun. Heaven knows he could use a little loosening up. You two are making him into a nervous wreck."

"He's, my son. Mind your own business." Connie spat back.

"You a stay out of this, Francesco," Nonna Josie whispered to her son.

The two youngest women in the house cleaned up while Bisnonna Nellie snored at the kitchen table. Her head was bent forward, and Vito noticed his bisnonna's false teeth slipping from their gummy grip. Before gravity pulled the dentures into her lap, Nellie awoke with enough power to jolt her head back and sucked her teeth into their rightful place. She did this regularly with the strength of a high-powered vacuum.

March 16, 2007

"Hello." an unfamiliar voice knocked Vito out of his daydream. The image of his bisnonna faded and Vito looked up to see a woman with the whitest hair he had ever seen.

"Yes?" Vito said. He couldn't help but notice that her long locks were ratted and piled high on top of her head into a beehive hairdo, which was popular in the mid 1960s. To keep this kind of hair one cannot wash it until the next setting. Vito knew this because his Nonna Josie, wore her beehive well into the 1980s, long after it went out of fashion.

"Is this seat taken?" the woman asked. Her lips were painted pink, and her eyes were shadowed with a bright shade of blue. She turned her entire body around until her ass was in Vito's face. Then bent at the waist, and leaned backward to take the seat before he could give her an answer.

"No," Vito stammered, "It's not taken." He quickly grabbed his briefcase and greasy lunch bag from the seat next to him before the woman plopped down. "You almost smooshed my sandwich," he said, although he wasn't sure why he was defending something he didn't even want.

"Oh." The older woman said and then added, "Maybe you shouldn't keep your stuff on the seat. Someone might wanna sit there." Vito had no response because, even though what she said annoyed him, he knew she was right.

Her hair was close enough to send Vito's heart racing. He did not like anything or anyone outside of his house to invade his space. Mostly, because Vito feared germs. He had read enough to know that germs, while they help you build an immunity, can infiltrate your system rendering you helpless. Unsure of what type of pathogens grew in a pile of unwashed hair, Vito decided to create them in his mind.

Through those strands of ratted dead cells on top of this stranger's head are nests of God only knows what.

Vito suddenly realized that her boney fingers covered in costume rings were in his face.

"I'm Nicki," she said, putting a hand out for him to shake.

"I don't shake hands," Vito replied, leaving her hand hanging.

"Oh," Nicki said. "Okay. Anyway. Glad to meet you."

Nicki pulled a flask out of her bag and shoved the aroma of bourbon into his post-breakfast face.

"Wanna slug? You look like you could use a drink."

The rim of Nicki's flask got close enough to Vito's face that he could feel the pathogens jumping off the surface and onto his nose.

"No, thank you. I don't drink." Vito turned his gaze back to the window, wanting to escape again.

"Well, you should drink," Nicki laughed, pushing the silver flask into his face again. "And you should start now."

"What is wrong with you?!" Vito yelled at Nicki loud enough for the people in the seats surrounding them to rustle or look their way. Vito scowled and did his best to politely push away her persistence.

Nicki pulled the flask away from Vito's face and took a long sip. After swallowing she leaned back into Vito's treasured airspace and said, "Your Uncle Frank always told me you needed some loosening up."

Chapter Two

Vito stared at Nicki. "What do you know about my uncle?"

"I know that he always said you were an uptight kid." Nicki replied.

Vito stood. "This is my stop."

"No, it isn't." she said.

Still seated, Nicki smiled and took another swig from her flask. "The paint factory is three stops away."

Vito sat back down wondering if he should scream to get someone's attention.

"Your uncle and I used to drink together at The Tap a long while back."

"Is that so?" Vito said, hoping the next three stops went by quickly. He leaned back and peered out the window as the bus began to slow down for its first stop.

"Yeah," Nicki said, digging into her purse until she pulled out an old picture in a dollar store frame. The mounting looked like it had spent eons on a corner shelf. Nicki shoved the picture in Vito's face. "See?"

Vito looked at the picture surrounded by a cloud of dust and debris once attached to the frame. There he was—his zio, Uncle Frank, beaming a rotted-toothed smile. The corners of his mouth were covered in a white foam seen only on the most dedicated alcoholics.

The bus doors opened, letting some passengers on and some off and out into the streets of Chicago.

"Listen, lady," Vito whipped his head toward the old woman, "I don't want to be rude …"

"Nicki," she corrected. The bus pulled away.

"Nicki," Vito said, hoping this lunatic of a woman would get up by the next stop, "I don't like talking about my uncle."

"That's too bad. A good talk might do you some good." Nicki took another quick sip from the flask and then sighed. "You can ignore me all you want, Vito, but the truth is going to find you, whether you want it to or not."

A stream of curiosity mixed with anxiety crept up Vito's spine. The bus pulled up to the second stop and Vito bit his tongue, eagerly waiting for the bus to pull away.

Finally, it pulled forward and Vito knew Nicki would have to let him get up at the next stop.

"You aren't the least bit curious about me?" Nicki asked, and she took another sip from her flask.

"Not if it has anything to do with my uncle," Vito replied. Frank left him years ago. That's where Vito wanted his uncle to stay. In the past.

"Well," Nicki said as she began to gather her belongings and depositing them back into her colossal satchel. The alcohol receptacle remained affixed firmly to her hand. "At least I can say I tried."

The bus began to slow down for the third stop, and Nicki pulled herself into a standing position.

Vito gathered his belongings and stood. He then took a step back, gave Nicki room to retake her seat, and held onto the bar for balance as the bus came to a stop. The doors swished opened.

"I'm sorry," Vito said, not sure why he was feeling guilty. He just knew that he was. "Maybe some other time." With these last words, Vito ran out the bus's double doors and joined his fellow Chroma employees for the long walk to the factory building.

Vito approached his cubicle, unable to get Frank out of his mind.

"Why hadn't Zio Frank ever mentioned Nicki?" Vito thought.

It was a question Vito forced himself to brush off until another day. He sat down and prepared for work. There were a ton of phone calls to make and new accounts to close.

Still, as the clock ticked on and the numbers were dialed one after another, memories of Frank kept flooding Vito's consciousness. No matter how hard he tried to focus on the glossy, periwinkle shipments being ordered and the primer packages he had for his best accounts, all he could think about was the last night he saw Frank.

May 14, 1988

It was the night of Vito's high school graduation. His mother and grandmother had been slaving over the kitchen stove for days, and Vito prepared for the feast of his life.

He had been waiting for this meal for months—not only because they were preparing his favorite dishes, but because this was the night he was going to tell them he was moving to New Orleans.

"What?" his mother asked, chopping romaine lettuce for the salad.

"I want to tell you something before dinner," Vito said. At eighteen, Vito was a man now. And he wanted his mother to be the first to know he was leaving.

"I don't have time right now," Connie said, brushing him off, "Monsignor Benevento will be here soon."

Vito sighed and slumped into a nearby kitchen chair. "Why do we have to invite him to everything?"

"Vito!" Nonna Josie scolded. "He's a man of a God. He's always welcome in-a our home."

Connie stopped chopping the lettuce and put her hand on Vito's shoulder. "Father Vince is coming too."

Vito smiled in relief; his happiness restored.

"Good," Connie said, "No son of mine is going to be sad on his celebration day."

Shortly thereafter, the doorbell rang, and Vito hurried to answer it.

"Good evening, Vito," Monsignor Benevento said as he entered the front hallway, stepping inside from the warm dusk air.

Father Vince followed suit, winking at his young protege as he too, entered their home. "Hello, Vito." Father Vince shook Vito's hand. "It's so nice of your family to welcome us like this for your celebration."

"We're glad to have you, Father," Vito said and then quickly added, "to have you both."

He led them into the living room where Bisnonna Nellie was snoring softly and Nonna Josie was pouring wine.

"Welcome to our a home," Nonna Josie shouted with a smile. "It's an honor to a 'ave you a both."

The men smiled and returned her graciousness. They all sat on plastic covered furniture as Nonna handed out glasses of wine. Connie emerged from the kitchen and the men stood again as the sound of squeaking plastic coverings echoed through the room. They switched positions so abruptly Father Vince nearly spilled his wine.

"Welcome." Connie announced. She walked over and shook both men's hands and said, "Relax with some wine. Dinner will be served shortly."

The monsignor smiled brightly and said, "I have no doubt everything is delicious and well worth the wait." Connie smiled and quickly ran back to the kitchen as Nonna Josie followed. The men sat down again. Vito took his seat next to his bisnonna, who whistled as she snored.

"So, your mother tells me you were accepted to DePaul and several other schools," the monsignor commented.

"Yes," Vito replied. He knew the less he said, the longer he could keep from making his announcement.

"Have you decided?" The pious man asked.

"I was going to make that announcement at dinner," Vito explained, exchanging a glance with Father Vince. The younger holy man already knew the answer to that question.

Father Vince taught English to the juniors and seniors at St. Luke's High School, and Vito had grown quite close to him. Over the past two years they bonded over their mutual love of literature. When most students ran off to hang out at Ricci's Red Hots, Vito and Father Vince would discuss their favorite writers and the stories that moved them.

Connie and Nonna Josie started bringing in the many plates of food they'd prepared for this celebratory meal. The men stood sending plastic sound waves through the air once again. Then they made their way to the dining room and took their places at the table. The seating arrangements were assigned so the men sat furthest from the kitchen. The women sat closest to the connecting door so that they could get up and down with ease to clear dirty dishes and serve more courses. The men's only job was to enjoy their meal.

Each platter was filled to the brim with the likes of meatballs, sausage, homemade ravioli, arancini, braciola—and this was only the first course.

Once all the food was set out, the women sat down and bowed their heads, ready to let the holiest man in the room give thanks.

"Benedici, Signore, noi e questi doni che stiamo per ricevere dalla tua bontà. Per Cristo nostro Signore. Amen."[6]

---

6   "Bless, Lord, us and these gifts we are about to receive from your goodness. Through Christ our Lord. Amen."

"Amen," the rest of the feasters repeated in unison.

Immediately thereafter, the platters were being passed around until everyone had a little bit of everything. Next, more red wine was poured for all, including Vito, the guest of honor.

"So, Vito," Monsignor Benevento said after his sip of wine transcended down his holy gullet, "have you given any thought to the discussion we had on your last day of school?"

Connie and Nonna Josie stopped chewing and looked toward Vito in anticipation.

Vito sipped his wine without responding.

"Vito," Connie said, "Monsignor Benevento asked you a question. Answer him."

"Yes, sir," Vito replied reluctantly. "I have thought about it."

"So, what is your decision?"

"I am not going to be a priest," Vito stated flatly.

"We said you can think about that," Connie answered. "He might change his mind," she said to the monsignor.

"Well," The monsignor said from his seat at the head of the table, "I suppose we can revisit this after you've spent some time at DePaul."

Connie shot the monsignor a look and he quickly added, "Oh, that's right. You were going to make an announcement about what university you've chosen."

"Don't keep us in suspense," Connie added.

"Well, I wanted to wait until Zio Frank got here so I can tell you all at once."

"Vito," Connie interjected, ignoring the food on her plate, "it's not nice to keep the monsignor waiting. You know the trouble he went through to get you into DePaul."

"With all due respect," Vito said, attempting to muster up the tone he believed an eighteen-year-old man should possess, "I didn't ask anyone to do me any favors. I already told everyone DePaul was my last choice."

Angry, Connie averted her eyes and took a sip of wine.

Nonna Josie, who always ate like a bird, looked sad and nervous. Meanwhile, Bisnonna Nellie focused on her plate with the appetite of a growing teenage boy. The two holy men, however, sat for a moment without uttering a word.

Then, Father Vince broke the silence. "I think it takes strength to leave your home and experience the unknown."

The monsignor swallowed a mouthful of braciole. "No one asked for your opinion, Father."

"I'm sorry, monsignor," Vito said. "I do appreciate everything you've offered me."

"DePaul is an excellent school," the monsignor interrupted. Then he took a quick gulp of his vino. "But I understand if that campus doesn't appeal to you. That's why I've decided to do what I can to get you a scholarship at DePaul." He popped his purple chest out with pride.

Connie nearly shot out of her chair.

"Grazie Dio!"[7] Nonna Josie squealed.

"But DePaul is only a few L stops away from here," Vito said before taking a bite of his meatball to hide his disappointment. He chewed slowly, wondering why Frank wasn't there yet.

"Vito," Connie shot eye-daggers his way before nervously glancing toward the monsignor, "DePaul is a fantastic school."

"So is Tulane." The words slipped out of Vito's mouth before he could stop them. Eighteen years' worth of pent-up repression was no longer capable of being contained.

"Tulane?" Connie's eyes grew wide. "When did you apply there?"

"At the start of the year," Vito said with the softness of a mouse. He then took a big gulp of his wine. "They offered me a partial academic scholarship. With the money I've saved from sweeping up the paint factory, and the grants I was awarded, I should be able to swing it."

Nonna Josie looked at everyone, puzzled. "Non copisco,"[8] she said, touching her daughter's arm.

Connie turned toward her mother. "Tulane no è a Chicago, Mama."[9]

Nonna Jose looked Vito's way with question marks in her eyes. Tears began to roll down her cheeks.

"Nonna," Vito started.

"And joost where is this Tua-lane?" she demanded.

---

7   "Thank you God!"

8   "I don't understand

9   "Tulane isn't in Chicago, Mamma."

The monsignor stared down at Vito as his sanctified gullet tore apart a large forkful of Nonna's arancini.

Vito ignored him and focused on his nonna. "It's in New Orleans," he answered quietly.

"What?!" Nonna screamed. "But you have a no familia[10] there, Vito."

"I know that."

Coming to the rescue, Father Vince smiled and held his red-reflected crystal glass in the air. "Well, Tulane is one of the best schools in the country, and I want to be the first to raise a glass to congratulate you, Vito. That's quite an accomplishment."

"Thank you, Father." Vito smiled and lifted his own glass, while the others just looked at them.

Monsignor Benevento put his hand on Father Vince's arm and forced it down with ease. "What the good father is trying to say is that while this is a great accomplishment, Vito, I don't see how you will be able to accept such an offer. Tulane is not a Catholic school. It has no religious affiliation whatsoever."

"Well, while Tulane isn't Catholic, there is a Catholic center for students like me. They even offer Judeo-Christian studies."

"They have mass in a center?" Connie turned up her nose. "I don't know how I feel about you going to a school that isn't at least Jesuit or Dominican."

"I'll be living in the second oldest diocese in the country," Vito argued. Why were they making it so hard for him to live on his terms?

Vito continued to state his case. "They don't have counties down there like here. Louisiana is divided up by its parishes. Even Chicago isn't as deeply rooted in Catholicism."

Father Vince smiled at his former student with pride. "I see you did your research. Vito."

"Still," the monsignor interjected, ignoring his subordinate, "Tulane is just too far away from your family. You're going to have to call and tell them you can't attend."

"The Hell he is," a voice came from the front hallway of the home.

Vito's face lit up. "Frank!" he cried, relieved that his zio had arrived.

---

10   Family

Frank walked over, smiled a gin-soaked grin, and put a hand on Vito's shoulder. He then fixed his gaze on the monsignor, looking him straight in the eyes. "I don't understand how that's your decision to make. Vito is eighteen now. Legally a man. He can make his own decisions."

Connie bit her bottom lip in anger while Nonna Josie looked around the table with visible nervousness. Bisnonna Nellie snored softly, her face nearly resting in her bosom.

Frank guffawed as he reached for the wine, poured himself a glass, and then dropped into his seat. He tossed back a quick sip, which turned into a giant belch.

"Francesco!" Nonna Josie scolded.

"Scusi, Mama."[11] Frank gave his mother a smile and wink. Her anger forgotten; she smiled back at her Italian prince with the love of a million mothers. Frank took another sip of wine, spilling a little on the mustard yellow tablecloth.

"We haven't seen you at mass for some time, Frank," Monsignor Benevento said, giving Frank a smile, although it was far less genuine than Nonna Josie's.

"No, you haven't," Frank admitted while eyeing the platters of food on the table.

The monsignor swallowed his latest mouthful. "And why is that?"

Frank kept his attention on the food. "So, what have we got here? Braciole! Ravi-oh-li! All my favorites!" He tipped his head back to finish off the rest of his wine, then reached to pour another glass. Once his goblet was full to the brim, Frank fixed himself a plate.

Connie lit a cigarette. "You're late," she said to Frank, her tone just as cold as the food on her plate. "You would think you could've made it on time for Vito's celebration."

"That's okay." Vito placed a hand on his uncle's back. "He's here now."

"I had to see some friends," Frank explained before shoving a fork full of food into his mouth.

"You had to go to the bar," Connie assumed as she took a drag from her cigarette.

The smell of gin on Frank's breath spoke the truth, so he said nothing and took another gulp of wine.

---

11   "Sorry, Mama."

"Well," Monsignor Benevento started, "if you came to mass ..."

"This is none of your business," Frank said, looking the holy man dead in the eye.

Monsignor Benevento pressed his lips tight and glared back.

"I realize my sister has been working for you for twenty years," Frank said, while keeping his eyes steady, "but you are not a part of this family."

"Francesco!" Nonna Josie scolded. "You say you sorry to the monsignor, right a now!"

"I'm a grown man, Mamma," Frank told his mother.

Nonna Josie bit her lip to hold in all she would say to her son once their company left.

Vito put a hand on his uncle's shoulder again and felt the tension in his body release like slow air seeping out of balloon. "I tried to wait for you, but I let the news slip."

"He already knew?" Connie looked to her son, and then to her brother, dumbfounded. Her voice became a shriek. "Are you telling me you knew he was planning on leaving, and you didn't tell me?"

Frank fixed his gaze on his younger sister. "He's been telling you his whole life, Connie. You just chose not to listen."

Silence fell upon the table, only disturbed by the sounds of Bisnonna Nellie's deep breaths as her head lolled forward in slumber.

"God is our refuge and strength," Father Vince spoke. "A helper who is always found in times of trouble. Psalm 46:1."

"Father Vince is correct!" Monsignor Benevento said, taking the opening. "And, as it seems, the trouble lies with Vito wanting to abandon his family."

Connie began to cry softly. Her mother put her arm around her and whispered, "Andra Tutto bene figlia Mia, Andra Tutto Bene!"[12]

"Abandon is a bit harsh don't you think?" Frank chimed in. "I don't see how Vito is abandoning his family just because he has a desire to see the world."

"The boy's uncle is right," Father Vince said, adding a little more weight on Vito's side of the table.

The monsignor shot daggers at his colleague. "Not now, Father."

---

12   "Everything will be fine, my daughter. Everything will be fine!"

"What if Jesus didn't follow his calling?" Father Vince argued.

"Are you daring to compare this boy with our Lord and Savior?" The monsignor turned his head toward his subordinate.

"No, monsignor, but he is a smart boy who knows his destiny. That's a gift from God, and we would be doing him a disservice by convincing him otherwise."

"That's not for you to decide, Father." Monsignor Benevento poked out his sanctified chest as Connie and Nonna Josie hung on his every word.

The monsignor looked around the room piously before returning his focus to the younger priest.

"His mother feels he should stay. Do you know better than the child's mother?"

Father Vince left the question hanging mid-air.

Monsignor Benevento turned back to Vito. "I know your father abandoned you, my son, and we all know the effect this has had on you."

Vito's face reddened, but this only fueled the parish leader's fire.

"What about your mother, Vito? Honor thy mother who has honored you by giving you the life you want to live so badly," the monsignor said, proud of his retort.

Vito looked across the table at his mother.

Connie's silent tears had turned into audible sobs. She dried her eyes with her napkin and let her cigarette smolder in the full ashtray. "Please, don't leave me, Vito."

Nonna Josie shook a bony finger at her grandson. "You donna 'ave familia anywhere but a 'ere," she said crossly while still trying to console her only daughter.

"I want to have adventures," Vito said, hoping to calm two of the three women in his life. The third and oldest hardly paid attention. She was too busy eating as if she'd been asleep for a week.

"Vito," the monsignor said while cutting deeply into his second braciola, "I know you have this desire to see the world, but God has put you in a specific position and expects you to do what he has intended for you. Sure, you could leave tomorrow. Jump on a bus and head away from here, never to look back. But I promise you, my son, God has his ways of punishing those who don't abide by his wishes. He will make you pay for disobeying your mother. Remember the Fourth Commandment, young Vito. 'Honor your father and your mother, that your days may be long in the land which the Lord your God gives you.'"

Connie and Nonna Josie smiled in approval as if the light of the Lord himself was shining through the monsignor's words.

"It takes a strong man to follow his destiny," Father Vince said in a lowered voice, cutting into the monsignor's speech with opposition.

"THAT IS ENOUGH FROM YOU, FATHER!" the monsignor roared. The dominating cleric turned his eyes to his young parishioner. "I promise you, Vito Glandell, you go against the wishes of the Lord thy God, and He will bring his vengeance upon you."

Frank stood abruptly. "I've had about enough of this bullshit." He then took his wine glass, emptied what was left into his mouth, and gave his nephew a wink.

Having had enough as well, Vito stood and followed his uncle out of the dining room, into the kitchen, and down the basement stairs. That wink had filled Vito with all the confidence and self-assurance he needed. He was eighteen and knew that his uncle was right.

In a short time, Vito was going to walk away from his job at the paint factory and head down to New Orleans never to look back.

Chapter Three

Friday, March 16, 2007

Vito looked at the clock above his cubicle wall. The big hand was on the five and the small hand on the ten. Around him, he could hear his colleagues saying things like, "How many gallons of the mustard yellow did you need?" and "Hi, I'm calling from Chroma Paints, how are you today?" Their insincere gaiety was robotic.

Eyeing the color samples in front of him, Vito sighed. He needed to make endless calls for re-orders, new orders, and any other orders he could drum up because that was the very nature of sales.

Vito thought back to that night after his celebration dinner.

May 14, 1988

'Vito had decided to sit in the basement with his uncle to avoid what he knew was waiting upstairs. Even though a door and an entire floor separated them. Vito could feel the cold shoulder from his maternal enemies in the kitchen. Frank, Bisnonna Nellie, and Nonna Josie had lived in their brick bungalow ever since he could remember. The three of them moved in not long after Gus walked out.

While his grandmother liked to tell all her church friends that they moved in to help her poor abandoned daughter and grandson, the truth was Zio Frank had been slowly drinking and gambling away any savings Papa left Nonna after he died. Eventually, Nonna lost the house, and they were forced to move in with Connie and Vito. Nonna Josie and Bisnonna Nellie shared the third bedroom, while Frank took up residence in the basement. Frank had moved from job to job as his body grew weaker and his skin yellowed.

"Are you nervous?" Frank asked that night, his eyelids looking like weighted sandbags.

"Yeah," Vito answered, getting up from the sofa so his uncle could take claim of the couch that served as his bed.

"You're gonna be great," Zio Frank said as he shifted his body into his favorite sleeping position.

Vito put a blanket that Nonna Josie crocheted over his beloved zio. Frank's eyes closed as Vito walked back up the stairs.

March 16, 2007

"Vito!"

He heard his name barked loudly behind him. Vibrations shot Vito out of his memory and back to his thirty-seventh year of life.

"I've been standing here calling your name for over a minute," the voice complained. It was a voice he knew better than he cared to.

Vito slumped, keeping his back turned to the speaker.

"Well?" this person said in a way that let Vito know this was the last time they were going to say it.

Vito turned around to see exactly who he expected, his manager, Anthony Passarella.

"Uhh …" Vito stammered, unsure of what to say.

Anthony walked into Vito's cubicle, rested his ass on the desk, and laughed. "You haven't changed a bit since we were kids."

Vito looked to the floor and kept quiet, knowing full well his cubicle neighbors were listening while pretending to be on the phone.

"I haven't seen any new accounts from you in a while," Anthony continued while Vito remained silent. "You know," Anthony crossed his arms and looked down at his subordinate, "when I was promoted to run this department, I took a good look at everyone's numbers. While your steady clients continue to order enough to keep you afloat, I can't say that I've seen an increase in revenue from you in the last twelve months."

"I've only missed my quota once so far this year," Vito said.

"I'm not talking about quotas, Vito. I'm talking about creating a splash, going outside of the box, and making a real name for yourself. I was wrong. You have changed since we were kids. I remember how you talked about how you were going to leave and have—what was it?" Anthony smirked and made air quotes. "'Great Adventures?' Ha!" Anthony clutched his stomach as if his laughter was going to cause his abdominal muscles to fly out and slap Vito in the face. Once his laughter died down, Anthony stood and turned to leave. Before he did, Anthony glanced back at his former childhood neighbor and schoolmate. "Have you gone *anywhere*? Have you done *anything*?"

Again, Vito didn't answer. He was surprised that everyone in the room didn't hear his heart crush under the weight of his reality.

Anthony tossed a few sheets of paper onto Vito's desk. "Here's some leads. I want to see you make something happen. Otherwise, we're going to have a serious discussion about your future here at Chroma." With that, Anthony walked out of the cubicle. Vito collected the sheets Anthony had thrown and stacked them into a small pile on his desk. He stared down at the type, but the words all blurred together through the tears collecting in his eyes.

"He's a tool," said another familiar voice behind Vito.

He turned to see Patrick, the new guy who'd been assigned the cubicle next to him.

"And you look like you need a drink," Patrick added.

"I don't drink," Vito said, which was the most he'd spoken to Patrick since he'd started working there.

"Okay," Patrick said. "So don't drink. At five, a bunch of us are going to head to this place down the street called The Tap. Ever hear of it?"

"Heard of it?" Vito thought to himself. "My uncle lived there when I was a kid."

"Yeah," Vito answered. "I've never been there though."

"Well, you can cross it off your bucket list, because you're going there after work with me." Patrick smiled and moved in his rolling chair back into his own cubicle.

Vito thought about sneaking out at four to avoid the whole thing, but he couldn't deny that he had been curious about that place for decades. Maybe it was time he had an adventure.

Focusing his eyes on the new leads he was given, Vito tried to stay in the moment. But his mind moved back into the past.

May 14, 1988

That summer night, after his celebratory dinner, Vito emptied the jars of change he had been saving for years. First thing in the morning, he would take the bus to the bank, deposit all this silver and copper, and talk about transferring his nest egg to a bank in New Orleans.

He crawled into his twin bed and tried to sleep, but excitement proved to be a powerful drug for his anxiety. Vito tossed and turned for an hour or so, but slumber never came. Giving up, he decided to get something to eat.

Walking into the kitchen, Vito found his family gathered around the table in silence. His mother and Nonna Josie were playing Gin while Bisnonna Nellie snored softly.

The maternal duo didn't look at Vito when he walked through the kitchen door, and he was able to push out a "Hi" on his way to the refrigerator. The two women threw curses at him with their eyes and resumed their game as if he were not there.

Vito made a couple of sandwiches while listening to the cards being shuffled. He then slipped past his mother and grandmothers again, avoiding looking at them entirely despite the way his heart raced.

He'd hoped they would eventually give him some shred of understanding, but their silence was deafening.

With his head hung low, Vito opened the basement door and headed down the stairs.

"Don't worry about your mamma, Vi," Zio Frank told him as he took another swig of the martini he'd been sipping. Awake again, the seasoned drinker took the olives out of his gin and offered them to his nephew.

Vito took the olives and smiled. Chewing on gin-soaked olives was an experience he'd had since his uncle first moved into the basement. Vito knew the taste of gin almost as early as he knew his mother's milk.

"Don't let your life pass you by," Zio Frank lectured. "You don't want to end up like me."

"I'm going to miss hanging out with you down here," Vito admitted, finishing off the olives and chasing them with his Coke.

"Me too, kid." Zio Frank leaned over and put a hand on Vito's shoulder. "More than you know."

After a moment of emotional silence that was too much for any Sicilian man to handle, Zio Frank shot up with a burst. "I have a little going away present for ya."

"Zio, you didn't have to do that."

"But I wanted to." Frank said. He set his martini glass down on the carpet, reached under the sofa, and pulled out a shirt box wrapped in the Sunday comics section.

Vito smiled as his uncle handed him the box. He tore it open to find it full of cash.

Shaking his head, Vito shoved the cash-filled box back toward his zio. "Frank, I already have money saved."

"Having a little more won't hurt."

"But what about you?" Frank stood from the sofa with the empty glass and walked over to the hutch that served as a bar. "I have a couple of jobs lined up," he said, pulling ice from the bucket. Frank loaded his glass and picked up the bottle of Bombay, only to realize it was empty.

"What kind of jobs?" Vito asked, noticing with dismay that he sounded like his mother.

"The kind that pay, kid." Frank sifted through cabinets with growing fury. He then came to a halt as if something had hit him in the face. "Wow, I haven't seen this in years."

"What is it?" Vito asked. He looked to see his uncle holding a flat, slightly rounded silver container adorned with gems and stones. Every color of the rainbow was generously represented on this receptacle.

"A flask," Frank answered. "It was a gift from some friends a long time ago." He turned and passed the flask to his nephew.

While most flasks were silver, square, and the perfect size for discreet pockets, this one was all those things and so much more. Different-sized gems and stones were affixed to the surface. Frank could hide it quickly, but once any type of light reached the colorful jewels, it shone as if it were a candle lit from the inside. The colors didn't just shine; they flickered.

Vito looked up from the flask to find his uncle staring into the distance as if he had forgotten where he was.

"Hey, kid," Frank said suddenly, taking the flask back from Vito, "I have to run out. I forgot to do something. Do you mind if I cut this party short?"

"Not at all," Vito remained seated and watched his uncle cover up his white dago-T with a nice bowling shirt. Next, he pulled on some dress slacks and dress shoes; Frank never wore jeans, because he thought they looked sloppy.

Lastly, Frank slipped his London Fog cardigan over his shirt and affixed his star sapphire pinky ring onto his finger. Once his watch was in place, he folded his bills, secured them with a money clip, and shoved it in his front pocket. "Give your zio a hug." He held his arms open to Vito.

Vito stood and fell into his uncle's embrace. Then they gave each other a kiss, because that's what Italian men do. Shortly thereafter, Frank ran up the stairs as Vito gathered his sandwich plate and followed.

In the kitchen, Bisnonna Nellie was alone at the round table. Wearing a basic black dress covered with her pink floral apron, she peeled an apple with a paring knife. The skin came off in one swirl while the lighting from the small-screened television colored Nellie's face an iridescent blue. Noticing Vito, she gestured with the knife for him to sit next to her.

He did as she commanded with silence, and once he was seated, she handed him a slice of apple.

Bisnonna Nellie couldn't speak much English, and Vito knew very little Italian. He could barely understand his bisnonna, but he loved to sit with her when no one else was around. Known as Nicoletta when she lived in Italy, Vito's great-grandmother migrated to the United States in 1939 with her daughter in tow.

Nicoletta first sailed to South America, then came through Ellis Island, like millions of immigrants before her. She'd left New York upon arrival and traveled with her young child to Chicago. There, she met up with a cousin who had departed the Old Country decades earlier and opened a bakery. Nellie had just turned thirty-four, and her daughter, Giuseppina, was fourteen when they made the windy city their home.

Bisnonna Nellie met her Sicilian husband, Nunzio, at this bakery. Vito's bisnonno—or great-grandfather—owned a liquor store. He did so well Nellie no longer needed her job. Since they did all their living and working in one Chicago neighborhood, Nellie didn't need to learn English. Italians owned all the markets, stores, restaurants, and businesses Nellie dealt with, so it was easier to speak Italian.

But Nunzio felt his new daughter, Giuseppina—whose name evolved into Josie over time—had to learn English. It would ensure her a promising future in America and make Josie more desirable to the men in the neighborhood. So Nonna learned to speak enough English to get by. But she confined herself to their home and area once she married Papa Angelo, so she continued to communicate in Italian and never lost her accent.

Papa Angelo took his father-in-law's opinions even further. His children were American, and they would have an American future. Papa insisted that English was the only language used in his house, except when his wife needed to talk to her mother. Connie and Frank learned some slang and Americanized versions of Italian words like 'ree-gawt' instead of ricotta, and 'gabagool' for capicola.

In the end, Connie and Frank knew some Italian but couldn't write it at all. And by the time the generations shifted again, Vito was never taught Italian in his home or neighborhood. Granted, he did call marinara 'madinahd' and mozzarella 'mootz-ah-rell'. But that was how everyone his age in his community pronounced these words.

Nevertheless, the verbal wall never affected Vito's relationship with his bisnonna.

"Bambino,"[13] Nellie said softly, pointing to the basement door with her paring knife—a dagger that anyone would have sworn was another appendage. She made a gesture as if tipping a half-empty bottle down her throat. Then she took the knife and moved it across her throat with a quick slit-like motion without making contact with her skin. "Capisce?"[14]

Vito smiled and nodded yes. Then they sat together at the Formica table for an hour or so watching TV as the night grew darker. Eventually, Vito woke his beloved bisnonna and walked her to her room before heading to his.

March 16, 2007

"You ready?"

Once again, a voice knocked Vito out of his daily dose of procrastination, forcing his consciousness to return to his cubicle at Chroma. This time, however, he was grateful to return to 2007. All the time he'd spent living in the past exhausted him. He turned around to find Patrick waiting.

---

13   "Child.
14   "Do you understand?"

"Almost," Vito replied. "I have to finish up a few things. Can I meet you there?"

"Sure," Patrick said. "But you better show up, or I'll make you sorry on Monday."

"I'll show up," Vito promised. He wondered whether Patrick was joking or not. Vito hated get-togethers and small talk and actually considered skipping the work meetup in favor of wandering downtown. But he always wanted to visit The Tap to find out what Uncle Frank had loved about the place.

Vito's desk phone rang. "Chroma Paints. This is Vito," he answered.

"Vito," his mother was on the other end. "When are you coming home? We have dinner for you."

"What? Ma. I told you I wasn't coming home for dinner."

"But I made meatballs and sausage with lasagna. You seemed so upset about the no meat thing this morning, I thought you'd be happy. God can give you dispensation for your birthday."

"I already told you; I'm not coming home."

Vito heard his mother put her hand over the mouthpiece, muffling her voice. "He's not coming home for dinner," she said.

"What?!" Nonna screamed as if she'd just been told that he had been in an accident. "Why a not? It's a his birthday!"

Vito sighed. He just wanted to be alone, or to do something different. But he knew the women in his family didn't want to hear that, so he lied. "Anthony is taking us all out for our monthly birthdays. It's a new employee appreciation thing the company started. It's mandatory."

"Oh," Connie said. "Well, work comes first. I'm glad to hear that he's finally being nice to you. He was such a little shit when he and his Dad lived next door. Remember that?"

"Yes," Vito said, wishing he could forget. When they were kids, Anthony tortured Vito in the school halls and once Anthony beat up Vito in the area where their front lawns met. To this very day, Anthony had never even told Vito why. And now that Anthony was his boss, Vito didn't want to ask for an explanation.

"Okay. Well, Nonna and I are going to bingo later. I'll leave something for you in case you're hungry when you get home."

"Thanks, Ma." Vito felt guilty for lying, but tonight, for this birthday, he was determined to do something different.

"Love you," Connie said.

"Love you too," Vito replied. He hung up the phone and turned back to his computer. The leads he didn't call sat on his desk as he shut the machine down. Then he stood and went out to meet his new friend, Patrick, at The Tap.

***

Even though he had never been inside, Vito had walked by The Tap many times, pondering what it was about the place that made Zio Frank spend so much time there. When Frank was gone, Vito was underage and wasn't allowed inside The Tap. By the time he was twenty-one, he had grown used to Frank's absence and just wanted to put it all in the past. Besides, his mother told him that dark bars are where filth lives. She was a bit dramatic, but he had no doubt in his mind that multitudes of bacteria lived happily in this den of drunkards. They danced through the air and on surfaces undisturbed by a rag or splash of Lysol cleaner just waiting to pounce and make him sick.

This was the point when Vito decided he wasn't ready for this. Walking through this door required overcoming too many things. Not only did he have to do his best to ignore whatever germ inside could possibly kill him, it also required facing the pain of Frank's leaving. It was too much.

Then, Vito looked up to the glowing Old Style sign advertising COLD BEER. The blue and red of that sign reminded him of cans he used to see in the fridge, when his uncle lived with them. That was the moment a long-lost voice popped into his head.

"Hey, kid. You've been living in the past for the last nineteen years. I think it's time for an adventure. Consider it a present for your birthday."

Vito felt a hand push him toward the door. He turned around to see no one. He looked left and then right. The street was empty. Being raised in an Italian-American Catholic home, Vito was more than familiar with the concept of spirits, angels, and signs. Did he believe in them? Sometimes. He wasn't like his mother or nonna, who took everything as a sign from God, or Papa, or someone they loved who had passed away. But there was no denying there are some things that cannot be explained in the physical realm. He found it was best to accept these things and move on.

Pulling the heavy, leather-clad door open, Vito put his fears into a place in his head he created. A box where he could hide them away just for the moment, but which he knew had a weak lock. He stepped over the threshold into the dark, musky unknown and stood for a moment as the door shut behind him with a weighted thud. The small window on the door let in a few streams of the setting sun.

The barroom was lit only by dim overhanging lights with green glass domes. The bar was a large wooden square with scattered stools around it. Some stools were holding up drinkers who were either beginning their dive into an evening out or had been there for a while. Neon signs that shouted out beer names decorated the walls. The High Life Witch sat firmly on the moon toasting the blinking stars around her. The Budweiser Clydesdales kept time with the rhythm of the neon. The Hamm's sign depicted a smiling bear floating down a river in the land of sky-blue waters. Under the neon were walls of wood paneling that reminded him of the den in the bungalow when he was a small boy

"Hey, Vito! Down here!"

Vito spotted Patrick at the bar with Tammy from accounting and Gustav from shipping. Vito approached the trio.

"Hey," Patrick smiled. "Have a seat."

"How's it going?" Tammy asked.

"Hola!" Gustav said.

"What are you having?" Patrick asked.

Vito took a package out of his pocket. He tore it open and pulled out an anti-bacterial wipe. He cleaned the seat thoroughly while the others watched him silently. Once he took a seat Patrick laughed, "What was that?"

"Don't pay attention to him," Tammy said. "He's smart you know. This place doesn't look very clean."

"Hey, Lucia," Patrick called out to someone Vito couldn't make out.

"Be right there," an intoxicating voice replied in their direction.

After a moment or two, a woman unlike any Vito had ever seen appeared through the darkness. She had short hair, straight as an arrow, cut in the bob fashion of the 1920s. The color was the kind of red only found in a bottle, and Vito wondered if she was wearing a wig.

She wore ripped jeans with a black tank top. A poster from *The Creature from the Black Lagoon* was silk-screened on the front of her shirt. Her shoulders were covered in rose tattoos, and she had stars climbing up her wrists.

"What can I do for you?" she asked, staring Vito directly in the eyes.

The intensity of her dark blue irises forced him to look away. "Uh, y-yes. May I have a Coke, please? I don't drink, and I've never been here before, but my uncle used to hang out here."

"Well, I'm glad you're here now," Lucia smiled. "One Coke."

After Lucia walked out of earshot Patrick once again let his amusement get the best of him and laughed. "Vito, she didn't ask for your life story, man."

The rest of the group snickered.

Vito felt blood rush to his face, and he was sure his skin was bright enough to light up the dark barroom.

"Well, I thought it was a lovely story." Lucia smiled walking back with Vito's Coke. She placed it in front of him and winked. "I'll be back so you can tell me all about your uncle."

Vito smiled brighter than he had in decades. Lucia smiled back and then turned to take care of another customer.

"How did you ever get into sales?" Patrick asked in a rhetorical way that insinuated he didn't care for an answer.

Vito didn't plan to answer anyhow. He let his eyes follow Lucia until she returned.

"So, what were you saying?" she said as she affixed her gaze on him.

Vito stared at her, unable to believe this woman wanted to talk to him. He never considered himself ugly and, from what his mother, grandmother, and great-grandmother said, he was quite handsome, but Vito carried himself in fear, which is repellent to most people. Vito opened his mouth to say something but was cut off.

"Hey, Lucia, we need another round over here!"

She glanced over her shoulder and then turned back to Vito. "Sorry, hon," she said with a smile. "Some other time."

Before he knew it, she disappeared into the darkness to serve a group of men on the opposite end of the bar.

"Well, what do we have here?" Another voice Vito recognized interrupted his thoughts. He turned around to see the woman from the bus this morning standing next to him.

"Hello, Nicki," Vito replied, although he wasn't interested in starting a conversation.

"You know my aunt?" Lucia asked. Vito turned to find her standing in front of him again.

"Yep," Nicki chimed in, climbing onto the barstool beside Vito. Next to them, Patrick, Tammy, and Gustav were discussing office politics.

"This is Vito," Nicki said to Lucia. "I knew his uncle back in the day, although he and I just met this morning on the bus."

"Yes," Vito said, "Nicki and Frank were good friends, from what she told me this morning."

"Your uncle is Frank?" Lucia said, impressed.

Vito didn't understand what was going on, but he decided the less he said, the better. So, he nodded, and the women smiled with glee.

"Well, I have something for you," Lucia said to Vito and then looked at her aunt. "I should give it to him, right?"

Nicki smiled and nodded.

Shortly thereafter, Lucia ran to grab a stool. She then brought it behind the bar and placed it before the built-in wooden shelving centered in the middle of the square bar. The liquor, cash register, and other memorabilia were kept there. It was the place where the kind of things that bars are given over the years are left to collect credibility and dust. Like police patches, underwear, odd glasses, and an occasional book, toy, or statue. The Tap had a collection that was nearly a century in the making.

Taking a closer look, Vito noticed some of the memorabilia were urns with plaques featuring names he presumed were of deceased patrons.

Lucia climbed onto the stool and seized a large book from the top shelf. With the book in tow, she climbed back down and brought it over to Vito. "Here. Your uncle wanted you to have this."

Vito stared, speechless. The book's cover read, *Fiaschetta Magica*[15].

---

15   Magic Flask

"Open it," Nicki urged with a grin that made Vito's skin crawl just a bit.

Nevertheless, he opened the thick book. Inside, resting comfortably in the middle of cut-out pages, was his uncle's jewel-adorned flask.

Chapter Four

"Where did you get this?" Vito asked without taking his eyes off the flask.

"Frank gave it to me," Nicki informed. The smile left her face. "We've been waiting for you to come in here and find us," Lucia interjected, smiling like a child who'd found a bag of Halloween candy.

"Would you bring me a gin martini, Lucia, dear?" Nicki asked and added, "Extra olives," phrasing her question like an order.

"Sure." Lucia ran off to fix her aunt's drink, although it was clear she was keeping her ear on the conversation between Nicki and Vito.

"I remember the last time I saw this," Vito said, tears swelling up in his eyes.

"Frank instructed me to let fate play a hand. He didn't want me to bring this to you. He said you'd find it when you were ready." Nicki stared deep into Vito's eyes. "Go ahead. Take it. You're ready."

Vito slowly pulled the flask out of its snug book bed. Memories of his graduation dinner returned. At that same moment, someone opened the bar's door, and sunlight hit a blue bead on the flask. The gems gleamed so brightly Vito had to cover his eyes.

Lucia came back with the cocktail, of which Nicki immediately took a healthy sip.

"It's full," Vito observed of the flask. He turned to Nicki, perplexed.

"Yep. We put it up there and had a rip-roaring night until the sun came up. That was the last time I saw Frank." Nicki took another sip of her drink. "What was that, twenty years ago?"

"How come I've never seen this case before?" Vito closed the front of the book and stared at the illustration on the cover.

"I always kept that here. This is my bar. Frank said he didn't need the case because alcohol was legal now, and he could flash his flask around for everyone to see," Nicki said.

"What is that supposed to mean?" Vito reopened the case disguised as a book and inspected the inside more closely. There were words on the first page, but they were in Italian, which he couldn't read.

"Prohibition," Nicki said. "Using books like this was a way for people to hide their hooch. You tuck the book under your arm, the flask sits comfortably inside, and when you get to your destination, you have some delicious bathtub gin, and no one is the wiser." Nicki grabbed her glass. "Speaking of gin … Lucia, dear, auntie needs another martini."

Lucia, who had been listening in the background, reappeared.

"I have to go to the bathroom," Vito said in a tone loud enough that every happy hour customer at The Tap turned to look at him.

Lucia giggled and pointed. "Right over there. I'll watch your stuff for you."

Vito stood, feeling like the few sips of cola he'd consumed were going to be ejected from his body Linda Blair style. Hastily, he ducked into the bathroom. When inside he discovered his fear of what he experienced outside of the bathroom outweighed his fear of whatever was floating around by the stalls.

Grateful to see he was alone, Vito approached the sink and wiped the handles off with another wipe. Then he splashed water on his face, wincing a bit wondering what kind of crud was inside the pipe.

Someone knocked at the door.

"Are you okay in there?" Lucia's sweet voice called through the thick, swinging wood. "I'm sorry I laughed. Your proclamation just caught me off guard."

"That's okay," Vito replied. "I just need a minute or two."

"Okay."

Vito listened to the thuds of her thick-heeled boots moving away from the bathroom door. He then went to a stall and covered the seat with toilet paper, three layers thick. He sat, wishing he had an actual seat cover rather than the makeshift one he'd just created.

Tears rolled down his cheeks as his mind wandered back to a place he tried to avoid.

May 15, 1988

The morning after his graduation dinner, Vito woke with an enthusiasm he had never known. He'd been ecstatic that in a few months, he would be leaving the west side of Chicago behind for a life full of adventure and new experiences. Yet, as he cracked his bedroom door open, he heard the faint sobs drifting from the kitchen, courtesy of his mother and Nonna Josie.

Exasperated, Vito decided to get dressed before facing the guilt trip that awaited. He vowed to come back someday to visit, but leaving to start his new life was something he needed to do for himself. They would never understand, but Zio Frank was right. This was his life and his dream—he had to be strong and not let them deter him from it.

Once he was ready for the day, Vito headed down, ready for the glares and cold shoulders. Instead, he found a pious Monsignor Benevento and a dismal Dr. Bruni walking upstairs from the basement.

Vito realized the crying he'd heard was not on account of his moving to New Orleans. "What's going on?"

"Son," Monsignor Benevento started, "it seems that your uncle's drinking habits have finally caught up with him."

In the immediate wake of those words, Nonna Josie released a horrendous shriek of despair right before fainting.

Tears streaming down her face, Connie caught her mother, and Dr. Bruni dropped his belongings and rushed to help.

Once everyone was secure, the doctor laid it out for them. All Vito heard was Zio Frank … dead … liver failure.

A wave of grief rippled through Vito's body.

"God is punishing me," he thought.

Blinded with tears, Vito ran out of the house. He ran block after block until he found himself in front of the rectory at St. Luke's. He rang the bell. After a few minutes, the nun Vito regularly saw working in the school office answered the door.

"Yes, my child?"

"Father Vince," Vito stammered, trying to fight back his sobs, "I need to speak to Father Vince."

"I'm sorry, young man. Father Vince left for the airport about an hour ago."

"The airport?" Vito asked. "We just had dinner with him last night. He never said anything about going on a trip."

The sister smiled. "Yes, it was all rather sudden, but the monsignor said the Lord needed him elsewhere. Some mission in the

Horn of Africa." She noticed the fear in Vito's eyes. "Maybe I can help you?"

"Africa? When is he coming back?"

The nun hesitated for a moment. "He's not."

Stunned, Vito looked to the ground, trembling with disbelief.

The nun put a hand on his shoulder. "Are you sure there's nothing I can do for you? Monsignor Benevento will be back shortly. He's out on a call for last rights. Maybe you would like to talk to him?"

Vito didn't answer. He simply turned around and let his feet carry him back home.

March 16, 2007

"Hello?"

Vito flinched at the loud voice and the knocking on his bathroom stall door.

"Are you okay in there?"

Vito blinked, taken aback to find Patrick peering under the stall.

"That redhead behind the bar asked me to come find you," Patrick said.

Vito stood, opened the stall door, and stepped out.

"Feeling sick?" Patrick asked, placing a hand on Vito's shoulder.

"Y-Yeah. My stomach is bothering me. I think I'm gonna head home. Thanks." Vito walked past Patrick, leaving the bathroom, and heading straight for the bar. He picked up the flask from the bar, put it back in the book and tucked it under his arm.

By this time, Patrick had returned to Tammy's side to resume their conversation. Meanwhile, Nicki was nowhere in sight, and Lucia was stocking beer.

Not wanting to call attention to himself, Vito headed for the door before anyone could stop him.

He boarded the 315 and rode back down Harlem Avenue toward home. He got out in front of St. Luke's with the book and flask in hand. Before moving farther, Vito opened the book's cover and took a close look at the flask inside. It glistened from the mixture of early evening sky and flickering streetlamps. He then continued his walk home. And with each step he took, Vito relived the morning his life fell apart, recalling the way his eighteen-year-old feet beat the pavement as he returned to his family's bungalow.

May 17, 1988

Young Vito was convinced God was punishing him. He'd defied his mother's wishes, and now, not only was Frank gone, but so was Father Vince. The harsh reality stabbed Vito like a knife through the heart.

"You're making the right decision, Vito," Monsignor Benevento said while they stood next to the casket. "God took your uncle to show you how important family is. I'm glad you came to your senses. When I get back to my office, I'll put in a call to my friend at DePaul."

"Why did Father Vince leave so suddenly?" Vito asked.

"The Lord needed him elsewhere," Monsignor Benevento replied.

"But he didn't even say goodbye."

"He didn't have time, Vito. The only flight I could get him on was early that morning."

Vito narrowed his eyes. "So, it WAS you …"

"What?" the monsignor said.

"You made him leave because he stood up to you."

The monsignor glared at Vito. He cleared his throat before finally responding. "Father Vince has a calling to serve the Lord. Unfortunately, his services were needed elsewhere. YOU should be focusing on your service to the Lord, and what that will look like."

Vito nodded, unconvinced, but not daring to argue any further. He looked soberly at his mother, Nonna Josie, and Bisnonna Nellie. Each dressed in black, they sat on the beige sofa in the front of the viewing room. Constant streams of tears ran down Connie and Nonna's faces. A pile of used tissues was growing beside them.Every now and then, one of them would cry out a 'Why?' or a 'God, Please no!' into the air, disrupting the silence around them. Occasionally, their wails were in unison, as if their pain was connected, which it was. The agony Vito felt watching them convinced him that his feelings were bound to theirs.

The grief of losing someone so young was too much to bear. Connie fainted, propelling her mother into rapid hyperventilation. Nearby mourners surrounded them, some trying to revive Connie, while others focused on Nonna Josie. Some tried to push her head between her legs to lessen her breathing. This proved to be challenging considering what a life filled with pasta had done to her stomach.

Bisnonna Nellie, who had been asleep, was awakened by their cries. The near centenarian scowled at her female family members. Crying is contagious and their grief spread throughout the room. As the sobbing rose a few decibels, so did the chaos.

Vito sighed and walked toward the casket to get one last moment in with his uncle. This sarcophagus held an empty chest, as far as he was concerned. A yellow-skinned shell that used to encase his beloved Zio Frank lay there, mocking him, contradicting all that the inebriated yet wise man had ever preached.

March 16, 2007

When Vito came home the night of his thirty-seventh birthday, inside the refrigerator a full plate of food was waiting for him. It was Bingo night at St. Luke's—Connie and Nonna Josie's favorite. That meant Vito would be able to avoid all their questions about why he was so late and had missed his birthday dinner.

Bisnonna Nellie was sitting at the kitchen table alone, examining the newspaper. She had a magnifying glass in one hand and her paring knife in the other. She had just turned ninety-eight and could barely stay awake long enough to blot her bingo card. So, Connie and Nonna Josie stopped taking her with them on Friday nights.

"Bambino," Bisnonna Nellie said, smiling up at Vito when she noticed his entrance into the kitchen. She began to make quick motions for him as she lifted her newspaper for him to see.

"That's good," Vito said, patting her shoulder and glancing at the newspaper with no interest. He approached the kitchen countertop and set down the flask-concealing book. He then took the tin foil off his plate and put the dish in the microwave.

"NO!" Bisnonna Nellie yelled, banging her knife on the table like a judge's gavel.

Confused, Vito looked to his bisnonna and saw she was pointing to something on the page with the blade.

He set the microwave for two minutes and hit start. Then he grabbed the milk from the fridge along with a glass from an adjacent cabinet and poured himself a drink.

"Andiamo,"[16] Nellie said, growing agitated. Once he joined her at the table she shoved the paper into Vito's face.

He laughed when he saw it was the lost properties section. Bisnonna Nellie could not read English any better than she could speak it. Vito's curiosity left him as fast as it came though, and his attention went to the ding of the microwave oven.

As he stood to retrieve his plate of lasagna, Vito noticed his uncle's name through Nellie's magnifying glass. Quickly, he sat back down and took the paper from his bisnonna.

There it was, plain as day:

Frank Levatino
Midtown Bank
5522 Sheridan Road
Chicago, IL 60640

Underneath the address, it said *"Please contact regarding unclaimed properties."*

Bisnonna Nellie laughed and clapped—not from the excitement of unclaimed properties, but just for recognizing something in the daily Tribune.

Stunned, Vito couldn't believe that his Uncle Frank, who'd been dead for nearly twenty years, was so abruptly projecting himself back into Vito's life.

Vito gave the newspaper back to his great-grandmother and got his dish from the microwave before rejoining her at the table. While he ate, she fell asleep.

Once his dish was clean and the kitchen back to the way he found it, Vito grabbed the book, and the flask it held, from the counter and left Bisnonna Nellie sleeping at the kitchen table. He shut the door behind him and headed down the stairs to the basement.

---

16   "Hurry up."

Vito flopped into the old blue chair he hadn't sat in for years. It still fit him like a glove. He flicked on the lamp and studied the cover of this so-called book he had just acquired.

He read the title again. *Fiaschetta Magica.* Magica, he could figure that out. But Fiaschetta? He stood and went to a hidden bookcase in the deep wells of the basement. After a few minutes, Vito was able to retrieve his Italian to English dictionary from Italian class at St. Luke's. A quick stroll through the Fs and there it was, fiaschetta—flask. Magical flask.

The cover featured a golden frame encompassing an illustration of women picking grapes in a field, while one burned on a stake in the distance. A group of men stood around watching the burning woman, while another group of men holding whips and axes watched over the working women.

Inspecting the back, Vito found another gold-embossed frame that surrounded a creature that was half man, half stag. It had a rack of horns that would have been the envy of every buck in the Cook County Forest Preserves.

Vito opened the book again and aggressively pulled out the flask. He placed the book and flask on the coffee table in front of him.

He looked around the basement, noticing the minor changes his mother had made in an attempt to hide the fact someone died down there. Mostly it still looked the same, with the exception of being cleaner and having more storage boxes than he remembered.

It had taken Vito years to step foot through that door, let alone walk down the stairs. But of course, as time went by, there were instances in which he had no choice but to go into the basement. Whenever he did though, he made it a quick trip.

Vito's thoughts were interrupted by a hum. He glanced around, his heart racing. Soon he realized the humming was inside his head. He looked back to the flask, which seemed to glow in the dark basement.

Vito picked it up and hesitated for a moment. Then he opened the top and put his nose to the opening for a sniff.

"Gin. Not surprising." He snickered a bit, remembering how much Frank liked gin.

Vito brought the flask to his lips. He drank wine occasionally at dinner, but didn't partake of booze or the scene it revolved around. Still, something about the flask held his attention.

"One sip can't hurt," he heard a voice in his head say. It was a familiar voice, but it was not his. Vito went to take a sip and remembered that this thing has been sitting at the bar for nearly two decades. God only knew what kind of bacteria was growing on, or in, it.

"Don't worry about it, kid," Vito heard the voice in his head again. "That gin can kill anything." Then he heard the laugh. Vito knew that laugh and was afraid of where it was coming from. Vito stared at the opening for a moment and shrugged. He put the silver rim to his mouth and took the first sip.

Wincing as he swallowed, Vito noticed that the gin in this flask seemed much stronger than what he remembered from those olives Frank used to give him. A burning sensation moved through his chest and stomach. He began to cough, loudly and deeply. He wiped tears from his eyes as his reaction to the alcohol calmed.

As the laugh he recognized began to grow louder in his head, Vito's ordinary life took an extraordinary turn.

All the colors surrounding Vito began to fade. The brown walls bled to leave nothing but gray. The blue of the chair leaked out to nowhere, also leaving gray in its wake. The green shag rug, the mahogany dresser, everything he could see emptied its colors.

Vito closed his eyes and shook his head. "What the hell is happening?" he thought.

When he opened his eyes again, the color void remained.

Vito stood, ran to the wall, and placed his hand against it. It felt the same and looked the same, despite lacking color.

He slapped himself in the face. Still, there was no color.

Frantic, Vito made a mad dash for the stairs and barreled out of the basement through the familiar door that was now foreign to him. He found Nonna Josie and Connie still with their coats on, having just returned from their night playing Bingo.

Vito stared at his surroundings in shock and horror.

His mother and grandmother stared back with curiosity that quickly morphed into terror.

"Vito? What is it? Tell me!" Connie cried.

"Bambino!" Nonna Josie also cried. "You a scaring me."

In Vito's eyes, his mother's usual crimson hair was sans hue, Nonna Josie's housecoat no longer held its mustard-yellow brightness, and the flowers on Bisnonna Nellie's apron were no longer pink.

Vito's breathing grew heavy and fast as he stumbled to the wall and braced himself with a hand that was no longer olive toned.

The women rushed to help him regain his balance.

"Bambino, wassa matta you?" Nonna tried to lead him to a nearby chair that was once teal, but he broke free and ran out of the gray kitchen.

Reaching the front door, he opened it. "This can't be real," he muttered.

Vito exited the house and ran to the end of the walkway. The icy chill in the air told him that Spring wasn't quite there yet. Old snow crunching underneath feet sounded the same, and the scent of car exhaust smelled the same.

But all the color was gone.

Vito's body shook as he ran back into the house, hurrying past his mother and nonna. Rushing through the kitchen, he headed back to the basement, closing and locking the door behind him. "Vito! Vito! What's wrong with you?" Connie yelled, pounding on the door and jiggling the doorknob.

"Nothing, Ma," Vito hollered, still baffled by his colorless surroundings.

"Don't lie to me!" Connie hollered.

"It's nothing," Vito lied as he found the flask lying on the floor, still colorful as ever. "I'm just not feeling well and thought I was going to be sick."

"Do you want some pastina?" Connie asked. Pastina is an Italian cure-all for most ailments. But Vito sensed that the tiny pearls of pasta would not help him with this.

"No, Ma. I'm fine." Vito stared, mesmerized as the flask began to emit a blissful hum that reminded him of a tuning fork. It grew louder, and all other sounds disappeared until Vito could hear nothing else. Soon afterward Vito's sight blocked everything in its periphery. Except for the flask's hypnotizing colors. The beads and gems on it glowed and pulsated like a soul conscious of itself.

Chapter Five

March 17, 2007

"Vito ... Vito ... Vito …" Connie's voice gradually closed in.

The pain in Vito's head intensified with every call of his name. His mother's tone was like a sledgehammer on his frontal lobe. As his eyelids opened, his pupils pulsated from the harsh glow of sunlight. Vito blinked rapidly, slowly focusing on his surroundings.

Everything was still colorless.

He turned his head to the ceiling and pulled his stiff body to a sitting position. He was still in his work shirt from the night before, though his pants were on the floor. Vito noticed he wasn't wearing any socks, which was odd, but not as odd as the loss of his color sight. Vito climbed out of bed and walked to his oak dresser, which had lost every ounce of brown. The long oval mirror on the wall proved that this nightmare was indeed Vito's reality.

One look at his reflection sent a pang through his chest. The man before him was familiar, only he looked like he had stepped right out of a black and white film. He pinched himself hard enough to draw blood. The substance coming out of his arm felt like blood. He let it pool on his fingertip and placed it in his mouth. It tasted like blood, thick, salty, and metallic. But there wasn't one drop of red to be seen.

"VITO!" Connie's voice was loud enough to sound like she was right beside him, though she was on the other side of the house.

"Coming!" Vito yelled, although he took his time before heading to the kitchen.

***

"Vito!" Connie and Nonna Josie called in unison when he finally appeared in the kitchen doorway. Both nearly knocked over their coffee cups as they jumped up from their chairs.

Bisnonna Nellie awoke from the commotion and sucked her

teeth back into her mouth quickly enough to give her great-grand-son a bright smile.

"Are you okay?" Connie grabbed Vito's face and placed her lips to his forehead. "Well, you don't have a fever. What were you doing in the basement? You never go down there."

"Nothing." Vito pulled out of his mother's grasp and walked to the Mr. Coffee machine. He desperately needed a hot cup of adren-aline. Vito filled a mug and sat at the table next to Bisnonna Nellie.

Connie sat back down and stared at her son. "Nothing isn't an answer. You don't smell that great."

Vito nearly spit coffee out his nose. "Ma!"

Connie leaned back in her chair. "Well, you don't. In fact, it reminds me a bit of my brother, if you know what I mean."

"I know what you mean." Vito sniffed his pits. "I wasn't drinking."

Connie relaxed a bit. "Are you hungry? I have some bacon in the fridge."

"Sure." Vito looked at his mother, noting her smile was as bright as ever, despite her face being drained of its usual olive glow. He summoned a smile to give back to her, which made him feel a little closer to normal.

He sat at the table and watched a television news program in grayscale. "This isn't so bad," he thought—at least until his moth-er put his plate in front of him.

Something about his sunny-side eggs being less than their typical radiant yellow and orange didn't sit right with him. As he stared at his plate, unable to eat, he contemplated drinking from the flask again to see if it restored his color sight.

"Look at this bread I picked up at Liborio's. This ciabatta is baked to perfection!" Connie swooned.

Vito looked to the counter but could not see what his mother saw. He didn't see the light golden brown of a freshly baked cia-batta. He also didn't see red, green, blue, teal, magenta, or any of it.

All the colors he'd grown to know with the intimacy only a paint salesman could experience, were gone.

A tear exited his eye and rolled down his cheek.

"Bambino," Nonna Josie said, leaning in and putting a weath-ered gray hand on Vito's shoulder, "wassa matta you? Why you look a so sad?"

Vito looked at the three women he'd been sharing his life with for the past thirty-seven years. Suddenly, it no longer hurt not to see color; it hurt to see the fear in their eyes.

Their fear of not knowing why he was acting so strange—fear that stemmed from their undying love for him.

"I'm fine." Not wanting to worry them any further, Vito tried his best to perk up, putting on his best 'fake it 'til you make it' impression. He grabbed a fork, which strangely looked the same in his new visual world and began eating the bland-looking food. Fortunately, it tasted the same. But the whole experience remained nerve-wracking.

Vito's heart raced. He didn't want to lie to his mother and grandmothers, but he also knew he couldn't tell them what happened. Yet, as he sopped up the gray yolk and drab toast, he realized he did not want to carry this burden alone.

Vito chewed his colorless food, envisioning the scene that would transpire if he told the women around him that he could no longer see colors. His mom and grandmother were known to overreact to far less severe circumstances; there was no doubt they would all be driven to hysterics upon finding out what was currently going on with him. The kitchen would fill with their crying and screaming the very second the words left Vito's mouth.

This was clearly a problem they would not be able to handle.

Furthermore, they would insist that he see the doctor, and in his heart and soul, Vito knew no doctor would have the answers to his problem. Or worse, they would take him to the monsignor, and Vito had gotten good at avoiding him once he graduated from DePaul.

More importantly, Vito knew where the answer could be found.

After finishing his meal, he was about to head to his room for a Saturday morning color restoration nap when he heard a familiar sound behind him from the kitchen table.

Bisnonna Nellie was tapping her paring knife on the small plate in front of her.

Vito turned and saw she was holding the newspaper from the previous night.

"The lost properties!" he exclaimed. He ran to his bisnonna and reclaimed his seat at the otherwise empty table. Taking the newspaper from his great-grandmother, Vito's smile brightened. He kissed her on the head and gave her a gentle hug, making sure not to break her nonagenarian bones. He then hurried to his bedroom, unconcerned about dressing for the day.

Vito had kept his wardrobe in browns and blues his entire life, not caring about incorporating other colors. But now that all colors, with the exception of black, white, and gray, were missing from his closet, he missed them terribly.

Still, he patted himself on the back for making sure every shirt in his wardrobe matched every pair of pants. Vito knew that getting ready would be the least stressful time of his day.

It was early, but the bank was a hike up north and, from the address, Vito thought it might be near the lake. That meant a transfer or two, and he wasn't sure if he would need to hop on the L—Chicago's public transit system. It was going to take some research to find out, but Vito didn't mind. For the first time in years, he was genuinely excited.

Once cleaned and dressed for the day, Vito studied the schedules he kept in his room and found his best option to be the number 72 bus at North Avenue before transferring to the Red Line station at Clybourn. It would take a while, but the secret to seeing color again could be at that bank. He had to find out what it was.

***

"Where are you going?" Connie asked as he ran toward the front hall closet and grabbed his coat. "I thought you could come with me to the market. We need tomatoes for tomorrow's sauce."

"Uhh …" Vito stammered and turned toward his mother.

"There's a book reading I want to hit up North," Vito said.

"Oh, you and your books." Connie shook her head. "Fine, you can pick up the tomatoes on your way home."

"Ma," Vito began to protest, but thought better of it. "Fine."

"Good. We have company after mass tomorrow. Monsignor Benevento's sister is in town and they're coming to dinner. I'm making potato gnocchi."

"Why does he have to come here so often?" Vito complained, already irritated.

"Vito," Connie scolded, "we've talked about this. I won't have you bad-mouthing the monsignor in my home. I've worked in his office for almost forty years now. He was a friend to our family when I was a single mother, and he paid special attention to you in high school."

"I didn't ask him to," Vito said.

"Vito, he got you a scholarship at DePaul and followed you through your time there. He would've helped you join the seminary if only you …"

"If what?" Vito interrupted, his voice rising angrily—an occurrence that rarely happened while talking to his mother. "If I became a priest?!"

Connie ignored the question and instead replied. "I just don't understand what you dislike about the monsignor." She threw up her hands in exasperation and walked back into the kitchen.

"I don't understand why he needs to be so involved with our lives," Vito shot back, following his mother.

She spun around, her eyes blazing. "Maybe because he's watched you grow up, Vito! Maybe because when he decided to put an arm around an abandoned family, he became attached and feels like we're his family."

"But he's so judgmental," Vito said. "He tries to control everything. You say you're the one who pushed me to be a priest, but I know it was him coaxing you."

"He's a smart man, Vito. You should thank God to have him in your life."

Vito disagreed in his head but knew there was no arguing with his mother on this. He just had to begrudgingly accept that the monsignor was a stuffed, overinflated, egomaniac he just couldn't seem to shake.

Yet, as the thought went through his head, he began to hear a low whistle from somewhere.

"Besides, he's older and calmer now," Connie continued, oblivious to the whistling. "How much could he possibly have to say?"

"Plenty," Vito thought as a low frequency sound began to take over his ears. "Do you hear that, Ma?"

"Hear what?" Connie stopped pouring her coffee and looked at her son, puzzled. "Are you sure you're feeling okay? I've never seen you so pale before." She pulled his face to her and put her lips on his forehead again. The gesture usually annoyed him, but he was too distracted by how her hazel eyes were so dull in his new, colorless world.

Connie furrowed her brow suspiciously. "You must be feeling sick because you never let me do that anymore without a fuss." She returned to her coffee. "You're a little clammy, but no temperature."

"Thanks." Vito forced a smile, eager to leave and get to the bank, where he was positive the solution to his problem awaited.

But the sound grew louder, intensifying in his head and pulling him toward the basement.

Connie took her usual seat at the now gray kitchen table. "Aren't you going to be late?"

"Yeah, but I forgot something." Vito rushed past his mother and into the basement.

"Where is it?" he thought, ransacking the furniture, and turning everything upside down.

Finally, he found the flask in a drawer of the random old dresser that had been in the basement forever.

Once he had the flask in hand, the whistling ceased. He put the flask back inside the book cutout, closed the cover, and quickly restored the room back to normal before heading back upstairs, where his mother's concerned gray face studied him.

"Why are you spending so much time in the basement?" she asked.

"No reason," Vito lied.

"Don't lie to me," Connie replied with suspicion.

"I'm not." The container under Vito's arm began to vibrate. "I left my book down there."

His mother looked at the book under his arm. "Oh."

Vito yelled back toward the kitchen as he ran out the door. "I don't want to miss the bus. Bye, Ma."

"Don't forget the tomatoes!" she called out as the front door slammed shut behind him on the cold March afternoon.

Vito looked at his watch and hoped he could make it to the bus stop in time. As his feet shuffled along the city sidewalk, his mother's voice still lingered in his head.

Lying never came easy for Vito, but he had had to tell a few in the thirty-seven years he'd been living with his mother. The biggest lie he had ever told was when he lost his virginity to a woman he hired not far from where they live. Getting her to a motel on the bus wasn't easy. Neither was cleaning that hotel room. But he had to get her out of the neighborhood so he wouldn't see anyone he knew.

That prostitute would probably tell the tale for the rest of her life. Vito had no doubt that all her friends knew about the eighteen-year-old who had cried for hours in her arms about the death of his uncle.

The number 72 bus pulled up, and for the first time in his adult life, a surge of excitement built inside Vito's chest. He couldn't remember the last time he had headed somewhere unfamiliar in his own city. Chicago is huge. Who knew what awaited him?

***

Once he found a seat, Vito cleaned it off and sat down. He looked out the window and watched the sights on North Avenue move in a linear fashion as the bus headed east toward the lake.

The gas stations and businesses that he recognized had screaming gray neon signs and dull window displays as far as the eye could see.

The clouds hadn't changed, but the sky they covered was lighter without the ever-present blue covering the Earth.

Vito grew tired of seeing only gray and decided to focus on the only thing with color he could see. When he looked at the book, the colors were not just vibrant; it was as if they moved within the lines meant to contain them.

When he opened the cover, the first pages had an illustration with looming darkness hanging over the top with fire creeping upward. On the next page read, *Fiaschetta Magica* by Diana Antero. After that, the pages were glued together and cut out to fit the flask. Unable to read any more pages, he closed the cover and rested his head back on the seat.

Once he closed his eyes, the flask began to call out in a high-pitched whistle, just like before. Vito opened the book again and stared at the flask. The gems and stones appeared to move even though they were permanently affixed to the metal underneath.

Vito took the flask out of the cut-out and opened the top. Fighting back his nerves, he took a quick sip of the gin inside, hoping it would return color to his world. He also knew the drink would satisfy an immense thirst growing within him.

The gin slid down his throat, and Vito sighed contentedly. He screwed the top back onto the flask and looked across the aisle, noticing two passengers staring at him.

Vito checked his watch, seeing that it wasn't even eleven o'clock yet.

The bus driver announced Clybourn and Halsted as the next stop. Vito gathered his book and flask and made his exit.

***

Chicago's public train system, The L, was color-coded and a complete bitch to navigate with only black-and-white vision. Identifying which train was the red line was a total hassle, to say the least. For Vito, every transit line was merely a different shade of gray. He had to ask a homeless man who was missing a leg which train was the red line—a question that ended up costing him ten dollars.

Vito opted to stand on the L instead of sitting. He also made a mental note not to drink from the flask in public. Vito's thought was interrupted by all the revelers loading up the cars in shamrock hats and "Kiss Me I'm Irish" T-shirts. It was then he realized it was St. Patrick's Day. He didn't need to see color to know that the scene in front of him was saturated in Kelly green.

The ride on the L to the Bryn Mawr stop, where he had to get off, was only fifteen minutes, and the time flew in comparison to the near hour he had spent on the bus. Once his stop came, Vito grew excited and headed down the station stairs to a section of the city he'd explored as a kid but had not returned to in over a decade.

He headed down Bryn Mawr toward Sheridan and saw the sign for Midtown Bank.

After tracking down the right person and showing some ID, along with Frank's death certificate, a banker produced a pair of keys to a safety deposit box. The banker then led Vito to a small room with walls made of locked chests.

He used the keys to open one of the chests, pulled out the metal box inside, and set it on the table in the middle of the room. "I will be right outside if you need me," he said, leaving Vito alone with the long box.

Vito stared at it, terrified of what he might or might not find inside. Stalling, Vito looked around and wondered what colors the boxes surrounding him were. Then he turned his attention back to the one on the table in front of him, praying it would contain the antidote.

There was only one way to find out.

Vito opened the box and found a manilla envelope inside. There was one word written on it in ballpoint pen: *Vito.*

He picked up the envelope and could tell it did not conceal money or jewelry. Pushing aside his hesitancy, he tore it open. Inside resided a pamphlet, yellowed with age, along with another piece of paper—a letter written in the same penmanship as on the envelope.

It was a script he recognized as easily as his very own.

Hey Kid,
Looks like you found your way here, but this isn't where it ends. The Magic is yours now.
Love,
Zio Frank

Chapter Six

After staring at the letter for some amount of time, Vito rolled his eyes. He was not surprised there was not much information, so he shifted his focus to the pamphlet.

"It's in color," Vito thought, astounded. Ever since his world had gone black and white, the pamphlet was the first thing other than those gems and book that Vito could still see in color.

Fiachetta di Magica; Tutto quello che Devi sapere[17]

"Great," Vito thought. He scoured the few pages of the pamphlet, only to find it was written in Italian. Vito was sure the remedy for his gray life was right in front of him, but he could not read a damn word of it. He was just about to give up when he noticed an address beneath the words.

Biblioteca degli Amici. 1028 S. Oakley Avenue—right in the heart of Little Italy. Vito knew precisely where to go.

***

After two trains and an hour of wandering around the Taylor and Western area of Chicago, Vito found himself standing in front of a three-flat made of gray stone—a common sight in the city. Although he could see only gray Vito knew this building was built of stone that was gray in the real world. He knew this because this building was the type of solid multi-story dwelling that housed a multitude of families in every corner of Chicago.

Vito studied the pamphlet he'd brought along but could not find a recognizable name. Talking to strangers wasn't his thing, but he had come all this way and was unwilling to turn back now. He walked up the stairs and studied the name tags on a trio of doorbells. Not one of them said Biblioteca degli Amici. Instead, the names listed were Trentini, Cattaneo, and Vellemente.

Vito had decided to start with the first buzzer when a woman appeared behind him. She climbed the stairs carrying a paper bag containing a few grocery items and a loaf of bread. The second she

---

17   Magic Flask: Everything You Need to Know

stepped near Vito he could tell the bread was fresh as it steamed in the cool March air around them.

"Who are you?" the woman asked.

"Uh … hi. I'm Vito."

"Veeto?" the lady repeated. She studied his face and narrowed her eyes. "I don't know you." Then she ignored him and started searching through her large purse.

This woman's long curly hair was so black, Vito was sure it had hints of blue, even if he could not see them. There were spots, he could tell, where time had let white slowly creep in.

"No," he said, feeling unsure of himself. He held up the pamphlet. "I found this address on here. Do you know what *biblio-tay-ca deg-li Ami-ci* is?"

The woman stopped searching her purse. "Biblioteca degli Amici?"

"Yes." Vito held the pamphlet closer to her face.

"Stop that, you silly man." She pushed his hand away. "Of course, I know what it is!"

"I'm sorry," Vito said.

"Biblioteca degli Amici was my family's business during prohibition. It means Friends Library."

"I drank from a flask and can't see color anymore," Vito blurted it out in a way that seemed like the words had a mind of their own. To him it seemed his speach was beyond his control.

The woman looked at him curiously, scanning his body from head to toe. She then leaned in and took a long whiff. "You smell harmless," she announced, smiling the way his mother did when he was sick, to let him know everything was going to be all right. "I'm Allegra. It's cold outside. Come on in and have some pasta e fagioli[18]. I just made it this morning."

"But I don't even know you," Vito said.

"That's right," Allegra said. "But you can get to know me. And my sisters. We all live on the top floor. This is our building, and I can tell you about the flask, your inability to see color, and what you need to do to get it back. But the only place you're going to get that information is at my kitchen table over a bowl of pasta. It's cold out here."

Once she retrieved the keys from her enormous purse, Allegra turned to open the door.

---

18   Pasta and beans

"But I don't go into strangers' homes. I'm afraid of germs."

"Well," Allegra said without turning around. "You came here with questions. I have the answers. It's your choice. I can assure you our home is clean, and my pasta is delicious.

Once again, Vito found the strange women in his life to be correct. If he wanted to get through this, he was going to have to face some fears. First, the germs. Vito looked in his bag and saw he did not forget a package of disinfecting wipes, so he followed Allegra inside.

***

"Ginevra?" Allegra called out when she opened the door to the third-floor flat.

"Yes?" a voice answered from the kitchen.

"Set another bowl at the table. We have company.""We do?" The voice from the kitchen drew closer and soon, another woman appeared. Ginevra was slightly younger in appearance than Allegra, but Vito could not quite figure out how he could tell that. Neither had wrinkles and, he thought, they both could be anywhere between their early thirties to late fifties for all he knew. Ginevra had a lighter shade of hair that Vito could not make out, but he guessed it may have been some kind of red.

"Ooh!" Ginevra screeched and ran to Vito, grabbing his face with both of her hands. "And who might you be?"

Startled, Vito pried her fingers off his face. "I'm Vito." He took an antibacterial wipe out of his bag and cleaned his face. The sisters laughed.

"Well, hello Vito!" Ginevra said, growing closer to his ear and face. Vito moved away from her.

"Ginevra," Allegra started, "you leave him alone."

"Oh, sister," Ginevra kept her dark eyes on Vito while speaking to her sibling, "you know how I love to touch things. And the more you deny me something, the more I want it. It's human nature, wouldn't you say?"

Allegra sighed and walked into the kitchen with the bread.

"I asked you a question," Ginevra moved closer to Vito.

"Uh ... well," Vito stammered as Ginevra moved even closer. "What was the question?"

"I said, don't you think it's human nature to long for that which you are denied?"

Ginevra played coy while putting her fingers through his hair.

"I suppose," Vito agreed, trying to move away from her but unable to shift even an inch.

"Ginevra," Allegra scolded when she came back in from the kitchen, "I said leave him be!"

Ginevra rolled her eyes, plopped onto the floral sofa, and tucked one leg under her rippling skirt.

"Now, Vito," Allegra said, walking back to the front door, "give me your coat, and we'll all go into the kitchen. We can try to figure out how to help you over a nice bowl of pasta and beans."

Vito took off his coat and handed it to Allegra. She hung it on a hook in the hallway, and then the trio moved into the kitchen.

***

Soon, the three of them were comfortably seated at a round table that resembled the one in Vito's kitchen. Steaming bowls of pasta é fagiole sat before them.

"Before we begin, let's say a prayer," Allegra said.

Vito made a quick sign of the cross over his forehead and chest, preparing for prayer.

The sisters gasped.

"Oh no!" Ginevra buried her head in her hands. "You're one of *them*."

"One of what?" Vito asked, confused and alarmed.

"*Catholic*," Allegra spat before putting her hand on his, which he'd folded in his traditional prayer position.

"Aren't you Catholic?" Vito asked. He was not naive enough to believe all Italian Americans were Catholic, but he'd never met any who were not or at least did not pretend to be. St. Luke's had a few Creasters—people who came to mass only on Christmas and Easter—but everyone from the neighborhood came to the church at some point during the year.

"No," Allegra said. "And if you're serious about solving your problem, then you might have to abandon everything you think you know."

"Problem?" Ginevra's eyes lit up as she pulled her hands from her face. "This sounds like an adventure."

"Not for you, Ginevra," Allegra rebuked. She turned toward Vito. "You must excuse my sister. She may be nearing her next century, but she acts as if she's still in her nineties."

"*Nineties*?" Vito looked between the two women. They looked the same age as his mother. Or did they look the same age as Lucia from The Tap? He could not tell. The more he looked at Allegra and Ginevra, the more confused he grew as to how old they looked.

"Let me lead the prayer," Allegra said as she pulled Vito's hand to hers. While he knew her germs were invading his palms, Vito couldn't pull them away for a quick disinfecting. The three interlocked their fingers.

"Goddess! Hear us! See us! We are your sorelle! We consume this meal in your name and honor! Our good fortune is your bidding."

With eyes closed, the women started to hum and let their heads hang forward. Then, they flung their heads back in some strange vibration or dance. Something told Vito his mother would not be pleased he was part of this ritual. But he supposed what she didn't know wouldn't hurt her. So, Vito closed his eyes and let the sisters guide him.

Once his eyes were closed, the sisters' energy moved through Vito's fingers and into his body. Their energy fought off his anxiety, and before he knew what was happening, he felt like his body was floating above the kitchen table.

"Yes!" Ginevra yelled. "You're doing it!"

Vito, afraid of what that meant, opened his eyes.

He was indeed floating with the ladies, right above the kitchen table. His heart skipped a beat in panic, and suddenly, the three of them came crashing back down, falling to the floor.

"Ugh," Ginevra said, pulling herself back to her feet. "What did you do that for? We were almost there!"

"Almost where?" Vito asked as he got off the floor. He considered making a mad dash for the door and never setting foot back in Little Italy again. Whatever was going on, he feared it was too much for him to handle.

"You aren't ready," Allegra said as she sat in her chair and reached for a bowl of grated Romano cheese to add some to her soup.

"Ready for what?" Vito asked.

Allegra swallowed some food and wiped her mouth. "To go to the other side."

"Is that where I'll get my color sight back?" Yet, as he asked the question, Vito wondered where this other side was and whether it was worth going to.

How important was recognizing pigments again, really?

"You can't see color?" Ginevra began to laugh so hard that food spilled out of her mouth. She collected herself and wiped her face. "I'm sorry. It's just, we haven't seen anything like that in decades. Someone got you *good*."

Vito found her laughter infuriating, and before he could catch himself, his anger got the best of him.

"Who got me good?" Vito yelled. "I have no idea what is happening to me."

Ginevra focused her fiery eyes on him. "Where did you get the flask?"

Vito blinked. "How do you know about the flask?"

"I know more than you think. You have it on you, don't you?"

"How do you know *that*?"

"I heard its call the second you walked through the door."

That very instant, Vito heard the flask humming himself. He had the flask hidden in the book in his knapsack, which he'd left on the sofa in the living room. Gradually, the humming grew louder, and Vito had to fight every urge in his body to retrieve it and take a drink.

"It haunts you," Ginevra cackled. "I see it in your eyes. In the sweat that drips off your forehead."

"Ginevra!" Allegra interjected. "He is a novice to the way, and incapable of harnessing that power. Stop tormenting him."

"Oh, sister! Taunting is what I do. How dare you deny me of my desires."

Allegra scowled. "It's obvious to us you need a drink from that flask," she said to Vito. "Why don't you give in to your desires and take a sip?"

Vito wanted nothing more than to put the cold metal opening to his mouth, but he was afraid they would take it from him. He was seriously regretting ever entering their home. "Maybe later," he said. "First, tell me about your family and their connection to the flask."

Allegra took another spoonful of her soup as Ginevra sat back down at the table; her eyes firmly planted on Vito.

"Well, back during prohibition, Italians were known for all kinds of illegal activities. Some ran sugar and dealt with bathtub gin. Our ancestors also took advantage of the situation to make some money but in a different way. They forged flasks and created cases out of books for people to hide their wares while roaming the streets."

Vito remained silent as Allegra took a slice of bread to dunk into her soup.

All the while, Ginevra kept her eyes fixed on Vito. He noticed the hunger in her eyes, but it did not seem to be for the untouched bowl of pasta and beans in front of her.

"They would walk to the speakeasy, fill up the flask, tuck it in the book, and head home," Allegra laughed and looked off into the distance with the kind of smile only the best memories invoke. "Those were the days."

But just as soon as she went into the gaze, Allegra came crashing out and looked at Vito with intensity.

"The thing is," she said, "most folks who purchased a flask and book got just that—a flask and a hollowed-out book. It was quite a prosperous business. But our father couldn't help interjecting a little bit of mischief, which is why he created three special *Fiaschette magiche* … flasks of magic."

"Fia-shay …" Vito tried to repeat the words.

"Fiaschette Magiche!" Ginevra exclaimed. "You poor boy. Tua madre o tua nonna non ti hanno insegnato a parlare italiano?"[19]

Vito ignored Ginevra and launched into explaining to Allegra how he'd come into possession of the flask and book.

"Frank!" Ginevra jumped up. "You're *Frank's* nephew?"

"Now, this all makes sense," Allegra said as she finished off her soup. "Frank visited us regularly."

"I remember when we gave him that book and flask," Ginevra said, softening up and turning to her sister. "What was that, like forty years ago? I miss Frank."

"Me too," said Vito as he stared into his untouched soup.

"You should eat something," Allegra said.

But suddenly, the call of the flask grew louder in Vito's head. It pulled him, somehow letting him know it was time to go. "I'm

---

19   "Didn't your mother or grandmother teach you to spreak Italian?"

not hungry but thank you so much. Please, I just wanted to know, how do I get my color back?"

Allegra stood from the table, picked up her empty bowl, and took it to the sink.

Ginevra kept her gaze on Vito.

Vito tried to stand but could not move. His eyes were locked in Ginevra's, and bizarrely, he felt like she was gluing him to his seat.

"Why are you trying to leave so soon?" she asked, a touch of malevolence in her voice. Her eyes remained locked on his.

"Uh," Vito stammered and tried to move, but his ass was stuck in the chair like he had sat in a vat of Krazy Glue.

"Ginevra, let him go!" Allegra roared.

Ginevra rolled her eyes and stood up from her seat as Vito bounced out of his. He quickly ran to the living room, which sat in the front area of the sister's flat, otherwise known in Chicago as the "frunchroom." He grabbed his knapsack from the sofa and headed for the door.

"Vito," Allegra called, following him, "you don't have to run from us. We won't keep you here against your will."

Vito felt the flask tugging at his heart. "Good. Because I'm not sure what's going on."

"Listen, just go back to where this all started. You'll know what to do. The flask will guide you." Allegra unlocked the door for Vito as he stood silently.

Seconds later, Ginevra came running toward him, grabbed his face, and planted a cold, wet kiss on his lips. "Good luck, Vee-to," she said, smiling. She then jumped on the sofa with her legs tucked under her skirts.

Vito exited the sisters' apartment, dumbfounded.

"We'll see you again," Allegra said with a sneaky smile, just before shutting the door in his face.

When he heard the door's padlock secure in place, Vito headed down the stairs and let out his breath when he reached the street. He checked his watch and saw it was past four.

His mother was going to kill him.

He turned down the street to find the nearest L stop.

And that's when the humming resumed.

Vito tried to ignore it, but the more he struggled to ignore the sound of the flask, the stronger its pull became.

He ducked into Arrigo Park and sat near the statue of Christopher Columbus. He checked to see if anyone was around before deeming it safe enough to take out the book. Confident no one was watching, he pulled out the flask, whose colors shined brighter than any other he had ever seen.

He unscrewed the top and took a sip. The gin glided down his throat and the humming stopped. When Vito looked at the flask in his hand the gems lessened their glow.

Suddenly, he was startled by a woman's angry voice.

"You can't do that here," scolded a woman who was holding a baby and pushing an empty stroller past him.

"Oh! I'm sorry. I didn't mean to…" Vito did his best to secure the cap on the flask before putting it into the book, but as they say, when you attempt to do things hastily, you end up wasting more time.

"Get out of here, you creep!" the mother yelled, raising her voice so that passers-by could hear her. "If you don't get out of here now, I'm gonna call the cops!"

"Okay! Okay!" Vito left the park with the flask in his hand and book under his arm. He could still hear her yelling as he walked down the street, trying to stuff the flask and book back into his knapsack.

"That's right, ya drunk! Get the hell outta my neighborhood!"

Another voice appeared. "Are you okay? You want me to go after him?"

Not liking the sound of that, Vito walked faster toward the L, casting cautious looks over his shoulder along the way to ensure no one was following him.

Taking one too many looks backward, Vito slammed into someone in front of him. His bag and belongings went flying out into the brisk March air. Panicked, he dropped to the ground, quickly scooping up the flask and book.

"Oh, no … I tried to warn you I was there."

Vito glanced upward, noticing that this time, the voice was familiar. "Lucia!" Vito's stomach twisted into excited knots.

"I tried to get your attention," Lucia said. "But you were running down the street like you just robbed a bank."

Vito laughed nervously as he zipped up his backpack.

"I wouldn't find a couple million dollars in there if I looked, would I?" Lucia joked.

"Uh," Vito laughed nervously. He took one quick look back and no one even looked his way. "Okay," he thought. "I'm in the clear."

"I'm sorry," Vito said to Lucia, letting his anxiety lessen a bit. "What were you saying?"

"I was saying that if you just robbed a bank and have a lot of money in that backpack, I might consider running away with you."

Lucia laughed at her own joke and Vito, so enthralled by how cute she was, just stood there.

"Uh," Lucia said. "Okay."

"I do have a million dollars in my backpack," Vito said, not sure how he came up with that.

Lucia looked at him like he may be serious, and then she smiled and laughed. Vito laughed with her, and everything seemed to calm down.

"What are you doing out this way?" she asked.

"Visiting some old friends," Vito lied and did his best to turn the conversation to her. "How about you?"

"I live down the street."

"You do? And you come all the way to Galewood to tend bar at the Tap?"

"Well, my aunt owns the place, so it's a family business. She doesn't have any kids, and I think she's priming me to take over when she retires."

"Is that so?" Vito said robotically, wanting to cringe, and hating the words as soon as they left his mouth.

"Yes, it is," Lucia replied in a voice that mimicked a butler. Vito blushed.

Lucia giggled until noticing Vito was not laughing along with her. "I'm sorry, Vito. I was just teasing you."

"Oh," Vito replied, not knowing what else to say. He could feel himself clamming up —something he was prone to do when nervous. It was better than spewing verbal diarrhea.

"So, are you headed home?" Lucia asked.

"Yeah."

"I'm headed to the bar. Are you taking the L? We can ride together."

Vito smiled, wishing he could see the hues of her red hair and green eyes. "Sure."

They walked to the Red Line in a rather awkward silence.

***

It was a little after five by the time Vito got home.

"Veeto?" Nonna Josie called out. Her footsteps sounded from the kitchen to the living room area that adjoined the front hallway. "Where 'ave you a bean? You momma issa worried sick!"

"Vito!" Connie yelled from upstairs. "Is that you? Where the hell have you been? Why didn't you call me? I've been waiting for you to come home with those tomatoes!"

Vito scratched the back of his head. "Umm, about the tomatoes…"

Connie came to the front hallway as fast as her feet would carry her. "Where are my tomatoes?"

"I forgot."

"Vito!" Connie sighed. "Well, you better hurry. They close at six."

Vito's eyebrows shot upward. "You mean you want me to go get them *now*?"

"I'm having company for dinner tomorrow. How am I supposed to make a sauce without tomatoes?"

Knowing there was no point in arguing, Vito headed out the door again and set off walking toward Harlem Avenue, where Tom Naples' produce stand was. It was where everyone bought their tomatoes.

Vito glanced at his watch. Seeing that they would be closing in forty minutes, he picked up his pace, eventually breaking into a run.

***

Vito brought his tomato selection to the checkout girl.

"Hi, Vito," she greeted him in a friendly tone.

"Hi, Maria." Vito tried to remember what color hair she had. He was already so tired of living in a black-and-white world.

"Whatcha got here?" Maria looked at his bag.

"Tomatoes."

"They're all green. What's your nonna and momma making with these?"

"Oh," Vito tried to find a good excuse. "I'm so in my head, I didn't even notice."

Maria giggled. "Were you supposed to buy tomatoes for her sauce?"

"Yeah."

"After all these years of shopping with your momma, you don't know what kind of tomatoes to buy for a sauce?"

"Well," Vito started. But before he could finish, Maria took his bag back to the tomato area and returned his selections. She then went to another bin. "*These* are the tomatoes you want."

"Great." Vito began filling a bag with random tomatoes, all the while trying to ignore how the flask had been pulling at him since boarding the red line train with Lucia. Granted, resisting the urge had not been that difficult while in her presence. He'd been able to distract himself, listening attentively to Lucia talk about her life.

Maria gasped. "What are you doing? You can't just grab *any* tomatoes! You have to check them for color. Look how red this one is compared to that one."

A tear welled in Vito's eye. All the tomatoes looked the same to him. Trying to find the right ones was going to take forever, and he needed to get home to be alone with the book and the flask.

"I've got an idea," Vito said, turning toward Maria and feeling frustrated. "Why don't you teach me. That way, when I shop for my mother next time, I'll know what I'm doing. I know it's almost closing time though, so if you're too busy, I understand."

Maria smiled. "Oh, no. I'm happy to help you."

Vito looked down at her apron, which he knew was red; all the workers at Naples wore them.

He stood and pretended to listen to Maria explain which tomatoes were best for sauce, which were good for salads, and a bunch of other pointers. But the vibrations of the flask in his satchel had become too distracting, and his craving for it was stronger than ever.

"Okay," Maria said, "that should be enough."

"Great." Vito grabbed the bag and headed toward an open register.

"Oh ... Well, I guess I'll see you later, Vito." Maria called after him.

"Thanks, Maria. I couldn't have done this without you," Vito said over his shoulder.

After paying the kid at the checkout, Vito headed home and hoped he was done with tomatoes for the day.

Chapter Seven

"Okay, hand me the string," Connie instructed.

Vito did what he was told and watched his mother and grandmother put the many braciole together. He sat in that kitchen with them so often, it was a wonder he didn't pick up any desire to cook himself. But despite having watched them cook for as long as he could remember, Vito didn't even know how to make a meatball.

"After you stuff and roll the meat, you tie it like this," Connie said.

But Vito's eyes were on the basement door. He had thrown his knapsack down the stairs after his mother insisted, she needed his help making the sugo. Her complaint that he'd gotten home so late with the tomatoes had been a sufficient guilt trip, making him succumb to her request.

Still, the pull of the flask was growing stronger with every passing second.

"Are we almost done?" Vito whined.

"Why?" Connie put the freshly rolled braciola into the pan for browning. "Where do you have to be that's so important?"

"I want to get back to my book," Vito lied. As the words left his mouth, the pull of the flask grew stronger.

"You spend too much time with your nose in a book, Vito. It's good to spend time with your family. Besides …" Connie stopped mid-sentence so she could add the rest of the braciole to the pan.

"What?" Vito hated when she left sentences hanging in mid-air, as if he was supposed to guess what she was trying to say.

"You've been acting strange the past few days. I have no idea what you've been up to."

Vito did not reply.

"OH NO!" Connie shouted.

Vito looked up to see his mother had splattered tomato sauce all over her apron.

"Vito, quick, grab me a towel!"

He got up from his seat and grabbed the first towel he saw.

Connie looked at him. "Why would you grab a white towel? The tomatoes will stain it!"

"Uh…" Vito looked around for another towel, more acceptable.

Connie walked past him and grabbed a roll of paper towels.

Embarrassed, Vito took a seat at the kitchen table and clamped his mouth shut.

Connie cleaned herself up and washed her hands in the sink. Vito wanted to get up, but he could tell she was not through talking to him yet, and any movement on his part would cause an increase in the hysteria. So he sat.

When Connie finished cleaning herself, she turned around and looked at her son who kept looking toward the basement door.

"Fine," Connie sighed in agitation. "Just go."

Vito ran down the basement stairs and shut the door behind him. He then made a beeline for his knapsack.

Before he could open his book to retrieve his flask, the door to the kitchen opened with its trusty little squeak. Vito halted, feeling on edge as the ringing became more and more overwhelming.

"Just one more thing," Connie started to say, her pink backless slippers flapping as she made her way down the stairs. Her apron was still splattered with tomato sauce, whose color Vito couldn't see. She had a wooden spoon in one hand while the other hand rested on her hip. "I smelled gin down here." She shook the wooden spoon at Vito, as if threatening to brandish his hide with it despite his age of thirty-seven. She moved closer. "You're a grown man now, and up until this moment, you've been a mother's dream. So, I'm going to give you the benefit of the doubt and believe you when you tell me you weren't drinking down here last night."

Vito's guilt meter rose to a level of red despite it being a color he could no longer to see.

"But I'm telling you now, Vito," Connie continued, "I dealt with a brother who loved the taste of gin so much he killed himself over it. At forty-seven. That's only ten years older than you are now."

"I know, Ma. I was there," Vito said, annoyance replacing his guilt.

"Well, I doubt the smell of gin is lingering from Frank's last martini," Connie said, smartly. "But I'm gonna forget about that and leave you with this … Drinking will steal your job, your relationships, and anything else that gives your life color."

"If you only knew," Vito thought, releasing a sarcastic snicker. Suddenly, his cheek stung from an abrupt slap across his face.

"Do you think this is funny, you little shit?" Connie said, staring up at her six-foot tall son. "My brother, your uncle, your nonna's only son, *died* from his love of gin! I'll be damned if I let it take *my* son!" With that, she turned sharply on her heels and stormed back up the steps, closing the kitchen door behind her.

Collecting himself, Vito looked at the book, which was resting on the coffee table. The flask still hummed for him, but he knew now that he would need to find another way to get his color back. Ignoring the pull of the flask, Vito left the basement and went to his room to read.

***

When Vito's eyes opened, he found himself lying in his bed with his latest book on his chest and a bland 3:05 a.m. staring at him from his alarm clock. His vision still had not returned to normal, and he longed for the colors floating on the flask.

As if sensing Vito's yearning, the flask's ringing began. Before long, Vito was in the basement with the flask and its irresistible potion in his hand. Staring at it was enough to make him temporarily forget he couldn't see color elsewhere. His only focus at that moment was the brilliant colors the book and flask provided.

He took a sip, although he hadn't expected it to bring his color back. But maybe the second sip would?

Or perhaps the third?

By the eighth time his mouth touched the opening, he had emptied the whole flask into his stomach.

He looked around the basement and everything was a blur of different variations of gray. The dark, medium, and light grays that surrounded Vito began to dance and blend until they became a vast darkness of nothingness. While this experience would have normally sent Vito into mass hysteria, he was surprised at how calm he felt. He knew it was the gin that made him okay with all this supernatural shit that was happening. It made him not care. Vito was particularly surprised at how little he cared about germs or anything. He contemplated that until he passed out.

***

Once again, Vito's eyes opened. To his glee and astonishment, he could see all the colors. He jumped up from the sofa and saw that the half windows on the basement walls bled yellow sunlight into the room. It made the blue of the sofa shine and the red of the afghan give him visual warmth. Vito looked around the room with tears in his eyes taking in all the colors he so terribly missed.

He couldn't believe his luck.

If he had known draining the flask was all it took to get back to normal, he would have done so a long time ago.

Vito did not want to stop taking in all the greens and oranges around him until he noticed gray on the floor. It was the flask, suddenly sans color. He picked it up and studied it for a bit.

"It's beautiful, isn't it?" a voice said behind him.

Vito spun around, but no one was there. Shrugging the mystery voice off as a figment of his imagination, he moved to the coffee table, where he had left the book.

"Don't put it away yet," the voice returned. "We might need a drink later."

"Who said that?" Vito asked, panicked. And right as the question left his mouth, the flask grew heavy in his hand, as if being held under a running faucet for refilling. Confused, he reopened the top, finding that the flask was filled to the brim with gin again. "What the …?"

"Funny how it does that, huh?"

Vito spun around, spilling a little gin on himself as he tried to find the voice talking to him.

"Relax, kid. Have a sip." The unseen voice laughed as Vito felt the flask lift his hand to his face for another drink.

Unnerved, Vito opened his hand and let the flask drop to the floor. Its contents spilled onto the carpet.

"Damn," the voice said as Vito stared at a cigarette suspended in mid-air. There was a quick flash of a match strike. "That's a waste of good gin."

"Who are you?" Vito asked the invisible stranger who was apparently smoking a cigarette.

"Never mind that," the voice answered. "Pick up that flask and take a drink."

"But it all spilled on the carpet."

"That flask can't be emptied," the voice said with a bit of melancholy.

Vito picked up the flask, and once it was upright in his hand, it magically refilled itself. He peeked through the opening, stunned to find the flask filled to the brim once more.

"Go on," the voice goaded as a levitating cigarette ember glowed. A stream of smoke was exhaled into the air from nowhere as if the invisible man was standing right beside him. "You look like you need a drink."

Vito stared at the floating cigarette while gripping the flask.

"It's your life, kid. You can stand there talking to a cigarette that'll be snuffed out in less than five minutes, or you can finally take a leap." The cherry on the end of the cigarette brightened, bringing it closer to the butt.

"I'm clearly losing my mind already, so what the hell?" Vito closed his eyes, put the flask to his lips, and took the biggest swig of his life.

When he reopened his eyes, his jaw hit the proverbial floor.

The lower half of a man dressed in pinstripe slacks and wing-tipped shoes was standing in one corner of the room. The hips of this apparition were positioned against the wall in a way that only the late Dean Martin could imitate. Slowly, the top half of the body began to fill in until Vito was looking at his beloved zio, Frank.

"Surprise, Vi!" Frank laughed and took a final drag from his dying cigarette. "Didn't ever think you'd see me again, huh?" He let the smoke flow out of his nostrils as he began walking closer to Vito, who was frozen on the spot in shock.

Vito shook his head. "It can't be you, Frank. You're dead."

When Frank reached his nephew, he lifted his hand out to shake. Rather than taking it, however, Vito merely stared. A cold shiver ran down his spine.

"Aw, c'mon, kid. I ain't gonna bite ya." Frank put a finger to Vito's chin, shifting his nephew's head so they looked each other in their eyes.

The moment Vito's eyes met his uncle's, he saw the hazel tone he remembered. Their kindness and shape were still there too, surrounded by the familiar laugh lines Vito knew so well.

The tension left Vito's shoulders, and he shook his uncle's hand. Soon the handshake morphed into a hug, a kiss, and back-patting.

When the uncle and nephew released each other, Frank pulled a pack of cigarettes from his breast pocket and pulled out another as he walked around the basement.

Vito followed him like a puppy, unable to stop his nervous chatter. "Frank, how are you even here? Are you a ghost? How were you able to touch my face if you're a ghost? None of this makes any sense, Frank. Did you know I couldn't see any color for a whole day? What's up with that?"

"Shhh!" Frank put a hand in his nephew's face. "One thing at a time. Let me look around. I haven't seen this place in a long time." Frank lit his smoke and began checking out the basement's drawers and mirrors. "I see some things have changed." Frank eyed a basket of yarn Connie put down there after she had to give up crocheting due to her arthritis.

"Nonna and my mom are gonna freak out when they see you."

Frank turned to face his nephew. "They aren't gonna see me."

"So, you *are* a ghost?"

"Maybe." Frank took another drag of his cigarette. "Or maybe this isn't the basement."

Vito looked around, confused. "What do you mean? This is the basement. I came down here last night to make that thing stop hounding me."

"What the hell happened to you, kid?" Frank sat on the arm of the sofa and stared up at Vito.

"Nothing, really. I mean, I'm older, but I'm still the same person."

"Are you?" Frank gave his nephew a look of disgust. "You seem a nervous wreck to me. Here, have a smoke."

"I don't smoke," Vito said as a cigarette appeared out of nowhere, dangling from his lips. He let it drop to the floor.

"You have to lighten up kid," Frank said.

The cigarette appeared in Vito's mouth once again and Frank was instantly standing in front of him. Before Vito could say anything, Frank used his Zippo and lit the dangling cigarette in Vito's mouth.

Vito inhaled, letting smoke fill his lungs for the first time. When he exhaled, a rush of happiness filled his body. He smiled and placed the rolled tobacco between his fingers, almost forgetting his long-lost, deceased uncle who was standing right in front of him.

"See? It's a lot easier here, isn't it?" Frank put an arm around Vito.

"Is that really you, Frank?" Vito asked, putting a hand on his uncle's shoulder.

"Of course, it's me." Frank pulled a tiny gold flask from his inside pocket, unscrewed the lid, and took a long drink. "Ahh, I needed that," he said contently and then looked to his nephew. "I've been wondering when you would get here."

Vito lifted his head. "Here? What do you mean? We're in the basement."

"Are we?" Frank raised an eyebrow. "Why don't you go take a look out the window?"

Vito looked at the small, rectangular frames along the top of the wall. He headed over, noting that it already seemed dark. How long had he and Frank been visiting? Vito could have sworn he had just seen the morning sunshine when he'd first awakened.

Once at the window, Vito looked and knew he wasn't in his Chicago bungalow.

Outside the window was a vast universe, reminiscent of images depicting space travel. Vito's eyes feasted upon nebulae and supernovae that he had once seen in his dreams. He was able to recognize these star nurseries because somehow, he had traveled through them before.

"This is a basement, but it's not the basement you think it is. Sure, this place looks like the basement I died in, but it's a whole different world here."

"Come sit with me," Zio Frank said, beckoning his nephew to the sofa.

Vito did as he was instructed and took another drag of his cigarette. He exhaled and looked at Frank. "So, I'm dead?" Vito asked.

Frank chuckled. "No, kid. You're just not at home."

"Is that why my color came back?"

"Yes." Frank took another sip from his flask. "When you go home, you'll still be colorblind."

"So, I'm going back home, at least. Well, that's good."

"Hold on, don't get too excited yet. You still have places to go."

"Places to go? Like where?"

"Have a drink," Frank instructed, eyeing the beaded flask that no longer belonged to him.

Vito didn't argue. The colorless flask was full, and he took a sip, instantly feeling himself relaxing. Then he took another drag of his cigarette, letting a cloud of smoke envelop him.

"Now, tell me—what happened to the kid I used to know?" Frank asked once Vito came out of his haze.

"I grew up," Vito answered simply.

"No, you didn't. You gave in. And you gave up." Uncle Frank shook his head. "I never thought you would turn out like this. I remember sitting in the basement and listening to you brag about all the things you were gonna see and places you were gonna go." Disappointed, Frank stood and began pacing the room. "But look at you!" He pointed his finger at Vito's face. "You were gonna see the world and have great adventures. But where have you gone? What have you seen? Nothing, that's what."

Vito sat silent and let the words beat him down, just like he did every night when they made an appearance in his head.

"I'll tell ya, kid," Frank said, finishing off his cigarette before lighting another, "I'm glad I wasn't alive to watch you turn into this."

"God took you from us to teach me a lesson. So I would stay home like Mamma wanted," Vito said, a meager attempt to defend himself.

"Bullshit! I died because I was an alcoholic, and my liver gave out on me. Nothing more, nothing less." Frank walked to the window and gazed out.

"Where am I, Zi?" Vito asked after a moment.

"That's not important now. What's important is where you're going." Frank returned to the sofa and sat down. His adult nephew joined him.

"And where am I going?""On the great adventure you've always dreamed about, kid."

Vito stood. "I can't go anywhere. Mamma and Nonna need me at home."

"You won't be able to see color there, Vito. How are you going to sell paint?" Frank began to laugh uncontrollably. "Or are you gonna push the gray number 257?" He began to cough as he reached into his pocket for his heavenly flask of gold.

"I'm serious, Frank. I can't stay here with you," Vito stated, growing annoyed.

Frank swallowed his drink. "I didn't bring you here for me. I'm dead, and I couldn't be happier." The well-dressed man stood and walked to his nephew. "I can go anywhere and do anything I want." He looked Vito meaningfully in the eyes. "I brought you here for *you*."

Vito stared back at him silently, puzzled.

"I don't like the way you turned out, kid," Frank added.

"What do you mean?" Vito said, his heart dropping at the idea of disappointing his uncle. "I've been taking care of Momma and Nonna *and* Bisnonna Nellie. I've been doing everything they ask of me."

"Have I ever once told you to take care of anyone?" Frank gave his nephew a soft slap on the side of the head. "You were a boy of dreams. You wanted adventure. You wanted to live life. So, I decided that, even if I had to bring you here, I was going to give you a great adventure before it's too late."

"But I don't want that anymore." Vito's shoulders slumped in embarrassment.

"Why?"

"Because they need me."

Frank slapped his nephew again, harder this time. "Bullshit. Why?"

"It's true."

Frank's pinky ring hit Vito's temple. "Bullshit! *Why?*"

"I ... I'm, I'm afraid, okay?" Vito's voice came out a screech. Avoiding his uncle's gaze, he began to sob.

Frank sat down and took another sip from his flask. "Sure, that's okay. Courage is resistance to fear. Mastery of fear. Not the *absence* of fear."

Vito looked at his uncle in disbelief, recognizing the quote but unable to fathom how his dead uncle knew it.

Frank winked. "Mark Twain."

"I know it's Mark Twain!" Vito jumped up from his seat, angry for reasons he couldn't even comprehend. "Who the fuck are you to come here and start spitting Mark Twain at me?"

"Vito, relax." Frank stood and approached his nephew.

"Don't tell me to relax!" Vito shoved his uncle away. "What happened to my color, Frank?"

Frank sighed and lit yet another smoke. "I took it away."

Vito blinked. "Great. That was hilarious. You can give it back to me now."

Frank coughed out smoke with his laughter. "It doesn't work that way, kid. Sorry."

Vito sighed and flopped back onto the sofa.

"I wish I could help you, but once the spell is set into place, it has to be completed." Frank shrugged.

"What has to be completed?" Vito asked.

"The adventure."

Vito glared at his uncle. "I don't want to go on any adventures. I just want to go home."

"Well, you can do that."

"I can?" Vito stared at his uncle again, sensing there was a catch.

"Yeah. But if you do, you can't get your color back. You can go home and skip the trip we set up for you, but you'll live the rest of your days in eternal gray."

Vito thought for a moment. "Okay. Fine. I won't see color anymore."

"So, you're telling me you'd rather go back to your ordinary life, selling paint and living with your mother?"

"Yes." Vito stood and began pacing. "When I was younger, sure. I would've jumped at the chance to take an adventure. But that wasn't what God intended for me. I have to go back."

"Okay. You can go back. Just take another drink from your flask, and you'll go back to where you started."

Frank stood and put an arm around his nephew's shoulder. "Or you can head upstairs and walk through that door and have the experience of a lifetime. The choice is yours."

Vito looked up the stairs toward the door he had seen a million times. Typically, that door led him into the kitchen, where his mother and nonna were always creating something delicious. The door he looked up to now, well, Vito had no idea what waited for him behind it. He sat back down on the colorful sofa and took one last look around at all the hues he could take in. Did he really want to go back to a life of gray?

Vito unscrewed the top of the flask and looked at his uncle.

"So that's it, huh?" Frank asked as he crushed out the butt of his Camel.

"Try to understand, Zi. I'm too old now. I'm too scared. I can figure out how to make this work."

"It's your life, kid. Just remember, that flask has powers that are impossible to ignore. When it wants you, you won't be able to resist." And with that, Frank was gone.

Vito jumped a bit as his uncle faded. His eyes lingered on the spot where Frank last stood. Then Vito looked up at the door that served as a barrier between him and some unknown adventure he never requested.

He put the opening of the flask to his mouth and took a drink.

The colors surrounding Vito began to swirl, blending and separating until he was in the middle of a funnel. He laughed, looking at the kaleidoscope of the last colors he would ever see.

Then, everything faded to black.

Chapter Eight

March 18, 2007

Vito's head felt like it had been the victim of falling ice from the top of the Sears Tower. His eyes burned from the window's glare even though he saw only white, black and degrees of gray. It now seemed unfathomable to him how that same window had been glowing yellow only a day ago. Or was it two days ago now?

Vito rubbed his eyes and sat up to find himself lying in the basement that was once again void of color.

When he heard the clanking of dishes upstairs in the kitchen, he looked at his watch. It was past noon on a Sunday, meaning he missed mass and there would be hell to pay.

He forced himself to stand, and that's when he heard it—the low ringing of the flask starting in his head. He placed it in the breast pocket of the jacket he'd worn the night before, hoping his mother and grandmothers wouldn't be able to tell he'd slept in it. But he knew he was just kidding himself; they noticed everything.

Preparing to face them, Vito walked up the stairs and opened the kitchen door.

***

After four hours of lectures, crying, and the most robust attempt his mother had ever made to make him feel guilty, Vito eventually made it through the kitchen and back to his bedroom.

Shortly thereafter, he was standing at the front door, showered and in a fresh suit, shaking hands with Monsignor Benevento.

"I didn't see you in mass this morning Vito."

"Uh, yeah … I wasn't feeling well."

"Make sure you come to see me before mass next Sunday then. I won't be giving you any communion until you've made your confession."

"Okay," Vito answered and left it at that.

"Do you remember my sister, Laura?"

"I do. Hello, Sister. It's so nice to see you again." Vito pushed pleasantries through his dry lips, which yearned for a sip from the flask in his breast pocket. He had learned that as long as he kept the flask close, it seemed to stay quiet. And that's what he needed. He didn't want to take another sip and end up back with his dead uncle lecturing him.

He stepped aside to let his mother and Nonna Josie greet their guests. The group then sat around the living room while Connie and Josie ran back and forth to the kitchen, finishing dinner. Bisnonna Nellie sat next to Vito on the plastic-covered sofa.

"This morning's homily was wonderful, monsignor," Connie called out from the kitchen, in a way that let Vito know the comment was intended to further chastise him. "Don't you think so, Mama?"

"Si!" Nonna Josie yelled back as she added salt to a pot of boiling water. Then she put all the potato gnocchi she and Connie made the day before into the boiling water and gave it a gentle stir. "Joost a few a more minutes, and we can mangia[20]."

"Great." Monsignor Benevento smacked his lips while his sister, the nun, sat voiceless by his side. "Vito, since you missed mass this morning, I would be happy to share it with you while we wait for dinner."

"Um ... well ..." Vito searched for the best way to say thanks, but no thanks. He wasn't in the mood to hear a homily. But he knew his mother would consider that being rude to the monsignor.

"Sure," Vito replied reluctantly, and slumped back into the stiff sofa.

The monsignor took a sip of his wine, which Vito could tell was red since it appeared black to him. Then the holy man stood and began to speak as if he was on the altar. "A young woman came to me and said, 'Monsignor, I am having family troubles, and I desperately need your help.'" He paused to make eye contact with everyone. "Her husband was a drinker. A carouser! A man steeped to his neck in sin."

Bisnonna Nellie yawned and closed her eyes while Connie and Sister Benevento raptly listened to their hero. Nonna emerged from the kitchen for a moment, until a scent or sound prompted her to scurry back to the stove.

---

20   Eat

"As it says in the Book of Peter, 'Be sober-minded; be watchful. Your adversary, the devil, prowls around like a roaring lion, seeking someone to devour.'"

Vito listened, though he was slowly falling into a stupor as the pull of the flask grew stronger. He couldn't focus on anything the monsignor said. All he could hear was the humming as the room around him began to blur. He began to shake his head and rub his eyes, but it was still blurry. After a moment, his eyes were able to focus again, and Vito concentrated on his gray reality.

Everyone was staring at him, except Bisnonna Nellie, who had fallen asleep.

Vito blinked, immediately feeling defensive. "What?"

"Your mother says you've been spending a lot of time in your uncle's old haunt," the monsignor said.

"Huh?" Vito said, his brain fuzzy. "Oh, The Tap? I was there only once, on my birthday. A guy from work invited me to have a beer there."

"The Tap?" Connie stood, furious. "He meant the basement! What are you doing hanging out in a *bar*?"

Soon, Connie was pacing, throwing her hands in the air, and shaking her finger in Vito's face. But Vito tuned it all out as best as he could.

Monsignor Benevento interrupted, speaking to Connie about exercising patience. Meanwhile, his sister excused herself to use the bathroom.

Nonna Josie peeked in from the kitchen, trying to figure out what was going on. Her jagged movements forced some gnocchi to slip in the platter, and one fell to the floor.

Typically, guilt would have taken over Vito by now. But with the flask next to his body, he somehow felt comforted. He pulled the flask from his pocket and took a sip to ease the ringing in his head. Yet, before he could swallow, a collective gasp bounced off the walls.

The gin rolled down Vito's throat as he looked around the room.

The nun, who hadn't made it to the bathroom yet, came to a halt and started uttering a prayer while the monsignor went to console a crying Connie. Not until then did Bisnonna Nellie awaken.

"Did you not hear what I just said about being sober-minded?" the monsignor barked at Vito as Connie cried on his shoulder. "That flask will lead you down a path of regret and despair!"

"Why is everything so black and white with you people?" Vito asked, his confidence growing as the gin created a warm path down his esophagus. "A little drink never hurt anyone. Look at all of you. You're drinking wine right now!"

"A little wine on a Sunday afternoon isn't the same as passing out in the basement!" Connie hollered through her tears.

Vito surveyed the room, sensing anger and disappointment surrounding him like a veil. He could deal with self-disappointment, but everyone else's disapproval, especially Bisnonna Nellie's, was too much to bear.

Unable to take it anymore, Vito stood and went to the coat closet.

"Where do you think you're going?" Connie demanded.

"Out," Vito replied. He was thirty-seven, everything around him was gray, and he was tired of doing what everyone else wanted. It was time he saw someone who made him smile. He put on his coat and opened the door, stepping onto the front porch. Then he headed for the bus stop.

He walked, eventually noticing footsteps behind him.

"Vito," Monsignor Benevento caught up to him and put a hand on his shoulder.

"What do you want?" Vito snapped, refusing to turn around. He was sick of seeing the monsignor's face.

"I want to help you," Monsignor Benevento said. He tightened his grip on Vito's shoulder and forced him to turn around until they were facing each other.

"You've done nothing but make me miserable," Vito spat.

"I've helped you every step of the way," the holy man said, defending himself with a huff. "I made sure you were in the right classes and took the correct path through life. I still think you would've made an excellent priest. It's not too late, you know."

"See, that's what I mean." Vito pushed his unwanted mentor's hands off him. "I didn't ask you for any of that. I wanted to leave. To head out into the world. But look at me now. At thirty-seven I've barely left my neighborhood. I never asked for your help, but you had to push your way in. Why do you care so much?"

The monsignor grew angry. "You were a fatherless boy. Your mother is my employee, and a good friend. She needed help, and you needed the influence of a man in my position."

Vito turned around and sprinted to the bus stop. "Tell my mom I'll be home late!" he yelled over his shoulder just before jumping onto the bus.

***

"Hey there, stranger," Lucia said upon spotting Vito at her bar.

"Hi." Vito's heart began to pound with a rhythm that sent electric currents through his body.

"What are you having?" Lucia asked, putting a paper napkin on the bar top in front of him.

"I'll have a gin and tonic."

"Okay." Lucia smiled, grabbed a glass, filled it with ice, and picked a bottle from a group that all looked the same to Vito. Once she finished, she brought the glass to him, eyeing him curiously as she did so. "I thought you didn't drink?"

"I don't," Vito said after taking a long sip from the glass. "But I'm taking a break from being a non-drinker."

"You look like something's bothering you though," Lucia said, her expression growing empathetic. "You have the saddest eyes I've ever seen. And I've been tending bar for more than a decade, so I've seen some shit."

Vito forced a smile. "I'm fine."

"I don't believe you. But if you don't want to tell me, that's all right."

Vito sighed. "It's just … complicated."

"In this life, what isn't?" Lucia asked, making a very good point. Seconds later, the door opened, letting a bright stream of sunlight inside a place designed to comfort those who enjoyed darkness. "I'll be right back." Lucia winked at Vito, though he was starting to grow convinced that she flirted with all the men who came into the bar.

Vito took another sip of his gin and tonic, and the alcohol's warmth climbed his spine and crept into his shoulders. This was his first drink, outside of the flask, in a long time.

He remembered the olives from Frank's martinis, reflecting on how he'd always adored the taste of gin. But there was something about sitting in a dark bar at three o'clock on a Sunday that calmed him. It also silenced the call of the flask, which was a much-needed relief. Plus, everything in the room was dark, making Vito's inability to see color temporarily not matter.

"I thought we'd find you here."

Hearing a hiss behind his head, Vito abruptly turned to find Ginevra and Allegra behind him.

"Like uncle, like nephew." Ginevra laughed as she pushed her way to Vito's barstool side and began rubbing his shoulders.

"Ginevra!" Allegra scolded and pulled her sister off Vito.

Allegra reached into her bag. "You forgot this at our place."

Vito looked down to see her pull out the pamphlet he'd found in the safety deposit box. "I don't need that," he said, and turned away from the sisters to take a sip of his gin and tonic.

"But there are instructions in here that'll help you work the flask," Allegra insisted, shoving the little booklet in Vito's face.

Vito refused to take the pamphlet from her. "I don't need it. I won't be using the flask."

"What?" Allegra took an empty stool next to Vito. "What does that mean? Did Frank come to you?"

"Yes," Vito said, although he was still trying to make sense of this in his head.

"Well, did he tell you how to get your color back?"

"He did." Vito turned to look at Allegra, who'd placed the pamphlet on the bar in front of him. "But I'm not going."

"What do you mean you aren't going? Your uncle set this up before he passed to the other side. You have no idea what he went through to make this happen for you."

"I don't care. He gave me a choice, and I've decided to stay here, colorblind." Vito set down his glass, which now contained only ice. He then stood and left Lucia some money on the bar to cover his drink and a tip.

"It's not too late," Allegra said, pushing the leaflet in his face again.

Vito snatched it from her hand in irritation. "I can't read it anyway. It's in Italian."

"I'll translate for you," Allegra offered. "We both can, right, Ginevra?" She turned and saw her sister walking into the men's bathroom with a guy who'd had been sitting across the bar. "Hey!" Allegra yelled as she ran to her sister, pulling her away from the barfly.

"What?" Ginevra said. "We were just about to—"

Allegra rolled her eyes. "I know what you were about to do. And now is not the time, *mia sorella*."

"It's a perfect time. He's gone."

Allegra turned to see that Vito was no longer with them, and that he'd left the booklet with his empty glass.

***

Vito came home to find Nonna and Connie clearing the dinner table, with the monsignor and his sister nowhere to be found.

"I'm back," Vito announced as he hung his coat in the front hall closet.

But Nonna and Connie ignored him, their silence serving as retaliation for his sins.

Vito, however, chose to ignore the guilt and appreciate the quiet. Loud yelling and drama were so constant in this house that calm was more than welcomed.

Until Vito heard the call of the flask.He hesitated, not wanting to walk past his family to get to the basement. Resisting the urge, he went to his bedroom and hoped reading would provide a sufficient distraction.

Yet, when Vito got to his room, the call of the flask grew so loud he had no choice but to pull it out. He knew drinking from it might mean another colorful visit from Frank, but he also knew it was the only way to end the incessant ringing.

His willpower crumbling, Vito took a long drink from the flask. Suddenly, stillness enveloped him.

And there was no Uncle Frank.

Realizing he wasn't going to get any visits from dead relatives, he sat on the bed, kicked off his shoes, and leaned against the headboard before taking another sip. After drinking enough to satisfy himself, Vito closed the flask and set it on the nightstand.

Soon, his surroundings grew fuzzy, and sleep engulfed him just as the sun was setting.

March 19, 2007

Waking up in his clothes, Vito looked at the clock on his nightstand. It read "8:45", which would've been fine if it was post meridiem. But the bright "AM" meant ante meridiem was at hand, and there was no way he could make it to his desk by nine.

Calling in was a much better option.

Vito got up and went to his door. In 2007, most people still used landlines and there were two in their bungalow. He never had one in his bedroom because Vito never had anyone to chat with. Plus, he wasn't fond of the ringing interrupting his reading time.

Peeking down the hallway, he debated whether to sneak into Connie's room to call his office or face the pack of women in the kitchen. All the while, the flask rang like a faint foghorn in the misty distance. This time, he decided to ignore the call.

Vito darted to Connie's room, heading straight for the land-line, and dialed his workplace.

"Chroma Paints. This is Hillary. How may I direct your call?" a voice answered.

"Hi. This is Vito Glandell from sales. I'm running late this morning."

"Okay. What time can I tell Anthony you'll be in?"

"Who is that?" a voice in the background said. "Give me that phone."

Hillary hesitated for a moment, and then her voice was re-placed with a gruff, far less polite one.

"This is Anthony. Who is this?"

Vito wished he had just pretended to be sick. "It's Vito. I'm running a little late."

"Why?" Anthony demanded.

"I woke up, and I wasn't feeling well, so I thought about call-ing in."

"Blah, blah, blah, blah! Seriously, Vito, I don't give a shit. Get your ass in here by ten. I called a meeting." He slammed the phone in Vito's ear, ending the call.

Frowning, Vito hung up and quietly slipped back into his room to get ready. The flask kept ringing, but he had to resist the urge—at least until the workday was over.

***

Vito got to the office just in time to get into the conference room before the door closed and the meeting started. Unfortunately, he was still too late to find a seat. Since Anthony started as the department manager nine months ago, he'd nearly doubled the sales force.

"Thanks for joining us, Mr. Glandell," Anthony said as he shut the door behind him.

The rest of the group laughed with a mixture of discomfort and relief that someone else was the target of Anthony's malice.

Vito smiled nervously and caught Patrick across the room rolling his eyes. He made a face at Anthony when he wasn't looking.

"Mr. Grivas has come up with a new line of paints that are designed for home interiors, specifically children's bedrooms and nurseries," Anthony said, kickstarting the meeting. "Playrooms. That kind of thing. The series of hues are fun and energizing, as well as soothing to look at. The entire line has been named after Grivas's newest granddaughter, Amaryllis."

"Are there swatch booklets available?" a voice broke into Anthony's speech.

"Yes. You'll get your swatches on the way out. First, let's go over the options and what sets them apart from child-themed paints of the past."

A collective groan went through the room yet remained quiet enough to miss Anthony's ears.

"Here, we have a short overview of the colors," Anthony said, pulling down a white screen with twelve large swatches taped to it. "As you can see, this new line of shades is bolder than our softer hues of the past."

Vito stared at the swatches. They all looked to be various shades of gray to him. Nevertheless, Anthony continued about how the paints were made with a new compound discovered in research and development.

"Safety is a top point when selling this new line," Anthony droned.

Despite not being able to see the colors, Vito tried to listen. But even that was becoming more difficult, thanks to the intensifying call of the flask in his head.

"Earth to Vito," he heard Anthony say as he pulled himself from his thoughts and refocused on the presentation he was supposed to be listening to. Anthony was fixed on him with a stern stare. "What did I just say?"

"I'm sorry. I missed that."

"I asked how you would pitch this line to your clients. Could you give us a quick demonstration?" Anthony reiterated, his voice cold and impatient.

Vito had no desire to do a demo, but he knew that there was no way Anthony would let him out of it. So reluctantly, he went to the front of the room to look over the swatches.

To his horror, there were no names under the swatches. The cards showed only blocks filled with colors everyone could see but him.

Nervous, Vito faced his co-workers and merely repeated everything he could remember Anthony saying about safety and why that was an important line to carry.

The group clapped, and Vito bowed his head in thanks before returning to the back of the room.

"Hold on," Anthony said. "I'd like you to talk about *every* color and why they were chosen for this line. Like this one." He pointed to a square. "What would you say is positive about this color, Mr. Glandell?"

Vito swallowed and thought fast. "I would say that it brightens any nursery."

"Brighten?" Anthony laughed. "Sure. But we'd like for *all* our colors to brighten a room. So be specific."

Vito thought for another moment. "It's the type of color that would make any room feel home to a nature lover."

Several guys nodded their heads in agreement, and someone in front muttered, "That's true."

Anthony stared at Vito. "Impressive, Glandell. Now, how would you describe this color?" He pointed to another gray swatch at the bottom of the group.

"That color would make any little girl smile," Vito said. As a paint salesman, he knew colors had genders assigned to them, specifically blue and pink. Hence, he was taking a big chance, assigning a gender to a color he couldn't see.

"I agree!" someone to Vito's left said while others rambled, "uh-huh" and "yep."

Vito breathed a sigh of relief. He was on a roll.

Anthony watched Vito with a stare reminiscent of a cat waiting to pounce on a mouse. "Okay… And how would you sell *this* specific color?" He pointed to yet another square.

"Pure sunshine!" Vito asserted.

The room grew quiet, and Vito knew that he had finally missed the mark.

What now? Should he admit, he couldn't see color anymore?

The silence in the room was broken as a couple of his co-workers began laughing.

Anthony smiled. "Well, I suppose blue backs up the sunshine, but I'm not sure that's the right direction to go in when selling this color."

Vito forced a laugh and hoped his fifteen minutes of fame were up.

"Now," Anthony said, turning his attention back to the entire group to resume his presentation.

Almost instantly, Vito's peers forget about him and refocused on the boss.

A relieved Vito stood against the wall for the rest of the meeting, praying he would blend in with the gray background.

Chapter Nine

Retreating to his cubicle, Vito looked at the walls, which were always bland, even when every color in the rainbow was available to him.

Then he saw Anthony walking toward his desk.

"Hey, Vito," Anthony said, before putting his butt on the nearest place it would fit. "How are those leads going?"

"Uhh …"

"What is it with you and the 'uhhs'? Come on. Don't you want to work here, Glandell?"

Vito stared down at his lap.

"Hey, Anthony," another voice interrupted.

Vito looked up to see Hillary coming their way.

"Can you sign this for me?" she asked. "I need it now so it can go out in today's mail."

Anthony took the slip of paper in Hillary's hand. He scanned it for a moment and then took a pen from her to sign the bottom of the sheet. "Pen's out of ink," he announced. "Vito, give me a black pen."

Vito pulled a random pen from a cup on his desk and handed it to Anthony.

"I said a *black* pen. That's red."

Vito held his breath and reached for another pen, hoping luck would be in his favor.

"Hillary, can you give us a moment?" Anthony said abruptly. "I'll sign this and bring it to your desk in ten minutes, all right?"

Without argument, Hillary walked away.

Anthony turned to Vito and gestured to the pen he'd just picked up. "That's blue."

Vito sat silently.

"Grab that red binder over there," Anthony instructed.

Vito put his hand on a binder and knew immediately he'd made another mistake judging from his boss's reaction.

"You can't see color," Anthony said.

Vito took his hand off the binder, knowing he couldn't hide his affliction any longer.

"No," he confessed. "It happened the other night. I don't know how. I just woke up on Saturday morning, and everything was gray." Vito decided that was as much as he was going to say. He didn't want to get into the flask and all of that. The less Anthony knew, the better.

"I hate to tell you this, but you can't sell paint if you can't see color," Anthony said.

"I know," Vito replied.

"Have you consulted a doctor?"

"Not yet," Vito replied. And right that instant, the call of the flask shifted from a low hum to a piercing scream. Vito put his hand to his ears and cried out in agony.

"What the hell is going on with you?" Anthony said, jumping to his feet.

"I don't know. Just let me hit the john. I'll be fine in a minute." Trying to regain his composure, Vito pushed past his boss and didn't stop until he was locked in a stall in the sales floor men's room.

He took the flask out of his pocket and drank as if he had just spent the morning walking the Sahara. As the gin slid down his throat, the cries stopped. He screwed the top back on and walked out of the stall to find Anthony in front of him, his eyes affixed to the shiny object in Vito's hand.

"What's that?"

Vito's mouth moved wordlessly.

"I want to see you in my office in ten minutes. And take a mint to get that gin off your breath." And with that, Anthony left the bathroom.

Vito returned the flask to his breast pocket and looked in the mirror. Staring back at him was a man who'd just been caught drinking on the job. No doubt he was on his way to getting fired.

His mother was going to be so proud.

Vito tried to push thoughts of his mother and family out of his head as he walked to the sink to clean up.

He splashed water on his face and then looked in the mirror once more, checking to see if he was at least somewhat presentable.

Vito took a deep breath, knowing there was no point in delaying the inevitable any longer. So, he left the bathroom and headed to Anthony's office.

***

"You've been with us for a long time," Anthony said, seated behind his desk.

"I have," Vito agreed, standing because he was too nervous to sit.

"I sense something's going on with you, so I'm giving you a leave of absence for one month or until your eyesight goes back to normal—whichever comes first. If your vision doesn't go back to normal though, we'll have to talk. So go see a doctor to find out what they can do. In the meantime, I hope you can get a handle on this new *habit* of yours because that shit doesn't fly with me. My dad was a drinker. I have no patience for it." Anthony paused, his face softening a bit. "You're an asset to this company, Vito. We'd hate to lose you after nearly twenty years."

The moment of kindness took Vito by surprise. "Thank you," he said, cautiously reaching out to shake his nemesis's hand. "I'll get my sight back to normal. I have to, because what else would I do?"

Anthony chuckled and returned Vito's handshake. "You'll be fine. There's always something to sell."

Vito nodded, left Anthony's office, and went to his desk to get his coat. He saw that Patrick was on a call, or at least pretending to be.

There was no one for Vito to say goodbye to—just a group of faces and names he knew on a surface level. Throughout all his years working there, he'd always spent his spare time with his nose in a book, effectively missing out on the opportunity to learn the stories of the people who'd surrounded him for nearly two decades.

Once he made it out to Harlem Avenue, Vito knew where he had to go. He hopped on the L and heading toward Little Italy.

***

"Veeto!" Allegra said as she opened the door and found him standing on the other side. "Come on in!" She let him step inside and then pointed up the stairs to her apartment.

"Hello," Vito said before making his way up to the third-floor flat. When he stepped in, Ginevra was combing the long hair of a woman who had curly locks just like hers and Allegra's. This woman's hair, however, was a few shades lighter. It was almost blonde.

"Ooh," the woman said, her eyes feasting on Vito. "I see what you mean, sister. He *is* an interesting subject, for sure."

"Freya, leave him alone. He needs our help," Allegra reprimanded and then turned her attention toward Vito. "Forgive my sisters, Vito. They never take anything seriously."

"That's okay," Vito said, letting himself be led into the living room, where they pushed him into an oversized wing chair.

"Freya, go and make us some espressos. We have a lot to cover," Allegra ordered.

The new-to-Vito sister scowled, but got up and did as she was told.

Ginevra moved closer to Vito, possessing the look of a ravenous tiger about to eat her prey.

Vito swallowed nervously against his dry mouth. "I came here because—"

"Oh, we know why you're here," Ginevra cut him off. "We just didn't expect you for an hour or so. Premonitions are tricky, but we knew you would come to this conclusion."

"What conclusion?"

"To take off on the journey your uncle promised. You want your color back."

"Are you witches?" Vito asked, tired of being polite.

"Witch is a misunderstood word, Vito. It can get a gal into a lot of trouble. We prefer to be known as the Sorelle, or Sisters. We're part of the Sorellanza Magicka[21], which is derived from La Vecchia Religione[22]. That's the old religion, long before the religions that dominate the world today. But like other healers and fixers everywhere, we were persecuted for worshipping in our way."

"They didn't like it when we got naked." Ginevra giggled and put her hand on Vito's thigh.

"Ginevra," the oldest sister drew out her voice, "not now!"

Ginevra rolled her eyes but grew quiet anyhow.

"Who we are doesn't matter, Vito," Allegra continued. "What matters is you came here to learn about this magical in-

---

21   Magical Sisterhood
22   The Old Religion

strument your uncle so generously left for you, and we're here to help."

"Why didn't I see my uncle when I drank again? I tried on the way here, but nothing happened."

"Where were you when Frank paid you that visit?" Allegra asked.

"The basement of my home."

"Okay. Was that where you were when you lost your sight for color?"

"Yes."

Allegra smiled. "That's the portal then. We'll go over this booklet together tonight." She pulled out the pamphlet she'd been trying to convince Vito to take from the pocket of her housecoat. "It's all right here."

"Espresso?" Freya returned with coffee for them all.

"Si,"[23] Vito said. "Grazie."[24]

"Prego,"[25] Freya replied and put his coffee in front of him.

"Do you have a pen and paper?" Allegra asked Vito as she added a few sugar cubes to her espresso.

"I do." Vito produced the items while Allegra condemned Freya for forgetting the biscotti. Freya ran back, got the biscotti, and then stuck her tongue out at her oldest sister when she wasn't looking.

Once they were all settled, Allegra started translating the writing in the faded, yellowed booklet. They had to be careful handling the delicate pamphlet, for it was the original one that came with the flask nearly one hundred years ago.

"Amici miei," Allegra began. "Nella vostre mani, avete il potere di ..."[26]

Vito blinked. "In English, please?"

"Oh, yeah." Allegra cleared her throat and began again. "Dear Friends, in your hand, you hold the power of the Sorellanza Magicka. After a few sips from your flask, a remarkable journey waits for you. This is a rare adventure, gifted to you by another, whom you will meet. The portal is easy to open and close, as you will see in the illustrations that follow.

---

23   Yes.
24   Thank you.
25   You're welcome
26   "My friends," Allegra began. "In your hands, you have the power to..."

"With the use of ancient metals, amulets, and stones that have carried out spells, incantations, and metaphysical journeys for hundreds of years, Dominick used his skills to forge these enchanted items into a flask, where you can hide your giggle water."

"Giggle water?" Vito questioned as he felt the ring grow louder.

"Booze. This set was made in the 1920s so the language is of that era. Around here, some chose to run sugar for the guys who ruled this neighborhood. Some people ran speakeasies. They gave people a place to get away from it all, you know? Our father, the Dominick they speak of in this booklet, helped the neighborhood people hide what they were doing in his way."

Vito listened as Freya got up to get more coffee, while Ginevra rolled her eyes and played with her hair.

"He made flasks like this one so people could hide them in books and bring gin home."

"Sorellanza Magicka has been in hiding for centuries," Freya chimed in as Allegra took her first sip from the tiny espresso cup her sister put in front of her.

"When people who enjoyed liquor were forced to live in secret, back in the 1920s, the Sorellanza Magicka, decided it would be safer to hide among them," Allegra explained. "So, our father started welding flasks and carving out books. He made tons. I think everyone in the neighborhood bought one."

"Do you mean there are hundreds of these causing havoc in people's lives?" Vito asked, in shock just at the thought.

"Oh no," Allegra said, shaking her head before swallowing some coffee-soaked anise biscotti. "There are hundreds of flasks around the world, but most were made with ordinary metals and gems. *This* flask was forged from melted coins of mystical power and anointed gems. There are only three in existence."

"Where are the other two?" Vito asked.

"We don't know," Allegra answered. "The one you have is tied to Ginevra. You see, each is tied to one of us three."

Vito stared at the flask, astonished. "How did my uncle get a hold of this? Was he a …"

"Frank was a friend to us. He helped us when we needed him, and, in turn, we gave him the flask. He couldn't take his eyes off it. He said it sang to him."

"Yes," Vito agreed, easily believing this part of the story. "It's calling me now. And it keeps getting louder. I try to resist it, but it's no use. When I drink from it, the calling stops for a bit. But then, it eventually just comes back stronger."

"You won't be able to silence it for good until you've finished your journey," Allegra explained.

"So, how do I begin?" Vito asked.

"From what it says here," Allegra looked down at the pamphlet, "you need to go back to the site where your journey started. I think we can all agree that's the basement of your house."

Vito nodded.

"So go home and sit in the basement. Drink from the flask, and you'll go to the next step."

"Okay. Does it say anything about what to do when I get there?" Vito asked, wanting to ensure he did everything right.

Allegra scanned over the instructions again. "Once you find yourself in that place, the door will take you where you need to be."

"La porta ti porterà dove devi essere,"[27] Freya said, putting a hand on Vito's shoulder.

Allegra stood, walked to Vito, and placed a hand on him as well. "La porta ti porterà dove devi essere," she recited.

The two sisters looked at their third sibling. Ginevra rushed toward them. She threw her arms around Vito, jumped into his lap, and joined the recitations. "La porta ti porterà dove devi essere!"

"What does that mean?" Vito yelled, panicked, and worried about where he was being sent.

"The door will take you where you need to be!" the three sisters said in unison before resuming their dialect. "La porta ti porterà dove devi essere! La porta ti porterà dove devi essere! La porta ti porterà dove devi essere!"

The sisters then began cackling, the sound of their combined laughter bled through their flat and seeped into the settling dusk.

***

Later that evening as Vito was walking out of their front door, Allegra pulled his arm. "You do realize we expect the flask and book

---

27   "The door will take you where you need to be."

back when you're done with your journey, right?" she said. "We gifted this to Frank for a short time. It's far past the expiration date. My sister is tied to that flask, and she needs it before her next birthday."

"When is that?"

"April second," Allegra answered. "The next full moon."

"That's in two weeks."

"I know," Allegra said. "It's a shame you didn't find us earlier. Now that the flask is in her sights, their bond grows stronger. If she had never seen the flask, her birthday wouldn't be an issue. But, now that it's arrived, she needs it. Otherwise ..."

"What?"

"Just get the flask back to us by the next full moon. As long as Ginevra drinks from it before the sun rises, she'll be fine."

"I just hope I make it back to give it to you," Vito said, cursing the day he took that first sip.

Allegra nodded. "Some people never complete their journey. Like Frank."

Vito's hadn't realized Frank had been on a journey of his own.

"I know you can do it," Allegra patted Vito on the back. They then said their goodbyes, and Vito ran for the train.

***

Back in the comfort of his own home, the silence of the house was disrupted by the wail coming from Vito's chest pocket. He walked into the kitchen and the call grew louder, as if the flask sensed where Vito was headed and couldn't wait to get there.

Bisnonna Nellie was sitting in her usual spot, peeling another apple. She looked up as Vito sat next to her.

His great-grandmother carved a slice of the fruit and offered it to him.

Vito accepted it and smiled for the first time that day. "Mama? Nonna?" he said, inquiring about the other women's whereabouts.

Bisnonna Nellie pointed her knife to the door. "Andavano in chiesa per la tavola di San Giuseppe."[28]

"Oh, right." Vito may not have been able to speak Italian, but he knew San Giuseppe—St. Joseph. It was March 19, St. Joseph's Day. Every year, St. Luke's hosted a table for the neighborhood.

---

28   They went to the church for the Saint Joseph's table."

His mother always brought the pizzelles, thin cookies that look like circular waffles, anise-flavored and topped with powdered sugar. Vito wondered why Bisnonna Nellie had been left behind from such a special event.

His bisnonna handed him another slice of apple.

"You?" he said, by way of asking why she hadn't gone with them.

"No. Mi sento male." [29] She made an icky face and pressed her hand on her stomach.

Vito understood she wasn't feeling well.

He also noticed that Bisnonna Nellie's presence had silenced the call of the savage flask.

She put a frail hand on his arm. Her face was stiff with concern, and her fingers tightened weakly around Vito's arm to pull him closer. Vito leaned in as a gaunt finger moved toward his face.

"Veeto. No," Nellie said, her eyes pleading for him not to go.

Vito smiled. He had to go, and Bisnonna Nellie knew it too; the look residing in Vito's eyes was the same as the one she'd seen in Frank's so long ago.

She smiled at Vito and released his hand, letting him know she understood. They sat together for a while, watching television until Bisnonna Nellie fell asleep. When Vito began to hear her gentle snores, he reluctantly stood and made his way to the basement.

***

It only took one drink for Vito to pass out. Yet, he was far less frightened than he'd been the first time he awoke in the colorful "other world" basement.

He glanced around, expecting Frank to show up. But as the minutes passed, Vito thought he might be on his own this time around.

What was he supposed to do, let the adventure come and find him? In all the time he'd been alive thus far, the one thing Vito knew was that it typically didn't pay to wait for anything to find you.

If you wanted it, you had to go out and get it.

---

29   "No. I feel sick."

The flask gave a little ding, and Vito knew it longed to be back with him. So, he put the flask back in his pocket and then began to look around the room.

The words the sisters sang to him replayed in his head.

La porta ti porterà dove devi essere. The door will take you where you need to be.

Vito knew there were only two doors in the basement—one that led outside and resembled the tornado door Dorothy stomps on in *The Wizard of Oz*, and the other led to the kitchen.

The entire "other world" basement, which served as a weigh station to the portal, was full of color. Everything had a bright hue, almost over the top. The reds were exceptionally vibrant, the yellows were blinding like the sun, and the blues were so cool it brought down Vito's temperature. Everything in his sight was full of the long-lost color.

Except for the top of the stairs. The door that typically led to the kitchen wasn't walnut colored like he remembered. It was gray, which indicated to Vito that this was the portal to his adventures.

Where did the door lead to now? Vito had no idea. What he did know was that this door was drained of color, like everything, back home, in the real world.

The flask rang loudly. Vito took it out of his pocket, opened it, and took a sip. The instant he swallowed, the door at the top of the stairs creaked open and white smoke drifted out.

Vito's heart began to beat wildly. He knew it wasn't the kitchen that awaited him.

He started to climb the stairs. As he got closer to the door, he heard voices on the other side—familiar, though he couldn't place them.

For a moment, he considered retreating and just finding a way to navigate life with no color. He could get used to it. As Anthony had said, there's always something to sell.

But suddenly, a feeling Vito hadn't experienced in years came over him. It wasn't as strong as he remembered, but it was there nonetheless—a tiny spark of excitement mixed in with his fear.

Somehow, Vito simultaneously did and didn't want to embark on this journey.

His heart created a rhythmic beat that filled his body and mind with nostalgia over the childhood dreams he had given up so long ago. Dreams he had tucked away deep in a place he hoped he would never find again.

Back and forth, the spark fought his fears, and in the end, Vito found himself at the top of the stairs standing directly in front of the fully opened gray door. He couldn't see through it, and little by little, the white mist seeping from the other side began to swirl around his body and pulled him forward.

As Vito moved through the door, juvenile laughs and conversation filled his ears as the smell of showers, sweat, and urinal cakes filled his nose.

Chapter Ten

Once Vito was through the door, the cloud surrounding him dissipated. His eyes came into focus, and Vito realized he was in a place he hadn't seen in nearly twenty years, the boys' locker room of St. Luke's High School.

There was no mistaking the place. He recognized it as soon as he saw the verse on the wall painted over the bland metal closets: *Reach down your hand from on high; deliver me and rescue me from the mighty waters, from the hands of foreigners. - Psalm 144:7*

Vito knew the letters were painted in red, although they looked gray to him. He made a mental note that the adventures would be colorless, even if the "other world" basement was colorful.

Vito had never been a jock, but he'd spent many Phys Ed classes in this room, pretending to be sick and reading a book.

Currently populating the room were the neighborhood boys he'd known in high school.

Vito lifted his hands to his face to wipe the mist clinging to his skin. When he drew his hands away from his eyes, they seemed less familiar to him.

His hands were younger. Not only were there no wrinkles, but the scars that came along with living for thirty-seven years were no longer there.

Bringing them in closer, Vito noted these weren't the hands he knew as a kid. The hands he looked at now were short and stubby. Vito's hands were always long with thin fingers and big knuckles.

Curious, he looked down at his body, astonished to see he was wearing a baseball uniform. Gazing around the room, he saw dozens of other boys dressed in uniforms.

Frantically, Vito tried to find a mirror. He saw a long one fastened to a wall across the room and he ran to it.

Once his reflection was staring back at him, Vito could not believe his eyes. He was not Vito anymore.

"We're gonna kick their asses today!" someone said behind him, following up the declaration with a firm slap on Vito's back.

Unable to take his eyes off the image he saw in the mirror, Vito muttered, "This can't be real." He lifted the hand he now possessed to the mouth of the face he saw.

But it was. The reflection in the mirror mouthed the same words that Vito felt leave his chest. Even the voice wasn't his. He knew it but it wasn't his voice.

Vito felt a little dizzy and learned what it meant to be light-headed from the realization that he wasn't Vito anymore. The reflection in the mirror that stared back at him was a young Anthony Passarella.

"What the hell is happening here?" Vito thought to himself, still lost in the reflection in front of him.

Vito felt another slap on his back, and this time, he turned around. A large boy Vito remembered well stood next to him. Michael Fiorella.

"Hey, Anth," Michael said with a smile. "Whatcha doin' over here?"

Vito smiled back, unsure of how he was going to pull this off.

"Hey man, don't worry about the game," Michael kept talking as he faux-punched Vito—or Anthony, rather—in the gut. The burly teen then took Anthony's, (or was it Vito's?) arm, and led him to the lockers. "You're gonna do fine."

Vito looked around in a panic unsure of where he was supposed to be. Then he read *PASSARELLA #34* on a strip of masking tape across one of the lockers. He breathed a sigh of relief when he saw that it was unlocked already.

Michael punched him in the arm again and laughed as he turned and began to dig in his locker, which had *FIORELLA #27* above it.

A fumbling Fiorella took out his mitt and hat. Closing his locker with an obnoxious bang, the awkward adolescent moved through a crowd of teenage boys dressing for the game and horsing around with each other.

Vito opened his locker. Finding a hat and a mitt, he grabbed them and closed the door before hurrying after the Fiorella kid. Once he made his way through the rowdy crowd of teen ballplayers, Vito spotted Fiorella sifting through a pile of bats.

Vito looked down to the wooden implements and chose one at random as his massive locker neighbor moved toward where the other boys were congregating.

Vito followed suit and took an empty seat toward the back. He watched the teammates joke around and smack each other's asses. He remembered most of the faces in that room, standing behind Anthony whenever he was bullying someone, including Vito.

How many times had they called Vito a loser or knocked his books out of his hands?

He could remember a few of them laughing that time Anthony pushed Vito into the girls' bathroom. Connie had to go talk to Anthony's father, which was never a pleasant experience. They were both so happy when Anthony went off to college and his father moved.

When Vito had finished school and gotten away from these guys, he hadn't missed them in the slightest. He couldn't care less about any of these people. So why in the world was he here?

Vito listened silently as one kid recounted how he'd gotten into a fight at the roller rink. Another guy bragged about getting to second base with a neighborhood girl, while the group around him groaned and called him a liar.

"What the hell is wrong with you?" A voice came from Vito's left. He turned to find another familiar face. Bobby Cattaneo, a kid who was as much of an asshole as Anthony had been when they were growing up. Bobby and Anthony had been inseparable. "You gonna let Bellucci lie like that? I thought you'd call him out on his bullshit stories for sure."

"Uh … I ain't feeling too good."

"Pussy!" Bobby snarled at his best friend until a loud voice bellowed out behind the group.

"All right, you guys! Settle down."

Everyone quieted down and took a seat as a robed man walked into their circle. When the clergyman turned around, Vito lost his balance and fell out of his chair.

"Are you okay, Anthony?" Father Vince asked while the other guys laughed and hollered insults at him. Vito hadn't seen Father Vince since the night of his graduation dinner.

"Uh," Vito stammered as he jumped back into his seat. "Yeah. I'm fine."

"Good. Okay," Father Vince started, "we all know how important this game against Sacred Heart is. And I know how much it means to a lot of you." He focused his eyes on Vito with a knowing look.

"Does he know it's me?" Vito wondered.

Father Vince broke eye contact with Vito to look at the rest of the boys. "But remember, try hard, stay positive, and, most of all ... I think you all know what I'm going to say."

"Have fun," the group finished for him with a groan.

"That's right." Father Vince laughed. "I know some of you think winning is the most important thing." Again, he looked at Vito.

"Why is he looking at me?" Vito thought. But then, he remembered that he was Anthony. Then Vito recalled how competitive Anthony was when it came to sports.

"But try to remember that there's more to life than winning games," Father Vince said. "Okay, boys, let's gather around and pray." The priest motioned for them all to surround him.

The group gathered around Father Vince and bowed their heads.

Father Vince closed his eyes. "Lord, give these boys the strength, courage, and determination they need to win this game. Bless us, St. Luke, patron saint of our school, and help us see our way through by trying hard, staying positive, and no matter how much they hate when I say it, having fun. Amen."

A collective 'Amen' filled the locker room. Then Father Vince took a bat and tapped it on the floor. Then he tapped the heavy part of his bat on the floor again. The other boys did the same, even Vito. He didn't think to do it, which gave him the indication that Anthony might be somewhere inside this body, too.

Father Vince tapped a beat, and all the boys joined him in doing the same. The tempo of the wooden instruments grew louder and louder until they vibrated off the walls around them. Vito allowed the rhythm to take over and tapped the head of his bat on the floor with the rest of the team.

The priest swung open the locker room door, and all the boys ran out into the hall, cheering.

Rushed by the emotion and the powerful energy of the group, Vito ran out too, shouting through the hall and joining the rest of the team as they bled onto the field. Once he reached the dugout, Vito looked out to the crowd in the stands. And as gray and colorless as they were, their excitement still soared to the sky.

A few boys took seats on the bench while others ran onto the field.

"What am I supposed to be doing?" Vito thought nervously. His fear returned. Having no idea where he was supposed to be, he decided sitting on the bench and not doing anything was the best course of action. In high school, Vito had learned that if he did and said nothing, he could usually go unnoticed. That tactic had worked for him his entire life, and he hoped it would now.

The problem was, he wasn't Vito anymore; he was Anthony. As he turned to take his seat, Father Vince and all the boys stared in confusion.

They were waiting for him to take the field. Anthony was a great athlete and always in play, but Vito couldn't remember his position.

Vito at least knew the game though. When he looked out to the field, he saw that there was no one standing out in right field.

Vito stood and began to put on his glove.

Father Vince walked over. "Anthony," he put an arm around Vito's shoulders, "don't let last week's game get to you. Everyone is allowed to have a bad day. Just shrug it off, go out there and have fun!"

Vito looked up to that smiling face he'd once admired so much. He had missed how reassuring Father Vince could be. Smiling back, a surge of confidence came over Vito. He ran out onto the field. The cries of the crowd escalated as he took his position.

Standing in right field, Vito felt strange and awkward. But beneath these feelings was an unfamiliar sense of youth and vibrancy.

The pitcher struck out the first two batters from Sacred Heart, which gave Vito time to think.

The grass out on the field smelled just as he remembered—that dewy, fresh aroma that smacks the senses whenever someone cuts their lawn.

All the while, Vito felt the crowd's anticipation. He glanced over to the concession stand and remembered the pizza slices they sold. Nonna always claimed it tasted like cardboard with ketchup and didn't understand why Vito ate it when she made perfectly good pizza at home.

Nevertheless, Vito had loved to sit in the stands under the sun, listening to the crack of the bat.

CRACK!

Vito snapped out of his dream. And without even initially realizing it, his legs began to shake and set off running like they had minds of their own.

Anthony had to be somewhere inside of this body, knowing what to do and operating on muscle memory.

Amazed at how young and strong he felt, Vito ran toward the flying ball quicker than he'd ever been able to run in his life. And he ran with such precision and skill—qualities that he'd never possessed when he was living life as Vito Glandell.

As the ball plummeted down from the sky and back toward the Earth, Vito threw his fourteen-year-old frame down with fierce ease. He stretched his adolescent arms out until the leather-clad orb landed directly in his gray mitt.

Vito lay there in amazement as the crowds went wild.

He did it!

He picked himself off the ground and ran to the dugout with the rest of the team, smiling brighter than ever. The team cheered and gave him congratulatory thumps on the back when he got there.

"Good job, son," Father Vince said with a smile.

Moving through the crowd of back slappers, Vito took a seat as a flame of red flickered in the corner of his eye.

Red?

Vito saw red!

He jumped out of his seat and turned to look at the long-missed color. And the moment he did, he caught the eye of a girl sitting in the stands. Unlike the rest of the blurry crowd, she was not overpowered by gray. Her hair was long and strawberry red, her lips were rosebuds, and even from the distance, Vito could see that her fingernails glowed a bright, fire-engine hue.

They stared deeply into each other's eyes from across the field, and Vito could feel her pull. Her flowery lips curled into a soft smile, and at that moment, it was as if no one else existed. It was just the two of them.

Vito smiled back, and her grin grew even more radiant.

"It's about time you did something right," Vito heard a harsh voice behind him. Two powerful hands grabbed his shoulders and spun him around, taking the strawberry-hued girl out of his view.

Before him now, was a large man Vito recognized right away—Anthony's father, Mr. Passarella.

There was something about Anthony's dad that had scared Vito as a child, although he couldn't put his finger on it. He towered like a mountain and was always grunting under his breath. Vito remembered Connie and Nonna Josie scowling at Mr. Passarella when he walked past their house.

"He's not a good man, even if he is Italian," Nonna would growl.

No one in his family ever knew Anthony's mother; the Passarellas moved into the neighborhood after she died from complications when Anthony was born.

As Mr. Passarella towered over Vito, he began to feel small and helpless.

Anthony's father leaned in close and grabbed his face with a tight grip that shoved his teeth into his cheeks. "Don't get cocky, boy. This game isn't over. You'll probably fuck it up again." He smacked Vito on the back of the head and then went back to his seat.

Some of the boys whispered and stared, while others pointedly looked away.

Father Vince was talking to Monsignor Benevento, but the righteous gentile wasn't listening. Although Vito couldn't hear what was being said, he had seen the two men interact like that before. Remembering the red girl, Vito shifted his gaze, trying to spot her again. But she was gone.

Vito searched the crowd. But still, he couldn't find another glimpse of her crimson color. She had disappeared.

Vito's heart turned just as gray as the world around him.

St. Luke's scored two runs in the bottom of the inning and Vito found himself running back onto the field. He watched the game from his post, trying not to let his mind wander. All the while, Mr. Passarella followed his every move like a mantis shrimp waiting to devour its kin.

A ground ball headed toward Vito as the Sacred Heart player ran past first base and headed toward second. Without a thought in his head, Vito ran for the ball and threw it to the shortstop, who hurled it to second base.

The batter was out, and the crowd cheered and jumped in jubilation.

Anthony's father, however, remained seated, staring at him with disdain. With every glare, Vito swore he felt Anthony's pain in this body, along with agony and fear of what would happen if he screwed up. And beneath all these feelings, Vito sensed Anthony's torment from the knowledge that his birth killed his mother—and left him with Mr. Passarella as his only parent. He could tell that Anthony often wondered what his life would be like if his mother was still around … whether she would have counteracted his father's harshness.

But of course, he would never know.

The game went up and down. From the top of the second inning through the bottom of the ninth, it was everything a great baseball game was supposed to be. At one point, St. Luke's was up by one. In the next inning, Sacred Heart was leading by three. Then, there were triple plays and a home run.

Vito loved every minute of it.

It was the first time he had ever been part of a team that worked as one. But every time he lost himself in the sheer fun of the game, he would spot Anthony's looming dad in the stands.

The top of the last inning rolled around, and Vito's team was up by one run. Sacred Heart was up to bat, with no outs. The batter popped it right to Vito, who let Anthony's body run and catch the ball with ease. As he threw the ball back to the pitcher, Vito's ego soared.

Running to guard his position, Vito flashed a confident smile at Anthony's father. Mr. Passarella's hard eyes sharpened in return.

"He wants me to fail," Vito thought in alarm. He then wondered if the thought had truly been his, or if it was Anthony's.

Vito looked back at Mr. Passarella, a distinct stubbornness coming over him. No matter how harshly the man stared back at Vito, Vito refused to be intimidated. Anthony may have been afraid of him, but Anthony was not alone anymore. He had a grown man inside of him—a man who could be just as hard and bitter as anyone, including Mr. Passarella.

The next batter for Sacred Heart also popped the ball to Vito, who caught it without issue. He tossed it back to the kid on the mound, and the crowd's cheers grew louder.

"I'm going to win this game for them." Vito imagined the team lifting him on their shoulders like a hero.

Vito waited in right field, willing the ball his way, and ignoring Anthony's dad.

The third batter hit the ball, and it soared over Vito's head.

He ran, trying to get under it. He stretched out his arm and reached. "I'm going to catch it!" Vito thought as he positioned his mitt under the trajectory of the ball. He could feel more confidence in this body than he had ever experienced in the thirty-seven years he was Vito.

Vito took a leap of faith and jumped up to catch the ball, only to trip over his other foot. He stumbled oh so gracelessly, and the ball fell to the ground.

Sacred Heart scored a run. The game was tied.

In an instant, the attitude of the St. Luke's team changed. It was like a dark cloud had suddenly appeared out of nowhere, even though the sky was clear.

No one had to say it—the lowered heads and dragging feet made it evident that Vito's team no longer believed they could win. And, as it is with any game, your belief in yourself is essential. Unless you hold onto an unfaltering belief that you can win, you've given in.

Two more Sacred Heart batters scored, giving their enemies the lead.

"We have a chance to win it back," Father Vince said to them in the dugout. "Who's up next?"

Fiorella was up to bat, and he went at the ball with all his might. He could hit the ball decently if he ever got hold of one. The pitcher knew that and decided to hit him instead.

"He did that on purpose," Bobby shouted.

"Are you okay Fiorella?" Father Vince shouted.

"Yeah," the burly Italian kid shouted back as he took his base.

Bukowski was up next. He made contact, but the Sacred Heart turned a double play.

"You're up next," Father Vince was staring at Vito. Well, Anthony. But Vito felt the fear of having to bat move through the body he now called home.

Vito had no choice but to stand up and grab a bat, mostly because he let the soul of Anthony, who was running the show, lead him where he needed to be. But Vito's fear of failure still filled this brain. Whether or not that had anything to do with the fact that Anthony struck out and the game was officially lost, well, that he couldn't say.

Vito walked toward the dugout, watching his teammates sulk. He wanted to apologize. If only he had caught that ball, they would have won. He wanted to speak up, but before he knew it, a large pair of hands grabbed the back of his jersey and dragged him away from the team.

Vito didn't have to look up to know it was Mr. Passarella.

The man dragged him into the parking lot. They moved through all the gray cars until they came to the Monte Carlo that Vito remembered parked in their driveway.

Without a word, the large man opened the passenger's door and shoved Vito inside.

As they drove away from the school, Anthony's dad said nothing. Vito didn't know what would happen, but he could feel fourteen-year-old Anthony's fear.

The car pulled up to their street—the very same street Vito now lived on. He stared out the window at his own house. It looked so different, unlike the weather-worn place Vito knew it to be as a thirty-seven-year-old.

As they got closer, Vito saw his mother walk out the door. Even with his gray vision, Connie looked so young and fresh. She knelt, tending to some flowers in the front yard.

Mr. Passarella pulled the car into his driveway, shut off the engine, got out, and walked to the passenger side. He opened Vito's door and grabbed him by the shirt to pull him out.

The second he was on his feet, Vito pulled away from Mr. Passarella and ran toward Connie. "Momma! Momma!" he called out.

Connie looked up, confused. She clearly heard the call, but she didn't see Vito. She looked right into his eyes but didn't see her son.

Mr. Passarella hurried over and seized him, putting a large hand over his mouth to muffle his cries. "What did I tell you about crying like a fucking baby? You know you have it coming for fucking up. Take it like a man!"

Vito was a man in his mind. But his body was that of a fourteen-year-old kid. It occurred to him that physically he had no chance against Mr. Passarella.

Suddenly afraid in his own right, Vito squirmed, wanting to escape Anthony's father and run towards Connie.

But it was no use. She couldn't save him. She didn't even know it was him. She merely watched with sad eyes as Mr. Passarella dragged him into the house.

Vito found himself inside a strange and unfamiliar living room. Before he could even take his surroundings in, a hard smack across the face knocked him to the floor. He looked upward and found Mr. Passarella towering over him, removing his leather belt.

Vito scurried to his feet, ran to another room, and shut the door.

But Mr. Passarella just laughed, the maniacal sound reaching Vito's ears despite the door separating them. "You can't hide from me, you son of bitch. I'll get in there. Running only makes it worse. If you take it like a man, I'll go easy on you,"

Vito, not trusting anything this man said, kept his back to the door.

"Okay," Mr. Passarella said, "have it your way."

There was a hard bang on the door, and it flew open instantly. A startled Vito tried to run, but Mr. Passarella easily cornered him.

Mr. Passarella whacked him with the belt. One. Two. Three. Four times.

Over and over and over again.

Each time the leather hit the baseball uniform, a slap soared through the air and sent Vito wailing. The pain was too much to bear, and Vito fell to the floor.

He couldn't tell how many more times Mr. Passarella hit him after that. Each smack just blended into one constant force of agony. After a while, Vito couldn't even scream anymore. He just curled into the fetal position, wishing he could melt into the wall while the belt continued beating not only his body but also his pride.

Vito wasn't sure when the beating stopped. He just eventually noticed there were no new pains, and that he could hear Mr. Passarella's labored breathing.

"Maybe that'll teach you a lesson, you useless piece of shit." With that, the horrible man left the room.

Lying on the floor, holding in his sobs, Vito's anger mounted. He wanted nothing more than to get up and punch Mr. Passarella in the face. But he couldn't. And in that moment, he understood Anthony's helplessness and shame.

After some time passed, Vito finally crawled out of the corner and allowed his tears to escape.

Then, he realized that with Mr. Passarella no longer in sight, this was now his opportunity to escape.

Vito bolted out of the room, and then out of the front door, thinking about his mother. And even though it was Connie he was envisioning, he suspected that somewhere inside of the mind where he was currently residing, Anthony was longing for his own mother as well.

Angry and hurt, Vito ran across the lawn with tears burning his eyes.

Suddenly, he bumped into a gray blob and knew it had to be Mr. Passarella, coming to take him back. Reflexively, Vito felt himself take over this body and began to punch the person in front of him. All the anger and hurt he felt from the humiliation and beating were thrown into each punch. Vito released the force of his loathing with every jab at Anthony's dad.

He was enjoying it so much he didn't stop when Anthony's dad fell to the ground. Suddenly, Vito was pushed off the blurry mass he was beating.

Vito wiped away his tears, letting his eyes focus on who was in front of him.

The mass wasn't Mr. Passarella.

It was fourteen-year-old Vito Glandell on the ground, face covered in blood.

Vito had broken his own nose!

He stared back at his younger self in shock. The boy he saw wasn't him though. It couldn't have been. Could it? Vito felt beastly hands pulling his shirt as Connie and Nonna Josie rushed over to the mess he left behind.

Vito clutched the gray grass beneath him in an attempt to escape. He tried to pry himself away, wanting to get to his mother. But Mr. Passarella was too strong to escape.

Connie wasn't paying Vito any attention anyway. She was too busy doting on the *other* boy, unaware of which one was really Vito.

Through a sea of tears, Vito watched his family take the boy with his body into his house, leaving him behind with the monster.

Suddenly, Vito saw a life-size blur of red in his peripheral view.

The girl from the game!

He saw her standing across the street. A pink tear ran down her cheek as she watched Mr. Passarella pull Vito to his doom. Vito looked back at her as the imprinted butterflies on her dress fill in with the color pink. Then the flower beds surrounding her began to fill with pink as well.

So surprised to be seeing some color again, Vito briefly smiled at the pink sunset above, until Mr. Passarella threw him into the house. Vito twisted his body to catch one last glimpse of the girl across the street. Her gray eyes flushed with cotton candy colors floating around her.

Then the door slammed him into darkness.

Chapter Eleven

"Not what you expected, huh?"

Vito heard a voice while his eyes adjusted to his new surroundings. He didn't need to see to know it was Frank.

"What was that?" Vito hollered, standing from what he realized was the sofa in the now fully colored "other world" basement of his house. He looked up toward the door that usually led to the kitchen.

"Reality," Frank answered as he walked to the cabinet that held his gin. "You want a drink?"

Vito ran up the stairs and went to grab the door handle, but then stopped.

"What's behind this door now?" he wondered and lowered his hand from on the knob.

"You won't be able to open it," Frank called from his seat in the blue Lazy Boy.

Curious, Vito tried to turn the handle and found Frank was right. The door was locked. He was stuck.

Vito went back down the steps and looked at his uncle. "Why are you doing this to me?"

"I already told you why the last time I saw you."

"But I wanted adventures, Zi!" Vito's voice grew louder with each word, and he began pacing the room in frustration. "I wanted to maybe start in New Orleans and move my way around. I didn't want *this*!"

"Have a drink." Frank stood, took his nephew's elbow, and guided him to sit back on the sofa. Then he went to the buffet and began making another martini. "You're right," he said as he poured the gin into the shaker and grabbed ice from a bucket they hadn't used in decades. "This isn't the journey you wanted. But what did Mick and Keith say?"

"Who?" Vito asked as his uncle placed a fresh gin martini with three green olives on the coffee table.

"*Mick and Keith*. The Stones! Seriously kid, didn't I teach you anything?"

"What are you talking about?" Vito said, quickly losing the last of his patience.

"Okay, calm down."

Still annoyed, Vito took a swig of the martini.

"I'm talking about life not always giving you what you want," Frank explained. "What you need is far more valuable."

"So, I needed to become colorblind for a few days? And what's the point of this thing?" Vito pulled out the flask, which was stark gray with a few hints of pink. Vito blinked, startled by the flask's new look. "This pink wasn't here before."

"You're not where you think you are, kid," Frank said. "This is just a place in between."

"In between where?"

"Your world and ours."

"So, you're telling me our basement is purgatory?"

Frank rolled his eyes. "Come on, kid. With all the reading you do, it didn't cross your mind that this place can be anything of their making. We don't get a choice."

"Am I dead?" Vito asked, wanting to get to the point.

"We already covered this."

"Well, go over it again," Vito insisted.

"You're not dead," Frank began. "At least not physically. I think you died the same day I did. You gave up on your dreams and did everything *they* told you to."

"But Mamma was alone."

"Was she?" Frank asked and then sipped his drink.

"What's that supposed to mean?"

"Nothing." Frank stood with his martini in hand. "What's important here is you already started your journey. Now, all you have to do is finish it."

"Are you kidding? Whose body will I get stuck inside next? This is too weird. I don't want to do this anymore."

"You can't stop now. Once you start, you have to finish."

"Are you saying I won't go back until I can see all the colors again?" Vito asked, trying to understand.

"No." Frank finished off his last olive and then headed back to the cabinet for another drink. "You'll stop back home once in a while. You'll know you're there because all your color will be gone, except for the ones you've earned back."

Vito grimaced, trying to wrap his mind around what Frank had just said. "This is giving me a headache."

Frank chuckled. "It's not that bad kid. How about this, we'll call this basement the Intermondano[30]."

"Intermondano? What's that mean?"

"The in-between."

"In between what?"

"Worlds. The Intermondano is full of color. The basement back home is gray. As you earn colors, they'll drain from the Intermondano, and the flask, and find their way back into your reality.

"Why would you do something like this to me, Zi?"

"Look at it this way, you're getting an opportunity of a lifetime. To see life through another person's lens. Not many people get to experience that. I only know of two. You and Scott Bakula."

"How do you know about Scott Bakula? *Quantum Leap* didn't come out until *after* you died."

Frank came back to the sofa with a fresh martini in his hand. "Come on, Vi. Do you really think that people who die aren't around you? You loved that show. I watched every episode with you."

Vito smiled at the thought of his uncle hanging out while he clung to the television. Then Vito thought about it and was a bit embarrassed.

"What's the matter kid?" Frank asked, even though he already knew the answer.

"I didn't live my life at all," Vito admitted.

Frank put an arm around his nephew. "That's okay, Vito. You have a second chance at life right now."

Vito gave his dead uncle a half-hearted smile. He guessed he didn't have much of a choice.

"I'll be happy when I can see all the colors again," Vito admitted, trying to get himself excited about walking up the stairs again.

"Wait until you actually do die. Where I live now, there are colors you never imagined existed."

"How can you be around me when I'm watching television and in your new home?" Vito asked, not grasping this whole dead thing.

Frank laughed. "That's a talk for another time." Then he took a sip of his fresh pool of gin. "It'll blow your fucking mind!"

"What about Anthony?" Vito asked, getting back on track.

---

30   Intermundane

"Who?"

"My neighbor," Vito said. "My friend. The kid from the last door."

"What about him?"

"Am I going to be him every time?" Vito felt terrible for him and all, but he really wasn't eager to live or learn more of his life.

Frank laughed. "No. You'll see."

Vito sat in silence with his uncle for a minute, like they used to when he was a kid. Vito didn't sip martinis with him then, but the overall feeling was still the same. "I miss you, Zio," Vito said quietly.

"I miss you too, kid." Frank let the smirk on his face droop. "But I'm always with you. Even when you can't see me." He tossed back the rest of his drink and then stood. "I've gotta get going."

Vito panicked. "What? What do I do now?"

"When you take a drink from the flask, the door will open for you."

"Oh," Vito said, following his uncle to the staircase. "Will I see you again?"

"I don't know, but you see me now." Frank smiled before fading away. "And then you don't," Vito heard Frank say with a chuckle. Even though his uncle was no longer visible he had to have the last word.

Vito stood for a moment, looking up the stairs at the doorway. Then he took a long, hard look at the flask before opening it. After taking a cautious sip, Vito walked up the stairs, wondering what would happen next.

The door opened and Vito walked into a cloud. His vision obscured; he couldn't see where he was. He could, however, smell burning coal and melted metals. And wherever he was, the place was stifling with heat. He could hear the clanging of heavy machinery.

Being more than familiar with the sounds of a working factory, Vito let his anxiety subside for a moment. But he knew he wasn't in the paint factory.He waved his arms around, trying to deplete the fog. Fortunately, it started dissipating on its own.

Finally able to see, Vito found himself standing in front of an assembly line. Small motors passed before him, and he lifted his glove-clad hands to his face. He turned to look behind him and discovered working men assembling something he couldn't recognize.

Drab metal stairs climbed the ashen walls up to offices with shut doors. Vito glanced around again, just in time to see a woman passing by.

"Hello," she said with a smile.

Vito smiled back and took notice that the women around him, with their broad shoulders and twisted-back hair. Just one look and Vito suspected he had landed sometime during World War II. It looked like he fell into a movie set.

The blast of a steam whistle overpowered the commotion in the factory, and everything came to a halt. The workers were quick in their movements—taking off gloves, hats, and goggles while laughing with the kind of excitement established by a workday coming to an end.

The crowd began to walk toward a pair of open doors at one end of the factory. Vito followed along, trying to blend in while wondering who he was this time. As he made his way through the double doors, a mighty arm wrapped around his shoulder. "Hey there!" a voice boomed.

Vito turned toward the voice and instantly recognized the face it belonged to. He had seen this man and his easy, approachable smile in pictures Nonna would pull out to show him. This man was one of Papa Angelo's dearest friends when he and Nonna had lived in Indiana.

"Hey, Jed!" Vito said, surprised at his mental agility.

Jed chuckled. "Angelo, you look like you just saw a ghost!"

A sudden jolt of excitement jump-started Vito's heart upon the realization of who he was.

Behind Jed, a vending machine confirmed Vito's guess that he was in the 1940s during the war. The machine was round at the top and had a glass window, revealing the cola bottles. In the window's reflection, Vito saw a face he'd loved his entire life. The reflection greeted him with the same grin he felt himself making.

"I'm Papa," Vito thought, his chest swelling with pride.

Vito had never known his grandfather. Connie's father, Angelo, had died from strep throat when she and Frank were young. He'd learned all about him through Nonna's stories and the old picture books she kept in her nightstand by her bed. He could hear her voice in his head, explaining how Papa had died.

"They send all the medicine to the po'boys ova seas fighting that a bastard Mussolini, they had none left to give poor Papa."

Vito welled up a bit, thinking about Nonna.

"Are you okay?" Jed pulled his arm off Vito's shoulder.

"Yeah," Vito answered, still staring at his reflection on the vending machine. He looked at his friend and smiled. "I'm fine."

"Good. You were starting to scare me." Jed began to walk and talk, eager to leave work behind. "Is Josie still cooking tonight? I'm looking forward to that ara ... aranni ... what do you call it again?"

Vito laughed and fell into step beside Jed. "Arancini[31]. *AHRR-rahn-chee-nee*. And yes, she's still making dinner." Or at least Vito presumed that was the case. Nonna cooked every day. Why would this era be any different? Besides, Nonna always told him that Jed loved that dish—deep-fried rice balls with cheese, meat and pea stuffing, smothered in a sugo.

"Great." Jed smiled as they headed out of the locker room and onto the street.

Any concern Vito had about getting home faded as he relaxed into the nondescript conversation with his Papa's friend. Vito listened more than he spoke, not wanting to give away his unfamiliarity. They moved together down the street as the cars and trucks drove by. The Andrew Sisters singing about rum and Coca Cola called out from someone's radio.

As Vito took in his surroundings, he began to notice small pink items blinking from every direction. Flowers, dresses, bows in a little girl's hair.

He smiled, thrilled about the returning color and excited about what was in store for him this time around.

Soon, he and Jed found themselves on Hillside Drive until reaching Roosevelt Road.

Jed turned south and Vito started to follow.

Jed raised an eyebrow. "Where you going?"

"Oh ..." Vito said. "I live the other way."

Jed laughed. "Of course you do."

---

31   Deep fried rice balls typically with a ground meat, pea, tomato sauce center

Vito watched his friend walk south for a second before he turned to face north. "Where do I go from here?" he thought to himself. But then, he noticed his feet moving involuntarily, like they knew where to go even if he didn't. Shortly thereafter, he reached a residential area that could've been anywhere.

"Angelo! Angelo!"

Turning around, Vito found a young Nonna Josie running his way. He couldn't believe how smooth her skin was. Jet black curls hung past her shoulders.

"I need a chicory for the coffee," Nonna said to him as she wiped her hands on a gray apron dotted with pink flowers. She reached into her pocket and pulled out a dollar. "Angelo?" She snapped her fingers in front of his face. "Wassa matta you?"

Not knowing what to do, Vito leaned in and hugged her, still unable to believe this young woman was his nonna. As they hugged, he felt the bump in her belly.

It then struck him that Nonna wasn't his grandmother yet. She wasn't even a mother yet.

His mother, Connie, was still in her belly, waiting to be born.

They pulled away from each other, and Josie took a long look into her husband's eyes. She scanned his hair and his face, then took a step back.

A wave of apprehension swept over Vito. His whole life, he'd never been able to pull anything over on his nonna.

Suspicious, Josephine moved closer to him and put her lips on his forehead. "You donna have a fever." She pulled away from him again. "But you don't seem yourself." She stared at him a moment longer, then shrugged and handed him the dollar. "The chick-oh-ree." Nonna pushed him a bit and turned the other way.

Vito watched her walk back to a house that he had only seen in images in the hallway outside his bedroom—the one his grandparents had when they lived in Indiana. He smiled, feeling safe. Then, whistling down the street searching for a grocery store, he recalled Nonna's numerous stories about Papa.

In the beginning, Papa and Nonna lived on the west side of Chicago, where they met and married shortly before the Japanese bombed Pearl Harbor. All it took was one headline about that strike, and all the men in the neighborhood got in line to sign up for duty, including Papa.

But Papa would never fight in World War II alongside his friends because he had flat feet and was labeled 4F.

Vito could hear his grandmother tell him this story as he walked through the streets of Bloomington for the first time.

"The army turned him away. 'So a what!' Papa would holler." Nonna would throw her fist in the air, imitating her husband, and then giggling. "Angelo was gonna fight if it a killed 'im."

Vito's grandfather tried to enlist in the Navy, the Air Force, and the Marines, but his flat feet got him turned away time and time again. Then, he got word that a local shop signed a contract with the government to produce torpedoes. As a tool and die maker, Papa was a shoo-in for a job.

He was hired. But as the war escalated, another location was commandeered in Bloomington, and they sent Papa there to help get it started.

"I hated being away from my momma," Nonna would say tearfully, turning the photo album pages. "But a wife's duty is by her husband."

All his life Vito had listened to his family rave about what a wonderful man his grandfather was. His nonno's generosity and sense of humor was legendary in their neighborhood. Not knowing Papa was more disappointing to Vito than the absence of his father.

As Gus left his mind, Vito caught his reflection in the store window and remembered who he was—Papa Angelo.

Nothing could be better than that.

Chapter Twelve

Once he figured out where they lived and made his way back to their house, Vito was relieved when she kicked him out of the kitchen. That made it easier for him to not reveal who he really was to his nonna.

Vito sat in his grandfather's den, in a chair he assumed to be his, and read the newspaper as everyone did in the 1940s. Nonna had the radio going in the kitchen, and Vito could hear Billie Holiday singing "Strange Fruit."

By that evening, Vito was sitting at the head of the dining room table, listening to the dinner conversation around him as Jed and his wife, Bess, exchanged stories and laughter with Nonna.

Satisfaction soared through Vito's soul. Residing in the body of the man he'd always wished he'd had the chance to meet, Vito knew he would savor this moment forever.

In the middle of dinner, the doorbell rang.

"Who could dat a be?" Nonna Josie asked.

"I'll get it." Vito stood from the table. When he opened the front door, he found a small, bald man on the doorstep. "Can I help you?" Vito asked, although slightly distracted by the setting sun, which cascaded a pinkish hue across the horizon.

"You're new around here, aren't cha?" the man said in a gravelly voice. Vito presumed the man had to smoke at least three packs of unfiltered Camels a day. Nevertheless, it was the sky that continued to hold his attention. "Look at that sky," Vito uttered, forgetting where he was.

Confused, the man took a few steps back. He glanced at the sky but was not nearly as impressed with it. Suddenly, he snapped his fingers in front of Vito's face, trying to get his attention.

Vito returned his gaze to the man. "Sorry. What was that you said?"

"You and your pretty wife, you two are new to this area, huh?"

"We are." Vito smiled. "Are you a neighbor?" The question left Vito's mouth before he could stop himself. He hoped the man wasn't someone Papa already knew. The man didn't seem interested in answering though.

"It seems no one told you the rules around here," he said.

"Rules?" Vito asked.

The stranger didn't reply, but the look on his face made Vito uneasy. And within his body, he could feel Papa stirring around, agitated. "What do you want?" Vito asked, prompted by Papa's frustration. Vito could tell by the emotions he was feeling that Papa didn't find this man worthy of his time.

Chewing on a matchstick as if it was a toothpick, the short man smiled. When he spoke, tiny droplets of saliva jumped out of his mouth. "I'm here to inform you about the neighborhood rules. Seems to me nobody filled you in. We all just assumed you would know how we like things done around here. But it don't look that way, do it?" He stepped closer to the doorway, peering into the house, where Josie, Bess, and Jeb were still enjoying dinner.

Refusing to be intimidated, Vito stepped forward, forcing the stranger to take a few steps back.

The man chuckled. "I hear that you all are Catholics. I don't know how that one slipped by. But you bought the house, so I suppose now it's too late." He shrugged his shoulders. "At least you *kinda* look like us. But those people, the ones you got in there, they have to go. You understand?"

Vito kept his gaze on the short man. "What have they done to you?"

The man pointed a crooked finger in Vito's face. "Listen, those types are not welcome here, and I'll tell you, we have all sorts of ways of keeping them out. Ways that may make you reconsider living in this neighborhood."

Anger bubbled within him. "This is *my* home," Vito said, putting his finger into the little man's face. "My door will be open to my friends as long as it's mine."

The short man cackled, and suddenly a whistle sounded through the air. Knowing it wasn't the man in front of him who had released the whistle, Vito looked toward a truck parked on the street. A dozen dark figures in the flatbed stared back at Vito.

"I don't think you understand what I'm telling ya, boy," the man said as a foreboding smile spread across his face. "We know how to make you see things our way." The man removed the matchstick from his mouth and pointed it at Vito's face. "Think about it." With that, he turned and walked off the porch, jumped in the truck, and drove off.

Watching the retreating truck go down the street, Vito searched his memory for any of Nonna's stories that included this short man. But he couldn't think of any.

"Angelo!" Nonna called from inside the house. "Whoever it is tell dem to come on in. There's a plenty to go 'round."

Hearing the joyous laughter in the dining room, Vito closed the door and returned to the table.

"Who was at the door?" Jed asked.

"A salesman," Vito lied.

***

Later, when the night was over, Vito told Nonna he needed a little bit of fresh air. Really he wanted to walk Jeb and Bess back to their neighborhood.

Vito, Jed, and Bess stepped off the front porch, moving past the same spot where the tiny intruder had stood only a couple of hours ago.

"That wasn't a salesman at your door earlier," Bess said knowingly.

"We know that man," Jed said, looking down the dark street. "He makes his way to the west side now and again."

"I'm sorry," Vito said. "I should've been honest. But I didn't want Non ... I didn't want Josie to know. I was afraid it would frighten her."

"If she ever saw the things that man has done to people, she'd be more than frightened," Jed said. "My wife doesn't get to live in ignorance of the world's horrors. Bess has to know who that man is so she can avoid him. It could mean her life."

The trio walked in silence, all intuitively keeping a close eye on their surroundings until reaching Jed's and Bess's home.

Bess turned to Vito. "Would you like a cup of coffee and some pie?"

Vito smiled. "Of course I would."

Bess went inside to get the coffee going while Jed and Vito took a seat on the front porch. The weather was perfect, the stars filling the night sky and illuminating the street.

"What did that man say to you?" Jed asked.

Vito hesitated. He didn't want to tell Jed the truth. He loved them both and, while he wanted to be honest, it was hard to tell his friend that the man wanted him out of the neighborhood because he was black.

"You don't have to shield me. I get it every day," Jed said.

"How do you stay so calm?" Vito asked. "If I were treated that way, I'd be pissed all the time."

"Trust me, it isn't always this easy to turn the other cheek. I've just learned to put my faith in the Lord. 'Love your enemies and pray for those who persecute you.' That's from the Book of Matthew."

Bess returned with a tray of steaming hot coffee and three plates.

"When I was a teenager," Jed continued, "I was quick to get mad and get in trouble. But I learned being that way wasn't helping me or my family. So, I chose to educate myself about great men who learned to let their anger go. Jesus happens to be my favorite."

"Well, I'm not as quick to forgive as my husband," Bess chimed in. "But he's right. You can only fight hate with love."

Vito took a bite of his pie and couldn't believe something that looked putrid gray to him tasted so fantastic. "This is delicious," he said before swallowing his next bite.

Bess grinned. "Pecan pie. It's my mawmaw's recipe. I learned to make it as a girl when I spent my summers down on the bayous of Louisiana."

"I didn't know you had family in Louisiana," Vito said.

"Yep. Jefferson parish. Just south of New Orleans."

Vito smiled. "I've always wanted to go to New Orleans."

"You should. It's a city like no other." Bess proceeded to tell Vito all about New Orleans while he finished his pie. And once the hour grew late, he said his goodbyes and headed home.

Along the walk, Vito reflected on growing up in Chicago; even by 2007, not much had changed. He remembered how fast the black kids would ride their bikes through his Italian neighborhood, knowing it wasn't safe for them.

Lost in his thoughts, Vito was taken by surprise as several hands grabbed his jacket and pulled him down.

Someone shoved a sock into his mouth as he was dragged behind some bushes.

Vito flooded Papa's body with fear while guys with covered faces pinned him to the ground. Out of the shadows, a short figure emerged.

Vito didn't need to see his face to know who it was.

The small man held a baseball bat. He swung it at a few fireflies. A muffled chuckle sounded through the air as one of the ignited flyers was hit into oblivion.

Dread consumed Vito as he tried to pull free from their grasp. But there were too many of them. Maybe six or seven in total, he couldn't tell.

One of them balanced Vito's left ankle onto a cinder block.

"I kept hearin' about you Aye-talyans," a familiar, hoarse voice cracked from under the face covering. "Stubborn bunch, from what I could see." The man reached down and put his hand in Vito's hair, ruffling it as if Vito was a young boy. "It's greasy, all right!" the man yelled to his cohorts when he pulled his hand back up.

His friends roared with tobacco-filled snickers.

The man brought his hand under his face covering and took a long sniff. "*Oooh wee*! They reek of garlic too!" He waved his hand in front of the crowd, increasing their laughter. He then wiped his hands on his jeans and began swinging his bat at the fireflies again.

Another man placed a second cinder block under Vito's left knee.

"I didn't know how I could show you I was serious 'bout them people coming to our side of town. So, I think to myself and say, *'How would that greasy Aye-talyan understand that I mean business?'*" The small man stopped swinging the bat. "Then it hits me. Al Ca-poh-nee. Ain't that his name? He was that crazy wop over there in Chicago. That's where you're from, right?" The small man stared at Vito without even blinking.

Vito, paralyzed by the insanity he saw in the man's eyes, could only stare back.

"Answer me when I ask you a question, boy!" The small man grabbed Vito's shirt.

Vito nodded while trying to pull his lower left leg from the hands securing it on the cinder blocks.

"You dagos sure know how to make a point. I heard that Ca-poh-nee guy once bashed a buncha heads in with a baseball bat. Kinda like the one I got right here."

Vito squirmed, although he was losing hope he'd ever escape.

"So, I thought, a baseball bat to the head would send the right message." The short man dangled the bat near Vito's skull. "But then I thought, *'I'm not a savage like those greaseballs.'* The leg will do just fine."

Vito tried to scream, but the sock muffled his cries. He jerked his body, bucking his hips so much his leg finally came off the blocks. But the group worked fast to get it back up.

"Don't make this harder than it has to be!" the short man screamed. He raised the bat high above his head. "This is for Al Cah-poh-nee!" he roared, swinging the bat at Vito's leg with a power that only pure evil could induce.

Vito hollered in agony. "Next time, I'm gonna come for your wife," the short man said, and the beating continued as the faint pink dots surrounding Vito blurred into nothing.

***

Vito opened his eyes, not remembering where or who he was. When the room came into focus, he realized he was in a hospital bed. Looking to his right, the reflection in the window showed he was still Papa.

This portion of the adventure was far from over.

He saw a curtain drawn to his left, and from the sound of machines on the other side, Vito knew he wasn't alone.

A female figure approached, glowing in pink.

"Lucia!" he gasped.

She nodded.

Vito's heart jumped. It was her. Even though he had just met her, something about being near Lucia helped calm him. Her beauty was mesmerizing. Her lips were full of a soothing crimson glow, and her nails were red as apples.

"How did you get here?" he asked.

"I've been here this whole time," she replied.

"In the stands at the baseball game." Vito said, suddenly realizing the girl with red hair was her. "And you were across the street when Anthony's father was …"

"Shh," Lucia pressed a finger to Vito's lips and smiled. Then, to Vito's surprise, she backed away.

"Where are you going?"

"I'll be back," Lucia said, heading to the door.

When the door swung open, a young Nonna rushed in with tears streaming down her face. Vito looked past her to see Lucia move in a blur of red and pink down a gray hallway.

"Angelo!" Josie exclaimed, hugging him and blocking his sight. "Whatta 'appen to you?"

"Uh …" Vito hesitated, not wanting Nonna to know the truth, "I had an accident walking back home."

"I wassa so a worried," Nonna said.

"I'm okay," Vito tried to reassure her. "You can stop worrying."

"Angelo?" Vito heard Jeb's voice at the doorway. He looked over and breathed a sigh of relief knowing he was okay.

"Josie, will you go get us some coffee?" Vito asked. Even though he was occupying his grandfather's body, Vito knew he was making the choices. What amazed him was how easy it was to become the person he was inhabiting.

Nonna said nothing and hurried out of the room.

Jeb stepped inside and stood next to Vito. "How's the leg?"

"I don't know," Vito said, and then he added. "I'll be okay. I think I'll have a limp though."

Jeb didn't say anything. Then Vito said, "I guess I'll see you back at the plant."

Jeb looked at his friend and there was pain in his eyes. "Yeah, I guess I'll see you."

They both smiled and shook hands. Jeb wanted to say he knew he wouldn't be coming over to Angelo's house for Italian food anymore, and Vito could hear it, all right there in his Papa's head.

This adventure made Vito privy to his thoughts. Angelo never invited Jeb and Bess over again. It wasn't long before Papa and Nonna moved back to Chicago, back into their neighborhood. Papa never talked to Jeb again, and Vito was disappointed, knowing the reason. He always considered his Papa to be a stand-up guy who fought for his friends. But Vito could also feel the worry Papa had for his wife, and how he had to sacrifice his need to be on the side of right to protect her.

Vito then remembered Nonna telling him years ago that Jed had disappeared shortly after Papa's "accident."

Vito let his eyes focus on a vase on the windowsill. The flowers inside were gray. But an intense sorrow devoured him. He could feel the pain his Papa experienced over the loss of his friend and the disappointment he had in himself. At that moment, the gloomy petals Vito saw began to glow a bright lemon yellow.

Chapter Thirteen

"My dad was a hard act to follow."

Vito heard his uncle's voice as he opened his eyes in the Intermondano basement. "What?"

"Never mind," Frank said. "How ya feelin'?"

Vito stood and walked to the window, wanting to see something other than the basement. But outside the window, there was only darkness. He sighed. "I'm tired."

"I understand."

"Do you?" Vito rounded on his uncle, his anger flaring. "Because this is some fucked-up shit you signed me up for!"

"I know."

"This wasn't the type of adventure I had in mind, even as a kid!"

Frank said nothing as he walked to the cabinet to pick up a martini Vito hadn't noticed was there. He took a long sip. "Are you done?"

Vito looked around, wishing a gin and tonic would appear for him. And miraculously, as soon as the thought entered his head, the drink materialized in his hand. He took a sip and then sat on the sofa.

"So, I can conjure up anything I want?" Vito asked.

"Yup," Frank replied, taking a seat next to his nephew.

Vito thought of meatballs and a tray appeared on the coffee table before them. Frank's eyes lit up. Two plates, napkins, and silverware appeared. Frank grabbed a few meatballs from the tray and started to eat.

"Why should I ever go back?" Vito asked. And then Lucia appeared. "See, I can have anything I want right here. Right now."

Frank swallowed his meatballs and put his plate down. "Sure, kid. You can. But I wouldn't advise getting stuck in this place too long. You'll get trapped here. Trust me."

Vito wasn't paying any attention to his uncle. Instead, he was standing in front of Lucia. When he reached out to touch her Vito realized she was an apparition.

"You can't just make a whole person come here," Frank tried to explain as he led his nephew away from the image of Lucia, who faded the second Vito turned his gaze.

"You made me come here," Vito retorted.

"I set it up for you," Frank corrected. "You took the first drink."

"How was I supposed to know?!" Vito yelled. "Why didn't you warn me?"

"No one told me either," Frank insisted. "And I got stuck here. I don't want that to happen to you."

Vito pulled away from his uncle and took another sip of his drink.

"I realize this isn't what you think you signed up for, but the truth is, kid, you decided to take this journey long before you were even conceived in your mamma's womb," Frank said.

Vito stared at his uncle, dumbfounded. "*I* decided to do all this?"

"None of that matters, Vi. You're in it now. You can't turn back."

"How many more doors do I have to go through?"

"That's not for me to say," Frank said in that ethereal way Vito was beginning to loathe.

"Frank, I have to go home at some point. Will I be done when I can see all colors again?"

Vito's uncle laughed so hard, he spat out his martini. "I don't know kid." He wiped the excess liquid off his chin. "The only way you're gonna find out is by going forward."

"Great! Just great!" An exasperated Vito jumped up from his seat.

"Hey, the good news is you'll only be here for the length of one night in the "real world," no matter how many doors you move through. Once morning comes in that world, you go back home for a day. Then, when evening hits and you fall asleep, you'll come back here."

"I'm not following. Is this a dream or something?"

"I didn't say that. Could you see color when you were awake after you first came here?"

"No," Vito admitted.

"That's evidence that this is much more than a mere dream." Frank took another sip of his martini. "Although, I'm not making light of the importance of dreams. That's a different kind of door."

Vito took another sip of his drink. And at that moment, he decided to wait in the Intermondano until morning. He felt safe in this colorful replica of the gray basement back home. Vito looked around and Frank was gone. "Good," Vito thought. He loved Frank and wished he felt more grateful to see him again. Vito just didn't want to argue about his decision to wait in the Intermondano. Because that's what he was going to do. He would wait however long it took to get back to his gray reality. He'd had enough of the doors.

March 20, 2007

"Get up!" Vito felt himself being pulled until he hit the floor. His eyes darted open and found that he was in the real basement—still mostly gray with the exception of some pink and yellow splattered here and there.

"Vito!"

He heard his mother yell. Shortly thereafter, a wooden spoon smacked his ass.

"Ma!" Vito hollered, jumping up and then nearly falling again.

Connie made another attempt to spank his rear with her utensil.

"Hey!" Vito yelled again, moving out of her reach. "Stop it! I'm a grown man."

"Then act like one," Connie said through gritted teeth.

"What are you talking about?" Vito stumbled a little. The strange color combination of gray variations, pink, and yellow was making him dizzy. It felt like he was living in a half-filled coloring book.

"What am I talking about?" Connie scolded. "Look at you. It's 10:15 on a Tuesday morning, and where are you? Passed out in the basement. How drunk did you get last night that you're still stumbling around?"

Vito suddenly remembered his leave of absence, which he obviously hadn't told her about. And mentioning it now seemed out of the question.

"You're going to lose your job!" Connie cried.

Vito went to her, feeling guilty. "Ma, I'm not going to lose my job."

Connie wiped tears and straightened her back. "I know you're drinking."

"Yes. I was drinking last night," Vito said after a slight pause. "But I won't do it again. I promise."

Connie rolled her eyes. "I've heard *that* before."

"I said I wouldn't drink, and I won't. We have a meeting at noon, and Anthony said we could start late today."

"Anthony." Connie snorted, "The guy who made you come in every Saturday for a month because you were tardy that time after we celebrated Bisnonna's birthday? He said you could come in late?"

"Well, we all met our quotas and …"

"Save the lies."

"I'm going to work, Ma. My job is fine. I swear."

Connie walked to the staircase. "Breakfast is on the counter," she said, her back facing Vito as she reached the first step. She hurried up the rest of the stairs and shut the door behind her.

Vito looked around the room. The fuzziness of the color he could see continued making him dizzy. There was also a slow ringing in his ears, the flask up to its old tricks again. A quick survey of the room revealed the demonic vessel was glowing on the hutch close to where Frank had picked up his last martini.

Some of the gems and stones on the flask were now gray, leading Vito to believe that when colors reappeared in his reality, they disappeared from the flask.

Seeing how many stones were still fully colored, he realized with dismay that his troubles were far from over.

The flask's pull remained strong. Yet, he remembered his latest promise to his mother.

He took the flask off the top of the hutch and closed it into the bottom drawer. Nevertheless, he could still hear the ringing as he ran up the stairs.

"Ignore it," he kept telling himself as he ate his room temperature eggs and toast.

Nonna Josie didn't have much to say as she cleaned the dishes, and Bisnonna Nellie let a soft snort escape her nose as gravity took hold of her dentures.

"It's not really there. It's all in your head," Vito repeated silently as the flask sang out to him while he dressed for the day.

Once ready, he said goodbye to Nonna and Bisnonna Nellie so quickly he hardly looked at their faces. He ran out of the house, planning to catch the bus to the paint factory. But he was too late and missed it.

Then he wondered why he was going to the paint factory in the first place.

He gazed around at his half chroma, half drab reality. Most of what he saw was in grayscale, though bits of pink and yellow blinked at him like a laser shot in the eye.

Glancing at his watch, Vito realized he had seven or eight hours to kill.

He considered heading to the Art Institute to see what *At the Moulin Rouge* and *American Gothic* looked like with only bits of pink and yellow. But then he convinced himself that viewing Seurat's pointillistic masterpiece, *A Sunday Afternoon on the Island of La Grande Jatte,* without color would be nothing short of depressing.

Cars were speeding down Harlem, splashing through puddles that Vito knew were gray whether he could see color or not. He looked around at the bits of pink and yellow surrounding him, but nothing he saw was full of the colors he never knew he loved so much. Everywhere he looked, Vito was reminded there was still so much gray to fill in.

Realizing there was no telling when this so-called adventure would be over, Vito sat on the bus stop bench. Millions of colors were detectable to the human eye—that part of his training at Chroma always stuck in his mind.

Still feeling the call of the flask, Vito was suddenly stricken with just how overwhelmed he felt. His odd colorblindness mixed with the cravings from the flask were too much. At this rate, they were going to get the best of him before the end of the day if he didn't find a place to hide.

And then it dawned on Vito where he needed to be.

***

"Well, you're here early, aren't you?" Lucia said, walking up to Vito, who had taken a seat at the bar. Just as he expected, The Tap was quiet and dark, which is what he needed. The walk over from the bus stop was like moving through an obstacle course. You don't realize how distracting colors can be until you can't see them anymore. Or, when you can see only a couple.

"Yeah," Vito said, feeling safe for the first time in a while.

"I thought you worked over at Chroma. Or did you come to see me on your lunch?"

"I was put on a leave of absence because I got caught sipping from my flask in the bathroom."

Lucia laughed in a way that made Vito question whether she believed him or not. "So, do you want something to drink?" she asked after a moment.

Yes, but I don't want you to think I'm a drunk. "I'll have a coke," Vito said.

Lucia grabbed a glass and filled it with ice. "It's funny you came in today. I had a dream about you last night."

"You did?" Vito asked, perplexed. "What happened in it?"

Lucia shot cola from the soda gun into the glass. "It was weird. There was this one where I was a candy striper. Do you know what that is?"

"Yes," Vito replied mentally telling his chin to not hit the floor.

Lucia put his soft drink on the coaster. "Well, I dreamt I was a candy striper in the forties, like during World War II. And you were in the hospital for something … I think it was a broken leg. How weird is that?"

"Huh," Vito said, taking a sip of his Coke and wishing it had something mind-altering in it.

"Wait," Lucia said, placing her hand on top of Vito's. "There's more."

Vito jerked his hand back.

Lucia stopped talking and it seemed, to Vito, like everything came to a halt. Seconds later, sunlight pierced the barroom as the door opened and a patron entered.

"Hey Lucia, would you grab me a High Life?" the newcomer said.

"Sure thing," Lucia called out. Then she turned her attention back to Vito. "Uhm …" she started with obvious awkwardness. "Let me go get that beer … and sorry about the hand thing." Then she scurried off.

Vito sat there and sipped his Coke as he called himself every name in the book from loser to idiot. Why did he react that way?

She was beautiful and now she thinks he doesn't like her. Vito was thankful for the darkness inside the bar so no one could see him blush from the humiliation.

Looking around, Vito noticed there were still sights of yellow and pink in random spots around the room. Mostly they were bits of a neon sign or poster on the wall. But in The Tap, they weren't as jarring as they were outside. Out there, the colors gave him a headache, the likes of which he'd never experienced. In here, he felt fine. Yep. This was the perfect place to help him disappear for a while.

"As I was saying," Lucia's words disrupted Vito's thoughts. "Oh, I'm sorry, I can leave you alone if that's what you prefer." Vito didn't prefer that.

"No," Vito replied trying to be courageous. "I like talking to you."

Lucia smiled brightly, in a way Vito wasn't used to when it came to women. They usually made the kind of face one does after eating something bitter. Or they ran away. It took him awhile to realize women don't want you to stare at them. When you do, it usually gets you labeled a creep, so Vito learned fast to keep his eyes averted from anyone of the opposite sex.

"Hello," Lucia waved a hand in his face. "Did you hear me?"

"Uh," Vito blushed and then clammed up. He knew he would ruin it.

"I said, 'I like talking to you too,'" Lucia took a moment and studied Vito's face. "You aren't like anyone I've ever met."

Vito didn't know what to say. He quickly thought that keeping his mouth shut was probably the best decision when it came to talking to Lucia. But the quiet made him uncomfortable, so Vito asked if he could buy her a drink.

"Oh, no. Thank you. Bartenders shouldn't drink on the job."

"Oh," Vito said. "I figured bartenders drank all the time."

"Some do," Lucia said. "And some don't."

Another quiet moment went by, and Lucia was the one to break the silence.

"I don't drink," Lucia admitted. "I mean, I used to but quit a few years back. I tried to make it work back home in Iowa, but I needed a new start. My aunt invited me to come here to Chicago, so I did. I just started working here three months ago. Anyway, it's nice to meet someone else who doesn't have to get wasted to have a good time."

"Vito?" another voice from behind intruded into their two-way exchange.

Lucia looked at the owner of the voice. He wished to just ignore it, but that wasn't an option.

"What are you doing here?" Connie ran up to him as the front door shut out the sunlight she'd let in moments ago.

Vito didn't know what to say. He looked across the bar to see Lucia and other barflies watching the scene play out. His strange vision mixed with imagination and panic created a sight of a dozen or more eyeballs, white against the dark background, some filled with a jaundiced yellow and others with thin pink lines. All of them focused on him and waiting to burst.

"I'm talking to you!" Connie's shrill yell bounced off the dark walls along with the snickering of onlookers.

"Ma …" Vito turned on his barstool to face her. "How'd you find me?" He looked at her silhouette until the door opened yet again and bright yellow sunlight blinded him.

"I called your office to apologize for this morning," Connie said with a sniffle. The front door closed slowly, and the dark figure shaped like his mother soon came into focus. Vito stared into her broken eyes. "Anthony told me he put you on a mandatory leave of absence."

A throbbing pain moved through Vito's chest. He averted his eyes to the floor, unable to handle holding Connie's gaze. "I'm sorry."

"Come home," Connie said.

"But I haven't even had a drink," Vito said.

"Go home with your mommy, little boy!" someone taunted through the darkness.

Connie momentarily pursed her lips at the stranger's comment. "Okay, we'll talk about this when you get home," she said to Vito. She looked around the room, then turned to head back out the door.

Wanting to escape the eyes staring at him, Vito grabbed his briefcase, put a twenty on the bar, and left, despite having no idea what to do for the rest of the day. He couldn't go home for several reasons, and, at the moment, he wasn't planning on stepping into The Tap ever again.

Not knowing what else to do, he walked a few blocks, jumped on a train, and found himself back in Little Italy, on Oakley, standing in front of the sisters' building.

Vito stood for a minute, staring at the front door, and internally debating whether or not to head upstairs. Before he could decide, the front door slowly opened.

Although Vito couldn't see anyone looking out, he suspected they knew he was there.

Finally making up his mind, he entered the building. Once he was inside, the heavy wooden door with the leaded-glass center closed behind him.

Chapter Fourteen

"Maybe I should tell her," Vito said as Allegra handed him what looked like a picnic basket. He took it dutifully, as if she was his mother.

"You can't tell her," Allegra said shaking her head. She reached for another bag, which looked to contain coffee grounds, broken eggshells, and hardboiled eggs.

"Why not?" Vito asked.

"Are you kidding? If you tell your mother or nonna about this, they'll have you in the middle of an exorcism before you know it."

"True," Vito said, defeated. Allegra handed Vito the bag, which he took. He was starting to feel a bit overloaded.

"I think that's everything," the eldest sister said.

"Where are we going?" Vito asked for what seemed to be the twentieth time to Allegra. In reality it was only the third.

"I told you," Allegra said, trying to mask her frustration. "We're heading to our other property up north. It's called West-field. You'll love it, it's right on the lake."

"Why is it called Westfield if it's so far east?"

"My mom had a sense of humor."

"Why are we going?" Vito asked, unable to get his head out of his problems.

"Ostara my boy," Allegra said. Then she picked up some other bags and led Vito into the kitchen. "I'm going to Westfield because my sisters and I are welcoming in the new season, as we've done in our family for centuries. You're going because you're looking for a place to hide."

Allegra led Vito to the pantry door.

"Then why are we in the kitchen?" Vito inquired. "The front door is that way."

"I don't travel the way humans do anymore. Not if I can help it. We'll use the portal."

"Portal?" Vito looked at the door in front of them. He may have just met these sisters, but he'd seen them go in and out of that pantry several times.

"Come on, Vito," Allegra said with zero patience. "You've used a portal before. Catch up, okay? Otherwise, you'll be left behind."

"Okay," Vito said. "But you have to cut me some slack. Sorellanza Magicka, portals, and magic flasks are all new to me, so I'm bound to be shocked."

"Fair enough," Allegra agreed. "Are you ready?"

"I suppose," Vito said, trying to convince himself. When he thought about it, this was his third or fourth time walking into another world he never knew existed. Allegra was right, you'd think he'd be used to it by now.

Allegra opened the pantry door, and, just as Vito expected, there was no more pantry. No canned goods, no jars of stewed tomatoes, no cans of olive oil, no pasta. There was the oppressive cloud of smoke that made Vito's anxiety skyrocket.

"Don't worry," Allegra said as she took his arm. "You're safe."

"Why should I believe you?" Vito asked, his feet glued to the ground. "I barely know you."

"True," Allegra started. "But you can say that about anyone really. Even the people closest to us have secrets and skeletons in their closets and pantries."

Vito stayed silent, frozen with fear.

"You came to us, Vito," Allegra said, not letting go of his arm as the wind began to pick up in her kitchen. The cloud in the pantry began to creep out and surround them. "Remember," she began to laugh wildly as the white smoke closed in tighter, "everything you want and desire is on the other side of fear."

With that the cloud clung to them in the same way it did when he became Anthony, and his Papa. The difference was this time, Vito wasn't alone. He could still feel Allegra's hand on his arm, so he gave into the fear. The moment he did, he was no longer afraid.

Before he knew it, the cloud was gone, and they both were in the kitchen of a log cabin.

"See how easy that was," Allegra said. She let go of his arm and took the bags from his hands.

"Vito!" he heard a familiar voice call out. He turned to find Freya and Ginevra sitting at an enormous island, working on what looked like coloring eggs with paint brushes, glitter, and other ornamental objects to create what looked to be an egg one could sell under the name Fabergé.

"Hi!" Vito returned their greeting. "Are you coloring eggs?"

"No," Ginevra smarted back. "We're washing our hair."

"Ginny," Freya hissed. "Be nice."

Ginevra pouted and kept at her work.

"I was only asking because Easter isn't for a couple of weeks."

"These are for Ostara," Ginevra hissed. "Don't be such a human."

"Ginny," Freya said. "It's not his fault he was never taught about Ostara."

"I don't care," Ginevra shouted. "I'm bringing my eggs to the circle." And with that she got up and exited via the storm door into the yard, which to Vito looked to go on forever.

"Did I do something wrong?" Vito asked Freya.

"You're human," Freya said. "She's not a big fan of your kind."

"But she was so friendly when I first met her. Overtly friendly if I'm being frank."

"You're not being Frank, you're being Vito."

"Huh?" Vito was confused.

"I'm being punny," Freya snickered to herself.

"Seriously," Vito wanted to get back to Ginevra. "Why was she so nice in the beginning if she loathes humans so much?"

"Because you have her flask."

"Oh," Vito said, realizing this was more serious for them than he thought.

"What happens to Ginny if she doesn't get the flask back in time?"

Ignoring Vito's question, Freya put her last egg into the basket she had been filling for hours.

"It's a shame you can't see any of these in their full glory."

Vito looked at the basket, which had a speckling of pinks and yellows, but for the most part, they were gray.

"Whether or not I can see all the colors, they're still beautiful," Vito said.

"Thanks," Freya smiled. "I'm gonna go find my sister."

Vito watched Freya exit the storm door.

"Oh," Freya leaned back in for a moment. "Don't call her Ginny. That really pisses her off."

He smiled and hoped Ginevra would be his friend again someday.

"Vito," he heard Allegra call. "Come here."

Vito followed her voice through the grand kitchen in this log cabin. The wood was red, and the logs were huge. The vaulted ceilings reached higher than Vito had ever seen. Allegra was sitting in a small nook nestled into the corner by two windows. Outside you could see the ever-giving blue that is Lake Michigan.

The Lake, as the people in this area like to call it, is one of a collection that serves as the lifeblood of this region. Vito always felt he came alive when looking upon the expansive water.

"This is a beautiful place," Vito said, taking a seat at the table.

"Thank you," Allegra said, as she dumped a bag of shiny envelopes on the table. Upon further investigation Vito discovered that they were seed packets.

"This place has been in our family for generations, but our mother truly made it what it is today."

"Your mother sounds like she was an amazing woman," Vito said, realizing that, in this specific situation, his living with women his entire life benefitted him. He wondered in what other ways his experience of living with women had helped him.

"Get your head out of the clouds and help me," Allegra said, sounding more and more like his mother with each interaction. "I poured you some coffee, it'll ease the monotony."

"What do you need me to do?"

"We're sorting seeds," Allegra answered. "When we have each varietal in its right place, we'll head over to the greenhouse and start our seedlings for the season."

"What seeds are we starting?"

"Marigolds, zinnias, tomatoes, peppers, eggplants, zucchini, and much more. Here's the list." Allegra pulled out a pad with a list and then she explained where to place each packet. They got to work and drank their coffee.

"It's a good thing you came to see us today," Allegra admitted. "We can help you get through this safely, and in a timely manner. Then you can give us that flask."

"I've been thinking about that," Vito said. "I don't want to do this whole 'journey' thing anyway. I'll get the flask back to you tomorrow. I don't have to see color."

Allegra stopped working and put her hand on Vito's. "You are a good human, Vito. I wish I could take you up on that offer. But unfortunately, you must finish your journey before we can use the magic for Ginevra."You see, all things are filled with energy, including the flask. You must start thinking of it as a being, not just a thing. The flask you have was instructed, via magic from my very hands, to provide you with this journey."

Vito stopped working. "You did this to me?" He was shocked. "I thought Frank did this."

"He did," Allegra said. "But he couldn't instruct the flask. You have to be Sorellanza Magicka to give the instruction. Frank wasn't, so he came to me."

"All this time, why didn't you tell me you did this?"

"Because it was a mistake! All right!" Allegra was losing her temper and patience. "I thought you would have found it by your twenties and gotten this over with. That gave us plenty of time to get it back by Ginevra's birthday. You didn't find the flask until you were thirty-seven. You're a late bloomer, Vito."

Vito looked at the lake and said nothing.

"None of this matters anyway," Allegra said. "You are tied to the flask until you complete the journey. Until you do, the magic will not work for my sister."

Vito sighed and took a sip of his coffee. "I still think that I should tell my family what I'm dealing with here."

"No," Allegra said. "You're free to do what you want, but you are taking a great risk by telling anyone. Not only are you risking yourself, but you're also risking them too. Besides, *The Sorellanza Magicka*, and your journey, your family would see all of this as ..." Allegra frowned. "Hmm ... How should I put it?"

"Unholy," Vito finished her thought and understood her point. She was right. No matter how hard it was for his mother to believe he was a drunk, the alternative was much worse.

"I think that's all of them," Allegra announced. "Let's get to planting."

"What is the So-ray-lahn-za?"

Sorellanza Magicka," Allegra corrected. "Grab your coffee and follow me. I'll explain it while we plant."

Vito followed Allegra out the door into the most expansive garden he had ever seen. While everything was still in the final stages of hibernation, Vito could tell that this garden was luscious in the summer.

"It's tradition to plant the first seeds of the season on Ostara. Since we live in the Midwest, we can't put any seeds into the ground yet. It's much too cold. Instead, we start seedlings in the greenhouse. The important thing is that we plant with intention. As you put the seed into the ground, I want you to think about your journey, what you want to gain from it. Our belief is that the goal you set when planting a seed will be obtained when that plant first blooms."

Freya and Ginevra were sitting at a table with a basket of decorated eggs. Vito could see some of the yellow and pink, but the eggs looked liked they were covered in gray blobs. As he followed Allegra to the garden beds, he saw Ginevra and Freya each take an egg. Then they hit their eggs together on the pointed side. Freya's cracked and Ginevra jumped up laughing.

"I win!" Ginevra shouted.

"No," Freya tried to take Ginevra's egg from her. "Yours cracked too. We play again."

"It did not," Ginevra snickered as she started to run around the yard. Freya tried to chase her, and they romped and played as if they were children. Vito couldn't believe these women were older than his nonna.

"Here we are," Allegra said when she and Vito reached the greenhouse. Vito couldn't believe how big it was. It was almost as large as his family's bungalow.

They stepped inside and Vito was amazed at the lush life that lived in these glass walls. Vito looked at all the hanging foliage and trees tucked away in every corner of the massive room. They had tropical plants and he even thought he heard a couple birds call from behind the bushes. Vito knew there was more green in here than he'd ever seen in one place at one time. But he couldn't see a drop of it.

Allegra set down her basket and motioned for Vito to follow her.

They reached a row of raised garden beds with fresh soil. Vito couldn't see the color, but he allowed the fresh dirt to permeate his senses.

"Have you gardened before?"

"Uh huh. My mom and nonna keep a garden in the yard. We grow Romas, basil, peppers, and eggplant mostly."

She handed him a hand shovel, gloves, and a packet of seeds. "We'll start here. You're going to plant marigold seeds and move to your right. I'm planting zinnias and will move to my left. You do three rows of marigolds, and I'll do three rows of zinnias. When you're done, we'll switch sides, and I'll do three rows of marigolds, and you do three zinnias."

"Why wouldn't I just plant all the marigolds?"

"I'll explain in a minute, but this next part is important so pay attention. You're going to plant three seeds every ten inches. When you dig the hole, set an intention. Then, as you place the seeds into the hole, give thanks to our Mother Earth for she is our connection to the universe. Finally, as you cover those seeds with the generous gift of soil, bow your head in awe of her. Do this for every hole you dig."

Vito looked confused.

"In the Sorellanza Magicka, Earth is our deity. There is a force in this universe that has a hold on us all, including asteroids, stars, and planets. But us, we are of this Earth, so she is our connection to the source. But it's not just us in the sisterhood. Humans, plants, animals, rocks, everything on this Earth is connected. Some call that universal energy God, others call it source, some don't call it anything because they know, it's something too huge for the human mind to comprehend. Are you following me?"

"Yes," Vito said. "But what does this have to do with planting and us switching sides?"

"We celebrate the first day of Spring by planting," Allegra continued. "When we plant seeds, we set an intention. We give thanks and Mother Earth makes a promise that the intention will grow with that seed. You are struggling with this journey, which was set in place for you by your dead uncle. So be mindful of that when you plant marigolds and set your intentions."

Vito was catching on and stayed silent. Allegra could tell he was finally getting it, and she continued.

"Zinnias represent friendship, endurance, and all the goodness in the world. Again, knowing this and keeping your struggles in mind, set an appropriate intention. All who belong to the Sorellanza Magicka are free to practice as they wish. Some are vocal about what intentions they set. Some don't share them with anyone but Mother Earth. I'm one of the latter. But I will break my tradition to say that the first intention I set with Mother Earth while planting zinnias will be for the continuation of our friendship, even after you return the flask. I'll give thanks to Mother Earth for you showing up in our lives, and bow in awe."

"Thank you," Vito said. "I will do the same."

"Great! Let's get to planting," Allegra said. Then she stopped, "Oh, and we don't talk while we plant. All our energy should be focused on what we're doing. For these planting rituals to work, you must be in the moment, giving Mother Earth every ounce of your attention."

"Are we casting spells?" Vito asked, unsure of how his mother would react to that. It's no secret how the Church feels about playing with the occult.

"We are not devil worshipers," Allegra started. "The Sorellanza Magicka are lovers of nature who use her gifts to manifest our destinies. Humans could do this too if they paid attention."

"You didn't answer my question. Are we casting spells?"

"No," Allegra said. "This is a ritual handed down to us from our ancestors."

"Oh," Vito said. "Okay."

"Besides," Allegra snickered. "You don't have any powers to cast a spell young man. Powers like ours don't come from putting one's hands in the dirt one afternoon. It's not as simple as all that."

"Oh," Vito felt embarrassed. "I didn't mean to belittle your beliefs."

"You didn't. But let's get planting. I may be powerful, but the Earth will hide the Sun from us in a few hours and we have a ton of seeds to plant this Ostara."

Vito was dutiful and began planting. Allegra yelled for her sisters to "get moving" and they stopped their egg game and joined the work.

Vito thought about his mother and how proud she would be that he was doing what he was told. Well, maybe not. Vito second guessed his thoughts. It's a Tuesday afternoon, and I'm gardening instead of working. Vito self-scolded. She's going to be so mad.

The moment the cool, soft dirt touched his fingertips Vito's mind shut down. He felt an overwhelming sense of calm that he never experienced in his garden back home. Maybe because his mother would use the time to try and convince him to become a priest, or, once she realized that was a lost cause, she'd grill him about why he wasn't married.

This moment of peace was the most powerful feeling he ever had. The second his hands connected to Mother Earth he knew this was not the moment to think about Connie, who was miles away. It was time to enjoy the sunshine and the ritual of setting intentions. For the first time in a long time, Vito smiled.

Chapter Fifteen

Vito and the sisters spent the afternoon in their monstrous greenhouse planting zinnias, marigolds, tomatoes, zucchini and a myriad of other vegetables found in most Italian American gardens. They also planted spinach, kale, and lettuce. When finished, they sat around the stone table in their backyard, drank lemonade, and ate a frizzelle salad and Easter Pie Allegra put out. Vito sat with the sisters, and enjoyed the delicious food and drink, while taking it all in.

"My sisters and I were born into The Sorellanza Magicka," Allegra explained. "It simply means 'magical sisterhood' in Italian. But it's so much more than that. For one, the Sorellanza Magicka is comprised not only of women. Our members also include men and people who identify as both, or neither. The reason why it's called a sisterhood is because it was started by a group of sisters, one of whom was our mother."

"So, I'm in the presence of royalty?" Vito asked.

Allegra laughed, "You might say that. But the Sorellanza Magicka is bigger than my family now. And just because our mother was one of the thirteen sisters who started this congregation of magic, the Sorellanza Magicka does not have leaders. We do not worship one another; we worship the Earth."

"Thirteen sisters?"

"I know," Allegra chuckled. "I have my hands full with two."

They both laughed and sipped coffee Freya brought out. The sun was setting, and the clouds were turning pink. It was one of the only two colors Vito could see, so he made sure to take it in.

"What other powers do you all have?"

"A sister doesn't reveal all of her secrets, but the longer you hang around I'm sure you'll figure them out."

Vito laughed, feeling much more relaxed than he probably should in the company of someone as powerful as Allegra. But he knew she was no one to fear. At least for now. He also knew that she was kind, but she had a goal. She needed the flask for her sister.

"It's probably time you head back home," Allegra said. She stood and Vito followed her to the pantry door, where they came in just this morning. "If you walk through there you'll go back to our flat in Chicago. Just lock the door behind you when you head out."

"Will you make sure I unplugged my curling iron?" Ginevra said and Freya giggled.

"Don't pay them any attention," Allegra said pulling Vito's face back to look at her. "You must go finish the journey Frank set for you, and come back to us with the flask, free of intention. Understand?"

"Yes," Vito said. He hung on to his backpack.

"Before you leave, I have something for you," Allegra ran to another room and started rummaging through piles of books strewn around a lone chair in the corner. Vito grabbed his coat and bag and got ready to leave. Allegra gathered four thickly bound books and handed them to him.

"These will explain a lot about our ways," she said, opening the pantry door.

Vito put the books in his backpack with adoration for all words on paper, particularly those that are bound within history and magic. "Thanks for lending them to me."

"My pleasure. You can give them back when you're done. Like the flask."

"Right." Vito nodded. "Okay. Caio[32]."

"Buona notte[33]," Allegra called as the pantry door shut behind him.

As Allegra promised, he was in the sisters' kitchen, back on Oakley in the Little Italy neighborhood of Chicago. He checked for any curling irons plugged in and locked the door when he left. Vito knew what he had to do and he was ready.

The streetlights filled the night with synthetic luminosity as Vito made his way through the predominantly Italian neighborhood. It was saturated with flickering lights and the sounds of Frank Sinatra, Perry Como, and Connie Francis. Even though they were experiencing a cold March, Chicagoans grow tired of hibernating. Many had donned their heavy attire to stand in line at a local vendor's stand as the smell of grilled fennel sausages wafted through the air. Distracted by the sights, sounds, and aromas, Vito was startled when he felt a tap on his shoulder.

---

32   Goodbye
33   Good night

"Hi," a familiar voice said.

Vito turned around. "Hi, Lucia," Vito said. Suddenly, the whole scene with his mother at The Tap played out in his mind. His face began to burn from shame as he wondered why in the world she would ever be interested in talking to him.

"You left so fast, you forgot your change," Lucia said, clumsily searching through her purse.

"Oh no." Vito put a hand on hers to stop her. "That was a tip." He may have never set foot in a bar before, but Vito learned about the importance of leaving a good tip from his Zio Frank.

"But a Coke is just a buck fifty. That was eighteen fifty in change," Lucia said, pulling her wallet from her purse.

"I know," Vito said without removing his hand. "It was for the commotion. I'm sorry my mother made such a scene."

"I'm sorry Roy was such an idiot." Lucia grimaced. "He has no life and spends all his waking hours in that bar. If his mother was still around, he would be following her every command. Don't let the people in that bar fool you. Their laughter was purely out of jealousy."

Vito released her hand. "Maybe so, but …"

"No buts." Now, it was Lucia who took Vito's hand. "If you won't let me return your change, then let me treat you to a beef sandwich."

"It's getting kind of late."

"It's only 9:30."

He didn't want Lucia to think he was a momma's boy. Then Vito thought about what awaited him at home, and decided the flask could wait. No sooner had he thought of it, than the ringing began to grow in his ears.

"Um …" He looked toward Al's, the local beef stand, in this neighborhood. "Okay," he said, remembering his Papa's strength and bravery. If he could stand up to violent racists when he was Papa, surely Vito could resist the flask for a little while longer.

"Great!" Clutching Vito's hand, Lucia led him to the restaurant, with big bold yellow lettering on a sign above reading: AL'S #1 ITALIAN BEEF.

"This is my first time here," Vito said as Lucia pulled him inside.

"Let me guess," Lucia replied as she stepped behind the last person in a long line, "you're a Johnnie's fan."

"How'd you know?"

"You live by The Tap. Everyone there swears by Johnnie's."

"Well, Johnnie's *is* the best." Vito shrugged.

"I disagree. I mean, don't get me wrong. Johnnie's is excellent, but Al's is the best. You can't truly know if you haven't tried both."

"True," Vito replied. "You sure are passionate about beef sandwiches for someone who just moved here from Iowa."

Lucia laughed. "My Auntie Nicki has lived here my whole life. That's part of why I moved up here. I knew I loved Chicago the first time I set foot here. Plus, beefs are good."

"Do you know the history of beef sandwiches?"

"Nope," Lucia said. "You can tell me over dinner."

Vito smiled and they went inside.

Behind the counter, workers in matching "Al's Chicago's #1 Italian Beef Since 1938" T-shirts scurried about to fill people's orders.

Vito and Lucia waited while the line slowly moved.

"Why don't you tell me now," Lucia said.

"Tell you what?" Vito asked. "About the history of beef sandwiches."

"Oh, yeah. Well, back during the Depression, Italians here in Chicago would have Peanut Weddings."

"What's a Peanut Wedding?"

"Back in the day, most people around here were dirt poor, so they'd have weddings in the church basement, or their home, or yard, and there would be peanuts with shells and everything. To stretch the food, they would roast beef with seasonings and then shave the beef thin and put it back in its juices. That way the beef would feed more people."

"That's smart," Lucia said as the line moved up a bit.

"Yeah," Vito agreed. "They don't sell beefs anywhere else in the country. Maybe there's a few places in Wisconsin and Indiana, but not many more than that. And they don't sell them in Italy either. It's a sandwich specific to Chicago."

"I think I heard that before. Philly has its cheesesteak, and Chicago has the Italian beef."

"Right," Vito said.

Lucia smiled and said nothing, which led to an uncomfortable silence. At least it was uncomfortable for Vito. And he was hoping this was some kind of date, so the silence was all the heavier on him. He was sure she could hear his heart beating as they again moved forward.

"There's this place on Harlem, up near the HIP, that has amazing beef sandwiches," Lucia said.

She met Vito's smile, and, at the same time, they yelled, "Luke's!"

Vito sighed and they laughed. Then they both looked and the workers behind the counter glared their way upon hearing the name of a competitor in their presence. This sent them both into even further fits of hysterics.

When it was finally their turn, it took all they had to stifle their laughter as they ordered two beefs, one dipped with hot peppers and another dry with sweet peppers.

Once they got their sandwiches, along with root beers and fries, they found seats and unwrapped their meals.

Lucia took a bite. "Mmmm. See what I mean? *So* good," she said around a mouthful of food.

Ignoring the unsightly gray tone of the sandwich, Vito took a bite, and flavors exploded on his tongue.

"At least they didn't take away my sense of taste," Vito said out loud.

"What?" Lucia looked at him puzzled.

Vito mumbled a "nothing" with his mouth full of beef, au jus-soaked bread, and giardiniera peppers." Then he made a yummy face hoping she'd change the subject.

"I swear," Lucia beamed, "the rest of the world is missing out on these delicacies."

"Some say that the guy who started this place was the first to sell beef sandwiches on the streets of this very neighborhood." Vito loved to spew out information that made him feel smart. He loved to feel smart and especially adored the way Lucia didn't mind. Other people he met made him feel weird and different, but she made him feel like it didn't matter if he wasn't like everyone else. She made him feel it was okay to be him.

"So that would make Al's the best beef in Chicago," Lucia said and smiled as if she were reading his thoughts. Then she bit into her sandwich.

"Nope," Vito said before taking another bite of his dripping Italian beef sandwich, not wanting to show Lucia how much he was enjoying it. He had to be loyal to Johnnie's after all.

"You didn't get yours dipped," Vito commented after swallowing. "It looks so dry." He held his up. "*This* is the way you eat a beef sandwich. It's supposed to be dipped in the juices, so the bread is wet and melts in your mouth."

Lucia shook her head and laughed. "No, your way is a mess. Your sandwich is falling apart!"

Vito looked down. His hands were full of gray giardiniera peppers and shredded beef dripping in its own juices. The Gonnella bread meant to hold it together slipped onto the wax paper in front of him. He joined Lucia in laughing. "And like gnawing on that dry piece of bread is any better."

"Well, that mess you have there wouldn't have happened if you didn't insist she dip it a second time," Lucia said, reminding him of the earlier exchange at the counter.

Vito laughed as he dropped the meat onto his bread pile and stood. He walked back to the counter, grabbed a few napkins and a fork, then brought them back to the table. "I guess I'll have to eat mine this way." He dug into his heap of meat, juices, bread, and hot peppers. "It's a good beef," he admitted, "but Johnnie's is still the best."

Lucia stared back at him in disbelief. "What is it with all of you in that neighborhood? Sure, Johnnie's is good, but it's no Al's."

"Correction, Al's is no *Johnnie's*."

Lucia rolled her eyes and took another bite. "You sure spend a lot of time in this neighborhood," she said after a moment.

"Yeah," Vito said, shoving another forkful into his mouth.

Lucia took a sip of her root beer. Overhead on the speaker, Dean Martin sang about an evening in Roma, and the tables around them began to fill up.

"So, what made you leave Iowa?"

"A lot of things," Lucia said, not smiling. "I needed a change of scenery, so I thought it was a good time for an adventure."

Vito smiled as his spark ignited when she said that. But then he felt the pull of the flask tighten and beckon him to come home. His smile faded. "Be careful what you wish for," Vito thought.

"So," Lucia started. "I don't understand. Are you a drinker? Or are you not a drinker?"

Vito hesitated. He didn't know how to answer that question. He didn't drink until he got the flask, that she gave him. But he did drink from the flask. He felt it wasn't the same thing because it's not like he was bellying up to the bar and downing martinis. The flask was a portal to get his colors back, which he needed. Even if he decided not to go back to selling paint after all this, Vito wasn't about to live the rest of his life seeing only partial color when the rest of those hues were out there for the taking.

"I don't drink," Vito said, feeling fully justified in his answer. What about the martinis you've been having with Frank in the other basement? Vito pushed his thoughts out of his head. He wasn't lying.

"Then why did you tell me you were forced to take a leave of absence for drinking on the job?"

Vito felt stuck. He didn't want to lie. But, once again, telling her the truth would be far more disastrous.

"And your mother seemed so upset that you were sitting at a bar," Lucia continued making up her own mind.

"But," Vito didn't know what to say. "Okay, I am going through a bit of a problem right now," Vito admitted.

Lucia smiled with warmth and put her hand on his. "I can tell," she said. "I've been there."

Vito kept his mouth shut, because it usually helped him more than opening it.

"If you ever need help," she said. "I'm here. This coming December I'll be two years sober."

He never knew anyone who had to stop drinking. Okay, Frank *should've* given it up, but he didn't. When he thought about it, the only person he knew who didn't drink was himself, and that recently changed.

"Congratulations," Vito said.

"Thanks," Lucia said with a forced smile. "I don't like to talk about it too much, but it ruined everything I had and loved in life."

Vito remained quiet.

"Don't let that happen to you," Lucia added and turned away from him. Then she took her napkin to wipe away a tear.

"I'm sorry," Vito felt terrible. "My problem will be over soon. I know it will."

"I hope so," Lucia said, turning back around, trying to hold in her sadness.

"How about you let me take you out?" Vito asked. This was the first time in his life he ever asked a woman out and he didn't know where he got his confidence. Then he heard the flask calling to him and connected it to his newfound self-assurance. "There's a place in my neighborhood that has the best ravioli."

"No," Lucia said. "I'm sorry." She paused for a minute, unsure of how to make an admission. "I am attracted to you," she started. Lucia took another pause that gave Vito enough time to linger on his excitement over her revelation.

But soon Lucia was able to pull Vito out of his thoughts and into her gaze.

"I thought you were a non-drinker," she admitted. "You ordered a Coke and didn't have any booze the first night I met you. But now that I know you're struggling, I can't date someone who drinks."

Vito was floored. This wasn't fair! Once again Frank's stupid little adventure messed up his life.

"What if I promised not to drink?" Vito tried to convince her.

"You can't make that kind of promise," Lucia said. "Not now. Maybe, if you were sober for some time, I'd consider it. But you would have to be completely sober."

"Okay," Vito said. He was going to stop drinking when he got all his colors back and gave the flask back to the sisters. That could be by the end of the week.

"Maybe you can help me become sober?" Vito suggested. What a great idea! He congratulated himself on the quick thinking. Sure, he wasn't really drinking, so he didn't need help. But he can hang out with Lucia and still get to know her.

"I'm not sure that's a great idea," she said, deflating Vito's self-assurance. "You just asked me out. For all I know you're just saying that so you can hang out with me."

"Okay," he said. "I'll do this on my own."

"I never said I wouldn't help you," Lucia reached out and touched his arm. "But you need a different sponsor. I can help you get one. There's a meeting tomorrow night and I just happen to be off. Would you like to go?"

"Yes," Vito said. He didn't see any reason to go to a meeting, but he didn't want to miss any opportunity to hang out with her. "I'd love to."

"Great," Lucia's teeth glowed as her smiled widened. "Meet me at The Tap at 7 p.m. That's when my shift ends. The meeting's at 7:30 and we can walk over from there."

Vito smiled and took a slow sip of his root beer. Somehow, with Lucia he could sit in complete silence and not feel anxious. She was the first person he'd felt safe with since this whole nightmare began.

So safe that he almost told her about his sudden colorblindness and the flask.

Almost.

Chapter Sixteen

Vito walked through the front door of his family bungalow, expecting to find the house lit up with a gaggle of women waiting to pounce. But instead, he found an empty kitchen and the basement door open.

Hearing rustling at the bottom of the stairs Vito rushed down, wondering where he'd left the flask and prayed he'd find it before his mother did.

When he got to the bottom step, he found Bisnonna Nellie bent over with a box of Morton's salt in her hand.

"Bisnonna?" Vito said.

The old woman looked back at him and spread what she could to complete a circle she created with salt around the sofa.

Vito walked over to her and pulled her gently back into a standing position.

"Non importa. Tutto fatto," [34] Nellie said, looking at him. And with that, the 98-year-old headed toward the stairs. When she reached the first step, she turned her small, frail frame around again. "No," she said, and then made the motion of sweeping. "Oh-a-kay?"

Vito looked at the crooked circle of salt she had made around the sofa, which had been serving as his bed the past few days.

"Fine," Vito said with a sigh. "I won't sweep it up."

"Bene."[35] Bisnonna made the sign of the cross and then turned back to the stairs, taking one step at a time to get back to the kitchen.

Vito followed behind his great-grandmother until she made it up the stairs. And with every incline, the flask's call grew more assertive as if it assumed he was leaving it behind again.

"Grazie, Veeto,"[36] Nellie said once she was in the kitchen.

Vito helped her to her seat. "You're welcome, Nonna."

"Sei un bravo ragazzo," [37] she said as she took a deep sigh.

---

34   It doesn't matter. All done.
35   Good.
36   Thank you, Vito.
37   You're a good boy.

Once she was content, with the television on and an apple for peeling, Vito shut the walnut door behind her and locked it. He ran down the stairs and slid to the cabinet, where the flask was calling him.

He didn't even remember putting it there, but due to its calling, it was easy to find.

Once safe in his den with the elixir in hand, Vito looked around the room. The speckles of pink and yellow were abundant. He spotted Nonna's collection of housecoats, all with a hint of pink, sitting on the top shelf of the closet. Nonna had put them down there for future pocket repair.

Shifting his gaze, he took a long look at a yellow leisure suit hanging just beneath a pile of aprons. Vito remembered Frank had worn it often when he hit the discos in the late '70s.

Why do we keep all this stuff? Vito wondered.

There were other small memorable items speckled with his newfound colors, but they were few and far between. For the most part, the basement was still filled with the oppressive gray, just like the world outside.

Vito was growing weary of it.

As he sat on the sofa with the flask in his hand, he inspected the pocket vessel. The colorful gems remained as vibrant as he remembered the last time he'd held it, but there were two rocks adhered to the side that he had never noticed before.

The flask, once filled with endless color, was now disrupted with a few dull, gray stones where the pink and yellow ones used to be.

He looked at the room. Yellow and pink blinked back at him through the murky darkness that only a basement can produce.

"Time to get the others," Vito thought. He opened the top of his flask and finally allowed himself to quench his unbearable thirst.

It didn't take long for the panacea to take effect

Vito removed his pants, sprawled out on the sofa, and took another drink. Then he laid back and closed his eyes.

Moments later, Vito opened his eyes to a basement full of color, but now with the exception of Nonna's pink housecoats and Frank's yellow suit. Those items were gray, indicating that they were restored in his reality, and, now, he was again in the Intermondano basement.

"You're starting to understand how this works," Frank's voice drifted to Vito.

Unable to see his uncle, Vito glanced around. "Frank?"

Vito waited, but no one appeared. Tired of waiting, he ascended the stairs.

He reached the top and found the door cracked. Vapor slipped through the opening as if there were a bucket of dry ice swimming in hot water on the other side.

Vito hesitated and then pushed the door open. Smoke billowed out, blinding him. But pushing aside his reservations, he stepped forward into the fog until he crossed the threshold.

He held his arms out in front of himself, trying to feel what was ahead. But at that instant, the fog disappeared.

He blinked, finding himself looking over a car and straight into the face of the last person he would ever want to see.

"Father," Monsignor Benevento said to him, "are you going to stand there all night, or are you going to get in the car?"

"Uh," Vito said, still dizzy from settling into this new reality.

"Father!" the monsignor belted.

"Yes," Vito said. He looked down, opened the door, and settled into the passenger's seat. When he glanced into the rearview mirror, a smile spread across his face from ear to ear.

In this adventure, he was his long-lost mentor, Father Vince.

"Father, I don't appreciate it when you undermine me in front of parishioners," Monsignor Benevento said from behind the wheel.

"I'm sorry, monsignor," Vito said, but only half meaning it.

Vito looked up from the mirror just in time to see they were pulling away from his house while Connie, Nonna Josie, and the eighteen-year-old version of himself stood on the front porch, waving goodbye.

The monsignor turned down Harlem Avenue. "When I was speaking to the Glandell boy in there, it wasn't your place to step in. His mother and I know what's best for him."

Vito said nothing, unsure of how to respond.

"Are you ignoring me?"

"No," Vito said.

"Well?" the monsignor said expectantly.

"Well, what?"

"We went there for dinner to talk that boy out of leaving his family and attending a university right here. You did nothing but undermine every effort I made. Why?"

Vito felt his anger rise. "Is it our place to interfere with their family decisions?"

The monsignor stopped the car in the middle of Harlem Avenue and glared at Vito.

Vito immediately deduced that clearly, the monsignor wasn't used to being spoken to that way. The senior holy man let the silence prevail for the rest of the ride. Turning his head forward, he began driving again, heading toward the rectory.

Once the monsignor pulled into the parking lot of the St. Luke's compound, he parked in his reserved space for the night. He and Vito got out and walked in silence until reaching the rose garden in the small, slightly hidden courtyard separating the rectory from the convent.

"Our discussion about your performance tonight isn't over, Father. But I'm expecting a phone call from Sicily and will be busy for the next hour. I want to see you in my office in one hour and ten minutes. Not one minute before and not one moment after. Do you understand?"

Vito nodded, amazed that the monsignor could always make him feel like a child no matter how old he was—or even whose body he inhibited.

The monsignor turned and walked toward his office.

Not sure what to do, Vito took a seat in the rose garden.

He remembered accidentally finding the garden as freshman. He'd been engrossed in a book and had lost count of his steps. The next thing he knew, he'd been surrounded by roses. One of the nuns found him and made him leave because students weren't allowed there. The garden was only for the clergy, so they had a place to contemplate.

Being in the garden now, Vito remembered how the smell of roses hit him in his teenage face so hard that he looked up from his book. They were the deepest shade of red he had ever seen.

But now, the roses were gray, and their true color was just a memory.

"Red is being weird," Vito thought, recalling how he could see it in Lucia's hair and once saw it on her fingernails. But now, he couldn't see it at all.

At least Vito thought that was the case.

Suddenly a flash of red came into the courtyard.

Vito turned toward the color—and there she was.

"Lucia?" Vito jumped to his feet and ran over to hug her.

She hugged him back. After their embrace, they took a seat on a nearby stone bench.

"What's all this?" she asked, looking at Vito's clothing. She laughed. "This is some crazy dream, huh?'

Vito grinned as he took in her clothing as well. "You're a nun."

"What?" Surprised, she glanced down at herself. "This getup is too much!"

They laughed as a warm breeze moved through the rose bushes.

"It's so weird how we know each other in our dreams," Lucia said. "You know what I mean? You know I'm me, and I know you're you even though we don't look like ourselves."

Vito shrugged. "That's probably a good thing."

"Do I look like myself to you?" Lucia asked.

"Yes." Vito smiled. "You look beautiful."

Lucia's cheeks reddened with a blush—a redness Vito was able to see. Yet, the roses behind her were still the color of granite.

"Why do you suppose we're having this dream?" Lucia asked.

"I don't know," Vito replied, unable to take his eyes off her.

Lucia giggled. "Well, at least we're in this together."

"Are we?" Vito pondered internally. "I wish this were only a dream for me."

"This isn't a dream for you?" Lucia lifted an eyebrow.

Vito blinked. "Did I say that out loud? Or can you read my thoughts?"

"Maybe both?" Lucia replied. "But you didn't answer the question. What do you mean you aren't dreaming? You believe you're physically here, in this place? Have you looked in a mirror? You don't even look like you."

"Forget it," Vito said. "It is a dream."

Lucia had already forgotten it, like one does in dreams, and was buried face deep in a rose bush. Vito thanked God he hadn't lost his sense of smell. The roses were the most aromatic he had ever experienced. The fullness of their scent overwhelmed him. He closed his eyes, hoping the lack of sight would heighten his olfactory system even more.

"Come," Lucia said, pulling his arm. "Put your face in here."

Lucia pulled Vito closer to her and put her hand on the back of his head. The second her palm was on his skull she pushed it ever so gently, so his face was buried as deep into the rose bushes as hers.

"Ow," Vito said. "These things have thorns you know."

"I can't feel them. It's a dream. Just wish them away."

Vito wished the thorns would stop digging into his side, and they did. Then Vito wondered what else he could make happen in this dream. He looked over to Lucia and felt warm and tingly all over. She was so captivating. He wished he had the courage to kiss her.

With that wish, Lucia looked at Vito. He could feel her eyes penetrate his and before he knew what was happening, he leaned in and let his lips touch hers.

"Father Vince?" a voice said behind them.

Forgetting that he was Father Vince, Vito kept his lips on hers and his eyes shut and ignored the voice.

A loud throat-clearing disturbed the peace around them and the two jumped out of the rose bush.

Vito's heart skipped a beat in panic, finding an enraged monsignor in front of them.

Lucia looked at Vito and he could see her leaving the nun's body. Her red hair drained of it's color right there. But it didn't matter if the red disappeared. Vito could see it in her eyes as the look of love and comfort she once held became one of unfamiliarity and fear.

"Sister, I think you are late for something," Monsignor Benevento said to Lucia.

The nun ran off like a kitten.

The monsignor shifted his focus to his main target. "I thought I asked you to meet me in my office at this time, Father?"

Vito stood, remembering this wasn't a dream for him at all; this was Father Vince's life. "I'm so sorry I missed our meeting."

"Well," the Monsignor started, "none of that matters now. I just took a call from a colleague in Sicily and was informed they need a priest in Catania. I was able to get through to an agent to book you a flight. It leaves at eight tomorrow morning."

Vito felt his heart shatter. "Why are you sending me away?" Father Vince asked. Vito was a mere bystander inside this priest.

Still, Vito remembered that painful morning Frank died, and how he ran to the rectory in search of Father Vince, only to find he was no longer there.

"You know why," Monsignor Benevento answered.

This was the moment Vito took over Father Vince's mind. He had questions of his own.

"Because I stuck up for the Glandell boy at dinner tonight?" Vito said. His broken heart added more guilt to his list of ailments, knowing he may have been the reason Father Vince had been sent to Italy.

"This has been a long time coming, and you know it," Monsignor Benevento said as he turned to walk away.

"Excuse me, monsignor," Vito said following him in a rage, "you can't just send me away. I'm not your toy!"

The monsignor sharply spun, blocking Vito's path like a tower of righteousness. "Oh, can't I? I suppose you're right then. I guess my only choice would be to contact the diocese and let them know the condition I just found you and Sister Angelle in."

"Condition?" Vito stared up at the man who'd been his nemesis his entire life. The monsignor was monstrously tall, while Father Vince had the curse of Italian shortness. The difference in Vito's perspective didn't alter the rage he felt inside. "What *condition*?" he spat. "It was a kiss. That was it. Completely innocent, and you know it."

"That's not what I saw, Father. From where I stood, you were both succumbing to the lust you vowed to reject."

The monsignor turned around and walked away.

"What is it with you and the Glandell boy?" Vito shouted after him.

The monsignor stopped and turned around again. "What's that supposed to mean?"

Decades of frustration from this man's interference in Vito's life sprang forward. "Why are you always so involved with his life? You never let the boy breathe! Tonight, you were insistent on helping his mother convince him to stay in Chicago and attend DePaul, but did you ever *once* listen to what *he* wanted?"

The question hung in midair for long enough to make them both uncomfortable.

"I don't think you understand the bond I have with this family, Father," the monsignor said. "Mrs. Glandell started working in my office before he was born. She wasn't even married when she started her job. When her husband left, I raised her salary so they could keep the house. Young Vito has been a part of my life since she first brought him to work and set him up in the corner of my office. She could've left him at home, but for the first few years of his life, she wanted her baby with her. So, Vito was here, in my office, every day."

Vito's jaw dropped. He had no recollection of any of that.

"But my stance on this has nothing to do with Vito," the monsignor continued. "I was attempting to persuade him to stay here with his mother because that's what she wants. While it may seem strange to you and me because we're childless, she depends on him being there. If he were to leave, the anxiety would be too much for her to handle. So, he needs to stay in Chicago. DePaul is an excellent school, and it's right here at home."

"But he wants to experience something new."

"I understand that. But as we all know, life doesn't always give you what you want." He paused before adding, "you should hurry along to pack your things and say your good-byes. I'll be driving you to the airport myself to thank you for all the wonderful years of service you've given us at St. Luke's. We leave at five a.m. sharp for O'Hare."

Vito's heart dropped as the monsignor turned to leave for good, having gotten the final say. Vito wanted to object, but there was no reason to; he knew how this story ended.

"Lucia!" he suddenly thought. He ran back to the rose garden, but she was gone. Vito looked back in the direction the monsignor had gone. "It's out of my hands," he thought.

Just before the monsignor was completely out of view, Vito glimpsed his gray robes fill to a deep and noble shade of purple.

Chapter Seventeen

A life without drama sounds relaxing to some but this type of existence can be a monotonous cycle for others. Just the right amount of drama, however, can make life feel fully lived.

Vito had tons of drama in his family. In his mind, Connie and Nonna could cause drama over a bad batch of sauce. If someone accidentally dumped more black pepper into the pot the maternal mafia would lose their minds. Their reaction would be on par to learning their water pipes just burst. Nothing that happened in their lives was short of tragedy or victory. Connie and Nonna didn't spend time in the in-between.

As for Vito, when he wasn't being dragged into their crises, he did his best to remain in a drama-free situation. Until he found the flask. Now, he had too much excitement in his life, and it was quickly growing taxing.

"How about a drink?" Frank's voice said.

Vito opened his eyes to find himself back in the gateway between this world and the real one. The Intermondano.

Or is the Intermondano real and that other world the fake? Vito noticed with some consternation that the two worlds were growing muddled in his mind, like cherries at the bottom of a lazy Old Fashioned.

"Did you say Old Fashioned?" Frank chuckled. "I haven't had one of those in eons."

"I don't think I've ever had one." Vito sat up on the sofa seat and looked around, searching for new gray spots in the basement where the purple used to be. "So, I suppose once I clear out the colors in this basement, my adventures will be over?"

"Maybe," Frank replied as he prepared two glasses with ice. He then took a silver mixer and added ice.

"There are several schools of thought on Old Fashioneds," Frank said as he took a bottle of rye out of nowhere and poured a hefty amount into the mixing tin.

"You have the original, which I'm making now." As he spoke, Frank added some dark liquid.

"What's that?" Vito asked

"Demerara syrup," Frank smiled and winked as he added a touch more. Then he picked up a bottle of Angostura bitters and added few dashes. As he mixed, poured, and garnished each of their Old Fashioneds with an orange peel and a maraschino cherry, Frank continued his lesson.

"Then you have your Wisconsin Old Fashioned, which can come sour or sweet. Of course, there's the whole debate on muddling over no muddling."

Frank walked over to the sofa and handed Vito a cocktail. He took a sip and smiled.

"I don't know what muddling means but this is a tasty drink," Vito could feel the magic fog of alcohol take over after the first swallow.

"Thanks, kid."

Vito took another, smaller, sip. "I'd rather stay here than go back through the door."

"I don't blame you," Frank said. "But this isn't a life. You must finish your journey and head back home to that nice girl."

"Lucia?"

"Lucia," Frank repeated. "I can't believe you're with Nicki's niece. That's great, kid. If she's anything like her aunt, you're in for a treat."

Vito wasn't too keen on the idea of Lucia turning out to be anything like Nicki, but that seemed inconsequential at the moment. Thinking about it, he took the tiniest sip of his Old Fashioned.

"I know I make a tasty cocktail, kid, but you gotta drink up. You can't stay in here forever."

"Why can't I just stay for another drink with you?"

Frank looked at his nephew, who was almost like a son to him in many ways. "I wish you could. I miss you more than anyone. But the fact is, you're bound to this journey until the end. That means you'll never break away from the flask until you get all your colors back. And you know where life in the flask goes."

"But these so-called adventures aren't what I had in mind when I was eighteen."

"So what?" Frank laughed. "Life doesn't turn out how most people expect. You're in good company."

Vito took a long sip and wiped the excess off his face. "It was my fault Father Vince was sent away."

"Why do you care so much?"

"Because I needed him. You died, and I had no dad to help me stand up to Momma and Nonna. Monsignor Benevento did nothing but support them. Father Vince was the only other person in my life who understood me. Once he was gone, I felt I had to give in to them. I had to stay home."

"That's just fucking stupid." Frank finished off his drink and slammed his empty glass on the coffee table.

"What?" Vito said, somewhat stunned.

"Everything you just said is bullshit. The only person you can blame for your decision to stay home with your mother is you. Aren't you learning *anything* here? You might think he was sent away because of you, but you assumed a lot of things before you started this adventure, didn't you?"

"Well, yeah … I guess."

"Have some of those assumptions been proven wrong? Like Anthony. You thought he beat you up that day because he was just an asshole."

"Yeah, I did," Vito admitted, remembering his first journey in this crazy place.

"But he was just running and thought you were his dad," Frank continued. "So don't start thinking you know everything because you don't. The day we realize we don't know shit is the day we're finally free. That's how it is. I don't make the rules. Okay?"

"Okay."

"Good," Frank said. "Now stop being such a whiner and drink up. It's time to go."

Vito chugged the rest of his whisky, relishing the smooth, calming effect it had moving down his throat.

When he focused back on his surroundings, his uncle was gone.

The walnut door at the top of the stairs creaked open, and Vito knew it was time.

***

After walking through the gateway this time, Vito found himself in a moving wheelchair while the gray mist that accompanied his other transitions surrounded him.

A sharp pain ran through his lower abdomen and groin, and Vito let out a cry. The spasms in his lower gut were so intense, it made him dizzy. He slumped forward in his seat like Bisnonna Nellie did when she started to nap.

When the gray mist lifted, Vito realized he was, once again, in a hospital.

"What's going on?" Vito thought as the pain moved through his lower body again. The spasms left him so weak, the specks of pink, yellow, and purple passing by him were an incomprehensible blur.

His wheelchair came to a stop, and Vito momentarily caught his breath. But without warning, an immense wave of pain soared through his pelvis again, this one even more profound than the others. Vito screamed in misery, vaguely noticing his wails were too high-pitched to be his own. Yet, they were familiar.

During a brief break from the pain, Vito pressed his hands down to his stomach and felt it protruding outward as if he swallowed a watermelon.

Another wave of pain hit, and he screamed again.

"Less than a minute between contractions," a familiar voice said behind him. "This baby is coming *now!*"

"Baby!" Vito hollered. "Who's having a baby?!"

Vito felt his chair turn around, and two sets of arms helped him stand.

"You're having a baby, Mrs. Leverteeneeo."

"It's Levatino," Vito corrected as he was helped to a hospital bed. "Pronounced LEH-VAH-TEE-NO." He wasn't sure what made him correct the nurse, but he had heard Nonna Josie rectify the butchering of her last name enough times to make it a habit.

"Wait," Vito thought to himself as he laid flat on his back. "I'm Nonna!"

The contractions decided to reward him with a shot of pain so intense it made Vito scream with abandon.

"Mrs. Levatino," the nurse said as she rushed to her side, "you must try to keep your screams down. You'll scare the other new mothers."

"New?" Vito asked. "So, this is my first baby?"

"Yep," Vito heard that familiar voice answer. He looked to his other side to see Lucia, perfectly herself, in a nurse's uniform.

"Hi," Vito said before getting hit with another contraction. He tried to stifle his cries as the pain moved through this unfamiliar body.

"Keep breathing," Lucia coaxed, taking one of Vito's hands.

"FUUUUUCKKKKK!" Vito screamed as more excruciating pain ripped.

One of the other nurses gasped, and Vito abruptly remembered that he was Nonna. She never used that kind of language.

"You're in your head too much," Lucia said, gripping his hand. "Just breathe."

"How is breathing supposed to help?!" Vito hollered as another pain ripped through this body.

"I don't know," Lucia admitted. "That's what they do on TV."

"Nurse," another nurse came by. "Did I just hear you say you don't know why she should breathe?"

"Uh," Lucia didn't know what to say.

"Don't tell me you're going to run out and boil some water too," the other nurse started to laugh along with another who was in the room.

The two senior nurses went about their business shaking their heads.

"How am I going to do this?" Vito asked, watching a team of strangers focus their gaze on his private area.

"Women do it every day, and most of them have lived to tell the tale," Lucia replied.

"But I'm not a woman," he told her.

"Well, you're a woman in *here*." Lucia squeezed his hand.

When the pain radiated through this body, Vito could feel his hand crushing hers like a steel winch.

Closing his eyes, Vito felt this body's instinctual knowledge of what to do.

Something solid moved inside him.

"Take a breath," Lucia's sweet crimson voice said.

"I'm trying," Vito replied through clenched teeth. The pressure of this thing in his body was so intense, it was hard to breathe.

Lucia leaned in close and whispered, "Pretend you're taking the biggest shit of your life."

Vito burst out laughing, and his body relaxed.

Another nurse handed a packet of tools to Lucia. "Get a vein for the IV."

"IV?" Lucia questioned.

"Yes. Strap her arms, and let's get the Twilight going."

Lucia stared back at her, visibly puzzled.

Frustrated, the other nurse—who was wearing pointy glasses and a colorless scowl—forced her way between Lucia and Vito. "Fine. I'll do it."

Before Vito knew what was happening, leather straps were being wrapped around his arms.

"What are those for?" Lucia asked.

"What were you doing in class, sleeping?" the senior nurse smarted. "These are to keep her down so that when we give her the twilight, she doesn't jerk herself off the bed."

"But what about a natural birth?"

"And make her deal with all that pain? Are you one of those anti-suffragettes?"

Vito could see the stunned look on Lucia's face as another contraction moved through Nonna's body and made him screech.

The senior nurse looked at him, and then back to Lucia. "Stop wasting my time. She's almost ready to have this baby." She grabbed some tools from a nearby station and began looking for a vein.

"But aren't the drugs bad for the baby?" Lucia pressed.

"Listen," the other nurse snapped, "this is 1941, not the '20s! Women fought long and hard to stop this needless suffering. Why should she have to go through all that pain?"

As if triggered by the word pain, Vito released a yell that was sure to radiate throughout the whole hospital.

"See what you made me do?" the elder nurse said. "Now she's scaring the other patients. You're relieved of your duty, nurse. Go home for the day!"

Vito looked to Lucia while the other nurse found a vein and inserted an IV. Then the anesthesiologist set up the bag.

The morphine and scopolamine dripped into Nonna's arm.

Lucia's smile disappeared, and Vito's brain grew cloudy. He wondered if his own consciousness would withstand the twilight in Nonna's body, but quickly realized that wouldn't be the case. Vito succumbed to the narcotics just the same as his grandmother.

When he woke, he was in a clean hospital room, in a different bed with fresh, white sheets.

For a moment, Vito thought he may have transitioned into someone else. He tried to get up, but his legs felt like rubber bands. When he put his foot on the floor, he fell with a bang.

The door of his room swung open, and several nurses rushed in.

"Mrs. Levatino!" a familiar voice he didn't want to hear cried. "Why did you try to get out of bed?"

The nurses helped him up, and when Vito was able to focus, he saw the older nurse and two others he didn't recognize. "Where's Lucia?" he asked as they guided him back into bed.

"Who?"

"The other nurse," he clarified.

That instant, yet another nurse came into the room, carrying some kind of small creature wrapped in a blanket. "Here's your baby, Mrs. Levatino."

Vito looked around for a familiar face, but there wasn't one. His heart rate increased as the nurse put the bundle on his stomach.

When he didn't react, the nurse asked, "Don't you want to hold him?"

"Uh, yeah." Vito put his arms around the newborn.

"There you go," the nurse who'd given him the IV drip said. "It's not easy when it's your first, but you'll get used to it."

Vito looked down at the bundle, and a tiny face he recognized emerged. "Frank?" Vito said, hoping the baby wouldn't offer him a martini.

"Is that what you're naming him?" one of the nurses asked.

"It's time for someone's feeding," the nurse from the delivery room announced when Vito's uncle began to cry. "Are you ready, mommy?"

Vito looked down at the baby and shook him a little, trying to get him to shut up.

"Mrs. Levatino?"

"Will someone please take this baby?" Vito said, the crying making him forget who he was at the moment. His agitation was distracted, however, when he felt a little moisture drip down his stomach. Suddenly, he recalled he was Nonna, and realized she was about to breastfeed her son for the first time.

"Mrs. Levatino, how about I feed him this time around?" The senior nurse reached for the baby, who was growing louder every second.

Vito tried to hand his uncle over, but his arms wouldn't budge. *Nonna* wouldn't let Frank go.

"No," Nonna said, as Vito felt the fullness inside her breast.

"Are you sure?" the nurse asked, standing cautiously at his side. "A moment ago, you didn't even want to hold him … I'm just a little concerned."

"You have *nothing* to be concerned about."

The nurse frowned. "That's strange."

Vito felt Nonna's blood begin to boil. "And what exactly are you finding strange?"

"Your accent. You had a thick Italian accent when you were first admitted to this ward. Now it's gone."

"Uh," Vito swallowed nervously. "Th-That a doesn't matter. I wanna be alone a with my a bambino."

He fought the urge to cringe at his poor attempt to mimic his Nonna's accent.

The nurses all silently stared back at him while Frank continued to wail.

"Pardon?" the elder nurse said.

"I want to be alone," Vito repeated, abandoning his attempt to fake accent any further for these women.

Reluctantly, the nurses left the room.

Vito stared down at his newborn uncle. At just a few hours old, this was probably the youngest baby he'd ever held.

Refusing to think too much about it, Vito undid his hospital gown and let one of his breasts free. A drop of milk sat at the tip of his nipple as pressure swelled inside his bosom.

The baby latched on with the ease of a kitten on a mother cat. Vito felt a tingling sensation as this infant fed from his mother's breast for the first time. They were supposed to be alone, mother and son; a part of Vito felt guilty for being there. He wished whatever forces were ruling this game jewould have let them have some privacy.

But just as the thought went through his head, Vito felt warmth like nothing he'd ever felt before engulfing this body he was trapped in. He imagined what he was feeling had to be akin to what the fabled Grinch experienced when his heart abruptly grew three sizes.

Vito looked at the newborn suckling at his breast, and as if on cue, the baby looked up at Vito. They held each other's gaze, and a powerful force shot into Vito's soul. Right that instant, he knew an unbreakable bond had formed.

Tears fell down his cheeks as he shared this incredible moment with Nonna and Uncle Frank.

Yellow sunlight beamed into the room, and Vito looked up at the rays. At the windowsill, there was a vase filled with white roses. Vito watched the leaves and stems of those roses vibrate into a dark yet spirited green.

Chapter Eighteen

When his eyes opened, Vito looked around and saw he was back in the Intermondano, with his uncle sitting next to him on the sofa.

"That was weird," Vito said.

"Weird doesn't even begin to describe it," Frank said. "Imagine it from my point of view."

"I'd rather not." Vito walked to the cabinet for a drink.

"What are you making?" Frank asked.

"A martini. Want one?"

"Does a bear shit in the woods?" Frank replied. "Are we going to discuss what you experienced in that last journey?"

"Do we have to?"

"No," Frank said. Vito handed him a drink. "I suppose we don't."

"Mm," Frank said after taking his first sip. "You make a good martini Vi. I taught you well."

"Is any of this real?" Vito asked after his first gulp.

"Beats me." Frank shrugged.

Vito tossed back a third of his drink. "So umm, were you in that last journey?"

"I thought you didn't want to talk about it."

"Well, I changed my mind. So, tell me, were you in the body of you as a baby?"

"Do you mean was I aware that I was a baby nursing on the tit of my mother, who just happened to be my nephew?"

Vito finished the rest of his drink and stood to make another.

"No," Frank said, finishing his martini as well. "I wasn't there cognitively. But you can't look at any of this from your perspective. You're not a participant. You're an observer, here to learn. I know it's difficult, but you have to take yourself and your ego out of it."

"I get that," Vito said as he opened the ice bucket and marveled over how it seemed to always contain the same amount of ice. "But why couldn't I have been some random woman giving birth? Why did I have to be my grandmother?" Vito stirred the martini and poured the gin into two new glasses that seemed to be right where he needed them to be. He then added a couple of skewered olives from the bottomless garnish tray and handed one to his zio.

"I don't know, kid," Frank said, never taking his eyes off the martini. "Do you remember anything when you were there, other than feeling creeped out?"

Vito sat again as he took a smaller sip of this drink. He wanted to inhale the entire thing and forget what he had just experienced, but he was tired of getting up to refill his glass. "There was a moment when I looked down to the baby and felt this overwhelming force take over. I don't know if that was happening to Nonna, or me. But it was an incredible feeling regardless."

"What do you suppose that feeling was?"

Vito contemplated over a few more sips of gin. "I was experiencing her feelings. What it felt like to be a mother."

"How many guys can say they've experienced *that*?"

"None," Vito answered. "Unless they've had a similar adventure."

"I suppose." Frank ate his final olive and sipped the last of his drink.

"Do you want another?" Vito asked, seeing his glass was empty as well.

"Nah." Frank set his glass down and stood. "I have an appointment with a friend."

"Come on. Just one more," Vito urged.

"I can't stay here forever, kid. And neither can you."

"No, but I can wait it out here until morning. I don't have to go back through the door."

"True," Frank said, walking to the staircase. "But maybe the only way to stop this ride might be resisting the call of the flask. Can you do that?"

"What do you mean?"

"Well, there's no telling how many doors you're slotted for. And there's a fine line. You have to know when it's time to leave this journey. Maybe the only way to get out of here for good is to stop drinking from the flask."

"You died when you stopped drinking from the flask," Vito said. "That's when you brought it to Nicki to hold for me. Then you came home and died in the basement."

Frank smiled. "That's right. I did."

Vito jumped up. "Will I die if I stop before I'm finished?"

Frank shrugged. "I don't know."

"You don't know?" Vito said, feeling incredulous. "You set me up for this stupid trip. What do you mean you don't know? Did you set me up to potentially *die*?"

"Be careful out there, kid." Frank patted his nephew on the shoulder. "Get those colors and get out. Don't stick around too long like I did. This place can become addictive."

"What happens if I don't get out in time?"

"Just promise me you'll stop this ride once you get your colors," Frank said after a slight pause. "Give that flask back to the oldest of the sisters. I'm starting to fade and forget her name."

"Allegra," Vito said, a sensation creeping up his back and giving him the impression that she was listening from somewhere.

"Whatever," Frank said. "You'll know when it's time to stop. Don't ignore the signs. Can you do that?"

"I'll try," Vito said, following his uncle.

"Good." Frank turned around when he reached the stairs. "This is where I say goodbye then."

"Oh," Vito said, realization dawning on him. "I guess if I don't drink from the flask, I won't see you again."

"Either way, kid, this is where my role in this journey ends."

Vito felt as if the wind had been knocked out of him. "Even if I come back here? If I decide to drink from the flask to get more colors, won't you be here in the Intermondano?"

"Nope."

Fear grew in Vito's chest. "Don't sound so broken up over it."

"Ha!" Frank snorted and patted Vito on the back. "You got your uncle's sense of humor."

"What the fuck, Frank! You set me up on this journey, and now you're leaving?" Vito just couldn't believe the unfairness of it all.

"Kid, all I can do is bring you here. The rest is up to you."

"Great. I'll just get drunk here until morning then."

"Okay," Frank said, a warning tone in his voice. "But the longer you avoid the journey, the more difficult it will be to resist the flask in the real world, and the harder it'll be to see the signs when it's time to end it."

Vito said nothing as he prepared and drank another martini.

Frank took Vito's arm and tried to lead his nephew back to the staircase. "Why avoid the inevitable? Complete your journey, and then all will be right again."

"But I'm doing it alone," Vito said, resisting his uncle's attempts to lead up the stairs.

"Everyone walks through life alone, Vito," Frank said, mounting frustration creeping into his voice. "Anyone who tells you otherwise is lying to you, and themselves."

Vito looked up the stairs and then to his drink. He turned around to the sofa, convinced that it was the safest choice.

Frank sighed. "It's your life. I set you out on this journey for your own good, but I can't make you face your fears. You have to find the courage to do it yourself." And with that, Vito's uncle trekked up the stairs and slipped through the door. "Don't worry, Vi," his voice drifted down toward Vito. "I have faith in you, even if you don't."

Vito watched the door at the top of the stairs close. He put the rim of his glass to his lips for another sip, hoping this would be the one to send him home for good.

But once he swallowed the last of his celestial hooch, Vito took a long look at the sofa. Then he looked up at the door and watched it open, smoke billowing out.

Vito's stomach burned with sheer dread, knowing there was no easy way out of his predicament. Sighing, he closed his eyes and waited for this journey to take him back home.

March 21, 2007

Once Vito's eyes were open, he could tell he was back in the real basement because he could see the colors he gained back. He took a moment to soak in the purples and greens he never noticed before all this craziness took over his life. As his eyes moved over the items stuffed downstairs, he noticed it was dusk outside the window.

"It's Wednesday morning," Vito thought as he stood from the sofa. The clock that had served as Frank's alarm when he was alive said it was ten to seven in the evening.

Vito ran up the stairs to find his family sitting around the kitchen table, playing a game of kalooki.

"Why didn't you wake me?" Vito accused his mother.

"You're an adult," Connie said without looking up. "If you want to sleep your days away in the basement, you go right ahead."

"Lucia!" Vito shouted, which prompted his mother to look up.

"What?" Connie said. "Are you still drunk?"

Vito ignored his mother's comments and ran to the bathroom. The mirror confirmed his suspicions that he looked like shit and there was no way he'd catch Lucia before the meeting.

He decided to try and find her at the meeting. Vito cleaned up as best he could without taking a shower and headed upstairs to put on some clean clothes. Once he was as presentable as he could get in fifteen minutes, he bolted out the front door.

Vito ran inside The Tap to find Nicki standing behind the bar.

"You're late," Nicki said. "I'm not surprised though. You remind me a lot of your uncle."

"Where's the meeting?" Vito asked.

Nicki looked him in the eye and said, "If you hurt that girl you're going to have to answer to me." And with that Nicki took a long sip of a martini that was sitting on the bar next to her.

"Hey," a voice called from the dark side of the bar. "Can we get some service down here?"

"Hold your horses," Nicki yelled and then she looked at Vito. "It's in the basement of St. Luke's."

Vito ran out the door as he heard her say, "Okay, what do you pains in the asses want now?"

***

Vito tried not to run through the church but rushed to get in. When he walked through the door of the church's basement, everyone in the room turned. All eyes were upon him, which is nerve wracking for most people, let alone a man who is hungover and showing up late to a sober meeting, where he was supposed to bring a girl he wants to impress.

Lucia was sitting in the front, and smiled when he caught her eye. Everyone turned back around and a man at a podium began to speak.

"As I was saying," the man began. He smiled brightly and looked right toward Vito. "I'd like to welcome everyone to tonight's meeting. Especially some of the new faces I see here."

Vito slinked down in his seat because he felt like everyone was looking at him again. Probably because they were. But then they were more than happy to turn their attention back to the man at the podium.

"Our first speaker is Sam," the man said. He then looked at another man in the crowd and said, "Are you ready?"

A man in the crowd nodded and walked to the podium. The speaker sat down, and the quiet man took his place. He paused as he looked out into the crowd. Vito could feel this man's fears emanate from his eyes and pierce Vito's soul. He knew that look. The look of desperation. The look of wishing everything in life wasn't so damn difficult.

"Whenever you're ready," the man who first spoke said from the audience.

"Uh," Sam said into the microphone and jumped back when the piercing EEEEEEEEEEEE!!!! of feedback hit everyone's ears. "Oh," Sam tried not to go as close to the mic as the first time. "Hi everyone."

"Hi," everyone in the crowd said back, except for Vito.

"My name is Sam. And I'm an alcoholic."

Everyone in the room replied, "Hi Sam!"

Everyone except Vito.

"Well," Sam began. "I've been sober for six years, three months, two days, four hours, and fifty-two seconds, but who's counting, right?"

Everyone in the room giggled. Except Vito.

"My story isn't any different than what you've heard. Crappy childhood, abusive parents who also abused booze and dope. So, here I am. But I'm glad I am still here because I have a family of my own, and I don't want this cycle to bleed down to my kids. You know?"

A cacophony of "yeps" and "uh huhs" rose above the crowd.

"Seven years ago, I wasn't the guy you see in front of you," Sam said with a smile. "Today I can go out with my wife and have a fun evening. Seven years ago, I would've probably ended up in jail. If I said I don't wish I could have a glass of wine when we're out for dinner I'd be lying. That's why I come to these meetings. I need them to keep me strong. Some people can handle their booze. I'm not one of those people. And, while I still struggle with the desire to drink, I know my life is happier without it."

Everyone started clapping, including Vito. But he didn't put his hands together until the crowd got going. He had no idea how to act in this type of atmosphere.

"Thanks," Sam said. After everyone quieted, Sam finished. "I just wanted all the new people out there to know that life without booze is doable. It's livable. And it's enjoyable. Thanks again."

Sam walked off the stage and took his seat. The man who was speaking when Vito came in took his place back at the microphone.

"Thanks Sam," the man said. "That was so inspiring."

Everyone clapped and agreed with grunts or yeahs.

"For anyone here that doesn't know me, I'm Denny."

The crowd erupted with a "Hi Denny!"

He smiled and said, "Hi." Then Denny continued to talk about why he hosts meetings and other things Vito didn't have time to listen to. He was too busy watching Lucia, who seemed to hang on every word Denny had to say.

Vito felt his jealousy rise but sat there and waited until he had a chance to talk to Lucia. Once the meeting was over, Vito rushed over to where she stood. Unfortunately, Denny made it there first. Vito took notice that he was taller, fitter, and much better looking than Vito.

"Vito," Lucia said when she saw him coming their way. "This is Denny."

"Hi Vito," Denny said pushing his way into Vito's space with an outstretched hand and a smile that had enough power to burn someone's face off.

"Hi," Vito replied with reluctance. He didn't want to be rude.

"So glad you made the meeting," Denny said and then took Vito's visual cue of recoiling as a sign to take it down a notch. Denny stepped out of Vito's space.

"Me too," Lucia smiled. "When you didn't show up at The Tap to meet me, I thought maybe I put too much pressure on you."

"No," Vito said. "I got caught up."

"That's fine," Lucia said. "You came. That's what matters."

They both smiled at each other and Denny took this opportunity to step away and mingle with the other meeting goers.

"I'm sorry I wasn't there," Vito said. He didn't know what to say so he said nothing.

"That's okay," Lucia said. "I understand."

"No," Vito said. "You don't. You can't understand what I'm going through."

"I may not understand the specifics of your situation, but I understand the feeling of desperation. Of being lost."

Vito said nothing and just let guilt overwhelm him. Maybe I should tell her. But even as the thought moved through his head Vito imagined the look she would give him, like he was insane. There was no way he could tell her the truth. He had to continue the alcoholism charade.

"Denny said he could be your sponsor," Lucia said. "If you're ready to take that step."

"Let me think about it," Vito said. And with that a low ting started to hum in Vito's ear. It grew louder quite fast, and he knew it was the flask calling him back. "I have to run."

"But you just got here," Lucia said puzzled.

"I know," Vito said, putting on his jacket. "But there's something I forgot to take care of."

"It's the drink," Lucia said.

"What?" Vito said, "No. You don't understand."

And with that, Vito turned and walked out of the basement. He heard someone follow him.

"Vito!" Lucia called. "Vito!"

Lucia chased Vito up the stairs and outside the church.

"Don't make me run after you," Lucia yelled. "I don't have a coat on."

Vito felt the chilly March air make the hair on his ears stand up and he felt guilty. He turned around and met her on the sidewalk.

"I know you think no one understands," she started. And then she looked to the ground and hesitated. Then Lucia revealed something that Vito would never forget. "I killed my fiancé."

There was a pause because the weight of that admission pinned them both down.

"I didn't mean to do it," Lucia said when she found the courage to continue. "We were out drinking. It was New Year's Eve. I was driving and thought we could make it over the tracks before the train ..." and she stopped.

Vito remained quiet. He wanted to put a hand on her shoulder. To hug her, but something told him to give her the space she needed.

"We were hit. He was killed instantly. I was in a coma for a few weeks but, from what the doctors said, his body shielded mine and that's why I survived."

Vito ignored his fear and put his arms around her for an embrace. She returned his hug and said, "Thank you."

They let go of each other and Lucia looked up to her new friend, "My fiancé was decapitated. And it was my fault. I haven't had a drink since, and I don't plan on ever harming anyone I love again."

"Thank you for sharing that with me," Vito said, knowing how difficult that revelation would be for anyone.

"So don't think I don't understand," Lucia said. And with that the flask began to call again, but this time he could feel its force pull at his body. As if it had invisible hands with long arms and the flask was trying to physically make him turn around and come home.

"My situation isn't like yours," Vito said. "I do have to go."

"If you just resist, you can beat this."

"I can't see color!" Vito shouted as a couple of people leaving the meeting stared at him, confused. Then he was alone with Lucia, who looked puzzled.

"What?" she asked. "What do you mean?"

Vito told her the whole story. He let it all out, from the moment she gave him the flask until his running into the basement of St. Luke's a little over an hour ago.

"Are you sure you're only drinking booze?" Lucia asked. "That sounds like an LSD trip to me."

"I'll prove it to you," Vito said. "Did you have a dream last night that you were a nun, and I was a priest, and we kissed?"

Lucia's eyes widened.

"Did you also dream that I was a woman, and having a baby?"

"What the fuck," Lucia said, shock decorating her face.

"Those aren't dreams for me Lucia," Vito said. "They're the doors and I have to finish them. But once I'm done. I'll be a non-drinker again."

Lucia said nothing, likely because there isn't much to say after someone tells you they're being teleported to another dimension via gin martinis to regain their color sight.

Vito felt the pull of the flask getting stronger.

"I have to go," he said, holding her again for a quick and innocent embrace. "But I'll find you when I come back tomorrow."

"Are you safe doing this?" Lucia asked. "You can live without color."

"No," Vito said. "I can't."

And with that, he turned and ran toward his home.

***

After waking up in the Intermondano, Vito didn't hesitate for more than a few seconds to run up to the door. While he was still suspicious of what would happen once he stepped through, he was beginning to feel it was best to just rip off the bandage. It would still hurt, but it was faster than the agony of a slow peel.

When the cloud that typically surrounded him faded, Vito was in darkness. Still, the obscurity that engulfed him was familiar.

Vito's eyes cleared. He was relieved to discover he was sitting in The Tap. "Lucia!" he called, sitting up on his barstool and spotting her instantly. "I'm so glad to see you!"

Lucia scowled at him. "That's not what you said last night, before I kicked you out of here."

Vito read the hatred in her eyes, and it cut him to the core. He also noticed her hair wasn't red, nor any part of her clothing or her nail polish. Every time he had seen Lucia while living out the journeys, she had red hair. This time, she was completely gray, except for her pink lips.

Lucia continued to sneer at him. "If I remember correctly, Roy, yesterday you called me a fucking bitch. And I kicked you out and told you not to come back again."

"I'm not Roy."

Lucia laughed. "Oh, that's rich. You sure look like the same asshole who was here last night. For the past few months I've been working here you've gone by the name of Roy. You sure look a lot like Roy. Tall guy, ugly face, likes to cause a lot of trouble."

"No. Seriously, Lucia. It's Vito. I'm *not* Roy." He stared at her, not understanding why she couldn't recognize him this time around.

Lucia rolled her eyes and walked away. "Don't make me call the cops. I'm not messing around this time. You can't talk to me like that. You're no longer welcome here."

Vito dropped his head and walked to the front door. He turned with one last attempt to appeal to her, but she had disappeared somewhere in the darkness, and the bar was empty. Defeated, Vito opened the heavy door and stepped out into the sunlight.

Once on the street, he had no idea where to go or what to do. Walking aimlessly, he turned down Harlem. The aroma of Scudiero's pizza hit him in the face. Following his nose, he entered the restaurant and approached the counter, his stomach rumbling with anticipation. He remembered coming in here as a kid, and how Mr. Scudiero occasionally would give him a free slice.

"What the hell are you doing in here?" Mr. Scudiero yelled upon spotting him. "I said you can't come in here anymore! Get out of my store!"

"Mr. Scudiero," Vito said, shocked, "I've never seen you act like this."

"Act like this?" The pizza maker ran around the counter toward Vito. A couple of guys seated at a gray table jumped up just in time before Scudiero smashed Vito's face. "After what you said to my daughter the other night, you should feel lucky I don't make you a pair of cement shoes!" Scudiero yelled through gritted teeth while the two other men held him back.

Vito looked at the men's angry faces and decided it was in his best interest to just get out of there. Scurrying out, Vito stumbled into the street and collided with a figure who gave him a hard push. "Watch where you're going, you stupid drunk!"

Vito fell to the ground.

Based on the way he couldn't seem to stay on his feet, Vito wondered if the body he was currently inhabiting was handicapped in some way. He tried to get up but lost his balance and fell again.

Suddenly, he felt a hand on his arm. "Let me help you up."

Once he was steady on his feet, Vito saw that his savior was Sister Angelle. Although Lucia had inhabited her in an earlier dream, prior to that Vito hadn't seen Sister Angelle since Frank died, when he ran to the rectory in tears looking for Father Vince.

"Are you going to be okay, sir?" she asked.

"Uh … I think so, sister."

"I would feel better if I knew you were heading somewhere warm and safe," she said.

Vito didn't know what to say. He didn't even know who he was right now. "I'm going home, sister," he said, simply because he didn't know what else to say.

She smiled. "You wouldn't lie to a nice nun who helped you off the street, would you?"

Vito shook his head.

"All right," Sister Angelle said as she started walking in the opposite direction. "God bless you, sir."

She looks so much older, Vito thought as he watched her walk toward St. Luke's. Once she was out of sight, he surveyed his surroundings. What am I supposed to do now?

"Driver's license!" he abruptly shouted, startling a man walking his dog nearby.

Vito ran his hands over his body, feeling for a wallet. Encountering a familiar lump in his back pocket, he inserted his hand and seized the wallet. Just as he suspected, there was a state ID inside, but no license. He looked at the photo and was shocked to see himself, Vito, on this guy's identification. He shrugged it off and tried to focus on the address and grew dizzy.

"What's with this guy?" he thought, until he felt the familiar pull of the flask.

Panicked, Vito began scanning every possible pocket on this guy called Roy. In his breast pocket he found a flask. The second his hand touched it, a surge of energy shot up his arm.

Losing sight of everything around him, Vito returned the wallet to his pocket and took the flask out instead. Without hesitation, he twisted off the lid. When the opening was in his mouth—or Roy's mouth, rather—he lifted the curved vessel and drank.

A woman was staring at him, but he didn't care. He swallowed and let the energy of it all radiate through his hand and arm. Just as it did with Vito, the liquid projected the same power through every vein and capillary in Roy's body.

With his eyes closed, Vito took a deep breath before opening them again. The woman who'd been watching him was now gone.

Vito examined the wallet again, this time focusing more closely on Roy's address so he could find the guy's house.

Soon he was standing at the front door of a building that read 1042. Roy's building. It was a six-flat, with a stack of three apartments on the left and three more on the right. Roy lived on the corner of Oketo and Belmont, next to Nottoli's delicatessen.

Vito was familiar with the area because once Connie discovered he could navigate his way around the neighborhood alone, picking up sausage at Nottoli's became a weekly chore for him. But he hadn't minded because it was one of the best parts of the city, as far as Vito was concerned.

"Roy?" a voice behind him said.

Vito turned around.

"Did you lose your keys again?"

Vito focused on the person speaking to him. A man was staring back at him, questioningly. "Uh … yeah," Vito finally responded.

The man pushed past him and used his own key to open the door.

Vito followed him into the building. The ringing in his ears started back up and he grabbed the flask and took a swig.

"I told you not to drink out here anymore!" The guy pushed the flask down, away from Vito's mouth.

Vito returned it to his pocket.

"Get inside you lush," the man snarled.

Vito looked around the hallway, puzzled. Peering down the flight of stairs in front of him, he could see two doors, which he presumed led to opposing garden apartments. He turned to look at another flight of stairs. These went upward, which he knew led to the other four flats.

Tired, Vito sat on the windowsill.

"You live down there." The man pointed to the garden entrance on the left before turning to head upstairs. "Geeze, Roy. You gotta lay off the sauce."

Vito watched the stranger until he was out of sight. Then he went downstairs to Roy's apartment.

"My apartment," Vito thought, somewhat excitedly, considering he'd never had his own apartment. He reached out to turn the doorknob, surprised it opened with ease. But then he remembered Roy had lost his keys. Hence, he'd had no choice but to leave the door unlocked.

Stepping inside, Vito was hit with a putrid smell he couldn't even identify. Smoke, piss, beer, and puke? Or perhaps all those things combined, along with a dash of rotting cheese on empty pizza boxes, and weed.

Taking a couple of steps forward, Vito heard little creatures scurrying about. But the call of the flask had returned, making him care about nothing but refueling. He found a light switch on the wall and was surprised the place looked even worse than it smelled. It was riddled with crumpled paper bags, take-out containers, beer cans, and empty whiskey bottles.

Vito sat on top of the pizza boxes covering the sofa. He took the flask out of his breast pocket. When he opened the top, he took a quick look inside, amazed how the flask never emptied.

He drank like he'd never drunk before, his stomach soaking up the fluid like a sponge.

Yet, Vito forced himself to lower the flask from his lips, knowing he couldn't sit on the sofa drinking forever.

Standing, Vito found the bathroom. The mirror on the medicine cabinet was cracked in several places and filled with water spots that had likely caked up over months, possibly years.

Taking a towel off the floor, Vito wet it and wiped the mirror clean. Then he took a good look at the face in the mirror. It wasn't much—just a face with a nose, a mouth with chapped lips, and tired eyes that he suspected would be bloodshot if he'd been able to see the red in them.

"Wait," he thought. "I could see red when Lucia was in my other dreams. But why not this time?" Before he could think much more about this though, the flask began to call to him again. He retrieved it from the sofa. It was glowing, and Vito sensed its anger over being left alone. In his hand, the flask's top opened on its own. Barely noticing, or caring, Vito placed his lips to the opening and drank until his jaw began to hurt.

Suddenly, the room started to spin.

Vito fell face-down into the bed of gray pizza boxes that were speckled with a bit of green.

***

When his eyes opened, Vito blinked away sleep crust from his lashes. His vision unclear, he felt as if he was looking through a cheesecloth. He sat up and looked around, remembering where and who he was.

It was daylight now, making Roy's apartment look even worse. The walls were yellowed from cigarette smoke, and it was evident that Roy hadn't cleaned the place in years. Fuzzy animal-like clumps of dust hung from the ceiling fan, and piles of crap were everywhere.

Most notably though, to Vito, were the lack of photos. Every morning when Vito started his day, he was greeted with pictures of loved ones. Roy, however, didn't seem to have a single photo of anyone.

Vito's stomach growled, calling attention to his hunger. He went to see if Roy had anything to eat. But then, it struck Vito that there was no way he could consume anything in *this* place. It was that moment Vito remembered he had a fear of germs and he wondered how he wasn't dying from anxiety. Then he heard the flask sing and Vito had his answer.

He took in the apartment's mess once again, spotting an answering machine blinking beside the telephone.

Curious, he approached the machine and hit play, hoping the message would give him some insight into who Roy was, and why his journey led him here.

"Hello, Mr. Ekard. I'm calling from American Bell. This is our fourth attempt to reach you. I'm sorry to inform you that your service will be shut off in one week if the bill is not paid. You can call us back at this number to make a payment over the phone, or you can send the payment via Western Union. The amount due is ..."

Vito listened to the rest of the messages, all from bill collectors.

"End of messages," a computer voice informed once they had all played.

Vito realized that Roy had to be the loneliest man in the world.

Vito looked around again, not knowing what to do.

Should he go out for something to eat? It didn't seem like Roy was welcome in many places. The thought of being kicked out of another business wasn't appealing.

Vito wondered if Roy was welcome anywhere. Judging from the conditions the poor man lived in, it seemed no one loved Roy. He could even feel the loneliness in Roy's chest.

As if drawn to Roy's despair, the flask began to call for him. He looked at it on the table, glowing with the colors Vito couldn't see in the rest of the world.

Vito went to the flask and picked it up. It was warm in his hand and provided a sense of comfort.

The flask was the only friend Vito—or Roy—had.

He took a drink to quell the call for a moment longer. After swallowing, however, Vito grew dizzier than usual. Stumbling slightly, he sat on the sofa.

Everything surrounding Vito disappeared into an endless sea of gray.

Chapter Nineteen

Seated in the vast gray nothingness, Vito squeezed his eyes shut, hoping that when he reopened them, he would wake up in the basement he knew. With his eyes still closed, he lowered his hands to feel his chair.

A barstool? Wasn't he just on Roy's sofa?

He opened his eyes and found himself sitting inside The Tap again.

"Roy is being gross again," Lucia said, walking up to him without a hint of red. "I can't stand that guy."

Vito peered across the bar and spotted Roy smiling back at him. His heart jumped, and he looked down to his hands. Pointy pink fingernails rested at the end of sausage-sized fingers.

Vito had an inkling who he was this time around.

"Let me kick him out of here," Lucia begged him.

"No," Vito responded not knowing where the decision to talk came from. "I'll talk to him," the person he now inhabited continued.

"I don't know why you let that scumbag hang out here," Lucia huffed as she went to wait on a customer who'd just entered.

Vito noticed the straight-up martini in front of him, barely touched, with a couple of olives marinating in the gin. His mouth began to water.

"She must've just made this," he thought, picking up the glass and taking a long sip. The refreshing pine flavor mixed with the saltiness of the olive juice made every cell in this body rejoice.

"Nicki."

Vito heard someone call to him as he swallowed, confirming his suspicion that he was the obnoxious woman he'd met on the bus less than a week ago. Lucia's Aunt Nicki. He turned around and found Roy standing in front of him.

"I don't know why she's so pissed at me," Roy said, pulling up pants that were too big for his frail body.

"What did you say to her?" Vito asked, noting that somewhere inside this brain, Nicki was asking the question, not him. Then he remembered what his zio had said and relinquished his need to control this situation. He was only there to observe.

"Nothing," Roy replied.

"I don't believe you. Now fess up, or I'm gonna ban you from coming in here. And we both know you aren't welcome in a lot of places, Roy."

Roy lowered his gaze to the floor. "I said I wanted to bury my face in her tits."

Vito waited, because he certainly didn't know what to say to that. To kill a moment, he reached for the martini and took out an olive. He savored the saltiness as it sat in this lipsticked mouth and let the gin and juice slip down his throat. After he swallowed the olive, Vito looked at Roy. "You're going to go over there, apologize to Lucia, and then you are going to finish your beer and go home. Don't come back for three days. When you do, you better never say anything like that to her or any woman in my bar again. If you do, you're banned for life. Got it?"

"Got it," Roy said, crestfallen. He walked away.

Vito didn't care if he was only supposed to observe. He thought Roy should pay for what he said, so he added a stipulation of his own. "And from now on, whatever you plan on tipping her, add an extra ten bucks on top of it," Vito added.

"But I'm living on disability!" Roy argued.

Vito held up one of Nicki's hands, dismissing Roy and his retort. He picked up the martini and took another sip as Roy walked over to his half-empty beer.

"That extra sawbuck would force him to come in less," Vito thought.

"I don't know why you don't just ban him," Lucia said, returning. "He's always causing trouble, and no one likes him."

"I know." Vito set his empty glass on the bar rail, letting Nicki say her peace. "But he's a lonely man with nowhere else to go. We can't just send him back to his miserable little life."

"Why not?" Lucia took the martini glass and put it by the sink. She walked to the ice bin, where she grabbed a shaker and loaded it with ice before reaching for a green bottle.

"Listen, you're young," Vito continued, realizing Nicki's words were coming out again. He took a backseat, simply listening. "You brush aside these people now. But one day, you're gonna be old too. And when you're an old lady like me, I hope you aren't lonely like some of the folks that come here."

They both took a good look around, noting the people inside the bar. Many sat alone, not speaking to anyone. They were a mixture of genders, races, ages, and ethnicities, having nothing in common apart from their affinity for sitting inside The Tap, drinking the day away, attempting to suppress their demons.

Lucia finished making the martini and put it in front of her aunt. Nicki picked up the drink, and both she and Vito felt a rush of comfort the second the gin and olives hit their tongue.

"I don't care if he's lonely." Lucia said. Vito noticed how her hair seemed to light up at the ends, even if it no longer looked red to him. "That doesn't give him a pass to verbally abuse me," Lucia continued. "It's 2007. Women don't put up with that bullshit anymore. Did you ever think he might be lonely for a reason?"

"Maybe he's had some bad breaks in life?" Nicki said.

"You know what, Auntie," Lucia looked him, her eyes flashing angrily, "you are the most anti-women woman I know."

"What's that supposed to mean?" Nicki said, affronted.

"You feel bad for Roy but have no regard for how his disgusting behavior makes *me* feel. I heard you tell him to tip me an extra ten. What the fuck was that?"

Vito felt a pang of guilt since that part had been his idea.

Lucia continued. "Is my dignity and respect worth a measly ten bucks?"

"This is what bartending is," Vito heard Nicki say, feeling her self-doubt creeping up. "It's part of the gig."

"I call bullshit," Lucia argued. "What happened to the aunt I knew? The one who was so powerful, she was the first female bar owner in this neighborhood? You were a trailblazer. Now look at you."

Vito felt Nicki's need for a drink as she lifted the glass and took a swig.

"You can't hide from the truth inside that glass, Auntie," Lucia said before storming off to the darkest reaches of the barroom.

Nicki stood, took her martini, and moved to the bar's backroom, where she kept a desk, sofa, and files. She sat at the desk and pulled her wallet out of her purse. All the while, Vito remained quietly in the backseat of her body, simply watching, and listening in on the thoughts bouncing around her head.

Nicki had a successful bar in one of the best cities in the country. All the booze she could ever want was right at her fingertips. Yet, there was a void in her heart.

She opened the wallet and pulled out a yellowing photo frayed at the edges. She focused on the image, but Vito couldn't quite make it out. To him, it was blurry. Nevertheless, he could feel that void within Nicki intensifying.

Vito made a conscious effort to see the face in the photo. After a moment, he realized it was his zio, Frank.

He'd never seen this photo of Frank before. He was standing with a woman much shorter than him. She had the legendary Farrah Faucet hair flip, with Daisy Dukes and a black T-shirt with white three-quarter sleeves. The front of her shirt had *LED-ZEPPELIN* printed on it in big yellow letters. Under the band's name was an angel screen printed on the black fabric. Beneath the celestial being were four symbols that Vito couldn't quite make out.

"Led Zeppelin Four," Vito heard inside this head, courtesy of Nicki, who was wondering what had happened to that shirt.

She took her eyes off the insignia she once owned and stared at Frank's image instead. Nicki's feelings and memories of Frank began to flood her body—so much that Vito was starting to feel uncomfortable.

The reality of who Nicki was to Frank became evident.

Seeing her thoughts, Vito didn't have to wonder why she hadn't been at Frank's wake. One glimpse into her consciousness revealed she hadn't been willing to accept Frank's death. She hadn't accepted it then, and she still didn't. The pain coursing through her body was overwhelming.

Nicki took the last swig of her martini, and Vito could feel her yearning for another. She stood and opened the office door just in time to hear Roy say, "Now I gotta tip that fucking bitch an extra ten bucks just to hang out here."

Vito never felt more enraged. He could feel Nicki's anger skyrocket too as they both began to yell with one body. "What did you say?!" Vito tried to take full control of Nicki's body, but she was just as mad. Even though both souls were doing the talking, it all came out as her voice.

"That's it! You're gone, Roy! Get out of my bar right now before I call the cops! I won't have you talking about my niece that way! And *you* …" Vito and Nicki turned their attention to the guy Roy was talking to. Vito had never seen him before, but he didn't care. "If you want to come back in here, keep your mouth shut and go back to your drink."

"But Nicki," Roy started.

"Stop! Lucia's right. Get out! I don't ever want to see you in here again!"

Head hung low; Roy walked out the door.

Nicki returned to the bar to see Lucia smiling.

"Thank you," Lucia said, running forward to hug her aunt.

"He deserved it," Nicki replied, and then held up her empty glass. "Would you make me another?"

Lucia chuckled. "Sure. But after you have a glass of water, okay?"

"Okay," Nicki replied. "I'll be back in a minute. Nicki went back in the office and picked up the picture of Frank. Once again, the pain of her loss moved through her chest.

A weary Vito realized he was tired of pain—his own, and especially other people's. And just as the thought crossed his mind, an intense jolt went through him. Woozy, he wondered if he'd had too much gin. Vito thought of the martini waiting for Nicki at the bar, and the ever-present gray around him abruptly vanished.

Vito was surrounded by nothing for what seemed to be an eternity, but then he felt he was somewhere. But where? As the nothingness began to form into something, Vito discovered that he was somehow back at The Tap. Yet, everything seemed different.

This time, a tall glass of Coke, or maybe it was a Pepsi, sat in front of him. Not caring which one it was, he thirstily grabbed the drink and took a long sip. That one swallow, however, informed Vito that while the beverage may have looked like cola, it had only enough to hide a gargantuan amount of whiskey. Vito coughed from the shock of the taste, nearly spitting it out of his nose.

"Are you okay, Patrick?"

Vito felt a friendly pat on the back following the voice he recognized but couldn't place. As his focus cleared, he saw he was sitting next to Tammy from shipping. "Yeah, I'm fine. Thanks."

"Good," said Tammy. "I was worried you were going to spit out a lung or something."

She picked up her glass, which was shorter than his, and drank its remaining contents. She then set the empty glass on the rail and waved for Lucia's attention. Vito saw her standing near some random guys. He waved, and she smiled and waved back. "Maybe she'll know it's me," Vito thought.

Tammy flashed a twenty to Lucia, pointed to her drink, and got off her stool. "I'm going to hit the little girls' room. If you want another drink, it's on me," she said to Vito before sauntering off.

Vito had vaguely sensed that he was Patrick—his work buddy from Chroma—even before Tammy revealed his identity. Perhaps all his adventures were finally paying off. He knew where he was, and he was feeling good. After morphing from Nicki to Patrick, Vito didn't feel any anxiety whatsoever. Vito smiled and considered the fact that he had no choices in here. It was appealing to him to do nothing more than sit back and go along for the ride.

He picked up the glass again and took a long sip, aware now that it was primarily whiskey. As Vito drank, he thought back to how he had initially mistaken the drink in his hand as a soda. He should have known better. "Who orders soft drinks at The Tap?" Vito thought. Then he giggled. "Oh yeah. I do." Vito giggled again and some of the drink dribbled out the corner of his mouth.

"Geeze, Patrick," Lucia said, laughing as she walked up with Tammy's drink. "Do you need a bib?"

"No thanks," Vito said, recognizing he was a bit tipsy. "I'm not Patrick, I'm Vito."

"What," Lucia said laughing. "I'm not sure you should drink anymore."

Vito noticed Lucia's hair wasn't red anymore, just like the past two journeys.

"Aren't you looking cute tonight?" Vito said, knowing it was Patrick who said that. Sure, he was thinking it, but he didn't say it.

Lucia shook her head as she picked up the twenty Tammy had left her. "Aw, come on, Patrick. I like you. Don't ruin it by flirting with me."

Vito laughed, and so did she. He took another sip of his drink while Lucia walked to the register to get Tammy's change. When she came back, she put the change in front of Tammy's seat and turned back to Vito. "Aren't you going to be late for dinner with Trish?"

Upon hearing the name, Vito saw images of a woman flash through Patrick's mind, and sensed Patrick's love for her. Vito gave Patrick's body a pat-down, trying to locate his wallet. Then he noticed it was lying on the bar next to the glass of whiskey and Coke.

Vito opened the wallet as Lucia moved on to another customer.

Examining the contents, Vito learned that Patrick lived in Franklin Park, a suburb not too far from the paint factory. Flipping through endless business cards, Vito discovered a photo that looked to be about a decade old. It was a studio photo with a slightly younger Patrick sitting next to the woman Vito had seen in Patrick's mind. Surrounding them were four children and a couple of dogs.

While Patrick's eyes scanned the photo, Vito felt a surge of love unlike any he'd ever experienced before radiating in Patrick's chest. The overwhelming happiness was so strange to Vito, like being hit by a lightning bolt of euphoria.

Vito marveled at the feeling, at the sense of comfort and security Patrick had when he looked at the photo. It struck Vito that he would give anything to have that feeling for himself.

So distracted by the photo, he hadn't realized Tammy's return. She was staring at him with eyes full of regret.

"Last night was a mistake," Tammy started and then stopped.

Vito didn't have to ask what the mistake was, or what they'd done last night. Patrick's memories were there for him to see, although he didn't really *want* to see either of them in that way.

Looking back at the picture, Vito tried to recapture the overwhelming, unconditional love he felt when he first saw it. But it was gone, replaced with a crushing weight of devastation and guilt. The negative feelings moved through Patrick like a smoke alarm, alerting him that his world was burning and crumbling away.

Vito wanted to escape. He wanted this part of the journey to end. But he was stuck with Patrick and his indiscretions.

"Yes," Vito spoke when he realized Patrick was at a loss for words. "It was a *big* mistake." Patrick hung his head, ashamed. He kept his eyes on the picture of his family, avoiding Tammy's stare.

"I'm glad you agree." Tammy finished her drink in one gulp and put her empty glass next to the change Lucia had left for her. "Okay, then," Tammy stepped off her stool and grabbed her purse, "see you at work."

Patrick tried to take his eyes off the picture of his family, but he couldn't. The more he tried, the harder his gaze focused on his wife and kids. He wanted to look away, to avert his attention to anything other than their trusting eyes, staring up at him from the photo.

Witnessing this, Vito felt the betrayal from his father's absence bleed into the experience. He thought about the obvious love Patrick had for his family, and how fragile such love truly is.

Once again overwhelmed with Patrick's emotions, Vito took a backseat in his consciousness, giving Patrick full control.

Patrick glanced around the bar, thinking about how no one else from work—or no one else, period—knew what he'd done. No one but Tammy.

Patrick finished his drink. Then he looked at the photo once again before getting up from the barstool.

"You taking off, Patrick?"

"Yeah," he said, not even aware who was speaking to him. He placed the photo back in his wallet and returned it to his pocket.

"Give the wife our best!" someone said as he stepped out of The Tap and onto the street.

It was dusk, and the sky was full of pink streaks mixed with gray.

As Patrick began to walk toward the factory to retrieve what Vito assumed was his car, the branches and trunks of the trees planted along the pathway started to fill into a deep brown that reminded him of chocolate cake mix.

Vito wasn't sure if he would have time to process all he had seen to regain this color, but he didn't care. He was happy to see brown again.

He took a few more steps, and the colors begin to surround him like a tornado.

"This is new," Vito thought.

A storm of yellow, pink, green, purple and brown swirled around him until it went black.

Then Vito noticed his eyes were closed. He opened them and saw he had returned to the basement in the real world, where he was sure his mother was looking for him.

"When was the last time I was here?" Vito thought, hearing footsteps in the kitchen.

Chapter Twenty

March 22, 2007

"I was wondering if you were ever going to come up here," Connie said when Vito opened the basement door. "Please, come sit here and have some coffee with us."

Vito eyed his mother, Nonna, Bisnonna Nellie, and the monsignor sitting at the table, looking like a firing squad. Without a word he took his usual seat. Typically, he would have welcomed the sunlight coming through the window. But today wasn't one of those days.

With eyes that darted back and forth like a fish in a net, Nonna Josie looked from her daughter, who had so much rage in her it looked as if she was about to explode, to the monsignor, who sat patiently waiting for someone else to begin. Meanwhile, Bisnonna Nellie sat in her favorite spot, wide awake, and dentures fully intact.

Connie stood from the table to grab a mug from the cabinet and the coffee pot. She poured her son a cup and set it in front of him.

Monsignor Benevento sat in the chair Zio Frank once used. To Vito, the monsignor looked like a cat waiting for the right moment to pounce. Apprehension mounted in Vito, wondering how this was about to play out.

"What are you doing?" Connie said, breaking the heavy and awkward silence.

Vito wasn't sure how to answer that question. He knew if they found out he was taking part in pagan magic, it would lead to a world of hurt he didn't feel like dealing with. He had enough on his plate trying to get his colors back.

"Veeto," Nonna Josie started, "we are a worried 'bout you, bambino."

"This is an intervention," Connie revealed, refilling everyone's coffee cups.

"Ah! In da tee-a-vee!" Bisnonna Nellie hollered, recognizing the word from one of her favorite channels, A&E.

"I don't think this is necessary," Vito said. "I know it looks bad, but …"

"But what?" Connie yelled. "You've lost your job, and you're drinking at bars *and* in the basement! Is this some kind of mid-life crisis because you're nearing 40?"

Vito kept his eyes on his coffee, afraid to meet anyone's gaze. How was he going to explain his way out of this one?

"I think," Monsignor Benevento began, "that you've always idolized that uncle of yours, and somehow, this is your attempt to emulate him."

"You don't know crap," Vito spat without looking his nemesis in the eye.

"Vito!" Connie scolded him with the same tone she'd been using since he was a boy. "Apologize to the monsignor, right now!"

A surge of power filled Vito's chest. No longer afraid, he looked directly into his mother's eyes.

"No."

The color in Connie's face must've been red, but Vito couldn't see it. He simply detected her face growing a shade darker.

"I think—" the monsignor began again.

"I don't care what you think," Vito cut him off.

"Vito!" Connie screamed.

Monsignor Benevento closed his mouth.

Nonna Josie burst into tears and jumped up from her seat. "Veeto, you a donna know what you're doing. Listen to you a mamma, Veeto, donna speak to Monsignor Benevento that a way, bambino. You donna wanna burn all' inferno."

Vito stood and hugged Nonna. He felt terrible for putting her through all this, but he was sick and tired of the monsignor and could no longer hide it.

Monsignor Benevento looked at Vito as he took another sip of his coffee.

Speechless, Connie lit a cigarette.

Vito fixed his gaze on the monsignor. "I think you've been putting your nose in my business long enough, and I am done putting up with it!"

In his periphery, Vito could see that his mother looked as if she was going to faint from embarrassment.

"Vito, I told you, apologize to the monsignor! Now!"

"No!" Vito said, the severity of his voice matching his mother's. He helped his sobbing nonna back to her seat.

Connie glared at her son in disbelief. "After all that he's done for us," she cried.

"I think I should leave." Monsignor Benevento stood. "I'll do as you ask, Vito. I won't be bothering you anymore."

"I am so sorry, monsignor," Connie said, following after her boss.

"Never mind," the monsignor said.

Connie proceeded to mumble words to the monsignor that Vito couldn't hear.

Vito sat down and finished his coffee, feeling more powerful than ever before. Basking in the glory of finally having stood up to the monsignor, Vito wished Frank had turned him onto the flask sooner.

Nevertheless, Nonna Josie was still sobbing. Her eyes closed, she squeezed her rosary and mouthed the appropriate prayer for each bead.

With Monsignor Benevento gone, Connie returned to the kitchen. She made a beeline straight for Vito and slapped him in the face. The assault made Nonna cry and pray harder, while Bisnonna Nellie, who'd been sound asleep, jerked awake.

"How dare you?" Connie said to Vito, who'd taken the blow without flinching. Connie glanced toward her mother. "Mamma, please take Grandma to her room. I want to talk to my son alone."

When Nonna tried to get her mother out of the chair, the ninety-eight-year-old tried to argue. But after a few 'andiamos' and tugs on the sleeve, Vito's great-grandmother gave in to her daughter's insistence and stood. The short gray pair passed by Vito on their way out of the kitchen, but not before Bisnonna Nellie looked to her great-grandson and said, "Dio ti benedica."[38] Both grandmothers then made the sign of the cross and headed out the kitchen door.

Vito and his mother stared each other down for a long moment. Once the grandmothers were out of earshot, Connie's voice came out, low and angry. "It's called respect, young man. I taught you better than that."

---

38   God bless you.

"I'm not a young man," Vito retorted. "And I've wasted my days living here. What was I thinking?" He shook his head, halfway speaking more to himself than to his mother. "I'm a thirty-seven-year-old man who has never lived anywhere but with his mother. Don't you see the problem with that?"

"No!" Connie yelled, her hands flying angrily in the air. "In Europe, children live with their parents until they're married. And when the parents grow old, they go live with the children. And that's the way it should be here."

"But it isn't," Vito said. "And you knew I wanted to get out there. Why didn't you let me?"

Connie's left eyebrow popped up high as she looked at her son as if he was crazy. Opposite to her typical demeanor, this time, when Connie spoke, she was surprisingly calm. "It's not my fault you chose to live here."

As if disappointment had weakened her legs, she sat.

"What?" Vito said, incredulous. "Of course, it's your fault! You fought me every step of the way."

"I don't know what you're talking about." Connie lit another cigarette and gripped her coffee cup.

"I can't believe you!" Vito yelled. "You cried! You begged, *'please don't move to New Orleans!'*" Vito made his voice shrill and whiny, imitating his mother. "What was all that then, my imagination?"

"Of course, I was like that then," Connie said. "You were only eighteen. A baby! I couldn't let you run out into the world."

"Tulane was a great opportunity," Vito insisted.

"It was," Connie agreed. "You stayed as I wanted, and I appreciate that. But what about afterward?"

"What about it?"

"After you graduated from DePaul, did I beg you to stay?" Connie asked.

Vito sifted through his memory banks and couldn't think of one instance.

"Vito," Connie put her hand over her son's, "I never asked you to leave, but you were free to go at any time. You chose to stay here."

"But, but," Vito stuttered as the truth hit him in the face. "You're always so controlling. Trying to make me become a priest, and then all those attempts to fix me up with your friend's daughters or nieces."

"I was trying to get you on a good path in the priesthood. But you didn't want that so then I wanted you to go out on a date." Connie chuckled. "You spend so much time with your nose in a book, you never meet anyone. You don't even have any friends."

"I have friends," Vito said defensively, but also failing to think of anyone he truly considered a friend.

Connie put out her cigarette and reached for another. "Oh, yeah? Who?"

"Patrick," Vito said, uttering the first name that came to mind. "He works with me."

"How come you never spoke of him before this?"

Vito shrugged. "You never asked."

Connie gave him a knowing look after lighting a consecutive cigarette. She took a drag, then let the room fill with a cloud of smoke. "I should've said something to you a long time ago. The truth is, honey, you need to get out into the world more."

"Then why did you have such a fit when I was at the bar?"

"Because you were there in the middle of the day when you should've been at work!"

Vito flinched; he'd forgotten about that part.

"You don't want to hang out with the type of people you meet in a bar. Trust me," Connie said. "Now, go get some rest. And not in the basement. We can chat when I get home from work." Connie drank the last of her coffee and took her empty cup to the sink. "I realize you have an issue with the monsignor, and I suppose that's a bridge I should've helped gap a long time ago. But you just don't know how much he helped us when you were born. How he was there for us when your father left. For that, I think he deserves to be treated with respect. Okay?"

"Okay," Vito said, though it pained him to do so. He didn't agree with anything she said, but he was tired of talking about it.

Connie came over and kissed him on the head. "Good. Since you're not working, you can clean up the kitchen," she said on her way out to work.

"Okay," Vito said again.

Alone in the kitchen, he took another sip of his coffee. He looked around at all the dirty pans and dishes, and figured he'd better get to cleaning sooner rather than later.

Then he heard that damned flask calling for him again.

***

Vito stepped into The Tap and blinked rapidly, trying to get his eyes to adjust to the darkness after coming in from the bright noon sunlight. He easily found a seat at the bar.

He noticed the place was empty. He didn't mind though. He loved the darkness and the ability to hide from the world.

He waited a bit, expecting Lucia to come forward after hearing the bell above the door announce a customer's arrival. But she never emerged.

"Hello?" he called into the darkness.

"Vito?" someone said from behind the bar. "Is that you?"

"Yeah."

"Come back here."

Vito recognized the voice as Nicki's, beckoning him from her office.

He went to her office, surprised to see Lucia passed out on the sofa, with Nicki sitting beside her.

"What's wrong?" Vito asked.

"I don't know," Nicki said, her voice hysterical. "She was sitting up, and then she was on the floor behind the bar."

Vito reached down to take Lucia's hand. "Was she drinking?"

"She bought a round of shots for those ladies," Nicki said, wiping sweat from Lucia's forehead.

"What ladies?" Vito asked, recalling how empty the bar was. "Did they leave already?"

"Those ladies. You know, the ones you were sitting with the other day."

"The sisters?" Vito said, shocked. "They were here?"

"Yeah." Nicki pulled covers over Lucia, who was shivering a bit. "You didn't see them? They were out there when I found her. I asked them what happened, but two of them just laughed while the other said to ask you how to help her."

"Me?" Vito said, putting his hand to his chest.

"Yes." Tears rolled down Nicki's cheeks. "You have to help me, Vito."

Vito stayed with Nicki while they called 911. The paramedics came, and Lucia was in the hospital by dusk with Vito and Nicki by her side. Yet, no matter what, Lucia wouldn't wake up and doctors couldn't figure out what was wrong.

Once the sun set, Vito left Nicki sleeping by Lucia's side and took the next train he could find toward Taylor Street, determined to make those sisters answer for this.

Seeing Lucia lying helpless in that bed created a rage inside Vito like he had never known.

When he got to their door, Allegra was already waiting on the porch. She was smoking a clove cigarette wrapped in dark brown paper. For a second, Vito had forgotten he was on a quest to get his color vision, and the brown-wrapped smoke had caught him by surprise.

"We didn't do that to her," Allegra said, sitting on a wrought-iron chair paired with a twin on their front porch. The chairs sat opposite each other, separated by a round table made of stone. "Sit with me," she instructed, taking a puff of her stick, and releasing a strong scent of aromatic spices Vito couldn't recognize.

"No," Vito determined to stay on-task. "Let her go!" Vito moved closer to Allegra, but not too close.

"I just told you; we didn't do that to her. You did."

"Me?" Vito said, confused. "How?"

"You told her it wasn't a dream." Allegra took another drag from her stinky butt. Her hair—darker than the night sky—whipped around in the breeze, providing a gray backdrop for the blackest eyes Vito had ever seen.

"I told her it wasn't a dream for me," Vito corrected.

"Doesn't matter. She's the one who gave you the flask. That gave her access to you on the other side, through her dreams. I told you that you had to keep this to yourself. Otherwise, you could drag someone else in."

Vito blinked. "You didn't tell me that!"

"I didn't? Are you sure?"

Vito thought back and couldn't remember Allegra ever mentioning anything along those lines.

"Did you read the books I gave you?"

"I've been running in and out of portals to other people's existences. Excuse me if I couldn't make time for the half dozen books you gave me."

Allegra shrugged. "Regardless, she's stuck like that now, until you finish your journey."

Vito took the seat Allegra had offered him, needing a moment to process what he was being told.

"When I was in there, I saw Frank. He said it's up to me to know when the end is coming. Otherwise, I can get stuck in there, unable to get out."

"He's not lying. Frank was stuck until death released him." Allegra finished her smoke and took a sip of the espresso in front of her. "Would you like to come up and talk over coffee?"

Vito agreed, and the two went inside to the flat Allegra shared with her sisters, Freya and Ginevra. Both were there, but they were preoccupied with a group of women seeking psychic readings and asking questions like: Is my husband in Heaven? and Will I ever get pregnant?

As Vito and Allegra passed them, Vito caught Freya saying, "I hear him now. His name is Alfredo."

"No, no, that's not his name," the woman across from her said.

Ginevra snickered.

Freya shot her an agitated glare. "Hush! I can't concentrate with these distractions!" She then turned an annoyed glare to Vito and Allegra, as if they too, were bothering her just from passing by.

Allegra led Vito into the kitchen, shut the door behind them, and started making more espresso. "You know," she said, "you complicated things a great deal by dragging Lucia past the idea of her only being in a dream. That cast a spell upon her. Now she's stuck in limbo until you end your journey."

"So, I'll stop now," Vito said. "I don't care about getting the rest of my colors back. I can live without them."

"I wish it were that easy," Allegra said, taste-testing the espresso. "But you must complete your journey, right to the end. Especially now that Lucia is stuck in-between, you must do it by the full moon. Otherwise, she'll be stuck there forever."

Vito was speechless.

"We told you that at the start," Allegra insisted. "But you also have to recognize when the journey is completed and then get out. If you go through another door after your journey is done, you'll get stuck too."

"You mean I'll never come back here?" Vito heart pounded in anxiety. How was he supposed to know when his journey was over?

"No." Allegra put her tiny espresso cup back into the saucer. "You'll come back and forth as you do now, but you'll never be free of the flask—and you know how that ends."

Like Uncle Frank, Vito thought. A cold chill ran down Vito's spine. Regardless of what the monsignor said, he didn't want to be like his uncle.

Nevertheless, he had to save Lucia, even if this was more than he had signed up for.

A pang of frustration ripped through Vito. Had he really brought this whole adventure on himself? His mother's words replayed in his head, about how he could have left home long ago. She'd wanted him to stay close for college, but afterwards, there had been nothing or no one stopping Vito.

He was the one who'd decided to stay home, doing nothing but working and reading. Never meeting people or going out.

That had all been his own choice. The realization sliced Vito in the heart like an electric knife carving a Thanksgiving turkey.

Chapter Twenty-one

When Vito walked through the front door, his mother was waiting in the kitchen. Although the whole day had gone by, and she'd already been to and back from work, Vito felt like she had been in that seat the entire day.

"Where've you been?" Connie asked. "I was expecting you to be here when I got home from work."

"Why?" Vito asked, not liking having to answer anyone's questions anymore.

"Oh, I don't know." Connie threw a hand up in the air. "Maybe because you don't have a job anymore."

"So." Vito poured himself a cup of coffee from the pot sitting on the counter and sat. "Just because I'm on a leave of absence from my job doesn't mean I can't leave the house."

"That's not what I said." Connie smashed out a cigarette that she had practically just lit.

"What are you getting at, Ma?" Vito asked, exasperated.

"Monsignor Benevento came back to his office after lunch and told me that he saw you going into that Tap place."

"And your point is?" Vito stared back at his mother and gripped his coffee cup, trying to ignore the flask that had just started calling out to him again.

"You don't see my point." Connie stood, started pacing the kitchen floor, and went on a rant about why hanging out in bars wasn't a great idea.

All the while, however, Vito hardly heard a word she said. The flask's call had grown too loud and seemed to be clutching Vito by his very soul.

The flask wanted him to drink, but Vito didn't want to. He sensed that something was changing, and it wouldn't be long before his journey ended. He wasn't sure how he knew this, but it seemed clear as day.

He just prayed he could help Lucia in time, and that he himself wouldn't overstay his welcome and wind up stuck, like Frank. The very thought scared him shitless.

"See what I mean!" Connie screamed, pulling Vito out of his thoughts. "You aren't even paying any attention to me!"

"I'm sorry, Ma." Vito realized he hadn't considered her feelings at all during this whole fiasco. Acknowledging what it probably looked like to her, Vito felt bad. But he still felt it best that she didn't know the truth about the colors and his adventures; it would be too much for her to handle. Plus, he couldn't have her falling into a coma too.

Connie took a deep breath. "Vito, I don't want you drinking anymore. Not in this house."

"I'm a grown man," Vito countered.

"I don't care. This is still my home. If you choose that lifestyle, then fine. But you can do it somewhere else. I won't watch my son kill himself the same way I watched my brother." Even though her voice had been stern, tears leaked from her eyes.

Vito stood and gave her a hug. No matter how much they didn't see eye-to-eye, Vito loved her so much, it killed him to hurt her this way. But he knew if he told her the truth, she would either fall into a coma, call Monsignor Benevento for an exorcism, or ask him to see a psychiatrist—although he truthfully thought the latter might not be a bad idea.

"I promise," Vito said, deciding he had no choice but to tell his mother what she wanted to hear. She couldn't know the truth, especially when he still had to save Lucia. Even now, the call of the flask was intensifying, reminding him of what he had to do. Still, the lie felt terrible leaving his mouth, and Vito hoped God wouldn't strike him down for it. "I won't drink anymore."

"I hope not," Connie said, her voice indicating she'd believe it when she saw it. "Otherwise, you'll force my hand, and I'll have to kick you out of my house."

Vito nodded, begrudgingly realizing that the sound of living somewhere else didn't sound appealing, at least not at the moment. Not only was he jobless, but he had this whole colorblindness thing going on and had inadvertently put Lucia in a coma.

Finding a new place to live right now wasn't something he could afford to add to his agenda.

Somehow, he would have to be slick about the drinking, making sure Connie wouldn't find out until his journey was done.

"Okay," Connie said, taking her coffee mug to the sink, "that said, I'm going to bed."

"Good night," Vito said, sitting back down to finish his coffee.

"You aren't going to bed too?"

"I will."

Connie narrowed her eyes at him. "You aren't planning on sleeping in the basement again, are you?"

"Maybe," Vito said, annoyed with the third degree. "What does it matter?"

"Because you literally just promised." Connie said through clenched teeth.

Vito sighed. "Ma, I've been a good son all these years, haven't I?"

Connie blinked, taken aback. "Yes, you have."

"Okay. So, I screwed up. Aren't I allowed to mess up occasionally?"

"But Vito, you're ruining all that you've built for your life in just a few days."

"Don't you think I can find another job?"

"I suppose."

"You suppose?" Vito's eyebrows shot upward. "You must not think very much of me."

"I didn't say that" Connie said quickly, now sounding confused. She clearly wasn't used to having this kind of conversation with her son. It was also evident he had picked up some of her conversation tricks of turning the spotlight around on another. As angry as she was, Connie couldn't help but be impressed with her son.

Vito paused to sip his coffee. "Maybe you've been messing with my subconscious all this time. Putting me down in little ways here and there, screwing with my self-esteem. And I didn't dare to leave."

"Well," Connie said, after a moment, "I still mean what I said, Vito. Don't let me wake up to find you passed out down there again in the morning. Because if I do, you're going to have to find a new place to live immediately. Got it?"

"Yes," Vito said. He was pretty sure he could take a sip, slip into the other side, and finish out this thing quickly. Then, after waking up, he wouldn't have to drink again.

The key, he believed, was moving through as many colors as he could in one night. It was time to stop dicking around. He had to get Lucia out of that coma. His guilt over what had happened to her was practically enough to make him need a drink regardless.

"Good." Connie leaned up to kiss her son's cheek. "I'm glad you see things my way."

Vito nodded and watched his mother head off to her bedroom. He looked at the clock. It was only a quarter to ten, giving him plenty of time for one last trip to get whatever colors he could and find a way to knock Lucia back into reality.

Vito prepared to head to the basement, until his great-grand-mother came in.

She settled into her usual spot.

"Bisnonna," Vito said. "It's late. Dormire."[39]

"No," Bisnonna Nellie said. "Vieni qui."[40] She patted the seat next to her. In her hand, she held two rosaries. While his sight was still dominated by the oppressive gray, the beads on both rosaries were purple, and Vito sighed at their beauty.

But then the flask sent a shock wave through his ears with a piercing scream. He shook his head from the vibration and said, "Nonna, I don't have time." It was a fruitless effort. Before Vito knew it, he was sitting next to his great-grandmother, letting him-self get lost in the meditative pattern of prayer the Rosary offered. He knew his bisnonna was worried about him, so joining her in prayer was the least he could do. The two had always been so close. Vito sometimes thought she knew him better than he knew himself.

Once they were done, she put a wrinkled hand on Vito's face. "Bene, mi amore," she said. Then she smiled and gestured for him to turn on the television.

Vito did as he was told, just in time for an *Intervention* mar-athon.

Bisnonna grew excited and motioned for Vito to get her some milk and cookies.

Again, he did as he was told and even sat with her for a little while. The whole time, however, the flask yanked at his innards. But whenever he tried to leave the table, his great-grandmother would put her hand on his, letting him know she wanted him to stay.

---

39   Sleep
40   Come here.

Vito's heart began to pound with worry, knowing he needed to get back to his journey. This was the end Allegra and Uncle Frank had warned him about. And time was ticking. He needed to reunite with Lucia on the other side, so that he could bring her back.

Lost in his thoughts, Vito didn't snap out of them until Nellie's soft snores reached his ears. Vito smiled, reflecting on how much he truly loved living here. Why would he want to live alone anyway?

Maybe once Lucia was safe, and if they dated, they could live together. But that was what his mother called putting the cart before the horse. Hence, Vito needed to focus on the present.

Slipping out of his seat now that Bisnonna Nellie was asleep, Vito made his way down the basement stairs.

***

This time, the strange mist covered Vito like a shroud. Patiently, he waited for the cloud to disappear and expose his latest adventure. But the smog clung tighter than before.

Vito waved his arms about, trying to make the mist dissipate, but to no avail. Only when he gave up did the cloud begin to thin.

The haze lifted and Vito's eyes took in the damp Chicago asphalt in front of where he stood. He didn't have to guess where he was any longer. When he looked down at his hands and body, Vito discovered that this time he was a woman, and he also knew exactly what woman he had become.

As if she could hear him inside her head, Vito felt his womanly legs start to run after a pair of red taillights that were pulling away from the curb. The unknown car sped off into the night air as he ran and heard her voice emerge from his throat, "GUS!" But the red taillights took a quick right and disappeared around the long row of bungalows.

Vito could hear a baby crying in the distance. The body he now occupied turned quickly and ran back to a house Vito knew. Once inside he felt his arms reach out and pick up the wailing infant. Vito felt sobs start in his chest as her arms pulled the baby tight to their bosom. They wept.

He looked down to a crying infant's face—none other than his own.

"What a happen?" A matronly, yet young Nonna Josie ran to him. "Mia figlia!"

Suddenly, both women were crying as Josie took an infant Vito into her arms and placed him in a nearby bassinet. Nonna then put her arms around Vito, who was inhabiting Connie, his mother. In the background, baby Vito sobbed along with them. Inside Connie, Vito saw it all through her eyes and recognized that this was the most pivotal moment in their lives. It was the night Gus walked out.

"He just drove away!" Connie cried, sobbing and holding her young son. Vito sat back like Zio Frank instructed.

"Why would he do such a thing?" Nonna asked.

But Connie just cried in response.

As an observer, Vito simultaneously felt his mother's anguish, as well as his own guilt.

Vito knew that Gus left because he didn't want to be a father. Connie never said that, but Vito knew in his heart it was the truth. He could hear his mother's voice, inside her head, arguing that he was wrong. But all he had to do was ignore it and her voice went away. Vito chuckled when he thought about how close this was to real life.

Nonetheless, if Vito was sure about anything in his thirty-seven years it was that if it weren't for him, Gus would never have left.

The doorbell rang, and Connie rushed to the front door.

"Did Gus come back?" Vito thought. "I don't remember her ever telling me this part of the story."

Vito sensed her hope that it was Gus returning. He hoped it was Gus too, even though he knew it wasn't. He knew it wasn't Gus, not because he grew up without his father around. Vito knew the person at the front door was not Gus because he could feel a strange anxiousness overtake his mother.

He mentally pushed the haunting aside and grew giddy at the thought of seeing his father for the first time. He had no idea what the man looked like, since his mother destroyed every picture of him when he left. As a small boy, Vito had once asked why there were no pictures of his father. To that, Connie replied, "Because he walked out on us, and for that, he deserves to be erased from our lives forever."

When Connie opened the door, however, Monsignor Beneven-to was on their doorstep.

"What happened?" the monsignor asked as he walked through the front door without invitation.

"How did he know so quickly?" Vito wondered.

"Monsignor Benevento?" Nonna Josie asked, seemingly surprised to see him at their home at such an odd hour. This struck Vito as strange; he had always known the Monsignor to pop in on them at any hour of the day while he was growing up.

"Mama," Connie started, "I need you to leave us alone to talk."

"But you need me here with you," Josie insisted. She stared at her daughter, sensing something was wrong, particularly as Connie seemed unable to look her in the eyes. "What is going on, mia figlia?"

"Mamma," Connie pushed the baby into Josie's arms, "right now, I need you to take Vito and feed him. His bottle is on the counter, and it's ready to go. Take him into his nursery. He won't stop crying, and he loves that room."

Josie took the baby, her worried eyes darting back and forth between her daughter and the Monsignor. But she eventually nodded, went to retrieve the bottle from the kitchen counter, and made her way to the room that now served as Vito's bedroom.

Once alone, Connie took the monsignor's elbow and led him into the kitchen. When she touched the monsignor's elbow, Vito was surprised by the feeling of familiarity that moved through her.

A sense of dread slithered through Vito's consciousness.

"Did you tell him?" Monsignor Benevento asked as he took a seat at the kitchen table.

Connie didn't say anything, and Vito tried to follow what was going on in her head. But he wasn't in control. She was.

"Tell him what?" Vito wondered, feeling creeped out for reasons he couldn't comprehend.

"Yes," Connie finally said. "He had a right to know the truth."

"The truth about what?" Vito still wondered, even though the answer to the question was staring him right in the face.

The monsignor took a sip of his coffee.

Watching, Vito was amazed at how quiet he was around Connie. With anyone else, the revered holy man dominated the conversation. But now, in hindsight, Vito realized he never acted that way with his mother.

It was as if he showed her a level of respect a man would show his wife.

"No," Vito thought. "It can't be."

But as he sat there, living this moment of his mother's life, the revelation hit him.

"I'm sorry," Monsignor Benevento said, looking downward in shame.

A shocked Vito sensed what the priest was sorry about, but he didn't want to accept it.

"I'm sorry too," Connie said, nervous energy coursing through her.

The two adults sat in silence. And that silence allowed Vito to experience the shock of his true identity. Impossible to swallow, like a bag of nails sliding down his throat and into his esophagus.

"What if Vito is my son?" the monsignor asked, acknowledging Vito's alarming suspicions.

"He can never know," Connie replied.

Those four words crushed Vito to the core. Once they were spoken, every ounce of trust Vito ever had in his mother vanished.

"But—" Monsignor Benevento began.

"No," Connie interrupted. "Vito is my son. We don't even know if he's yours. So, you don't get a say in this."

Monsignor Benevento once again remained silent.

Meanwhile, Vito's mind raced.

How could he have not known? The signs had been there all along.

Vito felt like he was going to throw up even though he wasn't in his own body. Sharing the feeling, Connie ran out of the kitchen into the downstairs bathroom, relieving herself of the few sips of coffee that had been in her stomach. Then, with her head hovering over the cold porcelain, she began to sob uncontrollably.

Vito felt a hand on her back. If it had been his skin being touched, he had no doubt he would have jumped away in disgust.

When the monsignor touched Connie, however, she experienced a feeling Vito didn't even want to let himself recognize. He blocked out his mother's emotions, still reeling from the revelation that the person he hated the most in the world might be his father.

This would surely put him in therapy, or the bottom of a martini glass, for a while. Let alone the fact that his maybe father was a priest!

"I'm going to leave the priesthood and marry you," Monsignor Benevento said, reaching down to help Connie off the bathroom floor.

Vito was shaken to his core. He didn't even know how he felt so much emotion was swirling inside of this body.

"Romualdo," Connie said as she splashed cold water on her face and wiped it clean with a towel, "you know you can't do that. Besides, I won't marry you. So, there's no reason for you to leave the church."

"But I sinned. I broke my vows by being with you."

"I know." Connie walked back to the kitchen and grabbed a glass from a cabinet.

"But I love you," the monsignor said, following her.

Connie felt a wave of nausea, partially triggered by Vito's disgust. Unaware an adult Vito was sharing her body, she prayed she wasn't pregnant again. "I love you too," she said miserably. "But you can't leave the church. We aren't meant to be together as man and wife. I tried to hide my feelings by marrying Gus but look how that turned out. No wonder he left us."

"Wait a minute," Monsignor Benevento began. "He left you not knowing if Vito was his child. There is still a chance he is, and he knows that. If he doesn't come back, then you'll know he never truly cared about being a father."

"I suppose you're right," Connie said softly.

An all-consuming rage swept over Vito so strongly, he was surprised he didn't cause his mother's body to spontaneously combust. He couldn't believe that finally, he knew the truth—either his father had never returned after Connie's betrayal, or his father had been there all along, hidden behind the robes of the Catholic church.

"Listen," Connie said, "why don't you go back to the rectory and let me sleep on this? I don't know what to do. All I know is that I want what's best for Vito. We both do, right?"

"Yes," the monsignor agreed.

"Okay, then. I need time to figure it out. Goodnight."

Vito's potential father stood. Connie looked up to him, and

when their eyes met, Vito felt how much they cared for each other. Their love was strong, no matter how many vows the monsignor had made to the church.

Connie walked him to the door and returned to the kitchen.

Nevertheless, Vito couldn't quell his anger. He forced Connie's hand to pick up a coffee mug and throw it against the wall. It shattered and left a bleeding coffee stain on the off-white paint.

"Damn, sis!" a familiar voice sounded from the basement door. "I didn't know you had an arm like that."

Vito turned his head to see his Uncle Frank, young and drunk, standing in the corner.

"I didn't know you were home," Connie said as Vito took a backseat in her mind again.

"Obviously." Frank pulled the flask out of his pocket. Vito took one look and felt the tug. "Wanna sip?" Frank offered.

Connie grabbed the flask and emptied the contents down her throat.

"So," Frank said, watching his sister, "Gus is gone?"

"Yeah." Connie handed the flask back.

"Are you going to marry Romualdo then?"

Connie didn't respond. Vito, however, felt his already overwhelming anger grow tenfold over the fact that his zio had known the whole time.

"Well," Frank said, "whatever you decide, I'll stand behind you."

Connie smiled even though Vito fought it with every ounce of rage he encompassed.

Frank hugged her, and she hugged back.

As they hugged, Vito's eyes caught a glimpse of a bowl of fruit in the center of the table. A few of the gray citrus orbs filled with a color he hadn't seen in some time. Orange. This change reminded Vito why he was here in the first place as everything around him faded into nothing.

Chapter Twenty-two

"Romualdo?" Vito heard someone calling.

"What a stupid name?" he thought to himself. Vito couldn't see where he was, but he was so thrown off by learning his mother's secret that he didn't care one iota.

When his eyes adjusted to his surroundings, Vito noticed the room he was in looked like it was made for a giant. There was a grand piano and a bunch of expensive furniture, randomly colored with his prized hues. Vito made a mental note of the colors he could now see—pink, yellow, green, brown, purple, and orange. Orange: a color he once associated with things he loved, like Dreamsicles, sherbert push-ups, and the glowing orb of life in the sky, will now be eternally associated with his unholy existence.

Hearing rustling in another room, Vito attempted to stand but found he couldn't. He concluded this latest adventure was much different than his previous ones.

He was sitting on the floor, on some kind of soft blanket surrounded by blocks that had letters and numbers. He retreated into the brain and discovered there wasn't much internal dialogue; there were mainly just visuals like shapes, animals, numbers, and the few colors he had gained back.

"There he is!" a large feminine voice overhead.

Vito's heart jumped, feeling the power of strong footsteps coming his way. He looked up, spotting a woman coming toward him. She was as tall as the Board of Trade building downtown.

"A giant," he exclaimed in his head. And to his surprise, the shock prompted him to cry.

"Aw," the woman bellowed, and lifted him off the blanket. All the while, his tears flowed with an intensity he hadn't experienced since he was a child.

"Poor Romualdo," the woman cooed. "Did you miss your toys?" She cuddled him, and Vito suddenly felt an overwhelming sense of peace come over him. His tears stopped and he let the warmth of this giant calm his nerves.

His eyes fluttered to the woman's face, and he felt the love she had for him. And in turn, he sensed the feeling reciprocated from himself through the infant he now inhabited.

"Domenica, you coddle him too much," a commanding voice behind them said.

The woman shifted her gaze from Vito to a man he couldn't see. "Aw, Giovanni, he's my Primo[41]. That's what a momma is supposed to do." She lifted Vito, pressing him to her shoulder and patting his back.

With this change in position, Vito found himself face-to-face with the owner of the male voice. He gasped, and a burp sprang out of the toddler body he now inhabited.

"Ah, there it is," the giant woman holding Vito said, and then walked into the other room.

Vito focused his eyes on a man, who was a dead ringer for the monsignor. Before he could get a better look though, the woman had entered a kitchen and placed him into a highchair that looked like it was made during World War II. He squirmed a bit and accepted with disdain that he was somewhere in the 1940s, in the infant body of the monsignor.

Vito tried to move into the background again, merely becoming an observer. But the child's mind was so easy to dominate, it was nothing to slip into the forefront.

"He's my son too," the monsignor's father said, walking into the kitchen, where the table was set for supper. "And I have plans for this child."

Vito felt a sudden urge to look at a circling fan. The rotation of the blades was so fascinating, turning and turning. Unable to pull his eyes away, Vito realized that perhaps this child's brain wasn't so easy to dominate after all.

The monsignor's mother moved around the kitchen, putting together a chicken dish with what smelled like garlic, white wine, olive oil, peas, and potatoes.

"We'll educate him here until he's of age for the school at St. Vincent's," her husband continued. "Then we'll enroll him into Fenwick, where he'll work hard so he can go to Dominican University before Seminary."

"Vesuvio," the monsignor's mother said, placing a steaming plate on the table.

---

41   First

Vito's stomach rumbled with hunger at the aroma; the food smelled as good as his mother's.

The monsignor's doppelganger began filling his plate, while the mother went back to bring the rest of the food. When she finally took her seat, she put a bowl full of orange mush on the tray of his highchair.

"We sinned, Domenica," the man continued as he tore into his chicken leg. "I was set to be ordained, and you were going to take your vows."

"But we fell in love," Domenica replied with a smile. She scooped a glob of the orange goop onto a small spoon.

"I suppose that is true," the man said with a smile that made him look uncomfortable.

"Nonetheless, by marrying instead of devoting our lives to God as we promised, we owe Him a devotee that will take great care of his flock. And Romualdo will do just that. I'll make sure of it."

The woman shoved the spoonful of orange pulp into Vito's mouth. Without knowing why, he began to cry again, so violently that he flung his head back and let all the orange mash fly out.

"What in the name of ..." the monsignor's father jumped up as the orange spittle flew his way.

"Domenica, can't you handle that child?"

"Mi dispiace amore mio,"[42] Domenica said, grabbing the nearest napkin to clean up the mess.

"No." The monsignor's father put his hand on Domenica's. "I shouldn't have yelled. I'm sorry."

They looked at each other for a moment, their love apparent. Vito knew that look of love reminded him of who he was and all that he found out about his paternity. He felt an overwhelming need to sob. So he cried and cried and soon, the look of love the couple shared was interrupted by their child.

Domenica picked Romualdo up and held him close. Once again, the touch of her body relaxed him.

Vito wasn't sure why he was crying. He pondered whether he was still reeling from the fact that the monsignor might be his biological father. Or was his anguish Romualdo crying out for a life he just started and didn't have any say in? Or maybe it was just the taste of strained carrots when he really wanted a bite of that chicken Vesuvio.

---

42   I'm sorry, my love.

Whatever the reason, Vito just wanted out.

Once he calmed down, Domenica put him back in his high-chair. She took her seat again and helped herself to a chicken wing and a few potatoes. While she ate and drank her wine, laughing with her husband, Vito watched her, absorbing every ounce of affection this baby felt for his mother. And as he did so, a deep cobalt blue overlaid itself onto Domenica's dress until it glowed so brightly, it was all that Vito could see.

***

"I thought you weren't coming back here," Vito said to his uncle, who was standing beside him at the hutch in the Intermondano, which was nothing more than an ethereal basement.

"Well," Frank stood and walked toward the liquor cabinet. "I guess I lied."

"I guess this isn't the first time."

"What's that supposed to mean? I told you I wasn't coming back because I wanted you to take the leap yourself. You can't use me as a crutch anymore Vito."

"That's not what I'm talking about."

"What am I supposed to do? Read your fucking mind? I know I'm not alive anymore, but we have our limits. Just spit it out."

"You knew," Vito accused.

"Knew what?" Frank said as he poured a pair of martinis.

"You knew that my mom ..." Vito couldn't continue. "I can't even say it."

"What," Frank snickered. "That your mom and Ramualdo were doing it."

Vito punched his uncle in the face. Frank reeled and stood shocked for a moment.

"Don't you ever talk about my mother that way again," Vito growled, feeling nothing but hate for his uncle in that moment.

"Okay," Frank said. He put his hand to his chin in that cartoonish way and made sure it was still working. "I'm sorry kid. I took that joke too far."

"Yes," Vito agreed. "You did."

"But at least you're standing up to your fears," Frank admitted. Then he took a long sip of his martini. "You look like you can use a sip, too."

Vito took a sip of his martini, and he felt better.

"I am sorry kid," Frank said. "For my little joke. And for not telling you. But you have to understand. Your mom made me swear to keep it under wraps. I gave her my word."

Vito took another sip of his martini.

"You do realize how much this is gonna fuck me up?" Vito said, not looking at his uncle.

"I know," Frank answered. Then he sipped his martini and put a hand on his nephew's shoulder. "Answer me this. Would you rather go back to not knowing?"

Vito didn't say anything.

"Only you know the answer to that, kid." Then Frank walked back to the sofa and sat. Vito did the same.

"I don't want this," Vito said. "I'm done with all this bullshit. My life was just fine before I ever took that flask out of Lucia's hands."

Then he remembered. Lucia. She was in a coma, and he had to finish to save her. It didn't matter if he was fed up. It didn't matter if he was afraid. What mattered is he had a responsibility to give Lucia her life back. So, he had to move forward.

"How is Lucia?" he asked, somehow knowing Frank would have an answer.

"Stuck." Frank took a sip his martini. "You want to save her?"

"Can I?" Vito said worriedly.

Frank sighed heavily. "I don't know. Maybe."

"That's pretty vague," Vito said, his fear mounting.

"What do you want from me?" Frank asked. "Everything is vague. I'm not even sure I'm real. Are you sure that you're real?"

"What?" Vito was losing his patience. "What does any of that have to do with Lucia?!"

"Seriously kid," Frank also began to lose his patience. "I'm just a dead guy, doing my best here."

"Well do better!"

"What the fuck do you want from me?!"

"Want from you?" Vito sprang up from his seat, decades of disappointment seemingly pouring out of him all at once. "You did this to me! I didn't want to come here or lose my color sight. When this all started, I thought it was just some fucked up game! But now, I find out that the father I've hated my entire life is probably not my father at all. And that's not even the half of it." Vito flailed around him in a way that would make any Italian proud. "My father might be a priest who broke his vow of celibacy with my mother while she was married!"

"I know how this looks," Frank started.

"How it looks?" Vito spat. "I can't remember a time in my life when it wasn't thrown in my face that Gus abandoned us because he didn't want to be a dad. When he really left because she cheated on him. With a priest!"

Frank sat quietly while Vito's screams bounced off the sublime walls. "Are you finished?" he asked when Vito paused for a breath.

Huffing with anger, Vito sat next to his uncle and picked up the martini that was waiting for him. He took a sip and said nothing because if he started talking again, it would be just like letting his finger off the dam of acrimony.

"Okay then," Frank said. "First, priests are human, with the same desires and emotions everyone else has."

"But …"

"I'm talking," Frank said, cutting Vito off. He put a hand in front of his nephew's face, silencing him. "I realize it's difficult to look past the enormous lie your parents have told you, but try to think about the situation from their point of view. You're on this trip to gain more than colors, you know. This was more than a means to reveal the truth about who you are. When you were your mother, how did she feel?"

Vito thought back. "She was scared. Alone, and worried."

"Worried about what?"

"Me."

"Come on," Frank said, not letting Vito off that easy.

Vito sighed. "She was worried about the monsignor."

"And why do you suppose that was?" Frank picked up his glass and took out the toothpick containing two green olives. He popped one into his mouth while Vito remained perfectly silent.

"She loves him," he said, when it was apparent Vito wasn't going to admit this. "And she didn't want him to sacrifice everything he worked so hard to obtain for her. So, she convinced herself that Gus was your father and put all her anger toward him so that she could suppress the truth."

This was all too much for Vito to handle, and more than he wanted to hear right now. He wasn't ready to forgive his mother for such a huge betrayal. He had sacrificed Tulane for her, all while she lied to his face. "I can't listen to this," he said. "Where's the flask?"

Frank took a final guzzle of his gin and held his last olive on the toothpick in his hand. "It's over there, kid. I guess that means you're going back?"

Vito ran to the cabinet, opened the glass door, and took out the flask. He opened it and placed the rim to his mouth. And as the liquid burned down his throat, Frank faded away.

March 23, 2007

When Vito's eyes reopened, he was back home, but not in the Intermondano he'd just left. Instead, he was himself and in the basement of his childhood home.

Determined to finish this journey and save Lucia, Vito jumped off the sofa and took the stairs two at a time. He burst through the door and found himself in the kitchen.

Sunrise was moments away, and Bisnonna Nellie was sleeping in the same spot as the night before.

Vito ran past her and headed to his mother's bedroom. "I know the truth, Ma," he yelled through the door. "I know about you and Ramualdo. I think you should meet me in the kitchen so we can have a long, overdue chat."

There was no response, but he heard the sheets rustling behind the door. For a moment, he feared the monsignor was in there. But he knew that was just his imagination running wild.

The monsignor has never spent the night here, or has he? Disgusted, Vito turned and headed back to the kitchen.

Unable to sit still, he busied himself making coffee. "Bisnonna, do you want some?"

When Nellie didn't reply, Vito turned to see if she had fallen asleep. He walked over to his great-grandmother and put his hand on her back. His touch moved her old body, and something fell off her lap and hit the floor.

Looking down, Vito saw her pink dentures coated in white film, lying on the speckled linoleum.

Chapter Twenty-three

March 26, 2007

"Your great-grandmother was a strong woman," a visitor said as Vito stood beside her casket, wondering how he'd gotten there. Everything was a blur to him at this point.

When Connie realized Vito had learned the truth, she'd come out of her bedroom to talk to him. But of course, that revelation was overshadowed upon realizing her grandmother had died. Seeing Nellie's lifeless body, Connie had screamed, causing Nonna Josie to come running in.

Then all chaos broke loose, and Vito had no choice but to brush the recently discovered truth about his father under the rug.

"I realize you're angry with me," Connie had said to him when they watched the paramedics take Nellie's frail, ninety-eight-year-old body. "But with all that's happened, this isn't the time to start digging into that."

Vito hadn't been able to reply. He'd just watched the ambulance consume the only woman in his life who truly listened to him.

The next few days flew by with Vito and Connie avoiding each other, which was easy to do since people kept coming and going, offering condolences with lasagnas and Midwestern casseroles.

The day of Nellie's wake came, and Vito took his spot in the receiving line. As her only male relative, he was the first person to greet visitors beside her casket.

Hours passed, and Vito's mind was starting to go blank. He said 'Thank you' in a robotic tone to the blue-haired woman in front of him, whom he recognized but whose name he couldn't remember. And throughout it all, even while standing next to his bisnonna's body, Vito could only think about the secret eating away at him.

Looking past the woman before him, Vito saw his mother greet the monsignor at the viewing room door. By the way she leaned in and how his eyes grew ten sizes larger, Vito knew that she had tipped him off. Shortly thereafter, they exited the funeral home together.

Vito looked around the room.

Nonna Josie sat alone on the sofa opposite the casket. The blue-haired woman being the last in line at the moment, Vito took the opportunity to sit with his grandmother.

"Hi, Nonna," he said, putting an arm around her.

She leaned into his chest and let her tears run freely.

Vito wanted to talk to her about what he'd learned, but he didn't have the heart to bring it up at a moment like this. Deciding it could wait, he let his grandmother sob into his chest until she came up for air.

"Veeto," Nonna said, wiping her eyes with a handkerchief she kept in a purse, "I a know that you and you momma think I joost sit around and not know what's a going on. But I know, my bambino." She gently pressed her hand to his face. "You momma, she a love you. All she a eva a wanted for a you, is for you to be a success."

"With all due respect nonna," Vito started there, because that's how you talk to your grandmother. "What does any of this have to do with her lying to me my entire life."

Nonna Josie sat for a moment and looked more contemplative than he could ever remember. Then she said something that shocked him."

"You a momma made a mistake. People make mistakes," Nonna said, and then he could see her anger grow. "All your life, your momma took a care of you, fed you, and loved you. When did your momma ever promise to not a be a human?"

"What?" Vito asked, shocked that his nonna wasn't angry at her daughter for her infidelities with the parish patriarch, but instead seemed to be frustrated with him.

"Veeto," Nonna said, releasing her irritation and putting a hand on his. "Even our genitori[43] are umani.[44] Joost a because you a momma made mistakes donna mean she love you any less."

Vito forced a wobbly smile, hoping it satisfied Nonna Josie because he didn't feel like engaging the subject anymore, at least not now. "Are you thirsty?" he asked, changing the subject.

___

43   Parents
44   Humans

She nodded. "Caffè, por favore."[45]

Vito went to the sitting room to fetch his grandmother a cup of coffee, and stumbled upon the monsignor, sitting alone.

He glanced up and spotted Vito halting in the doorway. "Hello, Vito," he said, clutching a Styrofoam cup.

Vito's jaws clenched. Without replying, he walked to the coffee machine and poured a cup for his nonna, and then added a few spoons of non-dairy creamer and a packet of sugar. He then used the little plastic stir straw to mix it.

When Vito turned around, the monsignor was standing in front of him, so close that Vito could clock him in the jaw.

"I'm so sorry for your loss," the monsignor said, and put out his hand to shake.

Vito looked him dead in the eye. "Thank you, Father," he said, declining the handshake. He then walked past the monsignor and headed out the door.

***

When stepping into The Tap later that afternoon, Vito could tell things weren't normal and that Lucia still wasn't there.

"Nicki!" Roy called out. "I need another High Life."

"I know, I know!" Nicki's voice responded from her back office. "I'll be right there!"

Roy rolled his eyes, which Vito knew were bloodshot despite not being able to see red yet.

Walking behind the bar, Vito found a cold bottle of Miller High Life, opened it, and placed it in front of Roy.

"Who said you could go behind the bar, momma's boy?" Roy said with a sneer as he grabbed the fresh beer and took a swig.

"I did," a voice behind Vito answered.

Vito turned around to see Nicki standing behind him.

"You promised not to be a pain in the ass if I let you back in here," Nicki continued.

Roy huffed something unintelligible and returned to his favorite illegal gambling machine.

Nicki grabbed a beer and settled her gaze on Vito. "Where've you been?"

---

45   Coffee, please

"My great-grandmother died."

Nicki blinked, taken aback. "I'm sorry. Life certainly hasn't been easy on you lately." Shaking her head, she turned around and headed back to her office.

Vito followed. "How's Lucia?"

Nicki looked sad. "The same. I wish I could get over to the hospital, but there's so much to do here."

Vito glanced around Nicki's office, seeing piles of receipts and papers on top of her desk. "I don't know how we let things get so out of control," Nicki said, her eyes sad.

"Don't worry," Vito said. "I'll help you. Where do I start?"

Nicki looked around helplessly. "Why don't you go out there and make sure everyone is taken care of. Then come back here, and we'll figure this stuff out."

"Okay." Vito turned to leave. Then he turned back. "I don't know how to tend bar."

"There's nothing to it here. Just open a few beers and pour a few whiskeys. On the rocks means with ice. Neat means no ice. I doubt anyone will be ordering a grasshopper."

"You put bugs into drinks," Vito was shocked.

Nicki laughed. "Just go."

Vito returned to the barroom and did as he was told. And she was right. Besides a few pints and a shot of whiskey, bartending at the Tap wasn't stressful at all. Once Vito had all the day drinkers taken care of, he went back to Nicki's office and attacked the pile of papers on her desk. Within a few hours, Vito had it all sorted by invoices (paid and unpaid), and other important documentation that was laying around.

"Wow," Nicki said. "You are quite the productive little guy aren't you."

"I'm six foot four, that's hardly little."

Nicki smiled.

He could see she was hurting and Vito felt bad for how much he'd disliked her. Nicki was probably the only true friend he had at the moment. So, he confided in her about who his real father might be.

"Your dad might be a priest?" Nicki said. "I think I need a drink hearing that."

Vito followed her to the barroom where Nicki stepped behind the bar. "Do you want a martini?" Nicki asked.

"Sure," Vito said.

"Keep talking. I can listen as I pour."

Vito let it all out without holding back about his discovery. Of course, when it came to the details of how he found out, he had to lie and say he overheard her talking about it. He wanted to confess the whole story to her but feared something horrible would happen to Nicki if he did. After witnessing what had happened to Lucia—someone he could potentially love—he didn't want to risk harming anyone else.

"Wow," Nicki said. Then she took a long sip of her martini. "I knew you were going through a lot, but I had no idea it was that deep."

"Yeah. My mom wants to talk about it, but I'm not ready." He sighed. "I hate that I have to go back to that house."

"Well," Nicki said, slapping him on the back in that crude way that had made Vito dislike her when they'd first met on that fated bus ride, "you can stay here if you'd like."

"Thank you, Nicki." Vito looked around the office. It was perfect. A sofa-bed. A television. A hot plate for food, and a coffee maker. "Can I pay you some rent?"

"No." Nicki took a sip of her beer. "Just being here to help me is payment enough."

"Well, since I'm not working, I can watch the bar for you too." Vito took off his coat, feeling the weight of the flask in the breast pocket. He'd tried leaving it behind, but the call was too much to take, and he'd felt forced to bring it along; the pull less forceful when the flask was with him.

"Sounds good to me. Speaking of, I'd like to go to the hospital in the morning in case she wakes up. Visiting hours start around 7 a.m. Here's the keys," Nicki handed Vito a beer opener key ring that said, "Old Style." On this ring were three keys.

"This key is for the front door. It also works on the back door. Unlock both when you come in. This key is for the beer cooler. And this funny looking one is for the alarm. When you unlock the front, you'll hear a beep. The alarm box is on the side of the front door. You have 60 seconds to shut it off before it starts blaring."

"Got it," Vito said hoping he'd remember all of that.

"You could come here and open the place at ten-thirty? Don't serve anyone until eleven though. I don't care how much Roy begs you."

"10:30 a.m. No drinks before 11. Got it."

"Thanks, Vito. You're as good a guy as your uncle was." Nicki's vision glazed over, and Vito could tell she was having a memory. When she came back, Nicki said, "You hang here while I spend some time with Lucia. I promise I won't hang there all day and give you a chance to head over and visit."

"Of course," Vito said. Then he looked at the clock. "Have you been to see her today?"

"No." Vito could feel the guilt radiate from Nicki. "I couldn't get away from here."

"You might have some time to get there," Vito said. "Why don't you go now? I'll stay here until you get back."

"Great," Nicki said. She finished her drink and grabbed her purse. Before she walked away, she said, "Are you sure you're okay with all this?"

"I am,' Vito said practically pushing Nicki out of the barroom. "Go ahead. I'll handle everything here." He rolled up his sleeves and took his spot behind the bar.

"Okay." Nicki headed for the door. "I hate to leave her all alone. Her parents still haven't come to see her."

Vito thought about how his maternal mafia would be at his bedside nonstop if he were in Lucia's shoes. Especially Connie. But as soon as his mother made her way into his mind Vito shoved her out of it. He was angry and deservedly so in his opinion. She didn't deserve any good thoughts as far as he was concerned. At least not yet.

"You're working here now?" Roy said somewhere in the darkness.

Vito laughed. "Yes. For the time being, I'm in charge."

Vito wished he could've gone to the hospital with Nicki, but after his flask-fueled exploits that night, he was planning to rid himself of this curse as soon as possible so Lucia could come out of her coma. With that in mind, Vito began cleaning the bar top.

"How do you know your journey will end tonight?" someone asked as he put an armful of empty glass bottles into the trash can.

Startled, Vito turned around to find the sisters seated at the bar. "Uh," he stammered. "Hi, ladies. Did you come in for a drink?"

"No," Allegra said, "but now that we're here, we might as well partake."

"What are you going to have?" Ginevra asked Freya as they both looked past Vito to the bottles on the shelf behind him.

"I'll take a glass of your darkest red," Allegra said, taking off her jacket and hanging it on the back of the barstool. "My sisters will have the same."

"I didn't say I wanted red," Ginevra objected.

"You like red," Allegra said to her sister, although her eyes were on Vito.

"I do?" Ginevra said. "I'm pretty sure I like chardonnay."

Freya whispered, "She wants us all to have the same to create energy. Plus, the red wine looks like blood."

"Everyone is having red!" Allegra shouted, her blood pulsating visibly in her veins.

Vito turned to retrieve the wine but realized he didn't know where anything was. He wasn't even sure if The Tap sold wine at all. He took a quick look around and found a few single-serve bottles of Sutter Home Cabernet sitting next to stumpy wine glasses. The tulip-shaped glasses were set upside down on the back bar. One look at the thick layer of dust on the glassware told him The Tap rarely sold wine.

"Let me wash these," Vito said, grabbing a glass and going to the sink.

Sensing the sisters watching him closely, Vito felt apprehensive although he didn't know why. These were the same sisters who'd helped him understand this strange journey. They were always there when he needed them. But they were also the last people Lucia saw before she fell into that coma. Even though they denied having anything to do with it, he suspected they were lying. Additionally, Vito sensed anger coming from Allegra.

Once Vito had the glasses, he placed them in front of the sisters.

"Thank you," Allegra said. "How much do we owe you?"

"Oh no," Vito said as he pulled his wallet out of his pocket. "I'm buying this round. You've hosted me so many times, it's the least I can do."

"We were wondering what became of you," Allegra said.

"Well, my great-grandmother died. I got tied up with a wake and funeral."

"Sorry to hear that," the sisters said in unison. Then they all took a sip of their wine at the same time.

"How's your journey going?" Allegra asked. "And how's your friend, Lucia?"

"Still in a coma. That's why I'm here. I'm watching the place so her aunt could go visit her in the hospital."

"You do realize I've been waiting for you to finish this adventure of yours so that the flask can finally be where it belongs, with my sister."

Vito stared back at Allegra, now understanding her mood. "You said you wanted it back by sunrise on April 2nd. That's a week away."

"A week from today to be exact," Allegra added. "Vito, that flask was made from an amulet that belonged to our great-grandfather. It belongs to us."

"I know," Vito said. "There's something you're not telling me."

"She's not telling you that Ginny will die," Freya interrupted.

Allegra turned her anger to her youngest sister. "We aren't supposed to tell him!"

"No," Freya argued. "YOU aren't supposed to tell him. There's nothing in the curse that limits me."

"That can't be right," Allegra said. "When did you discover this?"

"The other night when we were organizing all the loose papers in the library."

"Why didn't you tell me?"

Freya shrugged. "It's more dramatic this way."

Allegra rolled her eyes. "I'll have to check that when we get back home."

Freya rolled her eyes.

Ginevra, was twirling in her barstool like she was a little girl sitting on one for first time.

"Look at her Vito," Allegra said. "My sister is going back into childhood, just like humans do before they die."

Vito finally interjected. "Why didn't you tell me Ginevra would die?"

"Because I wasn't supposed to. I'm supposed to let you take the journey unhinged."

Vito was silent for a minute. He suddenly felt like he needed a drink to continue the conversation.

Ginevra tried to pick up her wine glass while she was twirling in her stool. The motion sent the contents of her glass onto her pure white blouse.

"Fuck!" Ginevra shouted. "See, Allegra? You know I always spill on myself. Why didn't you just order me chardonnay?" With that, she stormed off into the bathroom.

"Could I get some soda water, salt, and a clean rag, Vito," Freya asked.

She was always so quiet, Vito often forgot she was there. But, after her reveal about the severity of Ginevra's life attached to the flask, Vito began to believe Freya might be the smartest of all three.

He went to find everything she'd requested and handed it to her. Freya then gathered the supplies into her arms and headed to the bathroom after her sister.

Once they were gone, Allegra turned her attention back to Vito.

"If I don't get that flask back in my possession soon, there will be no time for Ginevra." Allegra said.

"I understand" Vito said.

"I don't think you do," Allegra said. "There's no telling how many journeys you'll have to complete to be free of the flask. It could take months. Do you realize how many colors are visible to the human eye?"

"I'm getting the primaries taken care of. They'll start to blend."

"Vito," Allegra persisted. "Ginevra must drink from that flask by sunrise on April 2nd, otherwise we'll lose her forever.

"Okay," Vito said. "I get it. I promise, I'll be at your place on April 1st to hand it over."

"Good. I trust you," Allegra relaxed a bit. "She's my little sister. She'll be two-hundred years old." Allegra looked past Vito reminiscing. "Where does the time go?"

Vito looked around the room, noting that some of the bar's patrons had unfortunately heard that. He made a mental note to get them wasted before they left so they'd attribute the comment to their hangovers tomorrow.

"Let's keep it down a bit, okay?" Vito said in a lowered voice. "This isn't *It's a Wonderful Life.* Witches are viewed a lot different than angels, you know? And even in that movie, they didn't treat the angel so well at that bar."

Allegra laughed. Vito noticed her drink was empty. He grabbed another bottle of Sutter Home, opened it, and poured it into her glass.

She smiled. "Thanks. Although this wine sucks. My father made better wine with his feet in the tub."

They both laughed. The two had an understanding and a familiarity that comes with growing up Italian in the United States of America.

"So," Vito started after a sip of his beer, "I'm curious. Why would your grandfather curse you with such a thing?"

"Freya's life is tied to the amulets on the flask," Allegra explained. "Not to the drink. All of us have some sort of ritual that we must complete every hundred years, otherwise we fade away. The curse we're talking about is the one Frank put on you."

"What?" Vito was shocked. "Frank put a curse on me?"

"What do you think this whole thing is? Some freaky ride at Great America?"

Vito felt crushed. He wasn't sure how many more surprises he could take.

"Are you serious?" he shouted.

Allegra winced as spittle came flying in her direction.

Vito handed her a handful of napkins. "Sorry."

"I realize you're upset," Allegra prefaced, wiping her face. "But you have to get a grip. My sister's life depends on it."

"You're right," Vito admitted. "I'll go back tonight and do my best to get into as many lives as I can. I won't let your sister die."

"Thank you, Vito," Allegra smiled. "If it were my life, I'd consider just letting myself fade into nothingness. It seems frightening, but it's also comforting knowing there'll be no anxiety, fear, regrets, loss, or pain. There's something Zen about feeling nothing, know what I mean?"

"Yeah, I guess."

Allegra sighed. "But this is my sister. I can't exist without her here."

"Does she know about all of this?"

"Yes. But we've been together so long, I'm always taking control. Her battle plan is, 'ignore it and it'll go away.' Besides, the closer she gets to her birthday, the more childlike she becomes."

"I'd give it to you now, but I can't leave Lucia like this. I have to finish for her sake."

"I know." Allegra finished her wine and called out, "Girls, it's time to go!"

Ginevra and Freya resurfaced from the bathroom, soaking wet and cracking up.

"We left you a bit of a mess in there, Vito," Ginevra said as the three ladies walked to the door.

Outside, the sun had set.

Vito suddenly noted the flask calling from the back room.

"I hear it too," Ginevra said. "You won't be able to reach the other side here. You have to complete your pilgrimage in the same room you started it. It's the portal. There's only one door to your quest."

Vito's heart sank, realizing he had to go back to his mother's bungalow and drink in the basement.

Chapter Twenty-four

"Hi, everyone," Vito said to the small crowd in his family's kitchen.

His mother was sitting at the table with the monsignor, both smoking cigarettes with half-filled coffee cups in front of them. Nonna was at the sink, busying herself with washing dishes. Vito didn't recognize the others present. It didn't matter to him anyhow, for his only focus was getting to the basement door; he wanted to get downstairs and put this flask to his lips as fast as possible.

"Vito!" Connie jumped up and ran to her son. "Where have you been?"

"Out," Vito said, taking his usual seat at the table, partially as a form of protest against her lies and partially because it was the only seat available.

"Do you want a cup of coffee?" Connie asked, going to the cupboard to fetch a cup and saucer.

"No, thank you." Vito looked to his left, where his potential father was seated, staring back at him. His Roman collar was perfectly white, and his cassock a stark black.

"Why don't you have a cup with us, Vito?" the monsignor asked.

Vito suppressed the urge to sneer, hating the sight of the monsignor in his Bisnonna's chair.

"Why?" Vito said crossly, not caring if the other guests noticed the tension between them. In fact, he hoped they did. "Is there something you want to tell me?"

Monsignor Benevento remained silent.

"I'll take your lack of response as a no," Vito said.

"Vito!" Connie interjected. "How dare you talk to the monsignor that way?"

Vito shot one glance at his mother, and she too, fell silent. Surprisingly, however, shutting his mother up for the first time in his life didn't feel as good as Vito thought it would. He wondered if they would ever get past this.

It was an issue to ponder another time though. For now, Vito couldn't be bothered. There was one night left to save Lucia.

"Well, I'm off to bed," Vito announced. "Thank you so much, everyone." He stood and approached the basement door without one word of disapproval from his mother. He then stepped through and locked the door behind him.

Once in the basement, he pulled the flask out of the breast pocket and made himself comfortable on the sofa.

Vito took a long drink, letting the spirit burn down his throat until he was no longer conscious.

*****

"Well, that was quite the scene," Frank said as Vito's eyes slowly opened in the other dimension.

"I thought you weren't coming here anymore," Vito said, running up the stairs and trying to open the door.

"I wasn't," Frank said, "but you seemed so needy the last time I saw you."

"Why won't this door open?" Vito hollered, ignoring his uncle's quip. For the first time, he didn't feel like drinking or chatting with him.

"I don't know," Frank replied. "Want a martini?"

Vito twisted the knob a few more times, but it wouldn't budge. Resigned, he realized that just like the mist whenever he went through the door, the door itself wasn't going to open until it was good and ready to let him through.

"No," Vito said. "This was a curse. You put a curse on me."

"I did," Frank admitted as he began making more martinis.

"Don't you feel bad? You betrayed me?"

"Did I?" Frank asked as he handed him a chilled glass filled with gin and olives. "Or did I open your eyes?"

Vito didn't know what to say, so he took a sip of his drink. The duo sat together for a minute, sipping their martinis in silence. Vito felt so tired, like he'd been running for days. He didn't even remember what day it was.

"I think this may be the last time though," Frank said, breaking the silence. "You know, the last time you and I hang out."

"I suppose," Vito said, trying to care but only wondering when that door was going to open. Time was getting away from him.

"Well, if that isn't a fine how do you do," Frank huffed.

"What?" Vito said, shocked at the flack he was getting from a ghost.

Frank stood. "Just thought I'd get a little love when presented with the fact that this is the last time you'll see me."

"You said that last time, Frank," Vito responded. "Besides, you knew about my mom and the monsignor, but made me go through this whole thing to find out. You could've just told me."

Frank finished his drink. "Okay, kid. Then I guess that's that." Without further ado, he faded away.

Vito watched his uncle vanish, chugged his gin, and put the glass down on the coffee table. Then, without a bit of hesitation or remorse, he ran up the stairs and opened the door.

***

This time, when Vito stepped through, the mist didn't surround him for long. He could tell he was once again in the basement of his mother's house.

Standing in the doorway, Vito looked back to the basement he'd come from, and then forward to the basement ahead.

He shut the door and walked down the stairs into a cellar he was beginning to hate. Peering around, Vito noticed the basement looked a lot different than the one he'd left just moments ago.

He approached the hutch where Frank had just made their martinis, only to see a reflection in the glass he didn't expect nor appreciate.

"FRANK!" Vito screamed. The irony of his failure to foresee living a day in the life of Frank didn't escape Vito. Still, he was too pissed to see the humor in any of this and just wanted to get it over with so he could save Lucia and resume his life without his family or the fucking monsignor.

"That's your name," someone announced from the basement bathroom.

Vito turned to spot a young Nicki, wearing the same Led Zeppelin T-shirt in the photo he'd seen when spending time in her existence, and a pair of short jeans that fit perfectly. A stunned Vito had to admit she looked great.

Laughing, she walked over and put her arms around him, one of her hands landing on an intimate part of his behind. Then she kissed him.

Vito stood frozen, not sure what to do.

All the while, he wondered why Frank had never brought her around the family.

Vito deduced that it was the late seventies. And with Nicki in front of him, young and hot, his carnal desires started taking over. His brain grew foggy, or maybe it was Frank's brain that was muddled. Vito couldn't tell, but he suspected a half-dozen martinis likely had something to do with it.

As their lips met, a surge moved through Vito. His own consciousness fought through Frank's, telling him it was wrong for him to be experiencing this moment—this kiss with Nicki. But Vito was powerless to her amazingly soft lips that tasted like cherries.

When they came up for air, Vito smiled. He couldn't believe that for the first time, this crazy journey was providing him a pleasurable experience.

Vito looked at Nicki. In his arms, she looked so gorgeous and in love. But abruptly, her expression shifted, filling with confusion.

"Vito?" she said.

He jumped back, startled upon being detected. What was going on? Nicki was supposed to be seeing Frank when she looked at him.

"It is you?" Nicki said, taking a step back. She laughed. "Why are you so afraid?"

"What?" Vito said louder than he wanted to, but it was hard to keep his voice down. This was the first time someone other than Lucia had recognized him.

The thought moved through his mind. "Lucia?" he guessed.

"Yes!" she said, just before a loud knock at the door interrupted.

Vito glanced toward the door at the top of the stairs. There hadn't been any calls or pleas from upstairs, just the angry knock that he remembered hearing from his room whenever a woman's giggle drifted up from the vents.

How had he never figured out that woman may have been Nicki?

"How long have you been here?" Vito whispered.

"Where?" Lucia asked, snooping around the different shelves of things that should've either been sold or tossed decades ago. Between housecoats, pans, ancient jars of canned tomatoes, and stashes of Christmas cookies in tins, the basement was a deluge of treasures waiting for discovery. "Where are we?" Lucia asked, pulling anise-flavored biscotti out of a can and taking a bite.

"This is my house. Well, not my house, my mother's house. We're in the basement."

"And you're Frank, and I'm Nicki," Lucia said, finishing her cookie. "This is delicious, but I could use something to wash it down."

"I can make you a martini," Vito said eyeing the hutch where the gin was kept.

Lucia looked at Vito hurt.

He was so used to letting the true owner of the body he inhabited take control, he let Frank slip that one in. "Stop it!" Vito thought loudly in his uncle's brain.

Stop what? He could hear his uncle reply with the same intensity and silence as his thoughts.

"She doesn't drink and you're making me look bad." Vito replied. Damn, if he knew he could converse with the bodies he was in a lot might be different. Or maybe he was just able to talk to Frank because he was the one who started this whole thing.

"I didn't know." Frank replied.

Vito looked back, "How about a club soda?"

It was too late. Lucia was neck deep in a walk-in closet looking around. "Where are we?" Lucia asked looking around.

"I'm not sure," Vito replied following her as she moved through the room, which was as big as a full level of their bungalow.

"So, this is where you live?" Lucia said, taking a seat on the sofa.

"Well, kind of. I live here in the year 2007—or at least I did." He settled his gaze on Lucia, frowning a bit. "Do you even know what's happening to you?"

"What do you mean?" She looked around the room. "This decor is crazy retro. I always loved the seventies. It's fun to get a chance to spend time here."

"When do you remember coming here, Lucia? To this basement."

She furrowed her brow. "I don't know. I remember us kissing and then you holding me in your arms. Before that, it's all blank."

"Do you remember reality? Not this world, but the world where you and I actually live. When I'm Vito, and you're Lucia?"

"Kind of. It's all jumbled in my head. What are you trying to get at, Vito?"

In the real world, you're on the brink of death. The words were right on the tip of Vito's tongue, but he stopped them. Lucia was in such a good mood, and they were having a good time; he wasn't sure he wanted to ruin it for her yet.

"Nothing," he said.

"What are we supposed to be doing?" she asked.

"I don't know," Vito answered. "Typically, I'm drinking with my uncle."

"The one who died?"

"Yeah," Vito said. "It's been a crazy ride."

He sat on the sofa and Lucia sat next to him. Vito felt the pull again. But this time it wasn't the flask. It was her. Lucia's very essence made his body tingle and he wanted nothing more than to kiss her.

"I like kissing you, Vito," Lucia said. Vito opened his eyes and found that they were in an embrace. He didn't remember how they got there, but that didn't matter to him now.

Vito thought about how awkward it could sometimes be, navigating toward copulation. But this was not one of those times.

Lucia's and Vito's mutual yearning for each other dominated, and soon, they were spread across the sofa, enjoying every hedonistic desire possible. And although it wasn't Vito's first time, it was the best he'd ever had.

As they held each other afterwards, limbs intertwined and bodies keeping each other warm, Vito knew this was the adventure he'd been waiting for. The great road that would bring him to the one place he needed to be—with Lucia.

"Why don't we just stay here forever?" Lucia murmured.

Unsure whether it was a rhetorical question, Vito remained quiet.

"What do you think?" Lucia looked to him, waiting for an answer.

"We can't stay here forever, Lucia," Vito said, sensing it was time to reveal the truth. "If we do, there's no telling what will happen to us out there. From what they're telling me, if I keep drinking from that flask, I'll become an alcoholic and probably die like Frank. And you," he sighed, "you're in a coma."

"What?!" Lucia shouted. "What does that mean?"

"I don't know," Vito admitted. "But it doesn't look good. The doctors say you may never come out of it."

Lucia stared at Vito, fear seeping into her beautiful eyes.

"Nicki's lost without you. We have to go back."

Then Lucia's eyes filled with anger.

Vito realized he loved her. He claimed the emotion—love.

Love so intense, it broke his heart to see her upset. He sensed her current anger so keenly it caused him to see red. Literally.

Every item in the room that had this lost color originally filled with the color red.

"Why didn't you tell me this sooner?" Lucia demanded. She pulled away from him and began looking for the yellow Led Zeppelin t-shirt. "Was I wearing a bra?" she muttered in agitation, still searching for her clothes.

Vito tried to gather his thoughts, knowing he needed to provide a sufficient explanation.

"It's the late seventies," Lucia mumbled to herself as she grabbed her denim shorts and pulled them over her hips. "No one wore bras."

"Lucia," Vito started.

She rounded on him with a sneer on her face. "At least I asked you to stay here with me. You tricked me!"

"Tricked you?" Vito got up to retrieve his own clothes now. "What do you mean?"

"Why didn't you tell me I was in a coma and might not get out of it?"

Vito lowered his gaze, ashamed. "Because we were enjoying ourselves so much I didn't want to put a damper on things."

"Damper? How am I getting out of this coma? Tell me that."

"I don't know," Vito admitted miserably.

"You don't know?" Lucia tossed her arms in the air, exasperated.

Vito stared down at his feet.

"All the time we've been doing this, and we could've been figuring out how to wake me up!" Lucia screamed.

Vito felt so stupid. Lucia had made an excellent point, and he felt terrible that it hadn't occurred to him while they'd been lost in the moment.

Another bang on the door made him jump. Vito suddenly remembered he was Frank and Lucia was Nicki.

"You know what really gets me, Vito?" Lucia said in a lowered voice as she stood up. "You didn't even give me the option to save myself. Who the hell are you, some stupid knight riding up to rescue me? If you think that's what I want, you're sorely mistaken."

"I get it," Vito said. "I'm sorry."

Lucia walked toward the stairs. Even though she didn't say it, Vito could tell she was contemplating whether it was worth walking up there alone.

She looked back to Vito. "I'm fully capable of fighting dragons, thank you very much." And with that, she ran up the stairs. Vito heard the door slam behind her.

He sat back on the sofa, unsure what to do. Looking around the basement he was growing to hate, he noted that from what he could tell, he had regained all of his basic colors. Hues like maroon and teal still weren't visible, but Vito didn't care.

All he cared about was Lucia—the woman he loved. He was painfully aware now that if he didn't get her out of here, she might get stuck forever.

In an instant, a martini appeared before him on the coffee table. Vito picked it up and took a big swig. He could think only of Lucia.

When her name went through his head, a splotch of red jumped out and danced in front of his face.

Vito took out the flask, deciding it was time for another sip. The booze descended his throat, and the droplet of red in front of Vito's face grew bigger. Then it began to fill with a cloud until there was nothing left but blackness.

Chapter Twenty-five

Before Vito opened his eyelids, a fine mist of water hit his face. Although he had never seen an ocean, he recognized the scent of saltwater.

His eyes opened to a fog surrounding him. But this fog wasn't the kind of moisture that had held him in at the beginning of his other adventures. This was sea air, thick, with the sun setting to his left. Or was it rising? He couldn't tell.

He realized he was on a beach he had never seen before. This wasn't North Avenue or Oak Street Beach on Lake Michigan back home.

The endless waves he saw crashing before him could be coming from any direction.

Was he facing south with the sun rising on his left, due east? Or was it north and the sun was setting in the west?

A moment later though, he noticed the sky growing darker, the ocean waters rushing under a deep blue.

"Blue," Vito muttered and sighed. He didn't want to think of the monsignor, but he couldn't help it. It was through that man's eyes that Vito had regained this color that he especially adored.

"Veeto. Andiamo,"[46] a voice said to Vito's right.

He looked over and down, spotting a man wearing a black turtleneck, tucked into black pants. Hearing additional voices, Vito glanced around.

Men in black shirts had Vito and the other man surrounded. They stood together, military-style. Glancing down at what he was wearing, Vito realized he was one of them.

A little man with the big mustache looked up at him and yelled, "Che cosa ti succede?? Andiamo!"[47]

A man standing behind Vito gave him a nudge. Vito looked to this other man; he had a little mustache over his upper lip that reminded Vito of a swastika.

"Eccoli,"[48] the man said.

---

46   Vito, hurry up.
47   What's wrong with you? Let's go!
48   There they are.

He said, *There they are.*

Somehow, Vito understood. He looked down the beach in the direction where the tall soldier had gestured. Though Vito couldn't see clearly in the dark, it looked like a group of women, at least seven, dancing in a circle around the body of another woman.

Vito peered at the woman lying in the middle of the raving, wild-haired women who were now chanting something he couldn't initially make out. But with concentration, he recognized the chant was in Italian—and he understood it.

"Dio della fertilità!"[49]

The women chanted as they held hands and swayed back and forth, around, and around. There were torches behind them, also in a circle.

Their eyes closed, the women were unaware of the soldiers' presence. They continued to dance and chant, "Accetta questo sacrificio nel nome della Dea!"[50]

"The wagons are just past the beach," the short man, the lead soldier, called out. "There are enough of us to round up these pagans. Witchcraft is against the law under Il Duce."

The crowd of men in black shirts moved in on the women and took them with little effort.

"Veeto!!! VEETO!!!" A familiar voice called out, but he didn't know where it was coming from amidst the chaos. He scanned the crowd and saw her. A soldier was trying to drag Allegra by her hair. Then he saw Ginevra and Freya. They too chanted his name. "Veeto! Veeto! *VEETO!*"

None of the other soldiers seemed to notice as they ran after the women trying to get away.

Meanwhile, one soldier approached the unconscious victim lying in the sand circle and picked her up. In the soldier's arms, her red hair moved away from her face.

"Lucia!" Vito screamed.

The man in charge came up to Vito. "Do you know these women, soldier?"

Sensing the truth would do them no good he replied, "No, signore," Vito was stunned at the ease in which Italian rolled off his tongue. He thought fast, letting a lie spring from his lips. "Pensavo

---

49   God of fertility.
50   Accept this sacrifice in the name of the Goddess!

che queste magia avessero rapito mia sorella. Mi sono sbagliato. Non è lei."[51]

Vito held his breath. Fortunately, the head soldier seemed to buy the story. Soon, Vito was helping carry Lucia to the horse-drawn carriage being loaded with the women. He needed to get them all out of there.

When no one was looking, Vito positioned himself close to Allegra. "What are you doing here?"

"Trying to get your girlfriend out of the coma," she hissed in his direction. "We brewed some tea when we got home that night and found her here. We were nearly done releasing her soul back to its body until your little group decided to show up."

Once all the women were on the cart, it headed down the road into the darkness.

Vito walked alongside, whispering to Allegra. "Where are we?"

"Sicily. Alcamo Marina," Allegra told him as she watched the women around her. Freya and Ginevra sat quietly with the other sorelle, while Lucia lay on the floor between them on a makeshift bed of straw.

Vito looked at the soldier in front of him, walking in time with the others. Freya blew the soldier a kiss. He sneezed, the force of it causing him to shake his head.

"He won't be able to hear us now," Allegra said, winking at her sister in appreciation.

"Who are these guys?" Vito asked.

Allegra motioned to Ginevra, who tasked herself with ensuring the soldiers were oblivious to their conversation.

Allegra turned her attention back to Vito. "They're Black-shirts, Mussolini's men. It's 1925, and they're taking us to the Iron Prefect."

"Huh?" Vito said, confused. "Am I supposed to know these people? I knew the other people I became. Who am I here?"

Allegra sighed. "I don't know. I've never had this happen before. All we can do is wait and see."

As the words left her mouth, the leader of the group spoke again. "There's one more—a local mafia boss's wife. Prefetto di

---

51   I thought these witches kidnapped my sister. I was mistaken. It isn't her.

Ferro instructed me to get her and bring her back to Palermo. Her name is Nicoletta Trapani. You," he pointed to a random soldier, "get into town and find her. You and you" he pointed at two others, Vito being one of them, "go with him and bring her back here."

The other two soldiers sped up, and Vito quietly followed suit.

Before long, they were moving through a little village. People ran when they saw them coming, a few of them shouting, "Camicie Nere!"[52] before scurrying off behind closed doors.

Vito watched as the other two Blackshirts accosted a few people with interrogations, asking where Nicolette Trapani was. While several were afraid to give up her whereabouts, one man was more than happy to point them in the direction once they knocked out a few of his teeth.

Shortly thereafter, they arrived at the home they'd been directed to.

Vito immediately noticed how much nicer the house was in comparison to the others. He listened to the soldiers discuss how scum bag mafioso were ruining Italy, and it was a good thing Mussolini was taking care of them.

"This was the house of Don Trapani," one said.

"He was shot point-blank by a rival in the village square," another added.

"Perché siamo qui se è morto?"[53] Vito asked.

"For his wife. They say there's a child too."

The soldiers laughed as they told jokes about how she and the child would be treated when Prefetto di Ferro got ahold of her. Apparently, she would be an example to others.

They busted down the door and took out the few guards waiting on the other side. Then the two black-shirted men Vito was accompanying dragged a young woman out of her home in tears. She held on to a young girl, no older than eight. The young woman held her daughter's face into her bosom in an attempt to shield her from painful memories.

Vito looked at her face and swore he had seen her before. As they dragged her through the streets, he searched for her face in his memory. At one moment, Don Trapani's wife struggled, and

---

52   Blackshirts!
53   Why are we here if he's dead?

Vito got a glimpse of a yellow gold necklace hanging around her throat.

It was the same as the one Bisnonna Nellie wore.

Nellie ... *Nicoletta.*

She was his bisnonna! The girl was Nonna Josie!

"Signore,"[54] the young girl said fearfully, "where are you taking me?"

The men gave her no answer as they continued pulling her through the streets.

One soldier grabbed the child and ripped her from her mother's arms. Nicoletta tried to grab her back but the other soldiers overpowered her. Soon, the wails from both were soaring through the night.

"Give her the child for now," the senior soldier demanded. "We'll let the prefect decide what becomes of them."

Neighbors watched the spectacle through their windows.

Vito slowly moved to her side and protectively put his hand around her arm, making sure not to yank it too hard. He didn't care if he was supposed to be an observer. It was time he got involved. Vito pretended to move Nicoletta along like the other soldiers, but he vowed he would kill anyone that touched either of his grandmothers. Once they got back to the carriage filled with the Sorellanza Magicka, Vito's great-grandmother was thrown into the back with the others.

He noticed Lucia was still unconscious.

"To Palermo!" the leader bellowed. "Abbiamo preso le streghe!"[55]

The driver steered the horses as they pulled the carriage of prisoners toward the capital of Sicily.

Vito moved closer to Allegra's position in the carriage again. "Can they hear us?" he asked.

"No," she reassured, looking down at the frightened young woman and her child who had just joined the party. "Who are your friends?"

"I'm not sure," Vito said with an exasperated breath. "I think it's my great-grandmother and my nonna. I tried to make out what those guys were saying. Something about a mafia husband. Don Trapani."

---

54   Sir

55   We got the witches!

"She's the wife of Don Trapani?" Allegra said with surprise.

The other women in the carriage stopped their chatter and bore their eyes into the fifteen-year-old at their feet. "Don Trapani burnt my sister alive," one of the enchanted women said.

"He hung my father because he worshiped the Old Religion," another said with anger in her eyes.

One of the Sorellanza Magicka lunged toward Nicoletta but was thwarted by Ginevra.

Glaring at Ginevra, the angry woman spat, "Don Trapani killed my son by firing squad for stealing an apple! Why would you protect her?"

Ginevra opened her mouth to reply, but another voice spoke first.

"Please forgive my husband for the crimes he committed against you and your loved ones."

All eyes turned to the newest person present—Vito's bisnonna.

"I can never make up for what he has done," she continued, "but rest assured, he is dead."

The women gasped.

"Dead?" one of them said. "Who was the lucky person to kill him?"

Nicoletta lowered her gaze in shame.

"Was it you?" Ginevra exclaimed with glee.

"Shhhh!" Allegra hissed at her sister. "They'll kill her if they find out!"

"Why?" Ginevra asked angrily. "Cesare Mori was sent here by Mussolini to make sure all the Dons were dead. She did the Prefetto di Ferro a favor."

"She's a woman who killed her husband. How long do you think she'll last with them?" Allegra pointed to the Blackshirts.

Murder? Vito couldn't believe what he was hearing.

"Si! I did. I killed my husband because he stole me away from my family and had them all killed so I would have nowhere to run. Now I'm alone with my child, and I don't know where these men are taking me." Nicoletta began to sob, still a child herself.

Vito listened. He didn't know how he would make it happen, but he was determined she would not be sailing from Palermo with the Camicie Nere.

Once they reached the metropolis of Palermo, Vito took his first opportunity when he saw his teenage grandmother being led off the carriage by another soldier.

"Scusi."[56] Vito tapped the soldier to get his attention. "Is it true Prefetto di Ferro is on the same ship we're sailing?"

"He is?" the soldier asked with excitement.

"That's what I heard. Are you going to try and get a glimpse?"

"I can't. I have to bring this prisoner to her cell." The soldier nodded his head toward Nellie.

"I'll do that for you," Vito offered, gently taking Nellie's arm. "I saw him in Rome last spring.

"Are you sure?" the soldier asked.

"This may be your only chance," Vito teased.

Taking the bait, the soldier excitedly walked away, leaving Vito alone with his grandma.

"I'm getting you out of here," Vito whispered as he quickly moved her through the crowded docks of Palermo.

"Who are you?" Nicoletta asked.

"That doesn't matter. We must get you on a boat." Vito turned to call a man on the deck of a ship. "Buonasera![57] Where is your boat headed?"

"Argentina. Are you looking to jump on?" the man said with a laugh.

"No, but she is." Vito pointed to the young woman in his possession.

The man, intrigued, came down to the dock. "Are you selling this girl?"

"No. This is the widow of Don Trapani. The Camicie Nere killed him on the orders of Prefetto di Ferro. Now they want to kill her and her child."

Another man on the ship turned his attention their way. "Don Trapani?" he said and jumped down.

Vito braced himself, prepared to defend Nellie.

"Don Trapani gave me a job," the other man said. "He also gave my brother a job. It helped us take care of our parents. If she's the widow of Don Trapani, I'll see to it that she gets to Argentina safely with her child."

---

56   Excuse me.
57   Good evening.

Vito breathed a sigh of relief and looked at Nellie. "This is your chance to escape."

Nellie looked at the ship and then back at Vito. "What's your name?"

"Vito," he said, wishing he could hug her the way he did when she was elderly and he was a boy.

"Thank you, Vito." Nellie kissed him quickly on the cheek before letting the two men help her onto the ship, where they hid her below deck.

Vito watched as the boat pulled out.

Why had he never known his great-grandmother had done something so heinous? He knew the rest of the story—that she'd sailed to Argentina and then sailed to America. Nonna Josie loved to talk about her childhood in the Italian neighborhoods of Argentina. Vito just hadn't known the prequel to the story regarding bisnonna having killed her first husband.

"Where is she?" a deep voice interrupted Vito's thought. The next thing he knew, multiple hands were pulling him to the ground.

"I knew you were up to something, Vito," the military commander growled, sending spittle flying into Vito's face. He proceeded to tie Vito's wrists together and throw him in the back of the empty carriage.

"The women? Where are the women we had here?" Vito asked frantically.

"On their way to Rome. Il Duce will deal with them." The commander leaned closer to Vito. "Luckily, he lets me take care of traitors."

The commander jumped in the driver's seat and steered the horses into the city.

Tied up, Vito watched the shore move into the distance. Further out, he could see the ship that held his future through the shape of a young woman and her child.

Just as he realized he may have lost Lucia forever; all the colors Vito was missing restored themselves.

His vision was back to normal.

The sky was deep midnight, and the moon held a greenish tint. The brown wood of the carriage he was in finally looked real. He touched it, making sure it all wasn't just an illusion.

Accepting his bout of colorblindness was finally over, Vito let tears run down his face. It had been such a long journey, and he was glad to reach the end.

"We're here," the commander announced as the carriage came to a stop in a dark field. The senior military man turned to hand Vito a shovel and sneered. "Start digging your grave."

Without complaint, Vito did as he was told. With every scoop of earth he pulled up, sweat poured down his brow.

"That's deep enough!" the fascist yelled. "Put the shovel down and meet your fate."

Vito dropped the shovel to the ground and turned to see the firing squad. This was the first time he'd faced death in his journey.

What would death mean for him back in the real world? Would he die in this body, unable to return to his own, just when he could see all the colors again?

"Pronti!"[58] the commander shouted taking out his sword.

Then he yelled "Mirate!"[59] as he lifted it to the air.

The squad focused their barrels on Vito.

Internal fear begged his eyes to close, but he couldn't. Vito wasn't the same person anymore. He was now the Vito who'd saved his family from certain death. He was the man who he was named after.

"Sparate!"[60] the commander commanded.

Vito closed his eyes tight and braced himself.

But nothing happened. He never even heard a gunshot.

"You can open your eyes now," a familiar voice soothed.

Vito's eyes shot open. Stunned, he saw the squad and the commander lying on the ground, tied and gagged. Ginevra danced around them, taunting them with branches and other foliage she collected from the ground.

"What? How?" Vito stammered.

Allegra laughed. "Never underestimate the power of the Sorellanza Magicka."

"Where's Lucia?" Vito looked around frantically.

"She's right there." Allegra pointed to a group of women. In the center was Lucia, smiling and laughing.

---

58   Ready!
59   Aim!
60   Shoot!

Vito began moving toward her, but Allegra grabbed his arm. "No," Allegra said. "You cannot interact with her here. It's not good for her. Besides, here, she doesn't know who you are anymore. Now, tell me—can you see color again?"

"Yes," he answered with a bright smile. "It's over. I can see just like I did before I took my first sip."

"Buono," said Allegra. "Can I have my flask back now?"

Vito pulled the flask from the breast pocket of his jacket, noting that he hadn't heard it calling out to him for quite some time. When the flask was free from confinement, he noticed it was void of its colors. The gems were clear, like cubic zirconia. He handed it over to Allegra. "Here you go."

The old witch's eyes lit up. Once the flask was in her possession, every gem and stone refilled with the brightest colors of the rainbow. "Thank you!" she squealed with delight. "Just in time for my sister's birthday!"

Vito still felt slightly unsettled though. He turned his gaze back to Lucia. "Since Lucia is okay in here, does that mean she's out of the coma back in our reality?"

"I don't know. You'll just have to find out when you get there." With that, Allegra pushed Vito with all her might, which was more than one would expect from a woman centuries old.

Vito fell backward into the hole he'd just dug. He never hit bottom and kept falling until the hole swallowed him entirely.

Chapter Twenty-six

When Vito's eyes opened, he was exactly where he wanted to be—in the basement of his family's home. Every color that had vanished from his sight in this very spot only days ago was now restored, as if none of it had ever happened.

Vito prayed the journey was officially over. But he wouldn't know for sure until he saw Lucia.

He couldn't wait. He ran up the basement stairs, unsure of who would be waiting in the kitchen. Vito didn't care though. He was simply ready to see Lucia's smile again.

When Vito reached the door that stood between the real basement and the kitchen he pondered where he had been. Then, even though he could still feel fear, Vito opened the door to find what was waiting for him on the other side.

Nine Months Later

"Hey, Vito," Roy called out from his usual seat at the bar. "Grab me another, will ya?"

"Sure." Vito made his way to the cooler and grabbed a High Life.

"Thanks." Roy smiled. "Here's a buck for you."

"Thank you," Vito said, smiling back. This new job of his was so much more relaxing than the sales team. There was a time when the paint factory had been the bane of his existence. Now, however, Chroma seemed like a distant memory despite all the years he'd spent there.

Vito walked to the sink and started washing the dirty glasses that were piling up.

"Thanks for getting those for me," Lucia said.

Vito turned to see her standing over him. "You're welcome."

She leaned in to kiss him. "I have to run out for limes. Be back in a little bit. Do you want anything?"

"Gummi bears," he said and handed her some cash.

"Nope. You got me last time." Lucia walked to the front door and turned around. "When I get back, we'll put up the Christmas lights." She opened the bar's door, briefly letting sunlight in as she exited.

Vito resumed his dish washing until he once again saw sunlight beaming in as the front door creaked open. In his periphery, he saw the silhouette of a couple coming inside. "I'll be with you in a moment," he said.

"No rush," a familiar voice responded.

Vito froze. Slowly, he turned his head, stunned to see his mother and the former Monsignor Benevento. The ex-priest hardly looked like himself though. He wasn't wearing any robes. Instead, he was dressed in jeans and a bowling shirt.

"It's good to see you, Vito," Connie said, fighting back her tears. She was dressed in jeans and a beige striped blouse.

"Thanks." Vito dried his hands on a nearby towel. "Would either of you like a drink?"

"I'll have some wine," his mother said and then turned to the former monsignor. "Romualdo?"

Vito cringed, hearing her call him by his first name.

"Uh, I guess I'll have some wine too. Red, please."

Vito began preparing their drinks.

Connie cleared her throat. "You didn't come to our wedding."

"No," Vito said, resealing the wine bottle he had just opened, "I didn't." He set the two wine glasses in front of his parents. "These are on me. Congratulations."

"Thanks," Connie said, tears in her eyes. "Please, Vito. I can't believe you've let all this time go by without returning any of my calls. I'm your mother."

Vito said nothing.

Connie stood as her tears began to flow. "Excuse me," she said before running to the ladies' room. Once the door was closed, Connie's new husband looked at him with concern.

"You should give your mom a break," he said.

Vito blinked. "Are you trying to teach me ethics, monsignor? Oh, wait. You aren't a monsignor anymore. You left the church to marry my mom."

"I did," the ex-holy man replied. "I suppose my time on the moral high ground has come to an end." He took a sip of his wine.

"That's it?" Vito said a few moments later. "You aren't going to lecture me?"

The former priest looked at Vito. "No. My lecturing days are over."

Vito let the statement hang in the air between them. For the first time, he felt like he had won an argument with this man who had been like a father to him—in more ways than one—his entire life.

"Do you remember Father Vince?" the ex-monsignor asked Vito, breaking the silence.

"Of course," Vito said. "He was a great mentor."

Romualdo smiled. "I wanted to be your mentor, but you rejected me at every turn. Father Vince knew how to listen to what you wanted. He was always a better priest than me. I finally realized it was because he wanted to be a priest. For him, it was a calling. For me, on the other hand..." His voice trailed off.

"What?" Vito asked, even though he had an idea of what his new father had to say.

"Maybe one day, I'll tell you about my parents." Romualdo reached into his breast pocket and pulled out a sealed envelope. "I want you to have this."

"What is it?"

"A paternity test I took when you were a baby. I've been holding on to it in case this day ever came."

Vito stared at the envelope containing the answer to his most burning question. The slip of paper that would reveal who his father was. Was it the former priest sitting at the bar or a guy named Gus that the flask didn't find worthy of a visit?

"What does it say?" Vito asked, unable to move.

"I don't know," Romualdo admitted. "In thirty-seven years, I've never opened it. Maybe I felt it protected me from my sins."

Vito's heart pounded so furiously he was pretty sure it would eventually go numb.

"I'm going to leave it with you," Romualdo said. "You deserve to be the first to know."

Seconds later, Connie returned, her wet face looking a bit more refreshed. Her eyes hopeful, she looked from Vito to Romualdo. "Did you two have a nice talk?"

"Yes, we did," Vito replied after a slight hesitation.

"Good!" Connie smiled and took a sip of her wine. Then she did something Vito never expected.

"I'm sorry, Vito." Connie said. "I was wrong to keep such a secret from you." Then Connie began to weep. "I'm your mother, I'm supposed to do what's best for you but instead I was selfish and…" She put her face in her hands as she sobbed. Her new husband ran to her side.

"You have to stop being so hard on yourself," The former monsignor said to his wife.

"No," Connie said lifting her head, wiping her tears with painted fingers. Vito noticed how pretty and pink they were. "I was wrong. It's time that I admit it. I just hope you know, I did it to protect you."

Vito stood frozen among all the other barflies who happened to be there this day. He didn't know what to say because he didn't know how he felt. It was all too much to process in this moment. And he needed to change a keg.

"Please forgive me," Connie said putting an emotional nail in the coffin that was her son's heart. Vito still didn't reply. Connie didn't push any further and gulped the rest of her wine. "Romualdo, it's almost time for mass. We don't want to be late."

"No, we don't."

As Romualdo Benevento took his mother's hand in his, Vito reflected on how he'd known this man his whole life without truly knowing him at all.

Mr. Benevento turned back to Vito; his eyes slightly hopeful as well. "Will you be joining us for Christmas, Vito?"

"I don't know," Vito replied truthfully.

Connie's smile dropped, but Romualdo interjected before she could respond. "Okay. You just let us know then." With that, they headed to the door just as Lucia was entering, passing her by.

She stood frozen with a bag of limes in her hands. Once the door closed, Lucia turned to him with a shocked gaze and asked, "Was that …?"

"Yep," Vito said.

Lucia hurried toward him. "What did they say?"

"Wanted to know why I didn't go to the wedding."

"I told you we should've gone. I think it's time you started getting over this. You can't punish your mother forever."

"My parents."

"Yeah," Lucia agreed. "Your parents."

"Hey, there, kids," Nicki called out, coming out from the back room. "Looks like Vito's shift is up. Didn't you two have plans?"

"Yeah, we have a meeting in half an hour," Lucia said, "And then we're headed to Al's for a beef."

Vito laughed "No. We're going to Johnnie's."

"Al's!" Lucia argued.

"Johnnie's!" Vito insisted while pulling her into his arms.

She laughed in his arms for a moment, until noticing the envelope on the bar. "What's that?" She pointed to it.

"Something we can look at later." Vito slipped the envelope into his breast pocket. "Let's get a beef."

~ THE END ~

About the author

Camille J. Severino was born and raised in Melrose Park, Illinois. A bartender for most of her adult life, today she works as a ghostwriter. Always on the hunt for new life experiences, Camille has lived in New Orleans, Louisiana; and Austin, Texas. She has a Bachelor of Arts degree in English Language and Literature from Northeastern Illinois University and Secrets of the Jeweled Flask is her debut novel. Camille lives in the northwest suburbs of Chicago with her life partner, their two black cats, and their cockatiel, Gandalf.